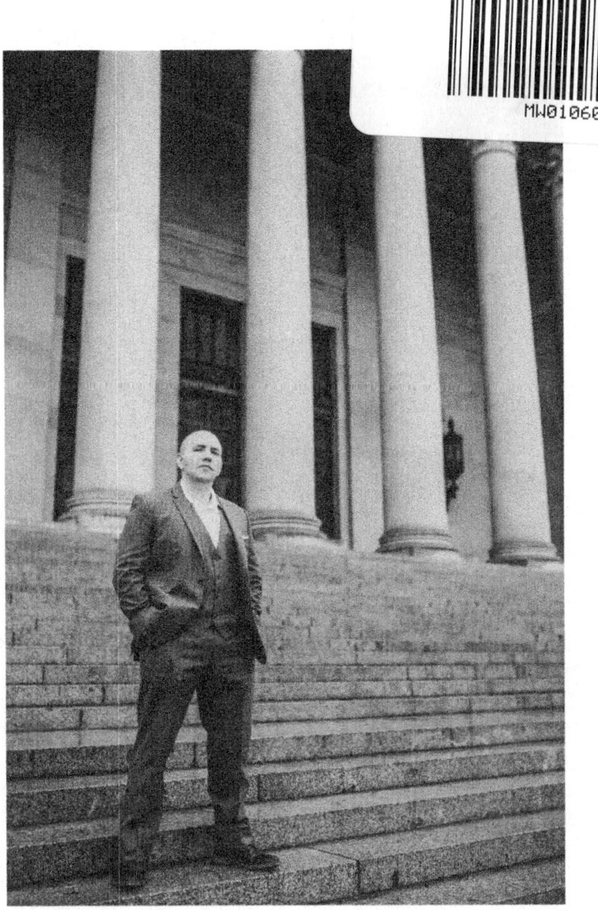

About the Author

J. L. Engel is not an award-winning best-selling author of numerous crime/action/suspense thrillers, or the occasional genre bending sci-fi/fantasy novel — YET. He is a lifelong writer who began doing so at the age of twelve. Under the enthusiastic tutelage of his sixth-grade teacher, who once got him the opportunity to be published, but he screwed it up because he was a stubborn child. Since he's grown up — some — he occupies his time as a single father, reading, writing, hiking, watching movies, pursuing fitness, and is an award-winning veteran corrections deputy and defensive tactics instructor in the Pacific Northwest.

A Dangerous Man

A Dangerous Man

J. L. Engel

Olympia Publishers
London

www.olympiapublishers.com
OLYMPIA PAPERBACK EDITION

A CIP catalogue record for this title is available from the British Library.

ISBN: 978-1-78830-870-0

This is a work of fiction.
Names, characters, places and incidents originate from the writer's imagination.
Any resemblance to actual persons, living or dead, is purely coincidental.

First Published in 2021

Olympia Publishers
Tallis House
2 Tallis Street
London
EC4Y 0AB

Printed in Great Britain

Dedication

To my grandmothers, Marilyn Karboski and Gloria Burris, I wish you were here to witness this journey.

Acknowledgements

A Dangerous Man would not have come to fruition if it weren't for the encouragement of who I do, and will, consider my number one fan — my friend, Julie F. Ten, years ago you helped me kill a gruelingly tiresome night shift with a mere suggestion for me to write, and everything I've written since has stemmed from that moment of reinvigoration. There is no limit to the appreciation I have for you, and what you would call your 'biased enthusiasm'.

To my dear friend and informal editor, Carol D. Your role in the completion of this novel was nothing short of angelic and magical. The guidance, honesty, and time you gave to assist me fueled my drive to not only complete this story — which originated as a short story with a much different ending — but to follow through on what I have been wanting to do since I was a sixth grade runt filling a class journal with my first story. (I do still have that.) Your position in my writing process has become essential and more significant than words, or the length of this page, will allow me to convey.

To my mother, Holly B. and my father, Larry E., I thank you for your constant belief in my creativity that has never swayed. The purity in this support helped me build belief in myself, which has never been stronger.

To my dearest daughter, Natalia, I hope my efforts in pursuing a lifelong dream will encourage you to never give up. Our paths in life do not always move in one direction and are often riddled with speed bumps, dead ends, and forks in the road. The path may change, but the destination does not have to. Follow your heart and find your happiness.

There are many others I could name who have been uplifting in my pursuit of becoming an author. If you're not named here know that I am thinking of you, and I thank you dearly for the time given to reading my product and giving me feedback, both good and bad. You know that I cherish the honesty, and it is appreciated beyond any measure of value.

Olympia Publishers, I thank you for choosing to pick up my novel, *A Dangerous Man*. It is my first effort as a novelist, and I am looking forward to this experience. I realize that this is a gamble you're taking on my work, and presenting me with the chance to reach the world is an undetermined one. I hope we can find success together and I cannot thank you enough for this opportunity. HERE'S TO CONQUERING THE WORLD!

To the READER: if you've made it this far, I hope that I have done my job to keep you invested as the pages continue to turn. I believe that I've constructed a ride you won't want to get off of, and I'm glad you've buckled up for the journey! Please enjoy!

Chapter 1
The Man Put Me Here

"9-1-1. What's your…"

The emergency operator's standard question was cut short by the sporadic sounds of gunfire. Although muffled, Regina Stratford was able to identify the exterior noise. She listened intently for a few seconds. The background sounded like a war zone, which she could attest to having served as an intelligence analyst in the Army seeing many missions abroad through hostile territory. She repeated her opening statement knowing someone had to be on the other end, or not, at this point. Nonetheless, her words spat out a third and fourth time, growing more desperate to gain an answer. Regina cursed at not getting a response while typing away on the keyboard in front of her to run a phone trace.

No dice.

She repeated her question again, louder and more aggressively. "What's your emergency?"

A faint whimper caught her attention and she was thankful the raging gunfire wasn't interfering. Regina listened harder, barely making out what a mother of three could only identify as a youthful cry. A child was on the other end of the phone.

"Can you hear me?" Regina asked. "This is 9-1-1. Speak to me, sweetie. Please. Talk into the phone." She took on a soft, motherly tone; coaxing and inviting. Regina waited, muting the line from her efforts within the bullpen, otherwise known as the dispatcher's workspace. "Does anyone have any reports of heavy gunfire? I have an active call. Multiple shots are being fired in the background. Child on scene."

She returned to asking questions to the call, begging and praying for that little voice to come through with a reply. The light of her monitor in the bullpen seemed to intensify in the dim lighting of the office area. Her eyes searched the call screen for any reports of gunfire after receiving no answers from any coworkers. She sat up straight and tall at full attention. The tail end of night shift had caught up to her until now. She had been teetering on the edge of exhaustion, but her adrenalin was now at a pace where she could keep up with a marathon runner. She could hear nothing more than the gunfire in the stillness of the call forcing her to second guess her prior conclusion. More effort was needed.

"Are you there?" she pleaded. "Come on, hon. I know someone's there. Talk to me. I'm here to help."

As the seconds ticked away Regina felt as though her heart was going to burst from her chest. She couldn't help but think of her babies, although they were well past their infancy, and made a mental note to hold them extra tight when she got home. But she wasn't going anywhere until this situation was handled. Her gut told her she was correct. There was a child on the other end of this line and he, or she, needed help, desperately. Regina's heart was aching as much as it was thumping. There was no way she couldn't feel connected to this call. Lord only knew what would happen to this child once the shooting was done. How the hell could there not be any other calls about this much gunfire?

And then it all changed with a frightened yelp. "Are you there?"

A girl. Young. Between seven and nine. Regina had been around far too many little girls these ages with her own two, Emily and Erica, not to recognize the age ratio. It was as if a specific tone were burned into her memory.

"Sweetie, my name is Regina. I'm the emergency operator with 9-1-1. Where are you?"

Sniffles and whimpering replied. Regina repeated her question, continuing to coax an affirmative response.

"I don't know where I am," the young girl cried. She squealed abruptly as a gun blast erupted close by. Regina jumped in turn as she heard the child cry out. "Help!"

"I'm trying sweetie, I am. Tell me your name? Can you do that?"

More time passed before an answer came. The stress was unbearable for Regina, but it was nothing compared to what this child must be feeling.

"My name is Ana Stewart… I'm scared…"

More gunfire echoed. It became less frequent, dying down, but closing in. Screams and yells rose and fell in the background. It sounded like people were dying.

Regina thought for a moment as her fingers danced over her keyboard noting the name. It sounded familiar. A missing child report maybe? She called it out in the bullpen asking for support as she maintained communication with the child. "Are you somewhere safe? Away from the gunfire?"

"A man put me in the closet of a room," Ana sniffled.

"What kind of room?"

"An office I think…"

A coworker called out from another workstation. "Ana Stewart, age eight. Reported missing three days ago."

Regina couldn't believe it. Something like this never happened. "Do you know the man who put you there, Ana?"

"No," Ana said.

"Was he the person who took you?"

"No. He gave me the phone and said not to hang up."

Regina was at a loss. She had run a phone trace but it came up empty. The phone must be a burner, which was difficult to triangulate with the basic equipment at Regina's disposal. She covered her mic on the headset she wore and asked for an advanced search. A coworker rolled up to the corner of her station and began working on a separate console. It would take time they told her. *But there was no time.*

"Ana," Regina began, pausing as she thought of what to ask the child. "What can you tell me? Anything can help. We're trying to find where you are, sweetie."

Ana seemed to hesitate. Between the shock and fear Regina couldn't blame her. Being so young and stuck in a life and death situation there was no telling what was running through the girl's mind. Regina was pleased she was even speaking and not frantically crying. She thought back to when she was a child and considered what she would do under these circumstances, concluding this child had more courage than she ever had at eight years old.

"The man said he'd be back," Ana said. "He… He… said not to make any noise."

"Okay, that's good, hon." Regina was thankful whoever this man was that he was looking out for Ana. But what was he doing otherwise, waging a war? "What else?"

Ana's breath came over the line long and heavy. Regina noticed she could hear Ana clearer than before, and it was then that the child told her what she already realized.

"The gunfire stopped..." Ana spoke in a hushed voice, eerily mature and poised.

Regina felt a chill as her thoughts and Ana's words collided. *The man said he'd be back.* The gunfire had stopped. There were no more screams, or yelling, either. There was only Ana's breath reverberating over the line, growing heavier and heavier with her anxiety as time ticked away. The dispatcher turned to her coworker for the trace, but there were no results yet.

"Ana, talk to me," Regina pleaded. "Are you okay?"

Ana's breathing stopped. Regina thought she could hear the child suck in all the air she could and hold it. *He said not to make any noise.*

"Someone's coming," Ana whispered.

The mother of three imagined the child curled up in the corner of the closet, eyes wide with terror, holding her breath to be quiet, waiting for the end. Was it the man who'd placed her there for her safety? Was it someone else who would want to do harm to Ana? Tears would be streaming down her flushed cheeks. Strands of her hair would be sticking to her face, but Ana would be too frightened to wipe them away. Tremors must be shaking her in her place, the fear growing, but holding her breath kept her still and silent.

In the background of the call Regina heard the high pitch squeal of old, sticky door hinges. The creak of the floor was barely audible, but present. There was a burden of pause Regina translated over the phone line, feeling the pressure of its weight in the moment. Someone was in the room with Ana.

"Ana, who's there with you?" Regina asked. She felt beads of sweat form on her forehead, some rolling down the side of her face beneath the dark hair of parted bangs combed off to one side of her round cheeks.

There were no words in reply, only a prolonged hush. "Shhhhh..."

The thumping of Regina's heart radiated up into her throat. Her pulse had quickened so much in the moment she needed to remind herself it was her job to remain calm. The terror she felt for Ana was nearly impossible to control. Her thoughts jumped to what Ana's parents would be thinking. This was their little girl, taken from them by some monster, or monsters, but by some form of saving grace she wound up on her line, on her shift, a mother of three with her own fears. But she was just as helpless now as she was before. She had no information to get Ana the help she needed. Her worst fear was that the last thing she'd hear from this call was Ana screaming for help, a blood curdling cry that would carry such a primal force with it (the kind that screamed out for the protection a parent was supposed to provide for their child) that Regina wouldn't sleep for weeks knowing she had failed this little girl, and she would question what safety she could truly provide for her own children.

A melodic thumping of heavy footsteps on hardwood floors infiltrated the call. *Thump. Thump. Thump.* Three steps and they stopped at the closet door. Hinges squeaked briefly, a higher pitch like a roller in a track, as another door opened. Regina sat rigid as a statue in anticipation. She felt her breaths shorten. Her heartbeats echoed in her ears, thunderous in respect to the stillness extended from the phone call.

"Ana?" Regina dared to speak. She needed to know the child was alright. She needed to know what was happening.

"No," replied a deep, gravelly voice. "Ana is safe."

"Let me speak to Ana!" Regina yelled into the line. Her fear overtook her professionalism. "Put her back on the phone!"

There was some rustling in the background of the call. Regina heard a man's voice. Then she heard Ana's, agreeing to what had been told to her.

"Ana?" Regina called again, impatient.

"I'm here," the child responded. Her voice was no longer strained or frightened. In fact, a sweetness that a child's tone naturally conveyed had been restored; comfortable and innocent.

"Sweetie, are you okay? Who's with you?"

"The man came back like he said." Ana broke away from the call as though she were interrupted. She spoke indirectly away from the phone in agreement before returning seconds later. "I'm okay. I'm safe."

Relief overwhelmed Regina. She collapsed her head into the palms of her hands, elbows propped up on top of her desk. She shook off the feeling, even wiping away tears she uncharacteristically shed as she regained her composure. She thought to herself, *you're not safe until I get you home, sweetie.*

"He wants to talk to you," Ana said.

Regina attempted to have Ana wait, not wanting the child to relinquish the phone, but she was too late. Not that it would matter.

"Listen closely," the man's voice boomed. He was authoritative and cold in his use of the words. No time to waste. "Ana is safe, for now. I'm going to give you an address where to find her and get her home."

Regina began to speak, interrupting the man, but he was not having it.

"I said listen. When the police arrive, they'll find Ana locked in the conference room on the second tier. It's up the stairs and to the left. What they'll find below is much more disturbing. I advise the police to enter with extreme caution."

"Are you planning to ambush them?" Regina asked, a fiery tone accompanying her words.

"No. I'll be long gone. As best as I can tell I've killed everyone else. Except for the other victims."

Other victims?

"Who are you?" the dispatcher asked. Her fingers continued to make notes on her screen.

"Not important."

"I'm sure Ana's parents would be thankful..."

"I'm sure they would be. Nonetheless, I don't exist. Ana needs you, so you need to listen."

Regina paused, finding that she now held her breath in anticipation.

The man continued to speak. "*Again*, the police should enter with extreme caution. The FBI will be called. The people they'll find are victims of a trafficking syndicate. They're going to need medical attention." The man waited as though to ensure Regina was paying attention. When she didn't interrupt him again, he continued speaking and gave her the address for Ana's location. Regina muted her mic and immediately made the call out. The building lay on the outskirts of an industrial complex in South Boston. It was an area notorious for not being patrolled regularly.

When the man finished speaking Regina finally chimed in. "Is that all? Is there anything else?" She wanted information, anything at all. Anything that would help stall this guy from leaving so police could arrive and arrest him. Someone like him couldn't be allowed to get away. He'd admitted to murder. Mass murder even!

"Yeah, there is," he said.

There was a sense of playfulness in his voice that was unsettling to Regina. She got the sense he enjoyed what he'd done. "What is it?"

"This is far from over."

And then the line went dead.

Chapter 2
Breach and Clear

First responders arrived on location within ten minutes of receiving information from emergency dispatcher, Regina Stratford. Based on the information all units were instructed to hold off from entering the premises, which turned out to be an old warehouse complex in South Boston. They secured the perimeter and waited for SWAT teams Alpha and Bravo to arrive on scene. The arrival of said SWAT teams took an additional five to ten minutes, an eternity for every patrolman who happened to be a parent or guardian. Knowing a missing child waited for them inside made things far more difficult. And then there was the additional information of this being a location used for a trafficking syndicate. The task of not entering the building seemed impossible, but of the half dozen officers on scene first, no one disobeyed their superior's orders.

Alpha and Bravo teams collectively were made up of a dozen elite officers, six per team, all itching to get inside as well. Team leaders, who took point, gave assignments for breaching and the respective directions each team would deploy. Alpha team would be responsible for clearing the front entrance leading to the upper tier and retrieving Ana Stewart for safe extraction. Bravo team would continue to clear the ground level, and then move forward to an underground storage space indicated in the blueprints obtained from the city's Housing Records Department. Based on information the dispatcher passed along, this secondary area was "disturbing." For the officers of each team the entire situation was disturbing. Fathers, mothers, aunts and uncles were titles they all shared, and like any case involving a child, particularly one who had gone missing, emotions ran high. It was paramount they kept their professionalism in check. Unless, of course, they encountered the son of a bitch responsible, then there may be a need for one more body bag.

The initial breach of the warehouse was through a singular steel door on the south side of the building. A small port window occupied the upper center mass of the portal with the cliché steel cover attached to the interior for checking who was on the other side. On this end of the weathered concrete structure, a score of Cadillac SUVs were parked, designating this door as the main entrance. Alpha team entered there. Along the opposite side, Bravo team entered through an office area which ultimately led to the open warehouse floor where they would intersect with Alpha team. Being that Alpha team entered the meat of the building first, they were met with the bloody sight that could only be the endgame to what Regina Stratford had described as a war zone on the emergency call she'd taken from Ana Stewart.

Alpha team encountered the scent of recent gunfire first before their eyes set upon the scene of carnage. It hung in the air like a heavy morning fog blending with the metallic aroma that accompanied the spilling of blood.

"It smells like a fucking slaughterhouse in here," one SWAT officer barked.

"Fuck me," another officer gasped.

When they entered the main floor of the warehouse, the haze couldn't hide the bodies that decorated the interior. Dozens of men lay about lifeless on the concrete floor in pools of their own blood. Multiple bullet wounds mutilated the corpses. Some were blown wide open to the point of being nothing more than overdressed slabs of meat. Limbs had been shot off, some only nearly gone leaving white bone exposed amidst crimson pools of human remains. Brain matter had been extracted violently. Splatter and gore littered the walls and floor leaving a massive jigsaw puzzle of dried spaces to walk. One officer peeled away from the formation to puke out his disgust. He was ordered to leave as Alpha team pushed on to their designated target.

Bravo team entered across the way from Alpha team, moving singularly as their counterpart, taking in the large-scale execution as their fellow officers had seconds beforehand. They moved as a unit even as they verbally conveyed their repulsion for the horror they walked into. Both teams struggled to step over bodies and around pools of drying blood to continue their assignments.

As the teams moved through the warehouse a chorus of "Clear!" rang out through the building indicating that no suspects or resistance had been found. Alpha team followed their plan to move to the upper tier, scaling a steel staircase with yellow painted railings on the west side of the building. Their boots moved in sync, a practiced and choreographed march, banging up the steps until they fanned out to either side of the upper tier. The point man led them speedily towards an open hallway where a series of small offices had been plainly built. It was indicated that on this side of the warehouse Ana Stewart would be found in a locked conference room. Every room leading to the conference room was searched in a leapfrog formation. Two officers entered the designated room for clearance while the two officers behind them moved to the next. This staggered series continued with a slight variation as each two-man sub-team repeated the pattern until the last door at the end of the hall was all that was left. Being that they were now down a man, the odd man out kept watch over the hallway as the team progressed.

The Alpha team leader approached the door with his back close to the left side of the hall, refraining from standing directly in front of the door and in the line of fire if an unknown shooter waited on the other side. The tactic was a well-practiced method to minimize target area. He then knocked loudly once he was in position. After a count to three he called out in his thick *Boston English*, "Ana Stewart, this is Officer Beaumont, Boston PD. Are you in there?"

There was heavy silence that followed. No reply. The worst-case scenarios went through every team member's mind. The girl wasn't there. Or she had been killed. Or they had been lured into a trap. With the rising violence directed at police officers across the country they did not overlook an elaborate scheme to place them in harm's way. But today was not that day.

"I'm here," Ana answered loudly. Her voice cracked as she called back.

"We're comin' in, Ana," Officer Beaumont informed the child. "I need to know first, Ana. Are there any devices attached to the door? Anything that you wouldn't see on a door usually?"

Officer Beaumont couldn't imagine the child knew what an explosive was, or any kind of improvised device, so he chose to keep his question as basic as possible. Ana didn't reply to his questions. Instead he found his answer in the form of a skinny blond child who opened the conference room door. Her tear stained face was flushed red, and large blue eyes gleamed back at the veteran SWAT officer like innocent beacons of hope. She had clearly been overwhelmed with fear and the disbelief of returning home, only to have these feelings replaced with the deepest sense of joy. Her clothes were dirty and tattered as though she'd been forced to be unkept. The child's lower lip began to quiver as she locked eyes with Beaumont, the first and closest officer to her. Tears overflowed from the lower lids of Ana's eyes; tears of indescribable happiness, tears that reflected the anomaly of a miracle. But Beaumont wasn't going to let those tears hit anything but his shoulder. The officer swept his rifle to his left, letting the tactical sling carry it around to his backside, and he swooped in to take Ana into his arms. He held the child tightly and felt her let go in the base of his neck as she wrapped her little arms around him and wept. Salty tears saturated the collar of his uniform, most of which rolled down his own neck, and he found that some of those tears were his.

"Yah're safe, sweethaht," Beaumont said softly.

Two Alpha team members quickly entered and cleared the conference room as a tactical precautionary measure. Once this task was complete the remaining four officers formed a human barrier around Beaumont and Ana, much like a Spartan phalanx, and they proceeded to lead them out of the warehouse to safety. Along the way Beaumont shielded Ana from the sea of bodies littered across the warehouse. It wasn't difficult as the child kept her face buried in his neck. The officer focused on reinforcing how she was going home, how safe she was now, and he wouldn't let anything happen to her. It took all the officer's focus not to break down as he was reminded of his own daughter, half again as old as Ana, but a similar blond little girl all the same.

It wasn't until Alpha team broke out into the daylight of the crisp spring morning that Officer Beaumont let the overwhelming feelings of sadness and joy overtake him. He reached the first paramedic station with the girl, set her on a gurney, and cried right along with Ana, overwhelmed with his own thoughts and emotions and sympathy for the child's courage. A large part also stemmed from a protective rage welling inside him, instinctually bound to keep others safe from such deplorable crimes. The ending to this tragedy couldn't have been better for Ana as statistics had placed her on the low end of survival following an abduction, let alone having any chance of being recovered and returned home.

Once the ground floor had been cleared and Alpha team moved on to their main objective recovering Ana Stewart, Bravo team leader, Sergeant Clarey, led his team to a thick steel door at the southern corner of the building. Blueprints of the building that had been studied *en route* indicated there was some kind of storage cellar in the building, which had been added in the 1940s towards the end of World War Two. There was no rhyme or reason for it that he could think of, but that wasn't his concern. His main task was to clear this area of subjects who either offered some kind of resistance or association to the rumored syndication of trafficking in this location, or rescue any so-called victims. It went without saying that Clarey and the members of his team wanted there to be resistance, to give penance to those responsible for such inhumane acts. But being a SWAT leader meant upholding the higher standard of saving lives, not taking them.

The door was old and rusted on thick, stout hinges. It held a resemblance to what might be used on a submarine or Navy vessel, locking airtight with a rotating wheel used as the means of opening the door. The point man held his rifle at the ready while standing off at an angle in the opposite direction that the door opened. The breaching officer positioned herself to the left of the point man to pull the door wide as quickly as possible so entering the portal could be done with ease. The remainder of Bravo team formed behind the point man fully prepared to follow him into hell.

A silent countdown was initiated via hand signal by the breaching officer, and as the final number came up, she wrenched the door open with all her strength. The heavy door came quickly forcing her to brace her feet against the wall to her back to keep it from crushing her. A pungent stench burst out of the cellar's depths, stinging the eyes of each member, burning their throats, and forcing Bravo team to take a step away from the doorway. Clarey turned away, dry heaving as the power of the smell quickly worsened. He'd smelled death before, as had his team, but this was something far worse.

"Masks!" Clarey yelled. As he shut off the words, he held his breath. The strength of the stench, he felt, could be tasted if he left his mouth open too long, and that wasn't a flavor he wanted to become familiar with.

Each member of Bravo team removed gas masks hanging from the rear side of their tactical belts. Once they were fitted, and only then, did Bravo team proceed down into the cellar. The masks only helped slightly as the rotted meat and scent of shit had already permeated everything it came in contact with. The strong hint of feces and urine in the air, along with heavy body odor, laced the stink even more as they moved down the stairs. It reminded Clarey of herding cattle on his grandfather's ranch in New Mexico as a child, except today it wasn't a tolerable country air kind of scent. Were it not for the darkness of the stairwell, he thought the smell could have been seen hanging in the air.

"Moving," called out the point man, raising his rifle and initiating his tactical light on the rail below the gun's barrel leading their descent into the unknown.

Extreme caution was exercised as Bravo team moved in unison. Bright LED lights illuminated the darkened stairwell, but not enough to reach the bottom. The stairs it seemed went down at least two flights. They reached a landing that redirected the stairs back in the opposite direction of the first flight. Time passed reluctantly as Bravo team continued on, hesitant to discover what waited for them at the bottom, yet cautious every step of the way. When the stairs ended with a final landing the point man held up a tight closed fist to silently gesture for his team to halt. What his light revealed beyond an opened doorway sickened him instantly.

"Holy shit," the point man said. His tone was completely awe struck, and disgusted. He turned to one side, tore his mask away from his face, and puked along the side of the stairwell.

Clarey rushed forward to investigate, aiming his rifle and tactical light into the darkness where the stairs ended. Beyond the short landing was a doublewide doorway acting as the gateway leading deeper into the abyss of the cellar. A thick line was painted just inside the interior. It was blackened with age in a macabre manner, crusty and textured, drawn in blood. The line was clearly made to send a message, which explained why there were no doors attached to the entrance. Fear was the only tool needed here to keep this line from being crossed. His light penetrated the space beyond the concrete framed doorway, exposing a sight of absolute repulsion. What Clarey saw reached into his soul and convinced him beyond any reasonable doubt that evil truly did exist.

"My god," the team leader gasped. His words were distorted by the enclosure of the gas mask, giving them an echoed tone, and making him sound alien to the English language.

The words hung in the air as the energy from Clarey's disturbance filtered back to the members of Bravo team. A primal, instinctive characteristic compelled Bravo team to move forward, descending in unison, aiming their rifles and bright tactical lights into the cellars abyss to see what had garnered such a troublesome reaction. The team stood frozen in abhorrence at the sight they collectively observed. Looks of disbelief were exchanged. *How could anyone do this*?

What lay in front of the secondary SWAT team was a twenty by twenty concrete room filled exclusively with the human product the dead men above ground sought to traffic to unknown destinations. Women and children were packed together with nowhere to relieve themselves except in the spot where they sat or lay, and in turn slept in their own waste. In the white haze of the flashlights some of the older women, mostly naked, or relieved of the majority of their clothes, shielded the children in their immediate grasp. Hair was matted to the sides of heads. Cuts and bruises were evident among the majority of the room's population, including the young girls and some boys. There was no telling how deeply these people were truly wounded. Their exterior and physical injuries would likely be the least of their problems as life moved forward.

Chapter 3
In Too Deep

As the Boston PD's Commissioner, Anthony DeMarte did not typically access active crime scenes. Not anymore. He was far removed from the investigative task. The day's event, however, forced him to change that standard. There was no getting around it. Exigent circumstances forced him to have a presence at the warehouse, which was a red flag in itself.

DeMarte exited the main entrance of the warehouse, where he had been informed Alpha team made their entrance. He wore a white jumpsuit over a fitted suit and rubber booties over black Italian dress shoes, all to protect his professional garb. A CSI agent escorted the Commissioner beyond the Cadillacs to the back end of the forensics van. His quick, long strides made it difficult for the CSI agent to keep up without appearing to hurry. There was no shame in being in a rush to get away from the warehouse. Both men's faces were pale and sickly after witnessing the massacre inside, all the bodies and the blood.

They reached the opened double doors of the large, square van where others worked on processing evidence taken from the scene. DeMarte was assisted out of the jump suit and booties by the CSI agent, looking like James Bond stepping out of one outfit and instantly ready in another, such as a Canali chalk grey suit. Deep beneath the wool material his body was sweating all over, not so much from the temperature, but from fighting off the feeling of sickness that overwhelmed him from what he had just witnessed. Disgust guiltily seeped from his pores.

With composure, the Commissioner thanked the CSI agent, and walked around to the side of the van. He took a deep breath and leaned against the cool steel of the vehicle. There was no way to describe what lay within the confines of that warehouse other than gruesome, and he wasn't talking about the dead men scattered about. That, beyond all ethical values, is what he called justice. What was so troubling was the cellar full of women and children, and the humanity that had been stolen from them. The sight was beyond putrid. Inhumane would technically be correct, but it suggested those responsible were human and, even though they may walk and breathe in such forms, they were monsters. The thought of them made DeMarte want to throw up. It tore at his guts as though his soul were being dug out from his physical being. It was torturous, yet he felt he deserved it because as he thought of those responsible for such a deplorable deed, he knew he belonged in the same mix.

A buzzing emanated from his right trouser pocket. DeMarte retrieved his cell phone and observed the screen. Recognizing the name on the caller ID made him even sicker. He couldn't answer the phone. He wouldn't. Now was not the time to speak to the devil. Not here. Seeing the name on the screen deepened the reality of whose pocket he'd been in for the last decade, and knowing that man was responsible for what was found here today reflected on him just as badly as having let it happen. DeMarte had never bore witness to the things he'd been paid to overlook. He never knew any details. He was only informed of what he needed to know, and he followed through with his end. Protection was provided. Patrols were reassigned. These were simple things easy to justify. He'd never had a hand in anything directly, but his role suddenly came with a far more tragic definition and secretly made him an accomplice to what transpired here. He was responsible, which made him a monster just as well.

Anthony DeMarte, Boston PD Commissioner, and human trafficker.

The Commissioner quickly began thinking of how he could distance himself from this mess. Over thirty-five years on the force with twenty of those years worked on the straight and narrow, and now his life choices finally caught up to his conscious. Before seeing this, he hadn't thought of his transgression as anything more than a business transaction. He had always been careful not to overthink things. He'd justified what he was doing in the beginning, looking to the future for himself and his wife, who had still been alive at the time he transitioned from being a good cop to a criminal. Miranda had never known what he'd started and never would have. Cancer ultimately saw to that. In the aftermath of his wife's death DeMarte lost himself in grief and, seeing the massacre inside and the treatment of innocent women and children, he realized he'd lost himself completely. There was no way to make any of it right when he was forced to face reality.

But there was a way to give him time.

DeMarte gathered his composure as the political wheels of his mind began to spin, returning a sense of confidence he typically radiated. There was only one way to deal with this situation. Turn the tide in his direction and wash his hands clean of his position.

The Commissioner walked away from the side of the van and found his assistant, Britney, in the same place he had left her near a cluster of ambulances where other brass had congregated after their tours. She was a fully commissioned officer, and a hell of a smart cookie. She didn't truly belong in the position she held. Her talents were being wasted, but she did everything well. *Britney makes me look good, especially now.* DeMarte spoke to her privately to have her arrange an immediate press conference, lifting the temporary media blackout. It was the only way to buy himself the time he needed. What happened here shouldn't have been possible, and he would be the blame in the eyes of a profoundly unforgiving sort of people having had a strained relationship since the Cold War.

Britney did her job well and within a few minutes had the notification for the press conference out to the appropriate designees. It wasn't a difficult task, DeMarte knew, because an entire army of press swarmed around the perimeter line that had been set at a healthy distance away from the warehouse. He heard a sergeant radio out to the line patrolman nearest to the reporters. The conference would be simple and straight forward. He would address the cameras directly, no microphone or podium. A real street level story about Ana Stewart's return, the massacre, and the victims found in the cellar. The single anomaly DeMarte didn't want to think about was the decision he was compelled to make on the fly, but he would address that last.

"They're chomping at the bit, sir," Britney said blandly, stating the obvious. "Have been all day. By the time we reach the caution tape they'll be huddled together and ready for your address."

"Thank you," DeMarte said. He smiled bleakly, catching his reflection in a window of an ambulance and noticed he still looked pale, which was the least of his worries. The Commissioner gestured with an open hand in the direction of the press. "Shall we."

Britney accompanied him on the long walk of nearly two hundred yards. A patrol sergeant followed. There were no words exchanged. DeMarte's assistant knew him well enough to know when to speak, and when to accept the silence. He was clearly in deep thought, situating his delivery of the information he would disseminate to the press. It was unprecedented having nothing prepared to study beforehand. Today was an exception given he had firsthand knowledge of the crime committed. There was no need for words to be prewritten for him. Tonight, everything would be raw. He sensed an uneasiness surrounding Britney, who no doubt suspected something was wrong. DeMarte flashed a grin to ease the tension, his handsomely weathered face creasing at the corners of his lips, crow's feet accenting the outside of his hazel eyes. She wasn't buying it as she expressed a fraudulent smile in return. It seemed as though his dishonesty was contagious, and sorely affected those he should have protected or guided much better. The caution tape of the police line was less than fifty yards away at this point. The walk took far less time than anticipated; it was the heavy thinking DeMarte was doing in transit which made it feel as though it were much farther. There was no turning back now.

****

"Reports are coming in surrounding the recovery of Ana Stewart, an eight-year-old girl reported missing three days ago, who made an emergency phone call from the place she was being held captive. Ana has since been reunited with her parents, giving a happy ending to such a traumatic circumstance. But, as miraculous as this story is, it isn't the end. It's only the beginning of something far more sinister that is rocking Boston to its core. As more details come in, I'll be here, on scene, to give our viewers the first alert. Back to you in the studio, Kurt."

The news reporter's focus was laser sharp as he looked into the camera, presenting the conviction of a good story teller, engaging enough to remain interesting, and leaving just enough information out to tighten the suspense as the camera cut away and returned to Channel 7's main anchors in the studio. Jamal Laurence was a veteran in the news world, celebrated for his investigative pieces, and well-liked by most who came into contact with him. Spinning the drama in a story was never difficult for him. Call it a gift, or talent, but it was his niche and he nailed it every time. The only difference with this story was that he had no more information to go on other than what he'd reported, and rumors were being spread around like buckshot. The Boston PD had unprecedentedly forced a media blackout of this situation. Even though he was one of the first on the scene hours ago, and had an "in" with a few guys on the force, no one was talking.

Laurence prided himself on reporting the news unbiasedly. It was another aspect to his reporting character that won him over with his viewers, and attributed to the ratings the station unabashedly claimed. He was their golden boy. He knew this and used it to his advantage when he needed to pull some strings to get what he wanted, but it wasn't a crutch for his career. Lawrence was dedicated to his craft, to being authentic, and truthful. He stood alone most of the time in the ways he conducted himself, being honest with the public, which made it hard for him to report on the rumors outside of Ana Stewart's recovery. Word spread fast of a blood bath within the warehouse. The details were unsettling. Horrific. Although, if he had to make a judgment call based on the chaotic scene surrounding the warehouse, he'd nail the rumors as being ninety percent accurate. Even from this distance it could be seen that every person who'd entered the warehouse had come out in a sickly, altered state. The involuntarily retched over position was unmistakably recognizable.

The police line for onlookers and the media was set far enough away from the warehouse, and there was no way to get any good shots without zooming in completely. They were set nearly two hundred yards away. Luckily the area was not well traveled so being out in the middle of the road held no safety concerns. And with the area swarmed by the police there was nothing to worry about. What distressed Laurence were the numerous officers, and other first responders, he'd seen throughout the day that had been working on the interior of the building and then abruptly quit. And not quit as in their jobs, but ceased to continue to work the scene. Some came out crying. Some came out heaving their last meal.

And some actually refused to enter. He could only speculate as to how terrible things really were within the warehouse. Seeing pale faced professionals brought to their knees was not something he was accustomed to, and he'd covered the carnage of the Boston Marathon bombing of 2013. Anything less than being on that level of tragedy had him stumped.

Unless he believed the rumors.

Ronald Baker, his producer, had been putting pressure on him to tell what juicy tidbits had been swirling around. Laurence refused. He had nothing to back the information. "Make up a disclaimer," Baker had said. "No one will know the difference." But Laurence would. However, his curiosity was beginning to get the best of him. Something big was going on — bigger than a child abduction. What could possibly have such a devastating effect on the police, paramedics, and firefighters? Why the information black out? There were too many questions that needed answers, but there was no way to get them.

A patrolman stood nearby like a stone-faced sentry overlooking the frenzied reporters pining to execute the perfect broadcast for their respective (or not so respective) networks. Laurence looked the man over indirectly so he didn't garner any unwanted attention. He had to be a greenhorn, fairly fresh to the force, or only recently indoctrinated within the last few months following the mandatory stint at the academy, to pull such a shit detail as keeping the public and reporters at bay around a crime scene. But every job held its importance. Laurence understood that, if not only in a way to use it to his advantage. In doing so, he noticed the patrolman held no service hashes. This confirmed he had less than three years of service for sure, so he was somewhere in between new and mildly experienced. The quizzical look in his eye told the reporter the kid was not used to this detail, or completely comfortable being alone. The experience was new to him. Probably even an overtime position given the heavy presence of Boston's finest, which meant there was a good opportunity to find him being complacent. The young patrolman closed his eyes and took a deep breath before he returned to being the serious officer. He was tired. *Perfect.*

Laurence sauntered over towards the officer, reaching into the interior pocket of his suit jacket as he moved. The young patrolman saw him approaching. The reporter greeted him with an upward nod and a flashy smile, but not too flashy to raise any suspicion. He presented a packet of spearmint gum and held it out as offer.

"I saw you yawning. Would you like a piece? Helps keep me awake." Laurence slipped open the sleeve of the gum packet with a swipe of his thumb and read the officer's name tag: Redmont.

Redmont looked hesitant. Taking free offerings was prohibited, per agency policy, but it was just gum. No harm there, right? "Sure. Thank you, sir."

Laurence nodded. "Of course. It's the least I could do. We've all been out here for hours." He looked around at the score of field reporters and their camera crews, more for effect than anything else, and then looked the patrolman dead in the eyes. "I don't want to overstep, but I'm heading over to get some coffee. Or, well, my cameraman is. Can we hook you up with some Joe?"

"Naw, but thank you," Redmont declined. He had a mild Bostonian accent that vaguely made its presence known, depending on the word. "I'm sure that would get me too much attention, an' I don' need any right now."

"Aah, I see." Laurence took the hint that the kid was under some kind of heat. Mistakes were in his past, and not the kind that could be easily overlooked. "Got all eyes on you, huh? I know how that is."

Redmont snickered. "Shoor ya' do. Yaw're on TV all the time, but not under the microscope like us. Definitely not like me."

Laurence deduced the patrolman had something to say and wanted to tell it. That was his 'in' now, so to speak.

"I get what you mean, but it's no different for me because of that. You and I are constantly under the public microscope, man. We can't scratch our asses without being judged." Laurence noticed Redmont seemed to soften his posture for a moment as he spoke. Sympathy. *Time to strike*. "Whatever you've done, or didn't mean to do, couldn't have been too bad. They kept you on the force."

"For now," Redmont said dismissively. "I'm only here because they need the bawdies."

Laurence returned the gum to its place in his left interior breast pocket. It was always a good opener. He turned, stepping in towards the patrolman, leaning against the yellow caution tape, again for effect more than anything, and said, "Look, it's not that bad being out here. Sorta' cush, right? You just have to stand around and keep us idiots from crossing the line. Pays the same as chasing down a junkie, or directing traffic, right? I don't think I'd mind it if I had what it took to do your job."

Self-deprecation: check.

Praising statement: check.

Redmont waivered, opening up to Laurence about what had happened. Turned out it was fairly serious, a wrongful discharge of his firearm during the arrest of a violent drug dealer resulting in said drug dealer being in the hospital and suing the city. Learning the patrolman's details was only a means to an end, but he felt for the kid. Even still, Laurence buttered the patrolman up a little more so he could go for the jugular and get what he wanted.

"Well, based on that I'd say I'd have to be pretty pissed about being here, too," the reporter abated. "You're overqualified for this shit."

Redmont thanked Laurence for the compliment, shaking his head in a way that said, '*Even this guy can see my worth*,' which only fed Laurence's objective.

"You know what," Laurence said, displaying a fantasy of frustration, again for convincing effect. "Neither of us belong here. There probably isn't shit going on in there anyway. Too many rumors flying around and no one really knows what's going on."

The patrolman inhaled in a dismissive manner, almost like a snicker of sarcasm. A gesture saying, he knew something, and you're wrong, motha'fucka'. Laurence caught Redmont's 'tell' in the man's body language, his unconscious way of telling Laurence he was correct. Something big *was* going on inside the warehouse. He had Redmont right where he wanted him.

"What?" Laurence asked coyly. "There can't be anything *that* important going on in there, can there? I mean, we'd know something by now if there were."

Redmont appeared to want to fill in the blanks for the reporter, surely not giving a shit whether he said, *'Yeah, there is,'* or not. He never had a chance to say a word as his mic squawked next to his right ear, clipped to a shoulder band on his uniform coat. He replied immediately on the radio, and then turned to Laurence. "Yaw're about to find out, pal."

****

By the time the Commissioner reached the police line the media hounds had been herded together. The field reporters stood at the forefront with their cameramen watching over their shoulders. The lines were staggered so everyone could get their shot of Anthony DeMarte. He took his place at the center of the mob, confidently standing before them as a veteran law enforcement officer should. When he'd transitioned from the street ranks up into administration, he'd learned he had a gift for public speaking. It never frightened him, but he only did it when necessary. His delivery had a more profound impact that way. He had never been a fan of the media spotlight, but it was an aspect of his occupation he had learned to embrace early on, and he did it well.

DeMarte looked over the crowd of reporters, sizing them up, and making his presence known. He was a tall man, still in fairly athletic shape as he believed that a healthy body made a healthy mind, although he couldn't say much for his soul at the moment. A helmet of thick, perfectly accented salt and peppered hair complimented his camera-friendly looks, much like a Hollywood leading man. DeMarte played the part with an array of facial expressions, knowing when to lighten the mood, and capable of deepening the look of his dark eyes when the subject matter was dramatically heavy. Right now, was just that kind of moment. He appeared to be hesitant on speaking, although he was simply letting the weight of the circumstances lend him the right amount of compassion he needed to display, and build an equally balanced fire of dismay and need for justice. The information was organized in his mind during the walk over, touching on just enough detail to wet the media hounds' appetites and to inform the public of what was going on in their city, all while appealing to the bleeding heart of the world. He looked over his right shoulder to his assistant, Britney. Her dark hair reflected the bright overhead lights that had been set up to light the area when the sun went down, giving her an angelic appearance, he hadn't noticed before. She gave him an assertive nod to begin and he turned his attention forward again. It was when he opened his mouth that everything fell apart.

Jamal Laurence was front and center at the makeshift press conference. His mic was ready for when DeMarte would take questions, if he did, but above all else he took notes. He always took notes instead of relying completely on his memory when he made a direct field report. Adlibs would be added to sell the story and fill in the blanks, guided by the notes he'd taken, therefore making his reports more accurate. For a brief second, he looked up from his notepad and locked eyes with the Commissioner. It was a surreal moment in time where a searcher like himself was given access to observing the soul of another. DeMarte's humanity bled from his eyes. There was a sadness there Laurence had rarely encountered. It was a prolific instance seeing such a strong figure shed his armor and become vulnerably naked for all to see. Laurence knew immediately that this was going to be a historic moment.

"Today," Commissioner DeMarte said, pausing as he fought the proverbial frog in his throat, but then he hesitated to scan the media as he controlled his emotions — his shame. "Today, a young girl by the name of Ana Stewart was returned to her family after having been abducted and missing for three days. Our cities finest worked tirelessly to find Ana, but their efforts unfortunately led them nowhere in that time. She had been swept away with the wind, and returned just as anonymously. It was discovered that Ana endured frightening conditions of such a nature I will not give them any publicity."

"Ana's return came by way of an almost equally terrifying 9-1-1 call, of which, when it is released, will give you chills, especially if you are a parent. With Ana's return there was a discovery at the heart of Boston's core that cannot be unchanged, forgotten, or excused. Ana was not the only abductee found on hand at this warehouse. With her, subjected to equally deplorable conditions, were two dozen women and children, mostly foreign, and some from surrounding areas. They were captives in a human trafficking syndicate's network. To what extent we may never know."

DeMarte took a breath and let his announcement set in. It was professional and vague enough like he'd wanted, but his message was far from over.

"To add to this despicable activity there were a number of men on scene who were found dead throughout the warehouse," DeMarte added. He looked into the mob of reporters; stone faced now. His shame was subsiding for a moment, with memories of the dutiful officer inside of him he'd lost long ago. "The number of dead found has not yet been confirmed, but it is estimated to be between twenty to forty men. All were shot or mutilated in some fashion. Some even suffered wounds of an explosive nature. They were torn apart. They were decimated. They were completely and utterly annihilated. These men are suspected to have been responsible for the captivity of Ana Stewart and the other women and children." DeMarte noticed a growl enter his speech with these last words. He paused for the slightest of moments, eyeing the crowd like a wolf ready to beset upon a herd of sheep. "They got exactly what they deserved."

An uproar rose among the reporters. Had the police commissioner just condoned the killing of Ana's captors? Questions shot from the crowd.

"Is this the kind of justice Boston PD stands for?"

"Do you have any idea who was responsible?"

"Have you identified any of the men in the warehouse?"

The questions came like verbal machine gun fire. DeMarte wouldn't have been able to keep up with them if he wanted to. The Commissioner stood firm and silent. He raised his hands to the hungry media hounds, waiving away their questions and silently calling for them to calm down. He waited patiently for them to stop before he continued. He noticed Jamal Laurence looking at him intensely. He'd always liked that kid.

"Typically, I would not have made that statement," DeMarte said. "It goes against everything I've sworn to uphold for the past thirty-five years. It goes against the ethics and the morals we believe in, and it goes against *everything* we stand for. But, in my time of service, I've never encountered anything like this. I always thought I'd fought every kind of evil there was until today. Today I saw true evil, and I am not the same as I was before this. These officers working the scene will never be the same.

"Beyond this, I firmly believe in the justice served to the men responsible for the crimes we've discovered. There would be no other kind suitable." DeMarte picked a camera, Jamal Laurence's, and spoke directly to the people through it. "This seems to be a form of vigilante justice on a scale which is beyond comprehension. Detectives have been in contact with the FBI and ties to similar crimes have been made. They are being reported as serial massacres. There are six other metropolitan cities across the United States that have experienced this type of extermination. All involve human trafficking. And while this is not the way we bring criminals to justice, it is justice for them, the victims, and their families. In my opinion, personally, it is acceptable for these types of men.

"Having made that statement," DeMarte continued, "there is something that Boston should be made aware of. This... This..." DeMarte briefly struggled to find the right words. "This vigilante cannot be allowed to operate outside the laws our officers' fight to uphold every day. The laws they give their lives for protecting the public every day. We will hunt this killer down, and he will be brought to justice. Not his style of justice, but the United States justice. Boston's justice."

When DeMarte paused again, gathering his thoughts, a question arose from the reporters' that he felt compelled to answer. "How can you condone one man's means of justice, going beyond the law, and still feel morally obligated to have him arrested for his crimes?" It made perfectly good sense, and it was likely the most important question he could have been asked. And, ironically, it couldn't have been more helpful. *Jamal Laurence always knew the right kind of questions to ask*, DeMarte thought.

The Commissioner nodded his head, grinning as he prepared to answer the question. He looked directly at Laurence when he spoke. "Great question, Mr Laurence. The answer is incredibly simple."

"And...?" Laurence asked quizzically. He leaned towards his cameraman and whispered, "Zoom in and get this." His cameraman, Bill, gave him a thumb's up. He was already on it. They made a great team.

Now came the hard part. The real bomb. The escape plan.

"The answer is," DeMarte hesitated. He couldn't believe what he was about to announce. The headlines alone would go nationwide, but as the details of the massacre were revealed he'd be old news in less than twelve hours. "The answer is that I can't. I cannot condone these actions and morally support the arrest of whoever is responsible for saving the women and children found captive in this warehouse today. I cannot support the arrest of whoever made it possible for Ana Stewart to return home to her parents. And since I cannot do this, it is with a heavy, yet satisfied heart, that I announce my resignation as Boston Police Commissioner." Another uproar overcame the media, but DeMarte ignored them as though they didn't exist. "That is all. Thank you for your time tonight."

Chapter 4
Ghost

It was clear that there was so much not being told to the public and the questions kept coming from phone calls and social media. *Follow us on Twitter and Facebook. Let us know what questions you have for the Boston PD about this horrific event.* Such was the way of the world. Every tragedy was nothing more than a headline for agendas and to gain followers on social media. The interactive methods did nothing for the news, but people needed to feel a part of something when the spotlight wasn't on them. The moment could never belong to the victims, and the internet would never let them forget.

In spite of the constant coverage, every channel on the television ran with the safe return of missing child, Ana Stewart. It had been on all day. Constant *Breaking News* alerts were overused as news stations offered up more speculation from their studio hosts, blind opinions, and innumerous politically correct questions highly regarded by the soft-hearted citizens with liberal attitudes. This was the kind of media coverage any major crime seemed to garner at any point in time in the United States. However, it differed severely in the most important manner of all: it was not a tragedy of innocent lives lost; rather it was quite the opposite.

The unofficial tagline given to the day's event was 'The Boston Massacre' when rumors of a body count came to fruition. It was a fitting tagline because it was exactly what had happened and, given the natural pessimistic reporting standards of the media, the number of casualties were the most reported aspect of the day, although highly speculated due to an informational black out of other crime scene specifics. The reporting of Ana Stewart was repeatedly peppered in as a reminder of a positive outcome, the sole factual story involved, while persistent and annoying attempts at contacting the family shamelessly continued. The

Stewart's simply wanted to be left alone, yet they unfortunately learned that was not the way the American media worked.

For the man responsible, dubbed this time as the 'Boston Vigilante,' versus the previous 'Seattle Vigilante,' 'San Francisco Vigilante,' or the equally uninspired, 'Austin Vigilante,' it was just what he had expected. It was a less than flattering title and, as it gave the impression connections between cities were being made by the media, it was clear they were not and were equally uninspiring as his previous hunting grounds. It was consistently accurate in its description. However, it lacked the *je ne sais quoi* a name should give an individual, especially one with such a broad skillset as his. Something more appropriate was a former call sign he continued to entertain. Given the haunting impression his work left behind he was otherwise known as Ghost. The moniker was simple, accurate, and quite literal. It was difficult to be tracked when you didn't exist, and even as unknown as his alias was it gave him the manicured quality of an apparition. And like the essence of a ghost, he had arrived and vanished in each city he'd strategically targeted without a trace. The vigilante's reaction was the same everywhere he went, culminating in today's event aimed at the heart of the beast he'd been hunting all along. This demonstration left a more direct impression:

I'm here, and I'm coming for you.

Ghost watched the television from a seedy hotel he'd acquired in South Boston. The old, dusty brown curtains were pulled tight over the windows. The rickety steel door was dead bolted and chained, for what that was worth. Not that it mattered. He'd put his own touches on a personal warning system in the form of a wireless electro-shock band with a motion sensor attached to the interior doorknob. If it turned beyond forty-five degrees it delivered fifty thousand volts instantaneously, and was capable of knocking a bull on its ass. He was big on proper security, and he hated to be disturbed, or caught off guard. Then there was his stainless steel Colt Python .357 Magnum revolver on the nightstand as a final option. The barrel length had been shortened to only two inches, better for close quarters combat, and the hammer had been modified for quicker firing recoil.

The man sat at the edge of the bed with his muscular frame leaned forward, elbows propped up on his knees. The glow of the aged box television was the only light in the room and cast a faded blue ambiance throughout. Ghost had slept in his clothes following this morning's activities, never climbing under the shoddy green blankets. The tight black tee shirt and functional black tactical BDU pants he still wore carried the heavy scent of gunfire and death. He preferred it to the piss smell of the orange shag carpet, and the moldy bathroom. Either way he'd smelled worse on himself, and across the world. His focus was on the news cast for the evening, which he'd purposely woke to watch. If all went as planned, he'd be going back to work soon.

Channel 7, WHDW, was tuned in on the television. For the past hour Ghost had noticed that the field reporter was a unique individual. Jamal Laurence appeared in the informational band on the bottom of the screen. He was an African-American man, mid-thirties, savvy, and intelligent. The guy didn't blow smoke up the viewer's ass. When asked his opinion he didn't have much to say. He wouldn't speculate. He wouldn't pander to the 'make shit up as we go along' generation. He continually stated he had no updates from the scene of the 'supposed massacre' as he put it, and there had been no solid details released at the scene. Laurence commented on the slew of rumors surrounding the situation but refused to indulge in them. Ghost praised the reporter's no bullshit attitude. He liked the guy's style and wanted to pay attention to what was to come because he knew there would be more worth seeing.

As Channel 7 segued back into the studio the news anchors had grown by two. Ghost unexpectedly found a new reason to keep his attention locked on this particular station in the form of the second female lead anchor. He zoned out when her name flashed across the bottom of the screen, and paid no attention when the male anchor said it. His captivation transitioned to her resemblance to his wife, Veronica. Long, wavy hair, raven black and shiny as it cascaded over her shoulders in a simple yet model-like fashion. Full lips pouted beneath a button nose highlighted by sharp, but large doe eyes. Hazel spheres looked out into the world and, while being a common color, the excitement for life in those eyes contributed to them being far too uncommon. And it all was held together by her glowing caramel skin.

Before long Ghost no longer saw the female — only his wife. The similarities were too strong to keep his mind from slipping into the memories of her. He saw Veronica on the screen, articulating the news with the voice of an angel, and when she looked into the camera, he felt she was looking back into him. The information the anchor delivered on the television no longer came in a prompted fashion, but derived from the man's history with his wife. Veronica spoke to him directly, repeating how she loved him, laughing whimsically at her thirst for life, all in the fantasy his mind's eye created.

It had been some time since anything, or anyone, had provoked his wife's memory. But Ghost did not have the strength to fight it off and remain in the true moment of reality where he stared at a newscast on what became the exposure of a human trafficking ring, even if the public had not been made aware of it yet. He knew it was coming — it had to. He couldn't help that he was overwhelmed with how much he missed his wife. This spark in his memory was dangerous. He couldn't afford to be so easily tempted to entertain her delusion. Except she was his wife. His best friend. She was the one who'd accepted him for who he truly was even when only a few in the clandestine world knew both sides of his existence. She took him for the secret that he was, alter ego and all, going so far as to honor him with her hand in marriage and taking the name of his civilian cover. Veronica knew his true identity. She knew what he did for a living; how he provided for his family. And she knew she would never get to take the name of the man she loved, or give it to the beautiful daughter they had shared. Once they were gone, Ghost had not just lost their love, but he was left devoid of meaning. Losing this intimate detail of his life set ablaze the rage inside a man who dared to stare into the abyss, and embraced the abyss staring back. Vengeance was all that was left, and in it he rediscovered his drive, his ambition, and his meaning.

He needed to focus.

Slipping to the floor of the motel room and kneeling before the television screen, he moved towards it with a hand reaching out. Fingers touched the screen, feeling the electric buzz and static of technology's past, caressing and tracing the face of his Veronica as she slipped away, seeing the female anchor, silently saying the goodbye he'd never had the chance to say. Snippets of memory clashed with reality as Ghost fought to hold onto the vision of his wife. He began to realize the woman on the screen was the female news anchor and not Veronica.

Focus.

When her voice slipped away Ghost remembered the way she said, 'I love you,' like he heard her say it every day. The words gave him a feeling of warmth, reminding him of what he still lived for. And then he went cold. Reality set in like the flip of switch. He continued to stare at the screen, only inches away, coming to his senses just in time for what he'd been waiting for. Ignoring the tears running down his chiseled face, Ghost sat back on the edge of the bed and watched intently.

The information bar at the bottom of the screen read: *Commissioner DeMarte addresses public on 'Boston Massacre.'*

The view came from the angle of Ghost's new reporter of choice, Jamal Laurence. The back of the man's head could be seen just off to the left of the camera man's position. Commissioner DeMarte looked over the crowd of reporters. The policeman looked nervous, and hesitant. There was a sad appearance to the man, who should have exuded confidence and authority. After all, he was the backbone of the Boston PD as its leader. When DeMarte spoke, he opened with Ana Stewart's brave story. He transitioned quickly into the two dozen women and children found in the warehouse's cellar. The dead were mentioned, number unknown. And then DeMarte said, "They got exactly what they deserved." The mob of reporters came alive at this confirmation. But not Jamal Laurence. The man stayed cool. Ghost liked him even more.

DeMarte waited for the commotion to die down before he continued speaking. His crowd-pleasing comment was a failed attempt at redemption. Ghost knew it, but it was their little secret. DeMarte spoke on the vigilante justice of the Boston Massacre, its serial properties, and touched on the FBI's involvement. He claimed that the Boston PD would bring the vigilante to justice, but it was only a rallying statement. Laurence stepped in and asked the question of the ages, which backed the Commissioner into a corner. Here was the moment of truth: what would DeMarte do? Come clean, or run?

Ghost knew all too well and wasn't surprised when the Commissioner resigned. It was in the stars, so to speak, and all part of the plan. This freed DeMarte up to hit the road and get out of town quick because it wouldn't be long before he'd be linked to the people operating the human trafficking syndicate. Ghost would ultimately see to that tonight. Little did DeMarte know that when he resigned it wasn't just from his position as the police commissioner of Boston PD, it would also be resigning from life itself.

Chapter 5
Stone

In the midst of the Boston Massacre, elsewhere in the world and beyond the media pummeling the subject into every household turned to the national news, life went on. In fact, many knew nothing of Ana Stewart's miraculous return home from three days of captivity, or the discovery of human trafficking in the same location where the girl was found. The world kept spinning, and the grand scheme of the universe never skipped a beat. People came and went from here and there, were stuck in traffic, cheered and booed at sporting events, or simply surfed the channels without regard to news of any kind.

And criminals never rested.

One such case was Jonathan Michael Stevens, a career criminal and sexual predator of the most heinous kind. Wanted by the United States Marshals Services, or USMS, Stevens found he could never rest. They were relentless, but so was he. Even with his youthful obsessions Stevens couldn't keep away from what he wanted most, and being a federally wanted fugitive only presented him with a deeper, darker challenge. Today it wasn't paying off as his latest attempts allowed the Marshals to close in on his latest child exploits, epitomizing their slogan, 'The hunt is on.'

Stevens' lanky frame burst through the screen door at the back of his home, slamming the door against the side of the brick house with a crackling retort similar to a low caliber gun shot. He leapt down the five steps to the concrete patio and pumped his long legs towards the shabby wood fence at the edge of the yard. The man-made border rocked as he scaled its six-foot height, only half a foot shorter than he stood. He quickly dropped to the other side in the alley and wasted no time traversing the chain link fence of the home directly behind his, bolting through the neighbor's yard. Stevens knew not to look back. He'd learned the hard way once before. Running from any form of law enforcement and being able to get away on numerous occasions was something he'd prided himself on, although he didn't allow any form of arrogance to set in. It was never easy, and these bastards were as persistent as ever.

"US Marshals! Stop running!" sounded from Stevens' back porch. The instructions carried quite a distance between the gap he'd put between them.

"Not today, fuckers!" Stevens said to himself, bursting through the front gate of the neighbor's yard.

A runner was always on the lookout for any tails, and he'd seen a few different vehicles in his neighborhood over the past few days that stood out. He'd watched as closely as he could, left at different times, never going the same way, often times crossing through other yards. Most times he'd found the vehicles in question were never around for too long, but they weren't as inconspicuous as they were meant to be. Today his gut had told him something was wrong, stirring his already growing suspicions, which had proven to be correct. He was ready when he saw the caravan of blacked out SUVs come to a quick stop in front of his home. He'd been waiting to leave to catch a glimpse of his newest treat following her cheerleading practice when the day's excitement kicked off.

Now Stevens crossed through multiple yards, scaling fences, and crisscrossing directions. Kitty-corner to the home's yard where he emerged was a rundown two storey house boarded up with plywood. Broken glass protruded from rotted windowsills giving the structure the resemblance of a scarecrow meant to spook people, rather than birds, away from the neighborhood. He crossed the street to the forgotten dwelling, rounding the eastern corner of the house's front side to the overgrowth of the back yard. The rear entrance was boarded up as well, but served as a squatter's haven. Stevens ducked into the old home through the pried open back entrance, peeling the plywood covering away from a wall on one side and pushing the broken door in without effort. He had never actually been in this home, but it was well known to be accessible throughout the neighborhood, and he needed to catch his breath. The Fruit Belt district of Buffalo, New York allowed him a certain amount of anonymity. There weren't too many who'd move to a crime ridden area predominantly home to African-Americans, but he was truly no different than many who already lived here. His tastes were just more particular, and he kept to himself anyway. How he'd attracted any attention at all, especially leading the Marshals to his doorstep, was beyond him. It didn't matter now as he was getting away, again. He had a stash of essentials in a locker in the Downtown district, which he'd make his way to later this evening and be gone.

Breathing heavily in the darkness of the rundown house, Stevens bent over, hands on his knees for support. As he tried to catch his breath, he presumptuously ran as many scenarios through his mind as he could so he could map out exactly how he would get out of town. Of course, he thought he could get away, otherwise he wouldn't run. There was no way he was going back to prison. He was lucky to have survived the first time, but it wasn't an experience he could live through a second time. Multiple scars littered his back from an attack he'd sustained due to his conviction. If he were thankful for anything it was the leniency of the judicial system on sex offenders, and the quick response of the corrections officers' whose care he was under. Sure, once they realized whose life they had saved he'd heard rumblings of, 'We should have taken our time getting here,' but he didn't mind. They'd saved him, and good behavior got him released earlier than expected, serving only two and half years on a five-year sentence. Stevens could complain about the probationary time, but he clearly wasn't sticking to those parameters, so there was no need. He simply had too much love to give.

In the darkness of the abandoned home Stevens watched the back door. His breath was under control fairly quickly, which was an important factor so his heavy breathing didn't give him away. Beams of day light filtered through the hem of the doorway where the outer plywood prohibited the door from sealing fully. He could barely see the remains of a kitchen beyond the doorway behind him complete with a dining table littered with used needles and dust. To his left he made out a washer and dryer that smelled as though they'd been re-commissioned as port-o-potties. The covered porch area he rested in was an old laundry room spanning the width of the home. A rusted dog kennel set to his right beneath a broken window that was also covered by plywood. The kennel had a ragged bed inside it with a decayed canine corpse.

Time to move. Stevens couldn't stomach being in here any longer.

The fugitive cautiously approached the back door. He inched the pliable board open slowly until there was enough space for him to see out into the backyard. The area was still and quiet. He was three blocks removed from where he resided, but he still needed to be careful. The Marshals would be patrolling the area, likely with Buffalo PD's assistance, so he couldn't relax yet. He waited a few more minutes and then peeked outside again. Nothing had changed. The immediate coast was clear.

Stevens worked his way through the door, careful to make as little noise as possible, and make no sudden movements. He crouched on the back porch at the top of the concrete stairs. Gray skies overhead were rolling in, foreshadowing rain. He could have smelled it in the air if it weren't for the stench of rotted dog and human waste. A shower was in need now as he felt dirtier than he ever had. Molestation was one thing, but encompassed by the foul odor of death was something he couldn't handle. Sure, violence came easy to him, and was sometimes essential to achieving his desires. But he wasn't a killer. At least not the physical kind. Perhaps of emotions, or of innocence, but he'd died inside long ago. Or rather he had been stripped by force in the same manner he inflicted upon his victims. Not unlike his abuser, Stevens rationalized his crimes as necessary life experience. Nothing was ever yours forever. Sometimes you had to lose what was most important to you to truly appreciate it. *Right*?

It was no matter. He needed to focus. His getaway was the most important thing right now. There was so much more he wanted to do. He'd scouted out so many more prospects. A twinkle of joy sparkled in his eyes as he quickly thought about the local coverage of high school sporting events. If they only knew how much he truly appreciated their work, and how helpful they were to his endeavors. He hated how his thoughts strayed so easily.

Time to move.

Stevens descended the stairs and crept to the edge of the abandoned homes boundary made up of closely planted privet hedges. The growth of the individual plants seemed to overlap, pressing into those on either side. It was not so thick he couldn't easily sneak between the individual plants to the other side and still remain hidden. The bushes were tall and tear drop shaped making it effortless to remain concealed. He took one more precaution as he remained close to the hedge, scanning the street from the cover provided. There was nothing to be alarmed about moving out towards the street and continuing towards downtown Buffalo.

The fugitive felt good about his chances. Today it seemed so easy. He kept in mind he was still in range to be found, and fell into a comfortable stride that would alleviate any suspicion. He was just another resident out for an early evening stroll.

Stevens never looked back. It was a rule for running. The idea itself would slow a person down and instill fear by taking away from the necessary task at hand: don't get caught. His stroll was natural and even paced as he blended into the neighborhood, passing by the small-frame and brick homes known for the area. Stevens was relieved that he had gotten away. He smiled wickedly, pleased with himself, bearing crooked yellow teeth to the crisp air of the mild spring day.

He should have looked back.

****

In the background of the dilapidated neighborhood a man followed the gangly sexual predator known as Jonathan Michael Stevens. He walked in pace with the fugitive at first, increasing his speed every other step to quietly catch up to him. He was cautious not to move in such a way any of the tools attached to his black tactical vest would jingle or jangle and give away his position. The man had quietly radioed in his position when he'd seen Stevens, asking that back up stand down until he was closer to the subject. He was on loan from the FBI as a member of the US Marshals Fugitive Task Force. The badge attached to his vest over the left breast along with the bold white letters, FBI, across the back of his shoulders identified him as a G-man. He and Stevens had history, and the man hunter intended on stirring up those old memories and injecting some déjà vu into Stevens' life.

It took two blocks before the FBI agent was close enough to move in to apprehend Stevens. He paced the fugitive with an M4 carbine rifle in his hands at the low ready position in front of his body. A single point tactical sling attached to the rifle crossed his chest over the top of his right shoulder, looping down and under his left armpit. It made for great weapon retention when he would need both hands to take Stevens into custody. The agent let the rifle dangle in front of him for a moment while he adjusted his hard knuckle tactical gloves, seating them in nice and tight, ready for action.

The agent quickly sprang into action as he ran up behind Stevens and knocked him to the ground with the butt end of the M4's short stock, hitting him square between his shoulder blades. The fugitive heaved forward in a beautiful arc sure to have inflicted a small measure of whiplash. Stevens slapped against the pavement like a rag doll, flesh hitting with a wet splattering sound as he skidded across the concrete enough to inflict a low-grade form of road rash across his forehead, palms and elbows. He was dazed by the impact, seemingly oblivious to what was happening. The FBI agent jumped on Stevens back directing a series of punches to the man's kidney area. He straddled Stevens as he quickly reached out and brought the predator's wrists together behind his back. Hinged handcuffs were applied tightly, by accident of course, and back up was notified.

It was only a matter of seconds before three black Chevrolet Suburban's came to a screeching halt in the street next to the G-man. A handful of grizzled men exited the vehicles, M4 carbine rifles in hand just like their FBI liaison. They surrounded the captured fugitive and assisted in removing him from the scene, a quick snatch and grab scenario where they didn't give the neighborhood much time to catch what was going on. Two Marshals escorted the disoriented Stevens to the nearest SUV. As Stevens was turned around to be tucked into the back seat, he saw the FBI agent. A look of shock distorted his skeletally thin face.

"Stone?" Stevens gasped. He watched as the agent flashed a middle finger his direction. Rage replaced shock in an instant. "Fuck you, Stone! You motherfucker!"

Memories came back to Special Agent Connor Stone as he listened to Stevens yell more obscenities before he was shut away in the back of the Suburban. Originally Stone had arrested Stevens for a series of violent rapes around the Central Park area in New York City when he was first promoted from patrol to a third-grade detective. The case briefly threw Stone into the local spotlight as the serial crime had persisted for a number of months. Stone remembered putting in extra effort when a family friend's daughter had been abducted, tortured, sexually molested, and arrogantly released. Stevens wasn't known for killing any of his victims, but he should have. The mistake he made was thinking fear alone would keep the girl, Alena Forrester, quiet like the many before her. Unfortunately for Stevens, his final victim came from a family with a strong back bone and Alena was anything but quiet. Her description of Stevens led to a widespread canvasing of the known area where an anonymous call directed Stone to the sadist's doorstep.

What happened between Stevens' apprehension and booking into jail nearly got the case thrown out on terms of excessive use of force. Stevens somehow thought he had been taken to an undisclosed location and was beaten with a bat by Alena Forrester. Stone doesn't remember such a thing, citing in his testimony Stevens had violently resisted arrest, and he had sustained mild injuries in the fight as well. Luckily Alena's testimony and his own pain had saved the case. Stevens then went to prison, albeit for not nearly long enough.

Damn, Alena sure could swing a bat, Stone reminisced.

Now, after Stone's friend, Mason Jones, who led the Fugitive Task Force, had called him in for their latest hunt, Stone once again brought Stevens to justice. Stevens wouldn't get off so easily like he had before. He was going into a dark hole where he belonged for a long time.

The team congratulated Stone on the apprehension before dispersing back to their vehicles. Mason Jones approached the G-man with a less than appreciative demeanor. He was a large man, over six foot and nearly two hundred and fifty pounds of beef. The guy had muscles on top of muscles and easily outweighed Stone by fifty pounds. His dark skin gave him the appearance of a living shadow as he stalked towards Stone intently, accompanying the movement with a grim expression and painfully dark eyes. He held a cell phone to his ear as he approached, nodding as he gave an affirmative answer before extending it to Stone.

"You need to take this, brother," Jones advised. "We've had our head in the sand all day going after this asshole. We missed out on the big news of the day."

Confused, Stone took the phone and held it to his chest, covering the receiver end of the phone. "What are you talking about?"

"Take the call. You need to hit the road." Jones pointed to the phone. "It's your director."

Shit.

Stone placed the phone to his ear, saying, "Special Agent Stone."

He listened intently as a firestorm of information was fed to him. He had never heard the FBI director speak so determined and brusquely. The situation certainly called for it. Stone was astonished he hadn't been called earlier, but then again, his phone had died hours ago and it was the least of his concerns. He nodded as he ejected a number of yesses into the phone.

"I'm on it, sir," Stone said, ending the call.

Jones took the cell phone from his friend and tucked it into a pocket on his tactical vest. "What's the verdict?"

Stone stared back into the dark eyes of his friend with a cold demeanor that made his blue eyes appear as though they were icy crystals. Jones shook off a chill.

"Looks like I'm going to Boston," Stone said.

"That the work of your guy?" Jones was slightly aware of the case Stone had been working for some time, jealous he wasn't invited to help.

Stone nodded in reply. "Seems like it. He's getting bolder and more violent."

Jones straightened, raising his chin a little higher, looking farther down on the agent in a display of his self-confidence. "Say the word and I'll be your liaison this time, brother. We'll take this asshole down together."

Stone wanted to accept the invitation. He could use Jones' help. Hell, in reality, he needed it. But the circumstances of the case were too sensitive. As much as he wanted his friend's help, he couldn't accept it. He didn't want to say it was too dangerous, but it was, reaching farther than anything he could legally explain without literally having to kill the man.

"Not this time, man," Stone said regretfully. "Out of my hands."

Jones shook his head and waved Stone to his SUV. "Well, you know where to find me. Let's get your super-secret wannabe-spy ass to the airport."

Chapter 6
Different City, Same Mess

In the wake of Jonathan Michael Stevens' apprehension, Special Agent Connor Stone was immediately taxied to the Buffalo Niagara International airport. A brief stop at his hotel was made prior to gather his things, which didn't amount to much as he frequently traveled and always kept a go-bag handy. His good friend, Mason Jones, knew the routine for urgent travel conditions, and entered the airport through a ground level entrance reserved for government access. The FBI director and the Security Oversight Committee Stone reported to was kind enough to have an executive jet ready and waiting ahead of time for Stone to immediately board.

"Sure you don't need any back up?" Jones asked, continuing to attempt to get in on Stone's action. He lugged his friend's gear from the back of the Suburban and tossed it into the G-man's open hands.

Stone shouldered the backpack and shook his friend's hand, returning the iron grip of the former weightlifting champion in good, competitive fun.

"I'm absolutely certain I need the back up," Stone assured. "But this definitely isn't something you want to get involved in. It's deep, and it's messy. I couldn't do that to you."

Jones scoffed at Stone's disclaimer. "Shit, you know that's how I like it. It's no fun unless you're getting a little dirty."

The agent and marshal shared a laugh. Stone enjoyed the banter of a real friend. Jones was exactly the kind of man he needed on his side right now. He was a pit bull, relentless and tough, but also incredibly intelligent. Jones' knack for tactical acuity was nearly impossible to duplicate, and Stone knew that would be an intricate factor in his man-hunt. The unknown subject, or unsub, was clearly a master of execution in evading the FBI for nearly three years, and Jones could significantly narrow the gap between apprehending the mystery fugitive and his continued evasion. But Jones was a friend, and Stone would never pull a friend into this kind of lion's den voluntarily.

Stone looked at Jones seriously, washing away the lighthearted mood the jokes provided. "I wish it were that easy. This isn't the kind of thing a family man wants to get dirty in. I've been chasing this guy across the country, and if it weren't for the body count he's leaving behind you'd swear he didn't exist."

Jones understood, nodding his compliance. "Funny you got this case and there's hardly any news about it."

Stone knew the comment was worded in such a way he'd be lured into elaborating about the situation. Jones could read between the lines, was playing his strength in tactics, but it was too obvious.

"Nice try," Stone said. "But that should tell you how deep this goes, my friend."

Jones shrugged off the dismissal. "I had to try."

The two men shook hands and half hugged, slapping each other hard on the back. Jones wished Stone luck as the agent jogged up the stairs of the executive jet.

"I'm working for the wrong agency," Jones shouted.

"Get your education and transfer," Stone said. "I could use a good partner in the mix. *Once* this is finished."

Jones gave Stone the finger. The marshal had bypassed having a bachelor's degree with over a year's worth of specialized experience to begin his career in the United States Marshal Services. He was only one year short of achieving a four-year degree from an accredited university to meet the FBI's requirements as a valid candidate. He'd need an age waiver for having exceeded thirty-seven years on God's green earth by a single year, but his fitness, stellar transcripts in academia, and veteran status would make him a standout. And Stone's reference wouldn't hurt, of course.

"Careful," Jones warned. "I may take you up on that. For real." Jones tilted his head with an expression implying he was serious.

Stone laughed as he reached the top of the stairs where a female flight attendant met him at the entrance and took his go-bag. The weight of it caught her off guard as her gentle poise nearly toppled her forward, dropping the bag to the floor. Stone quickly assisted her by taking the bag back into his possession, assuring her he would take care of it. The embarrassed attendant retreated deeper into the fuselage. The agent paid no attention to the woman, thinking nothing of her dropping the bag. It was heavy, somewhere between sixty to eighty pounds, much like the former ruck he humped around when he and Jones marauded their way through the Marines.

"Listen," Stone said. "Quit fucking around and get your shit together. You got the action on a daily basis, but if you're serious, I need you. But until you're qualified, I can't do anything about it." Stone grimaced and looked away. That was a partial lie. He could do something about it, but the timing wasn't right.

Jones snickered. "Oh, you got some pull now? Hook me up and move right into the big boy spot."

Stone nodded. "When I say this is serious it's just shy of compromising national security. It's no joke, and it runs *high* and *deep*."

Jones picked up what Stone was putting down with his verbal emphasis. He looked as though he'd been hit with a melancholic epiphany turning his jovial expression into a grim mask of austerity. The realization of knowing his close friend and former war buddy was into something so dangerous he couldn't speak about it, but had no one to really trust, was unnerving.

"Holler at me when you're finished and we'll get a beer," Jones invited. He knew Stone would catch on to what he truly meant, and the agent didn't disappoint.

"I hope you're on board before that happens," Stone said. Jones was asking him to let him know he was okay. It was something they'd communicated ever since they'd run operations in the Middle East post 9-11. "I have a feeling it's going to be awhile."

Jones nodded solemnly. "No way to tell then."

Stone shrugged, lightening the tone with a broad smile. "Keep an eye on the headlines. I'm close to this guy. It's about to get messy."

The former Marines exchanged a half-assed salute accentuated with the use of their middle fingers. Each man laughed heartily at their age-old goodbye salute, and then Stone disappeared into the jet.

****

The executive jet sent for Stone wasn't overly lavish, but it sure as hell beat the aeronautic herding of a commercial flight. The flight attendant worked up the nerve to show herself once before the G550 took off, apologizing for dropping his bag, and asked if he was in need of anything. The agent wasn't used to flying in the FBI's own private jet, and certainly didn't expect there to be an attendant on board. He kindly declined any services and asked to be alone. The woman conceded and never bothered Stone throughout the flight.

During the hour-long flight over four hundred miles Stone rested in silence. He wanted to relax, but given the day's previous excitement and what was to come the idea never came to fruition. Following the apprehension of Jonathan Michael Stevens, the circumstances were about to change drastically. Stone compared the two to the equivalent of experiencing a hurricane measured as a Category 1 and running directly into a Category 5. What lay ahead in Boston unnerved him. In all his years of military and law enforcement service he'd never thought to be caught up in a real conspiracy that pulled him in every direction imaginable. It was a wonder he hadn't broken down and eaten a round from his gun at this point. Stone was a so called 'boy scout,' always doing the right thing, with exception to Stevens' original apprehension, and everything was bigger than his selfishness. He was compelled to do for others before he did for himself, sacrificing more of himself than he could have imagined. Oddly enough, that characteristic is what landed him in this position in the first place, coupled with having no one to go home to. However, seeing this particular event through was not only for others, but for himself, and made life much more complicated.

There was an urge to research what had occurred in Boston; however, Stone felt he knew it all too well. He was only two months removed from the last location his unsub had worked his violent magic. Austin, Texas was rocked by the discovery of connections between cartels and a European crime syndicate specializing in human trafficking. It was no surprise to discover people being smuggled across the US—Mexico border. This was something nearly every citizen was aware of, and what the Border Patrol fought against to keep the borders secure. The level of violence used was exceptional. It was personal, as in previous locations, but it was increasing. The execution the unsub demonstrated was a display of years of intensive training and discipline with a skill level unlike anything Stone had ever witnessed. Hollywood could take notes for their versions of films depicting a one-man army. That's how efficient this man was. Stone fully expected the ante to be upped in Boston. His gut told him this crusade was coming to a head and, even deeper in the well of his emotions, he knew his involvement placed him in an increasingly more dangerous position with far less hope of survival.

Flying into Boston Logan International Airport tacked on an extra half hour of airtime as the FBI jet had to fall in line with the holding pattern of other flights. Once they'd landed and taxied to a non-commercial location of the airport, Stone immediately exited the jet. A black Chevrolet Suburban waited about ten yards away from where the jet parked. The government had no creativity in the vehicles they employed. Even though Stone was considered a boy scout of his profession, exuding the air of a government agent, there was nothing that stood out more than a government vehicle. They were all the same. Everywhere he went it seemed like he traveled to a different city just to ride in the same blacked out SUV to get shit done. And such was his life as an FBI agent.

Directions to the site of the massacre were preprogrammed into the SUV's navigation system. For Stone this was a standard operating procedure, or SOP. He had never been to Boston before, but it was a destination he'd wanted to visit being a half-assed history nerd. The circumstances dictated he would have no time to enjoy the sites of Boston. *Unless we destroy one in this town, too*, he thought.

The memory of the shootout he was involved in, in the oldest operating hotel that Austin, Texas had to offer, briefly played in his head. The Driskill was the location Stone thought he would apprehend his evasive suspect. Instead the agent wound up fighting through a wave of *sicarios*, hitmen exclusively used by the Mexican cartels. Luckily, Austin SWAT had been dispatched early on and they'd saved his ass before his head could be sawed off. Due to the sensitivity of his investigation the destruction the Driskill sustained never made any headlines. He wasn't sure how the news had been covered up, but it proved to him conspiracies truly were powerful when they were real.

In a matter of twenty minutes, or so, Stone ventured west on I-90 and south onto I-93 until he arrived in the historic Dorchester neighborhood of South Boston. The navigation took him to an area off the northern part of Dorchester Avenue corridor, a road that served as the major spine of the neighborhood, running south to north all the way through Dorchester to down town Boston. Stone found himself in a large area of low-rise industrial warehouses and staging yards for the South Bay Rail Yard on the eastern side of a neighborhood that seemed like a ghost town. There was a surrounding residential area of mixed ethnicity, however, the heavy police presence in the area injected a bustling feel to the industrial scene with bright flood lights set up to illuminate the area, along with the flashing of red and blue lights of patrol cars guarding the perimeter lines set to keep out on lookers.

When Stone made his final approach, a young patrolman waved him to a stop. The agent rolled down the automatic window of the Suburban and had his FBI badge ready along with a name for a local contact on the scene.

"Can I help ya', pal?" the patrolman asked, appearing especially guarded and cautious.

The patrolman approached from the front of the Suburban in a tactical stance, his torso facing away from Stone at a forty-five-degree angle, his strong hand covering his service pistol, ready to be drawn. Most would take offense to seeing an officer of the law appearing to be ready to draw their weapon, but considering the circumstances of what had taken place here earlier in the day it was a reasonable position for the officer to take. He was tall and also kept his distance, which gave him a better view of where Stone's hands were moving within the vehicle, and enough space to react and maneuver if he needed to. The agent was impressed with the patrolman's vigilance.

Stone flashed his identification as he replied, "Special Agent Connor Stone. I'm here…"

"We been expecting ya', sir," the patrolman interjected. He stepped aside and pointed beyond his patrol car stationed across one lane of the road as a partial roadblock. "Paa'k just outside the fence behind the forensics truck. I'll radio ahead to the lieutenant detective so he can meet you."

Stone nodded in reply and pulled away. The public barrier, the first in a set of three typical crime scene barriers, was nearly two hundred yards of open road where patrol cars and their officers lined the opposite side of the road. At first glance a bystander would think these guys were standing around with their thumbs up their asses, but they were keenly observant, feeling their eyes on him as he passed by. He parked as directed behind the forensics truck, which was a large boxed van similar to a UPS delivery truck. This was where the second barrier, or command area, began. The final aspect would encompass the core crime scene that began inside the warehouses perimeter fence and spilled into the building's interior.

The area seemed to be a demonstration of organized chaos on a grand level. Pockets of personnel were all over the grounds from forensic specialists, detectives, patrolman, paramedics, and even administration leadership. Admin always stood out from municipal agencies where they either wore nicely tailored suits, or their Class A uniforms emblazoned with shining buttons and commendations. Stone had seen large, busy crime scenes many times, but this was something else. He could easily say he'd not been on hand for a crime scene of this magnitude. The intimate details were beyond his reach so far, which was odd given the fact some form of briefing typically preceded his arrival. His familiarity with the unsub's actions mapped out the majority of what he expected to see and learn. In some fashion it would be far too similar to the previous three cities he'd visited on the vigilante's whirlwind tour of murder. Knowing what this man was capable of gave him a good mental picture, which he simply augmented into a more grisly image to prepare himself for the extent of violence he knew was inevitable.

On the south end of the public barrier there seemed to be some serious activity where the reporters were camped out. A makeshift press conference of some sort was under way. *What a mess*. Stone's contact was supposed to meet him, and according to the patrolman he'd radioed ahead to inform the lieutenant detective the FBI had arrived. The agent was itching to get started and began walking towards the gate's entrance. Another patrol officer stood at the gate as a sentry, checking ID's as people came and went. Those he recognized were let through without a hassle while forensic techs and detectives unfamiliar to him did not pass without flipping open their badge wallets or ID cards. Stone reached into his jacket pocket for his identification as he neared the sentry. He never needed it.

"Special Agent Stone," a raspy voice said, almost sounding more like a question than a statement.

Stone turned halfway around to his left. An older man dressed in a grey suit, tie and shirt collar both loosened, and a weary appearance to go along with a slow, loping walk. He carried two cups of coffee in medium sized Styrofoam cups fitted with standard white to-go lids. Steam perspired from the open drinking hatches. When Stone made eye contact with the man, he raised both cups accompanied by a hello nod. The obvious assumption was this man was his contact. The guy couldn't be half bad bringing coffee to the party right off the bat.

"Yes," Stone replied to the announcement of his name.

The older man flashed a grim smile. Stone guessed he'd been here for quite some time and, given the mood of the day and the circumstances, the man's tired expression was a dead giveaway to how dedicated he was to his job.

"Lieutenant Detective Randal McCrary," the grey suited man introduced himself. He extended a cup of coffee to Stone, which he eagerly accepted. "Some fuel to keep your motor running."

Stone thanked McCrary as they shook hands. "Connor Stone, thank you for being my liaison."

McCrary tipped his head to one side and then pursed his thin lips. "Ima' be honest. This was assigned to me since I'm the lead. It wasn't something I was too thrilled about."

A smile cracked across Stone's face. "Well, you know how to make a good first impression."

"Best ice breaker known to man next to whiskey." McCrary's eyes squinted shut as he nodded again, smiled, and raised the cup of Joe like a salute.

"And if it didn't work?" Stone asked.

"Then we don't work together. Can't trust a man who doesn't drink cawffee. Or whiskey."

A light laugh escaped from Stone's lips. "We used to say in the Corps that we ran on sarcasm, caffeine, and bad ideas."

McCrary enjoyed the nostalgia, raising his cup in a salute once more. '*Semper fi.*'

Stone gestured towards the warehouse with the cup of coffee as though it were guiding a beacon. "Shall we?"

McCrary grunted in reply, and turned without saying a word. Stone followed him through the gate without a single question from the gate's patrol sentry. The detective explained briefly how Stone's presence was expected. And he was with the lieutenant leading the investigation of the crime scene so Stone wouldn't be bothered by trivial questions. McCrary did make it clear how he'd be right beside him all the time.

"Well, I'd expect it, working together," Stone said.

McCrary stopped and turned to Stone. They were about the same height, just over six foot, but McCrary was likely taller in his prime as he slouched slightly. He had an old-world aura to him, almost as though he belonged in a gangster film. His presence was heavy, and being a large man, he easily stood out. The facial expression he wore was more of a permanent mask which, if Stone read it correctly, told anyone who approached McCrary to fuck off before he could tell them. Stone sensed he was about to be told.

"This is true," McCrary said, "but most don't care to work with an agent of the FBI. Past experiences have left a bad taste in most mouths. And being that you're the expert on this supposed vigilante, killer-whatever, there's a high expectation of you letting us know how much we don't know."

"Great, we're in buddy cop territory already," Stone joked. It wasn't well received. He continued to say, "Look, I may be the so-called expert, but don't think I'm here to just run the show. If I'm more successful in gaining ground on this asshole, I may be an arrogant prick about it, and I'd have a task force with me to lead the investigation. But I have neither. Have I been close? Once. That doesn't amount to shit in the grand scheme of things. I'll be happy to fill you in on what I've learned if you're happy to help me put this fucker in a pine box. Or behind bars."

McCrary sipped his coffee, dark squinting eyes dialed in on Stone's blue crystals. "We're gonna' get along jus' fine."

"Lead the way." Stone again gestured towards the warehouse with his cup of coffee.

The detective paused when they reached the warehouse entrance. He appeared to be sizing up the doorway before walking through it for the umpteenth time. Stone watched him exhale deeply and shake his head slowly. He understood. Scenes like these left behind by the vigilante were hyper violent, and hard to take in at first. Even numerous visits didn't make things any easier. Stone's experiences had made him numb to the level of violence, yet it was no less disturbing. With everything he'd seen he had expected to become desensitized over time. Perhaps it was morbid to think, but the killings never ceased to amaze.

McCrary convinced himself to walk through the door and Stone followed. They moved a few feet inside and paused again. It took a moment to absorb the murderous grandeur that had been accomplished.

There were taped off quadrants spanning the warehouse floor with smaller sections within each to better organize each area. These crime scene sections expanded beyond the floor into the lower office area, and to the deck-like upper tier. Stone attempted to count how many forensic agents were working across the space of the building. It wasn't worth the time. There were far too many and he guessed a good portion of them weren't actual crime scene techs. It was more likely each area was overseen by a forensic agent. It would make sense to have some brought in by the state police as well, but it wasn't a detail Stone concerned himself with. The crime scene investigators carefully maneuvered through their work areas due to the excessive crimson evidence left behind by the dead. Clear eye protection was worn by all, as well as blue booties covering their shoes. At their feet was a sea of yellow numbered markers tagging evidence ranging from an assortment of discharged shell casings, the various weapons used, chalk outlines and body parts separated from their owners that still needed to be cataloged. Designated walk-thru lines were taped off to gain access through the warehouse without disturbing the immediate areas where evidence collected.

To the left Stone saw a line of nearly two dozen black rubber body bags. Judging by the work being done by the Coroner there were still more to add to the lineup. He tapped McCrary on the shoulder and motioned towards the dead. "Let's start there."

McCrary seemed surprised. "What the hell for?"

"I want to see something."

McCrary reluctantly followed Stone. When the agent reached the line of body bags, he asked one of the forensic agents clad in white hooded overalls to unzip all the bags. The forensic agent appeared taken off guard by the request, and rightly so. McCrary had no idea what Stone was up to, even when Stone turned to him for assistance.

"Do it," the detective said.

The forensic agent motioned to another to help him open the body bags. "This is gawna' stink this place up even more."

The forensic agent was referring to the decomposition of the bodies that begins several minutes after death. The oxygen deprived cells ultimately led to the bodies' self-digestion and, given that it had been hours since death was administered, the process was well underway. Rigor mortis had certainly set in. As the forensic agents began unzipping the bags a rotting stench filtered into the air like a heavy musk. The smell was so powerful Stone thought he could almost see it form in a mist-like vapor. He and McCrary both used their ties to cover their noses and mouths.

"I could have done without this," McCrary mumbled behind his muffled mouth.

Stone moved forward and looked intently at the bodies. He motioned to the forensic agents to pull the body bags open wider to expose the brutality the dead had experienced. The first forensic agent began to object but McCrary quickly put a stop to the bitching with the wave of his hand. It was a testament to the respect he carried as a veteran detective. McCrary's order was unchallenged.

With the further exposure of each body, Stone moved in closer. He dropped his tie, ignoring the pungent smell of death, risking the acrid flavor hanging in the air. Each body had excessive bullet wounds, making it easy for the coroner to determine cause of death. Stone's concern was seeing the level of violence used in the execution. One body had half its torso blown wide open. Another must have been filled with an entire magazine of high caliber ammunition. At least three had multiple gunshots to the head. Some had clearly been shot in the face by a shotgun blast, most likely a heavy slug that expanded on impact.

"Why are you escalating so much?" Stone asked himself, yet

seeming to direct the question to his unsub. He stood and backed away from the body bags, surveilling the dead.

Beyond the unveiled organs, white protruding bones from fileted rib cages and torn apart flesh, Stone appeared satisfied with what he saw. He thanked the forensic agents and they immediately began securing the contents of the bags.

"I've been at this for a long time, Special Agent Stone," McCrary said, confused by what he'd just witnessed. "Mind telling me what that was about?"

"He's escalated his level of violence," Stone explained. He appeared to be just as confused. "You saw the bodies?"

"I saw them earlier, and again now, yes."

"What stands out the most to you?"

McCrary mulled over the question, believing it to be idiotic, especially for an FBI agent. "I don't know. What?"

Stone was disappointed by the lack of trying. "How many homicides have you worked over the years?"

"Too many."

"Any serial killings? Or have you had any behavioral training?"

"You mean like profiling? Yeah." McCrary was getting annoyed with the line of questioning from Stone.

The G-man shook his head. "The point is there's a difference in simply killing someone and purposely murdering someone. Everything this guy has done has been extremely violent. Brutal. But he's escalating, if you can believe that's possible. He's not just taking these guys out to take them out. The level of violence inflicted goes well beyond wanting them dead. It's personal. There's a level of rage instilled with each killing here."

McCrary nodded. "I understand that. But what if they're not random? He clearly intended to come here and do exactly what he wanted." He looked around, opening his arms to the vast space of the warehouse where there was little cover. "It's also hard to believe he didn't sustain some form of injury. Who the fuck kills over twenty men, or thirty plus, in a *personal* fashion in a wide-open area, and comes out unscathed? Pumpin' that much ammo into this many assholes is ridiculous."

Stone turned to the warehouse floor, scanning the area. Not even the steel beams supporting the structure were big enough to provide cover from multiple angles. Sure, there were some stacks of random pallets here and there from other shipped items, some riddled with bullets, but not enough to realistically give a sustainable amount of protection. He became lost in his vision of what could have happened. McCrary made a good point. There was no clear explanation how the vigilante could have been so successful. Let alone needing an incredibly high skill set, he would need a miracle.

"Unless…" Stone whispered to himself, expressing the beginning of a thought but cutting it short.

"Unless what?" the detective asked.

Stone disappeared into a trance, envisioning the assault. His exposure to the vigilante's capabilities put him in touch with how dangerous he was. This was clearly an elevated event where the guy showed what he was really capable of. In his mind Stone saw a tactically clad man moving with uncanny intent, wasting no time, shooting first with no regards for questions. He'd use bodies as meat shields to make his progression through the gauntlet of men. This would explain the extreme lead poisoning, but didn't exclude the vigilante from using overkill. Stone imagined the vigilante using one man against another, heavily armed, yet still inclined to disarm the men in the warehouse and use their weapons against them. He would have worn body armor as well. He would need to. There was no other way. And he started upstairs with the advantage of the high ground, working his way down and through the warehouse. Top to bottom.

"That's how you did it," Stone said, once more directing his speech to the unknown killer. His tone came across as impressed. He looked to McCrary and said nothing.

"You have some kind of epiphany, agent?" McCrary asked.

"Just a theory," Stone lied. "It's a little farfetched. Pulling this off is next to impossible."

McCrary snickered. "Yet here we are. I get the impression you have a deeper insight to this guy than you're letting on."

"It's all conjecture."

"What about multiple killers? A team?" McCrary suggested.

Stone shook his head, still surveying the warehouse floor. "No. It's definitely only one man."

"Which is next to impossible, right?"

"For most men, yes. For a dangerous man with a high level of intent and capabilities? It appears as though the impossible is possible."

"Why isn't it a team? That would make more sense."

Stone looked around. He had said he'd be happy to fill the detective in on what he learned, and he was a man of his word. How much he'd fill McCrary in on was different entirely. There was an important aspect he needed to check out, which would be impossible to do without informing McCrary.

"Where were the people found?" Stone asked. "The victims?"

McCrary nodded to the second floor that encompassed the back end of the warehouse. It was a simple upper deck lined with offices with a central hallway. "The room on the far left past the offices was where Ana Stewart was found."

So, you entered on the second floor. Stone shook his head.

The detective pointed towards the south end of the building where a large steel door was ajar. McCrary looked angry as he thought of what had been done to the victims. His voice cracked when he spoke, attempting to control an angry tone. "Down there is a cellar where the otha' women and children were found."

Stone began walking down a designated path towards the south corner of the warehouse, saying nothing. As he passed a forensic agent near the steel door he asked for multiple black lights. In a matter of moments, the forensic agent produced two black lights nearly two feet in length. Both were portable and powerful for their size. They were exactly what Stone needed. He handed one to McCrary and crossed the threshold of the steel door.

"Hold on," McCrary protested. "Where are you going?"

"We're going down here," Stone replied.

"I went down there once. That was enough."

Stone looked down the stairwell. Forensics had placed a series of flood lights on the landings to light the way. McCrary couldn't be afraid of the dark. There was too much light. Perhaps it was the scent. The thick aroma of human waste, body odor, and mold filtered out of the cellar, hanging in the air. It was a sickening smell, but Stone's recent exposure to such exotic scents nullified the full effect of what the cellar provided.

"We need to go down here," Stone explained. "I have to show you something. I take it the victims have been removed and taken for medical attention."

McCrary nodded.

"Then what's the problem?" Stone asked. "Come on. This is important."

McCrary was hesitant to join the FBI agent. Witnessing the horrors these people were exposed to did not sit well with him. It turned his stomach. The job was troubling enough at times as it was without having to find twenty women and children stuffed into a small room against their will and abused for God knows how long. Seeing them being removed and privately transported for medical attention had broken the detective's heart in ways he didn't know existed. It was easy to reduce his attitude to that of someone who wanted to look the other way for the killings today, but not McCrary. He would uphold his oath to enforce the law and find this sonofabitch.

"Fine," the detective conceded.

Stone led the way down to the cellar, appearing not to be affected by the smell. McCrary covered his nose and mouth with his tie again, taking his time in completing the descent. Once they reached the cellar Stone finally covered his face with the collar of his jacket. The source of the stench could not be denied. It was far worse than the body bags, having no ventilation whatsoever, and heavily concentrated. Portable flood lights were set up in three corners facing the entrance. Three forensic agents worked the room, all dressed in white hooded overalls, and all wearing respirators. McCrary watched his step as he walked into the room while Stone could have cared less. The remains of what was left behind from the captives were smeared all over, some in piles and others in puddles.

"This won't take long," Stone proffered. "Kill the lights, please. Then leave."

McCrary fought back the urge to gag before he spoke. "Shut 'em down real quick guys."

The flood lights went out a moment later leaving all in a deep abyss of blackness. “Hit your light detective,” Stone directed.

Within seconds the hazy glow of the portable black lights illuminated the cellar where Stone and McCrary stood. The forensic agents used the light provided to find their way out. Once they were clear Stone moved towards the wall directly in front of him, and McCrary, facing east, scanned the light up and down its length. The light exposed nothing.

McCrary asked through his tie, “What the hell are you doing?”

Stone turned towards the opposite wall and shuffled towards it. “Confirmation.”

“Of what?”

The black light revealed a series of letters painted on the concrete wall. It was a detail known only by Stone and a few others (not to be named) from the other cities, and something that distinguished the unsub from random acts of violence against organized crime. The vigilante had spawned a number of copycat killers where hits had been made on crime syndicates, in turn giving Stone’s unsub credit to take heat off of competing organizations. Most had not included human trafficking, which was his guy’s main focus, and the killings had been objectively less violent. These characteristics were what set him apart, but so far, he’d left a message behind at every major crime scene.

“Shine your light here,” Stone instructed McCrary.

What the detective read was probably the most shocking reveal of the day, which was difficult to pull off given the circumstances. He would have never expected to find something like this. McCrary looked to Stone, stunned at the revelation before them. “You got some explaining to do, Agent Stone.”

Stone ignored the comment, knowing all too well. He’d forewarned Jones of the danger this case provided. It couldn’t be helped to involve McCrary. He focused on the wall thinking, *Different city, same mess*. The message on the wall, though crudely painted in long, large letters read:

Welcome to Boston, Agent Stone.
It ends here.

Chapter 7
The Wolf

His eyes looked out from the darkness with a predator's gaze, his senses heightened from past years of elite training, taking in the sights and sounds of the ambient environment. The ongoing festivity that encompassed the courtyard outside the opened balcony of his den was not obnoxiously raucous, but exuded a volume unfit for the city. Perhaps it was the sprawling acreage the grand home set upon at the end of a winding private drive that absorbed the boisterous sounds celebrating the man's youngest granddaughter, Katyana. He adored the ten-year-old girl. Her life and spirit were so full of excitement and wonder, yet at the same time he was not incredibly close to his family. He provided the necessities luxuriously, holding close to the familial ties that bonded them in blood while maintaining a certain degree of emotional distance. As the patriarch he looked at his family as his pack, much like a wolf, which garnered him his rightful moniker; Yuri 'The Wolf' Kurikova. And much like his hardened history from the old Soviet Union, Yuri ruled with an iron fist.

Yuri sat deep in thought, allowing the celebration to give him a particular amount of distraction while examining the day's events. His business had taken a concentrated hit in the early hours, affecting operations of Greater Boston, which in turn created a chain reaction involving the entirety of his business. Though he lived on the outskirts of Sudbury, not more than forty minutes west from the Cradle of Liberty, Yuri felt the strike as if he had suffered it himself. His blood pressure had never been so high, and his adrenaline seemed to pump endlessly. Issues of rage had forfeited the Kurikova name from scaling the military ranks of the former Soviet Union, but not in the shadows of the criminal underworld. His fury was his calling card, and when the wolf struck, he was merciless. Now he was under attack. Playing the victim role was something he had become quite unaccustomed to. It had been a long time. There was an expectation that the fight would be coming to his doorstep and, even in its anticipation, it did not make the situation any less difficult to manage.

This "Boston Massacre" had seen almost forty good warriors, or *boyeviks*, meet their end. Yuri did not care much for this loss as these warriors were the lowest of his syndicate's *bratva*, or structure, and they were easy to replace. With connections in Mother Russia, the crime boss' far reaching influence in the import/export industry allowed him access to a virtual army. He would strictly employ Russians, typically with military or criminal backgrounds. When action was needed there could be no hesitation. He kept to his own, and his name was recognized with fear and respect. So, it was not the loss of the boyeviks that concerned him. It was the loss of product. And with the loss of product there would typically be concern of him being connected to the event, but with every man found dead there was nothing to attach to the Kurikova name. The warehouses ownership was tied up under a number of shell companies, none of which led back to Yuri. He had many legitimate businesses with garnered success, yet they were merely fronts for what happened in the dark corners that humanity wanted to ignore.

Vlademir Kurikova stood in silence near the opened balcony doors, eyes on a book lined wall at full attention. He'd stood here many times in absolute silence, facing forward without movement, and over time kept his attention by counting the volumes his father collected in his personal library. Vlademir had also read them all. Such was the way to success, his father had told him many times. Everyman who wants to be successful should read. Vlademir's favorite was Tsun Tsu's *The Art of War*. While having no military experience he had grown up under the steely handed coddling of a former Spetznaz soldier. This discipline allowed his statuesque ability to be thoroughly engrained. The patriarch's son stood so still it was difficult to tell if he was breathing. He'd recently delivered the bad news to his father about the extent of the warehouse massacre, and waited for orders. Many of the warriors they'd lost had been brought up directly under Vlademir's tutelage. Their passing was a disappointment, but mafia men worked knowing they were expendable.

"And the news?" Yuri growled from the shadows. "Any

developments?" His Russian accent was heavy, even after decades of exposure to American culture and practicing his English.

Vlademir quickly moved to switch on the television. As the flat screen flashed to life, Yuri's son was already adjusting the channels. A look of surprise washed over Vlademir's face as the screen introduced them to the warehouse scene with a familiar face. He looked to his father, who shared the same expression.

The Boston Police Commissioner was addressing the slaughter at the warehouse in Dorchester. Information scrolled across the bottom of the screen below a tag line that read: Boston Commissioner resigns after condoning vigilante violence. The news cast repeated Anthony DeMarte's announcement from earlier in the evening where he stated, "I cannot support the arrest of whoever returned Ana Stewart home to her parents today. And since I cannot do this, it is with a heavy, yet satisfied heart, that I announce my resignation as Boston's Police Commissioner."

Vlademir barked at his father, anger overstepping the soldier mentality that kept him in line his entire life. As family and blood, the patriarch dismissed the lack of etiquette. He didn't even react. His son displayed the Kurikova quality of ferocity, and it was not a flame to be extinguished. The young man was in his late twenties, muscular, and handsomely clean shaven from his chin back over the smooth dome of his skull. Vlademir seethed like an angry bull, eyes wild and primal. Yuri sat forward while advising his offspring to calm himself.

"He betrays us," Vlademir spat, turning back to the television. His fists clenched opened and closed, flexing the swell of his muscles beneath his Armani suit.

"This is unfortunate," Yuri said. His intense gaze froze Vlademir with pause, and he directed an index finger at the wolf cub. "You will deal with him."

Vlademir took a deep breath; heeding the prior instruction he'd been given to calm himself, and finding honor in his father's declaration. He closed his eyes and contorted his face into a frightful expression as he fought off the surging anger. Within a moment, counting far beyond ten, he returned to his stoic demeanor, and waited for instructions.

The Wolf watched the news cast return to the anchors in the newsroom. They discussed the commissioner's resignation and debated the idea the man introduced to the public: should this manner of violence be tolerated by the public given the nature and motivation behind it, or should it call for the true, law abiding justice?

The screen transitioned from the newsroom to a field reporter asking these questions to random citizens.

A man who clearly looked like a blue-collar worker, dressed in dirty coveralls and sporting a beard extending to the middle of his chest said, "Ya, know… If that were my kid, I'd want those men dead, too. People like d'em don't belong here. D'ey can't be allowed to prey on our kids. Dat's justice if ya' ask me."

A woman holding a young child on her hip wearing big looped earrings and chomping on gum agreed. "Someone -bleeps- with my kid. Takes them from me. Yeeah, they deserve to die."

A man and woman were next; both dressed cleanly, more along the level of being in a white-collar profession. "I don't think that kind of reaction can be tolerated. No." The man shook his head emphatically. "It sends the wrong message. We have laws for a reason. Sure, a horrible crime was committed. But does committing a worse crime wash it away? I don't think so."

The woman at the man's side followed up with, "I have to agree. This poor little girl, and the women and children found, gain nothing from the violence taken to return them home."

The reporter chimed in with, "Well, one could argue the violence was done on their behalf. Right or wrong, it is exactly what allowed them to be freed."

The woman shook her head, looking to the man for support. "No. Two wrongs don't make a right." The man nodded in agreement.

When the camera cut away the field reporter was alone. Large eyes full of life and surprise looked through the camera and out into the world to the viewers. "There's always one out there who doesn't get it. And I'm not condoning the violence. But, where would these poor victims be had this mysterious vigilante not acted? This is clearly a highly controversial issue. I'm Jamal Laurence. Back to you guys in the studio."

"*Tupaya ovtsa*!" Yuri cursed. "Stupid sheep."

Yuri waived his hand and Vlademir shut off the television. He waited to speak, processing the information and the entirety of the situation. There were few actions to take. With DeMarte resigning the only conclusion Yuri could draw was that the former commissioner was going to flee and, seeing how DeMarte never answered his phone or returned his calls, this told Yuri everything he needed to know. It was what weak people did. They were for sale, and they run. He couldn't allow this to happen. DeMarte knew far too much. Had the man done as he had on the newscast and then contacted Yuri it would be a different situation. Perhaps. He thought about that and came to the same, final conclusion.

"Take two men," Yuri said. "Find him."

"Bring him back?" Vlademir asked, even keeled and emotionless.

The patriarch stood and walked to the opening of the double balcony doors. He looked across the half-moon shaped deck, beyond its pearl white railing, and down at the courtyard. He saw the happiness his family enjoyed. Men, women, and children giving love to his granddaughter on her day of birth. Her uncle Oleg, on his son-in-law's side of the family and also Russian, pulled on Katyana's ears once for each year of her life. The old tradition had not filtered into the dust of history just yet. Not in this family. Yuri smiled. It was time to make an appearance as he had been preoccupied with the devastation to his business. He felt the presence of Vlademir's eyes on him, patiently waiting for instruction as his son stepped closer to his side.

"Yes. Bring him back," Yuri said, a whimsical smile overcoming him as he saw Katyana laughing with her friends. "Make sure he is breathing."

Vlademir said nothing as he turned away and disappeared from the den.

Yuri continued to oversee the celebration for a short period of time. In that moment he allowed the thought of his Katyana being in the position Ana Stewart had been in. His fury was instantaneous. Anyone who touched her would have met the same end. And what if anyone from his family had been found in a cellar, locked away in the dark, abused and forced to piss and shit at their feet like animals? No, he couldn't envision such a thing. Not his family. They could never be subjected to such conditions. They were family. They were not products of his worldly business ventures. Imagining such things was too derogatory. All that mattered was family, close or not, and the Wolf always protected his pack.

Chapter 8
"Where Do You Think You're Going?"

Fleeing had never entered Anthony DeMarte's mind until he spoke the final words during the impromptu press conference earlier in the evening. He almost had no control over the words he'd spoke, or so he felt. Racking his brain for the last few hours only fueled the fear of what kind of retaliation the Kurikova syndicate would offer. Or, as he began to rationalize the part he played, deserved. It made him frantic, but he wasn't about to waste time and find out.

The former police commissioner spent the last few hours following his departure from the crime scene collecting some needed essentials for his departure. He still wore his service weapon, a Glock 22 .40 caliber pistol. DeMarte had always remained proficient with it, qualifying regularly and holding himself to the same standards as Boston's patrolmen. Through the length of his career he'd drawn the pistol maybe a handful of times, and only discharged it twice in self-defense. When he was younger, moving through the ranks as a detective in numerous capacities, he'd been known as a gunslinger simply for his proficiency. Tonight, however, there was a new form of fear surging through him that was completely alien to a man of his experience. He wasn't sure he'd hit the broad side of a barn let alone be able to draw the Glock with any decisive speed. The adrenaline made his hands shake, and he'd been sweating almost constantly. He needed to put Boston in his rearview.

Home was a three story, light grey shingle style home built in 1905 and had belonged to his wife's grandparents. Over the years it underwent a number of upgrades and restorations. Miranda had enjoyed herself with the lawn care and gardening, always finding a way to make the home more inviting from the outside. Not that the quaint and extremely picturesque home didn't invite on its own. It seemed to be a blocky structure if not for the irregular massing that added a romantic appeal, the unexpected placement of a turret in the center of the home where DeMarte's den looked out towards downtown, and a connecting balcony which ran from the front of the home and along one side. Bay windows covered the back of the house where a privately fenced yard was immaculately manicured. DeMarte had forgone the lawn care and gardening on his own and paid a local company to tend to its upkeep in the wake of Miranda's passing.

Crossing the threshold of either entrance led into a spacious hardwood floor home. DeMarte locked the back door as soon as it shut, turned, and crossed the kitchen to the hall where a single set of stairs ascended to the upper floor. He bypassed the amassed collection of trinkets that filled the home without regard. None of them were his. Miranda had organized the cluttered antiques that had also belonged to her grandparents. Inheriting the home came with a lofty price for DeMarte, which meant keeping everything. But Miranda made it all work. She had that quality of exceptional organization, and tireless work ethic when keeping life together. This was her home, and after she passed DeMarte left everything the same. He didn't have the heart to change anything. It was his way of honoring and continuing to appreciate her. DeMarte rushed from room to room, grabbing hidden necessities as well as gold and silver valuables from the turn of the twentieth century he could travel with quickly and lightly. Since Miranda was gone and maybe looking down on him, he ignored the sense of shame he felt knowing these items were going to work as bribes for keeping him alive. His years of corruption had not only corroded his soul, but his spine as well.

DeMarte rushed into the master bedroom and stuffed a couple of items into an open suitcase. The black bag was nothing special except it had been a gift from his wife. Before her cancer set in, they had begun to travel, at least two major trips a year. Miranda knew, wanting to get out and see the world before she left it too soon. The former police commissioner put these thoughts behind him as he closed the two halves together and zipped the luggage shut. Another suitcase sat on the bed, larger than the first, but similar in style. Black canvas, generically similar to almost anything and everything else made, with the exception of red stitched letters on the outer pocket on the face of the luggage reading: DeMarte. It was a nice touch. Immaculately sewn, it made identifying the bag obvious. DeMarte chose this bag because it was going to carry the most valuable item he needed to disappear, money.

The large walk-in closet reflected a classical style. Gleaming dark wood encased the room from floor to ceiling. It was a favorite design, even to DeMarte, but Miranda was solely responsible for putting it together. She had pretty much run everything in the house, like the age-old stigma of who was really in charge. As a wife she had been more supportive of a police officer as a husband than DeMarte deserved. She'd always told him, 'You take care of the streets, and I'll take care of our home.' And she had done so very well. Much like his dealings with Kurikova, DeMarte hadn't told her of the secrets he kept in the house. There hadn't been much reason to. Miranda wouldn't have approved, but who would have? DeMarte sometimes couldn't believe he had gone down that rabbit hole, yet once he'd experienced the allure of what his criminal dealings had brought him, or rather the potential future it would provide, he became addicted. It wasn't that he didn't know the part he played and in what kind of industry. It was that he maintained a position that kept him from knowing the details, which made all the difference to him at the time. The massacre woke him up like a shot in the dark.

In the back corner of the large closet DeMarte turned to his right and dropped to his knees, sliding to a stop towards the back, left corner. Before him was a small glass doored cabinet no higher than his mid-thigh, and used as shoe display. Miranda had kept some vintage ballroom dancing shoes her grandmother had once worn in the cabinet. Seeing how it was so important and no one would dare touch these items, or face Miranda's wrath if it happened, DeMarte had brought in a contractor to install a safe in the wall behind the shoe display. The overall design of the walk-in closet was meant to fit this display case in the room. Knowing his wife's affinity for the antique case he'd convinced her of where it should be placed to be in a protected spot, all the while planning to put the safe behind it. DeMarte was thankful the contractor he hired had exceptional skills. It had taken less than a full day to install the safe while Miranda had taken the time to see old friends in the city, fulfill some appointments and run some errands. It was the day she learned she had lung cancer.

DeMarte pulled the cabinet out from the slot it fit snuggly into.

Normally he was careful with the case, sliding it cautiously and respectfully from its home. Not tonight. Tonight, it squeaked and rubbed as he removed it. He was shaking it free and frantically sliding it to one side as if it meant nothing. The glass door rattled violently, threatening to crack or chip, but holding fast and remaining safe. His anxiety drove him to dive into the alcove and unlatch a lock that would allow him to slide the above shelving to the right and provide more room to maneuver. Having done this, it exposed a thin line in the drywall. DeMarte leaned forward placing one hand in the upper left corner of the cutout, and another just right of the center. He pushed inward and removed his hands. As he sat back on his heels, he could barely make out a gentle click from behind the wall through the pounding of his racing heart. It was the first moment he took notice of how profusely he was sweating, and moved to wipe his brow with the rolled-up sleeve of his button up shirt. The section of the wall silently extended outward, protruding from the clean lining the contractor had cut out in the closet, and rested there.

Even in his state of agitation DeMarte drifted off in the moment. His pulse rhythmically hammered inside his head, hypnotically forcing him to forget what he was doing. A sense of clarity came over him as it will with the most inconvenient timing. His feeling of fear drifted away. His heart slowed to a more calming cadence. He felt light as a cloud. A vision of Agadir, Morocco was all he saw. It was a vacation Miranda had always wanted to take, but they never made it. The tourist attraction was on the Atlantic coastline with bright white buildings and palm lined boulevards. DeMarte saw the sailboat he had procured, and envisioned braving the beautiful blue waters on his own. The thought brought tears to his eyes. His Miranda wouldn't be able to share the experience, and even before her dying days took hold of her, he never afforded the effort to whisk her away to fulfill the dream trip she'd envisioned. Instead, in light of the current events, it would provide him a place to escape to. Morocco was exempt from United States extradition.

DeMarte swung open the removed section of wall. The piece was arranged on a sliding hinge so it could be moved farther away from the wall, and then folded to the right where it would give complete access to the safe. Beyond the threshold of the secret compartment was a wall safe only DeMarte could open. It required a five-digit code and his thumb print. He entered the code, pressed his thumb to the biometric scanner and received a light beep in response as he gained access. The safe door came open with minimal effort revealing the crowded contents of stacked cash. Over a decade's worth of money was there, which DeMarte estimated to be over two and a half million dollars, minus the five hundred grand the sailboat in Morocco had cost him. Another three million sat in a Swedish bank account under an alias a document forger had created for him. A glint of satisfaction shone in his eyes. Maybe it wasn't so bad having all of this to himself.

Again, his thoughts quickly transitioned to the threat Kurikova posed. The Wolf would be unrelenting in his pursuit, and merciless in his action. DeMarte needed to stay ahead of him, and that meant not wasting any more time. He needed to focus on getting gone. A dark cloud had fallen over him, throwing his entire life's work into a storm. It was all brought on by his choices, but nonetheless it was there now. The right choices would get him out of it, and see him through to a new life. He wasn't ready to die yet. He'd done too much bad to make up for, whether it was firsthand or secondary, but he was going to live like he could die every day. Death wasn't going to punch his ticket yet.

The bright lights of the closet dimmed as DeMarte took the money from the safe and put it into a pile at his knees. He sat up and looked to the ceiling where a shadow stood over him, looking down from its hulking stature with crazed fury in its eyes. DeMarte froze, wanting to yell. He wanted to take the Glock from his hip and unload the hollow point rounds into the figure. But he couldn't move. Perhaps death had found him after all.

"Where do you think you're going?" the shadow growled bestially.

There was no European accent. No Russian diction in the pronunciation of his words. He couldn't be one of Kurikova's men. Kurikova strictly employed Russian's from the Motherland. Had he contracted out for a killer? No, he wouldn't do that. Kurikova would want to pull the trigger himself, but only after beating him to a pulp.

DeMarte felt his Glock stripped from its holster. The shadow had barely moved, or so it seemed. He was quick; too quick for DeMarte to do anything about. He couldn't quite comprehend why he wasn't fighting back. It wasn't like him. He had always been the protector; a warrior people called for help. That was who he was. And as he thought about it in those few seconds it quickly dawned on him that it might have been who he once was, but not anymore.

****

Ghost stood over the former police commissioner, blotting out the direct shine of the closet's light, instilling himself in shadow. He wore all black from his boots to his ski mask. A tactical vest protruded from beneath a black coat displaying an assortment of pockets fastened to its MOLLE style mesh. The look on Anthony DeMarte's face showed he could see everything was over. DeMarte was going to skip town, which was expected from a piece of spineless shit like him, but his plans were spoiled. And Kurikova's would be, too. It wasn't hard to believe the Russian mafia boss would soon have someone pay DeMarte a visit. Likely his son Vlademir. He was Kurikova's muscle and enjoyed violence. And he was very good at it with weaker people. Ghost knew all about them in great detail. If there were any luck in the world, Ghost would send the Wolf more than one message tonight.

The Glock thudded against DeMarte's skull. Not hard enough to knock him out, but hard enough to let him know he had no control. Ghost then took hold of the man by the back of his belt and dragged him towards the bedroom. He tossed DeMarte through the doorway and watched him flop and roll until he crashed against the bed on his backside, slumped over like a drunken hobo in an alley. DeMarte put his hands up in submission, blood streaming down the side of his head from beneath the thick mat of his manicured hair. Ghost took hold of DeMarte's left hand by four of his digits, twisting them down and towards his back. The control technique manipulated the fingers by hyperextending them in the wrong direction, and the twisting motion locked up his left wrist. DeMarte screamed in pain, flinching as his body responded to the pain involuntarily and the maneuver forced him to his feet. Ghost directed him out the door, and down the hall.

DeMarte attempted to struggle, but his actions were futile. Ghost was far too strong, and far too skilled. These factors, combined with his sheer size, made DeMarte feel small and weak, and he was far from being a light statured man. The way Ghost manhandled DeMarte was impressive even as the former commissioner's fear transitioned from being hypothetical to all too real. When they crossed into his den DeMarte learned how helpless he truly was. Ghost launched him over the top of his desk from nearly five feet away. The assaulted man's body cleared the contents decorating desktop. He sailed across the den's furniture, overturning the black, high backed leather chair as he collided with the wall. His head left a softball sized indentation in the drywall, coating his hair with white, chalky dust.

"Get up," Ghost ordered.

DeMarte emerged from behind the desk, using the furniture to pull himself up from the floor. He appeared dazed, but continued until he stood. Both arms supported him as he planted his hands flat on the desk.

Ghost stared through the former commissioner. When their eyes met DeMarte looked away, shaking his head as though he couldn't believe what was happening. Ghost never looked away from the broken man even as he stepped closer to the desk. A gloved hand reached into his black coat, and Ghost removed a folded manila envelope. He emptied the contents onto the desktop. A pile of paper printed photos came out, and Ghost spread them out so they could be better seen.

"Look at them," Ghost ordered.

DeMarte wasted time trembling and staring at the floor. One of Ghost's large hands slapped DeMarte along the side of his head, knocking the man to floor.

"Get up," Ghost demanded. He tucked DeMarte's Glock in his waistband and removed his own pistol fitted with a suppressor from a holster beneath his left arm. The addition to the pistol extended the barrel another three inches. He aimed the silenced weapon over the desk, directing the barrel at DeMarte's head. "I won't tell you again."

DeMarte stood up again, the right side of his face red and throbbing. He looked over the pictures and, as he realized what he saw, his bewilderment changed from distraught to utter shock. A form of awareness seemed to come back to him, and he slowly redirected his gaze to the black clad man before him.

"Explain," Ghost said.

"Where did you get these?" DeMarte asked. Anger slipped into his tone as his voice cracked.

Ghost shook his head to either side. He raised the pistol and shot DeMarte in the left shoulder.

The hollow point slug ripped through the man and lodged into the wall. A spray of blood immediately washed over the same area, and DeMarte followed as the powerful impact tossed him backwards like a rag doll. The gunshot took his breath away. Pain surged through his shoulder as though he'd been speared by fire. The entry wound instantly gushed blood, and the exit was ten times worse. A thick crimson trail ran from where DeMarte hit the wall down to where he collapsed. The cry he emitted was brief, turning to a gritted moan through clenched teeth, trying to be tough like the old version of himself would have been.

"Who are you?" DeMarte screamed. He roared with anger, somehow finding a lost sense of courage forsaken to men of his former profession. It was short lived as his desperation retained its hold on him. "I can pay you money. Take it all! Please!"

A bribe? Ghost wasn't too surprised. DeMarte was just as pathetic as Ghost had anticipated. The former commissioner's descent into the criminal lifestyle had deteriorated his guardian instinct. Once he was a protector of the streets, trusted to enforce the law with high morals and a code of ethics, and now he was reduced to a bad man who'd found himself surrounded by worse men.

Ghost aimed the silenced pistol at DeMarte's opposite shoulder. DeMarte raised his right hand in an attempt to signal his attacker to stop. The man waited with his pistol aimed, unwavering.

"Okay," DeMarte shouted through the pain. "Okay."

Standing was a challenge, but DeMarte got it done. He stood over his desk again, supporting himself with only one hand while his breath came in short, sporadic bursts. He glared at the man in black, unsure where to begin. It was obvious it didn't matter. He was going to die tonight regardless of what he said. And judging by the pictures spread out across the desk DeMarte didn't need to explain much.

"What do you want me to say?" DeMarte asked.

Ghost said nothing.

"You clearly know a lot. Or everything." DeMarte paused, swatting at the loose pictures, attempting to catch his breath while fighting the pain searing through his body. "You must be him; the man who's responsible for this morning?"

Ghost weighed the many options he had, deciding against killing DeMarte just yet. He nodded affirmatively in reply.

"And you know who this man is?" Demarte pointed to a photo of himself with Yuri "the Wolf" Kurikova. He held it up.

Ghost nodded.

"I can pay you to keep him off my ass," DeMarte said, reworking the angle of saving himself. He pointed towards the wall indicating the closet they had recently came from. "There's two million dollars there. Take it."

Ghost remained silent, dismissing the pathetic offer. It was generous and he was going to take it anyway. He shot DeMarte in the right knee. The leg whipped backwards out from under the man followed by the other as the force of the bullet's impact swept the bewildered former commissioner off his feet. DeMarte's face bounced off of the desktop with a wet thud, crushing his nose and knocking out his two front teeth. He cried out; his diction immediately altered to a shouting lisp. Ghost wasted no time circling around the desk and hauling DeMarte off the floor. He righted the desk chair before he set his victim in it, and then slammed DeMarte up tight to the desk. Gloved fingers overturned a picture and provided a pen. Ghost leaned in close to DeMarte, rapidly whispering in his ear, and holding him tightly by the nape of his neck.

DeMarte took the pen in his right hand and began writing. Anything he did now wouldn't matter. Kurikova was no longer a viable threat. He wasn't going to last much longer. He could feel it hanging in the air, thick enough to cut, and nearly too dense to breathe in. His death was inevitable. When he finished writing DeMarte expected another nonchalant bullet hole in his body, likely in his brain pan, but he was hit with an entirely different surprise.

"You have a decision to make," Ghost said. He peered out the window facing towards downtown Boston. The view was horizontal to the front of the home where a black Cadillac Escalade came to a stop at the curb side of DeMarte's house.

DeMarte trembled from the shock, bleeding profusely from his nose and mouth all over his desk and floor. He became fully unhinged, tears welling up in his eyes, trying to think of a way out of the only outcome fate held for him. A stainless steel .357 revolver dropped onto the top of the desk before him, thumping over the paper pictures, and spinning until the ominous barrel pointed directly at him. He noticed the hammer had already been pulled back making the gun ready to fire.

Ghost walked away from DeMarte, stopping short in the doorway as he filled it like a black mass. "You have more visitors. And you have one round in that chamber. I suggest you make the right decision."

Chapter 9
More Than a Wolf Can Chew

Under the right conditions it takes very little to turn a frown upside-down. In Vlademir Kurikova's case all it took was seeing the lights on in Anthony DeMarte's home. He exited the front passenger side of the Escalade without saying a word, or looking away from the home. DeMarte had entertained the Wolf and his cub once or twice over the years for business purposes, and Vlademir looked to where DeMarte's den was located on the second floor on the south side of the dwelling. He could see a shadow moving around in the backdrop of the room indicating DeMarte's presence. The angle from the street wasn't ideal, but it told Vlademir everything he needed to know for the moment: the former commissioner was still home.

Two large, muscular men joined Vlademir on the sidewalk next to the Escalade. They were dressed professionally in suit jackets and slacks, but casually matched with tight black V-neck shirts underneath. Their garb betrayed who they were as former Spetznaz soldiers in the Russian military, but played up their roles within the *bratva* as personal guards to Vlademir. The youthful Kurikova did not necessarily need them for protection. He was raised to be incredibly capable. These men, however, initially served as his trainers, elevating him to an elite status. It wasn't until his aggression and prowess for violence allowed him to match and, quite possibly, surpass their well-honed abilities that Vlademir no longer needed their protection. But, having two of the most dangerous men Russia had produced in recent years as back up didn't hurt, either. Spetznaz soldiers were among the toughest soldiers the world had to offer, at times bordering on the thin line of insanity.

The larger of the two was nearly a head taller than Vlademir himself, with a cleanly shaved dome polished to a prideful shine. A dark, thick beard counterbalanced the lack of hair on his head, and was accentuated by a mustache with either end pinched down to sharp, needle-like points. The second guard had a dark mane slicked back into a shining helmet of hair extending down to the back of his neck. He was the complete opposite of his comrade and cleanly shaven as he stood eye to eye with Vlademir. Their dark eyes were full of malcontent as they surveyed the neighborhood until settling on DeMarte's home.

Vlademir directed the bearded soldier to the back of the house as he activated the screen to his cell phone. He brought up DeMarte's number and pressed the green phone icon to dial the number. His free hand flashed hand signals to the other guard directing him to prepare to breach the front door. The phone rang five times before going to voicemail. Vlademir cleared the call and slipped the phone into his back pocket with his left hand while his right drew a pistol from beneath his black leather jacket. Joining his guard at the front door Vlademir positioned himself on the opposite side of the entry, holding his pistol in a low-ready position at the center of his broad chest with the barrel directed towards the ground. He and the guard locked eyes, seemingly syncing their breathing in what transitioned to a count down.

3…

2…

BANG!

A gunshot thundered from within the residence. Vlademir and the guard both sat back on their haunches in an instinctual manner of avoiding gunfire and seeking cover. Seconds felt like an eternity as both men regained their composure. Vlademir tested the doorknob. It turned, but the door didn't budge. It was dead bolted. Without direction the guard immediately circled out to center himself with the front door, and then swiftly launched a heavy boot at a weak point next to the doorknob. The door crashed inward, ripping apart the door jamb where the deadbolt had secured the entry. It collided with the inner wall to the right so hard that it embedded the knob into the drywall. The two Russians breached the doorway, pistols aimed out in front while moving forward swiftly, clearing the room from one side to another, careful not to cross each other with their weapons.

The home opened up into what would have been a spacious living room if not for the vast collection encompassing the area. Beyond the sectional leather couch and big screen television from an earlier decade, the room was organized chaos; walls lined with knickknacks and antiques on shelves, as well as filing cabinets all about. Vlademir slipped into the adjacent room, which naturally transitioned towards the kitchen. The guard backed in behind Vlademir to cover their path, careful to look to his surroundings so he didn't run into the heavy mahogany dining table and chairs. They met up with their bearded partner who'd breached the back door at the same time. Thus far the house was clear.

Vlademir used more hand signals to direct his men upstairs. The guard with the slicked back hair took point with Vlademir directly behind him, and the bearded soldier followed. The three men moved in unison; a practiced formation drilled hundreds, if not thousands, of times. They ascended the stairs with the point man aiming forward towards the landing, Vlademir covered the opened hallway space bordered by the second-floor railing, and the bearded man covered their backs. They were taking no chances by rushing ahead without caution. Vlademir considered the idea of the killer being anywhere they would do business, which included tying up loose ends with DeMarte.

The young wolf was not unlike his father in the manner of thinking before acting. Among his favorite quotes was one by the Ancient Greek scholar and Athenian general, *Thucydides*, who wrote, 'The society who separates its scholars from its warriors will have its thinking done by cowards and its fighting done by fools.' Vlademir took this to heart when preparing any operation. He was neither a coward, nor a fool, and to underestimate the abilities of a man capable of killing nearly three dozen of his father's *boyeviks* in a single setting would have been the most foolish act of all. Caution was necessary even if such a dangerous threat was not in play, but being that there was one to seriously keep in mind, it made the standard much more necessary. A thinking man lived longer than a man who acted without thinking.

At the top of the landing Vlademir lined up with the slick haired guard. They turned their backs to each other and moved simultaneously as they both leaned over to scan the entire hallway. The guard leaned to his right and covered the direction leading beyond the railing. Vlademir leaned to his left covering the length of the hall leading to DeMarte's den. The motion was seamless and quick. When they established either pathway was clear they moved up to the top of the landing. Vlademir covered the hall while the guard separated from his back. The bearded Spetznaz soldier quickly moved to the landing and cleared the end of the hall with his counterpart. The sweep took only a few seconds before they returned.

Vlademir took point leading down the hall. He and the guards transitioned seamlessly as they overlapped each other to clear the rooms leading to the den.

The room nearest to the den was the only other room that had any lights on within. The two guards entered the room while Vlademir acted as the hall sentry. The room was DeMarte's master bedroom. Being a larger room, it took a little longer to search. The two guards exerted extra caution as they passed into the massive walk-in closet. They opened every door within the closet, and searched through every hanging piece of clothing. Circling around the island at the center of the room they found the path to be unobstructed. They overlapped the others search before clearing the closet. It seemed like forever, but the search took just under a minute. As they exited the room the bearded guard tapped Vlademir on the shoulder, silently signaling him they were ready to move on.

Vlademir moved forward towards the closed den door. His guards fell in position behind him. All three men moved slowly; knees bent to keep them mobile in case emergent action was needed as they pressed forward. It seemed strange to have the door closed when DeMarte had the entire home to himself. Vlademir knew about the passing of his wife. How she'd filled their home with family relics and antiques as her grandparents had asked her to. And he also knew how DeMarte had never told her of his dealings with the Wolf. It was no surprise the former commissioner had been twiddled down to nothing of a man, giving him all the more reason to run like a coward. Vlademir despised cowards, and he wished his father would let him kill DeMarte for him. But the Wolf still liked to feed every now and again.

Vlademir directed the slick haired guard to the opposite side of the door using only hand signals. They repeated their synchronized breathing, assimilating the countdown before they breached the door to the den. The bearded guard centered himself with the door, aiming forward as he closed in on the door. He would enter first, followed by his counterpart and Vlademir as they filed through the door and turned to cover opposite corners of the room.

3…

2…

1…

When the door whipped open the men executed their plan flawlessly. There was no threat to be found even as they entered the room where they had seen previous movement upon their arrival. What they found was a dead Anthony DeMarte arched back in his office chair, arms flailed lifeless to either side. The crimson and grey matter of his brains dripped from the ceiling. Meaty chunks of DeMarte's final thoughts fell to the desktop, striking the surface with a wet slap. Each man lowered their weapons, finally relaxing as they looked to the fresh corpse.

"Shit," Vlademir exhaled. "He was more of a coward than I thought."

He walked closer to the desk to see what DeMarte had left behind. Papers were scattered about, but none of them resembled a suicide note. Blood covered a good majority of the papers, saturating them so they were wet and floppy, but Vlademir could tell they were pictures. Not all were painted red. The pictures showed dealings between his father and DeMarte. Some even looked to have included him, but they were heavily sloshed in gore. Vlademir knew these couldn't be found by the police, who could not be too far away with a gunshot in such a well-to-do neighborhood. He directed one of the guards to put on some gloves and gather the papers.

The guard with slicked back hair reached into a pocket inside his jacket and removed a pair of rubber gloves. Vlademir saw the guard's response to his orders out of the corner of his eyes as he never looked away from the desk, focused on the mess before him. The man quickly worked to dispose of the papers. A tin garbage can quickly became a makeshift furnace.

Vlademir could only guess that they had just missed the man who'd been sabotaging his father's operations. His father had many enemies, but in light of the situation it was likely to believe this vigilante was the one responsible for the pictures and DeMarte's death. Had they arrived sooner Vlademir could have put this entire business to rest, and delivered the man's head to his father. What an honor that would have been.

Two metallic whispers cut into the stillness of the room. The sound of a gun slide clicking back came in tandem with the pistol spits of lead. Vlademir recognized the sound of the suppressor, even though it was often considered a silencer. Truth-be-told a gunshot could not be silenced, only suppressed, and it had the distinct sound of a gunshot with the volume turned down low. Out of his peripheral vision Vlademir caught the spray of blood to either side of him, painting the walls in a chaotic spread of brain matter and skull fragments. Both of his guards collapsed like falling oaks, elite training be damned. The essence of time came slowly as Vlademir reacted instantly, moving milliseconds after the spray of blood, and in sync with the falling bodies. He turned with his pistol leading the way, looking in unison to find the threat at his back. It was a failed attempt before he'd started it. However, Vlademir was not a coward, and he would gladly die if it meant killing the man terrorizing his father.

****

A third whisper spoke to the Russian as he spun around. His reaction was quick, but not quicker than the whisper. What the whisper said to him was of an incredibly intimate nature, forming a bond that would not be forgotten. The powerful word it spoke punched Vlademir in the right side of his chest. The bullet did not blow through the heavily muscled man; it drilled him backwards like a hit from a sledgehammer. The Russian's pistol went off as he went backwards, and then it fell from his grip when the bullet hit its mark and severed the connecting tendons linked to his grip. Vlademir's shot hit its target, but to ill effect. Ghost stood tall and firm as the bullet proof under layer of his vest absorbed the impact of the slug. His outstretched arm aiming a suppressed pistol never wavered. Vlademir cried out in anger like a wounded predator unwilling to concede.

The Russian surged forward full of fight in spite of his right arm being useless and dangling at his side. Ghost had no time for a struggle. A fourth whisper shot Vlademir in the left thigh, kicking back the powerfully built limb, and dropping him to one knee. The vigilante dropped a duffle bag overflowing with cash, and then swiftly followed up with a forward thrust kick to the center of Vlademir's chest sending him crashing into the bloody altar of DeMart'es desk. Smoke from the fire burning in the tin garbage cast a light fog in the room as Ghost stood over the top of the Russian like death prepared to doom a soul to hell. He pinned Vlademir down with a knee to his belly and mashed the suppressed barrel of the pistol under his chin. The heat absorbed by the suppressor from the gunshots burned into the Vlademir's skin, but he paid no attention to the pain.

Instead, defiance blazed like a fire in Vlademir's eyes. Ghost had seen this many times when men didn't know when they were defeated. They welcomed death as an honor, or overblown *bravado*, until it was truly time to die. Vlademir was not like these men. He would gladly die in his father's name as a soldier should. However, this would not be that moment.

Ghost listened to the young wolf curse him in Russian. He knew what the boy was saying, but words were not weapons in his line of work. He didn't care what Vlademir had to say right now. But he did care about what Vlademir would say later.

The sound of blaring police sirens came into earshot. Blue lights could be seen flashing in the distance out of the den's bay windows. There wasn't much time. Ghost jammed the pistol into Vlademir's jaw even harder, forcing the Russian to shut his mouth and curse through gritted teeth. The heat of the suppressor singed his flesh deeper now, and seemed to gain his attention.

"Listen closely, little cub," Ghost said. "We have a message to leave for your father."

Chapter 10
I Don’t Wanna’ Know… Or Do I?

“You got a lotta’ fuckin’ explainin’ to do, Stone,” McCrary said for the umpteenth time. His raspy tone teetered on the verge of frustration. It was something he always tried to keep under wraps and remain cool headed, especially on the job. The G-man was testing him tonight.

Their time at the scene of the massacre was short lived for Stone, and he had advised there was nothing else they could see that would do them any good. He’d seen it too many times and learned not to waste precious time on looking for what didn’t matter. The vigilante left the dead, and freed the victims. McCrary arranged for them to meet up with the Organized Crime Unit back at the precinct. All of the massacred were Eastern European, specifically Russian, and the majority wore tattoos to prove their association. There was only one prominent Russian syndicate occupying Boston. McCrary found it to be too obvious, but not everything was a complete mystery.

Stone grinned halfway after hearing McCrary’s comment. The left corner of his mouth curled upwards mischievously. He’d told the detective he was happy to share with him what he knew. In the moment the timing wasn’t right. The discovery of the vigilante’s message to him was a classified detail in a case that was redacted from all local law enforcement archives. It was a need to know informational piece in the narrative of the investigation. Stone had gone to great lengths to ensure there was no record of any prior messages in the hands of anyone except himself and the council he reported to directly.

“I will,” Stone said dismissively, “just as soon as we have some privacy.”

The conference room they were taking over at the precinct was being loaded with casefiles from the Organized Crime Unit. Three detectives were assisting in bringing in the last decade’s worth of information regarding the Russian crime syndicates Boston had hosted over the years. Yuri "the Wolf" Kurikova occupied the seat of the *pakhan*, or boss, for the past fifteen years. He was the equivalent to a *Godfather* in rivaling Italian organizations. It was only customary to site the Wolf as being responsible for the warehouse of horrors given the twenty plus bodies of Eastern European men that were left forever cold. Most of the men were not formally identifiable, likely to have been smuggled into the country themselves, or imported with false documents. Either way, the situation screamed Kurikova, but there was no definitive evidence to link him to the location. It was a standard within the Kurikova organization to not be specifically marked unless a worthy rank was held. None of the dead were worth the ink.

One of the detectives passed a flash drive to McCrary after the tenth and final case was set on the long conference table. He and the salty veteran had a short conversation before the man cleared the room, but not before he gave Stone a contemptuous look. It was clear the detective disliked not being invited to the party.

"You know their insight would be invaluable," McCrary suggested, hoping to change the agent's mind about keeping the investigation team as condensed as possible.

"It's nothing personal," Stone replied. He removed his jacket, hung it on the back of a chair, and began rolling up his sleeves. "There are details I'll be sharing with you that are on a classified level. We need to keep this small."

"Classified?" McCrary's expression screwed into a disgruntled version of confused. The wrinkles from his stress worn mug resembled that of a curious bulldog.

Stone began checking the case file numbers for labels concerning trafficking of any kind. He knew the detectives from the Organized Crime Unit would be incredibly helpful, especially with the direction they'd need to search. They had lists of associates and ranks, and he'd hoped to find those most known for being involved in human trafficking. But the depths of the case revolving around the vigilante went farther than Stone had revealed, and it meant keeping information under the strictest confidence. McCrary vouched for the men of the unit, having worked hand-in-hand with them on numerous occasions, but Stone wouldn't budge. It had to be them and them alone. He found a file marked 'Sex Trade' and removed it from the congested cardboard box. The folder was thick with reports dating back three years. The agent found the period of time to be oddly short. Human trafficking was a billion-dollar industry, dating back to the beginning of time right along with slavery, and they only had specific reports of players in such an atrociously lucrative criminal industry dating back three years? Something did not add up here.

The detective held an irritating stare until the G-man finally replied.

"Classified, yes," Stone said, giving no attention to McCrary. "Look, am I going to have to repeat myself because you don't understand, or is there a hearing deficiency I need to be aware of?"

The comment was not well received. McCrary's eyes flared in anger, and he physically displayed calming himself with a deep breath and clenching his fists.

"Sorry, I'm joking," Stone spoke sincerely, putting his hands up to block an invisible object. McCrary continued to glare at him until the agent offered more information. "So, here's the deal; this is officially an unofficial FBI investigation." He paused to let that set in. "I'm working this on a special condition, except I don't report to the director of the bureau. This is more than a war on the Kurikova crime syndicate. It's more than a vendetta. It involves national security of the utmost importance, in a way civilization as we know it will never understand, and I report to a panel of men in the intelligence field who report directly to POTUS. That's what this is."

McCrary didn't have to speak the words he thought when Stone revealed the truth behind the matter. His face dictated his feeling exactly, and Stone translated the thoughts exactly: 'Fuck you.'

Stone continued, "I'm dead serious. The man responsible does not exist. He's a rogue operative..."

"Fuck! This is some spook shit?" McCrary complained. The question was obviously rhetorical.

The detective's words stopped Stone in midsentence, warranting a comical expression he gladly provided. "That's one way to put it, yes. It's a long story, which I may get to later if needed, but this guy is literally the most dangerous man you, me, or anyone else in the world will ever encounter." A grim appearance cast across the G-man's chiseled facial features. "I was his domestic liaison as a CIA splinter cell operating in the states. I've never formally met him. But when things went wrong, he..."

Stone paused as McCrary yanked a chair away from the conference table and fell into it. He looked disgusted, as though he physically ached from what he'd just heard. Stone knew the idea was daunting. It was why he'd never disclosed so much information to anyone he'd worked with. The difference now was they had a real chance of catching the vigilante. They knew his exact direction, which could only end in a handful of ways, and one of those ways included them beating him to the punch and bringing him down.

"What the fuck did you drag me into, *Agent* Stone?" McCrary's tone bordered between threatening and explosive, and the way he emphasized the word 'agent' spoke to his dismay of the G-man's status.

The men shared a hard gaze mixed with malice, fear, and determination. Stone was at a loss for words in the moment, but McCrary was not.

"My time in the Corps exposed me to windbags like you," the detective began, growling away his frustration as he shook his head, like he was slowly stretching away the tension mounting in his neck. "Guys like you use guys like me as cannon fodder. This shit sounds like it's got going sideways all over it, and I'm gonna' take the heat for it 'cause it's my city."

Stone acknowledged McCrary's decree with a nod while he scanned the file he pulled, pursing his lips while he held his tongue. He was not one to be labeled. Typically, he came across as a *boy scout*, or gave the appearance, but he was not so innocent, either. McCrary's accusation couldn't have been farther from the truth. He stifled his reaction for a moment so he could gather himself. The fact that he understood the detective's point of view helped. Indeed, Stone was more responsible for the vigilante than anyone would ever know.

"You wanted to be kept informed, so I'm informing you. If I were to follow the protocols of most agencies, I wouldn't tell you shit." Stone looked McCrary directly in the eye, unblinking, and deathly serious. "If you can't handle this, I'll talk to your captain about being reassigned. I was under the impression whoever worked with me was the most capable."

The mild insult called McCrary's resolve and integrity into question. Stone presented a challenge, and as both men were former Marine's he knew it would force the veteran detective to rise to the occasion. Or he'd have the sense to get out while he could.

"Fuck you," McCrary barked, standing abruptly and knocking the chair away with sheer force.

McCrary took off his jacket and began to roll up his sleeves, following suit with Stone. He crumbled under the pressure of being questionably capable, certainly as Stone intended, but he wasn't going to let this pencil dicked special agent get the better of him. His big hands hefted a case around to one side to clear a space for the laptop the Organized Crime Unit had provided, and he began to work on the flash drive. Not his favorite area to start, but it suited him for the moment.

Stone snickered in victory.

"So, tell your story," McCrary grumbled, punching away at the keyboard one finger at a time as he typed in a command.

"Bottom line is this: the heat is all on me. I'm responsible. We get the collar, it's a joint arrest and you garner credit. Probably a commendation. Shit goes sideways, it's all on me. Sound good?"

"Whatever you say."

"You still want to know more?" Stone inquired, finding the question humorous.

McCrary looked up from the screen. "What I want to know is how we're gonna' catch this guy if he's such a bad ass. You got all this cloak and dagger shit on the table. So, how are we actually going to get him? If you remember, it didn't work out so well for the local yokels when they went after Rambo."

Stone felt the heavy atmosphere ease up with McCrary's wisecrack. The salty bastard did have a sense of humor referencing *First Blood.* "We follow what we know, detective. We know Kurikova is the key."

"And the message on the wall?"

"That is his declaration. 'It ends here.' There's nowhere else to point a finger at. It's blatant, but he knows there's nothing to connect Kurikova legally, so our hands are tied. The dead men with Russian mafia tats, the shell corporations owning the land; our guy knows the evidence won't hold up in any court if we try to use it to our advantage. He likes to taunt me by pointing me in one direction, and leading me into the dark."

"Still doesn't give me any clue as to how we're going to nab this guy. He 'doesn't exist,' you said. So we don't know what he looks like. And, if Kurikova is the end game, why not just go right for the jugular? Kill the Wolf and be done with it?"

Stone nodded in agreement. "He left me a message once in Seattle. I'd followed him there and found a shipping container full of women. Half of them were sick, nearly dead, if they hadn't starved to death already. His message said, "You'll see beyond the surface before this is over." And then, before I left Seattle, when his trail went cold again, he sent me a note to my hotel." The agent failed to finish his sentence, laughing at the idea held hostage in his thoughts as he remembered. It said, 'Keep up the good work. We'll get to the bottom of your fuck up soon enough.'

McCrary cocked his head to one side, looking around the laptop screen casting a white glow of illumination on his leathery face that gave him the appearance of a mannequin. "And what does that mean?"

The agent shook his head, ignoring the question. "That's another piece of the long story that doesn't fit the moment. We need to do some digging here. Chances are, I'd bet, he'll be active enough to lead us in the right direction. That's his MO. He does not like to waste time."

McCrary overlooked the G-man's manner of dismissal. He'd learned enough for the evening to know he already knew too much. His gut told him this case wouldn't end as well as they would hope. Boston wouldn't be the same. Hell, just from the massacre this morning the city had already changed. People were hyper-concerned about watching out for their kids. Precincts were getting an astounding amount of calls from parents saying there were perverts watching their children in the parks, at schools, in stores. Any odd look seemed to warrant a 9-1-1 call. It was always irritatingly refreshing to see the world open its eyes to the daily dangers presented to them when a situation like this kicked in the door to their safety zones. Unfortunately, the vigilance wouldn't last. It never did, and McCrary could almost feel another wrinkle form on his brow as the sadness of the thought set in.

Just as the two men got settled in their search, going through paper and computer files, the detective's radio squawked from the corner of the table to his right.

"We've got multiple reports of a gunshot and a residential disturbance," a dispatcher advised. An address immediately followed.

Stone and McCrary perked up. It was a call that was difficult not to listen to. Having worked the streets prior to the FBI as a detective himself, Stone had an ear for these calls, which typically called him to action. It was the address that lifted McCrary from his chair with an urgency that made Stone think a fire might have been lit underneath his feet.

"That's us. Let's go!" McCrary grabbed his jacket and clipped the radio to his belt while he rushed to the door.

Stone quickly followed as he swung his own jacket around his shoulders and slid it on, rushing to catch up to the detective. "What's so important about this call?"

McCrary shook his head in disbelief, fumbling for the keys in his pocket as they entered the elevator. "The address belongs to our newly retired police commissioner." They exchanged a look of uncertain concern. "He resigned tonight at the scene of the warehouse. It was *very* sudden."

The detective's tone held no grief, and waivered on the cusp of suspicion. Stone nodded to himself as he picked up McCrary's cue, quickly piecing the idea together. A massacre of a mob syndicate happens on his watch, unveils a horrific discovery of human trafficking under his nose, and as the commissioner cuts ties, he soon winds up dead. It might explain the lack of focus on any crimes involving human trafficking, at least until there was too much to ignore. It was speculation for the moment. What was certain was that their man certainly *wasn't* wasting any time.

Chapter 11
Over Watch

Choosing a vantage point typically endures a critical assessment process, but the congested housing of the neighborhood made Ghost's choice an obvious one. On the adjacent block from DeMarte's home, Ghost set up in an empty home marked 'For Sale.' The house was on the far side of the block behind two homes directly across the street from DeMarte's. It was offset in its position so it did not line up with either home nearest to the former commissioner's, and its position gave a clear view through the fifteen-foot gap separating the pair of residences. The half-moon hanging ornamentally in the sky shone bright enough to cast a pale spotlight on the overwhelming presence of the responding police units outside of DeMarte's home, and left Ghost's position in pale darkness. Tactically he couldn't have been handed a better card to play as there would be no suspicion of him watching the scene, and when anything added up to his involvement he'd be long gone. From here he could watch without the weight of any stress.

And while he surveyed the organized chaos of the scene Ghost took in as much as he could. Being that the home belonged to the former commissioner, who realistically wasn't completely removed from his position other than his verbal resignation; the situation garnered a heavy response from the Boston PD in force. He watched the patrolmen secure the boundary, taping off the area while their squad car lights flashed and woke the neighborhood like a criminal block party. Ghost had spotted some of the neighbors cautiously peeking out their windows and doors in an attempt not to appear too nosey, while others blatantly walked out into their yards wrapped in their robes. Detectives arrived soon after, along with crime scene agents, and then the dedicated administrative officers. Ghost was only interested in the presence of one man on the scene, and that man would be the one to piece together Anthony

DeMarte's role for the evening.

DeMarte had made his choice long ago. Ghost did not have the exact details on the length of the man's involvement, which had no overall bearing on his decision. DeMarte was a part of the problem, betraying his oath to the people and the office he held a prestigious position in, and to the legacy of the Boston law enforcement brotherhood. There was no other outcome for such a treasonous act. For God and Country worked for all men of service, both military and law enforcement, and Ghost could not have let DeMarte get away with what he'd done.

But DeMarte's course of action had been dealt with. There was no more time or reason to dwell on the dead commissioner. Ghost was interested in Special Agent Stone's arrival. He questioned if the man would make an appearance, no doubt with a local liaison of some kind. The cat and mouse game Ghost shared with the agent had been cold for some time, but only because he had reconnaissance to do on the area. Boston had never been a destination of his choice. He'd been all over the world in every armpit it had to offer cloaked in mud, blood, and body parts, but Boston had never held his interest. Operating on American soil was never supposed to have happened in his line of work. The evidence in the case he'd been working at the time, however, had led him here from Moscow, Russia, originally. This was his second visit, both for business, in one fashion or another, once professional, now personal. In a sense it was the closing of a circle for him as he would end things where they had initially gone terribly wrong.

Ghost's position, in what would have been the master suite of the empty home, had him looking out the back window where a built-in bench/storage chest combo had been built for lounging. He chose to neglect the comfortable appearance of the cushions by standing to remain vigilant, arms at his side, one hand gripping his Colt Python. Beyond the neighborhood the view gave way to the Boston City skyline. In the light of the evening it looked welcoming and mysterious. He stood there trying to ignore it, focused and encompassed by the crime scene he'd orchestrated. At a glimpse its calm overlooked the chaos of the scene like a weeping angel.

A muffled grunt caught Ghost's ear, causing him to turn. Vlademir Kurikova rustled on the floor a few feet away from his forced slumber. A heavy wrapping of duct tape kept the wolf cub from making any significant noise. Tightly cinched knots binding his wrists and ankles with Kevlar reinforced rope restrained the big man into a hog-tied position. Vlademir's body rolled to one side from his stomach. He didn't appear to be fully awake. Ghost thought of removing the other Russians from DeMarte's home, but they were too large to move in the short time he had, and truly were of no importance. And besides, they would help reinforce the connection between the former commissioner and the Kurikova syndicate. There would of course be denial on Yuri's part, and there was no evidence left behind to solidly suggest a relationship. Approaching Kurikova about DeMarte would have the same effect as whispering in the ear of a deaf man. Vlademir's crew had made quick work of the pictures Ghost had provided, which was also of no consolation.

Ghost turned his attention back to DeMarte's home. He stood like a stone sentry, never wavering from his focus of mission. Time seemed to pass by at a snail's pace, but so much happened so quickly he didn't mind. Stone was his focus. Would the agent show? His answer came moments later. He recognized the man as he approached from down the block following an older man of larger stature. The area was cordoned off so it was likely they'd parked some distance down the block. The pair moved hurriedly, flashing their identification to the patrolman at the home's entrance, and then disappearing inside.

Now that the agent was on the scene Ghost was confident he'd continue to play his part and steer the investigation in the proper direction. With this aspect now in order, Ghost redirected his focus on Vlademir. A few steps took him closer to the bound Russian, and he appeared to be waking slowly. As this happened, first came the look of uncertainty, followed by the realization of his situation of being tied up and gagged, and then the futile struggle to test the bindings. Sadly, Ghost had seen it too many times. He'd often been in this position looking down on a man he'd taken for any number of reasons; persuasion, interrogation, or simply to dispose of. Vlademir was of the latter reasoning. Ghost was intent on delivering a more direct message to Vlademir's father, one that would open the old man's eyes a little wider than the warehouse incident. At the end of the day Ghost's purpose was to let Yuri Kurikova know, once and for all, nothing he held dear was safe.

Struggling on his side, muscles straining to break free from the ropes that bound him, Vlademir finally looked up to see his captor. He stopped working against the unbreakable bindings that restrained him. While he paused to take in the appearance of the man in black, he did not flinch. He showed no fear, and the contortion of anger fueled his struggle to curse Ghost with words beyond the duct tape keeping him relatively silent.

Ghost watched Vlademir for a moment. He did not enjoy what he had to do, nor did he dislike it. He had no feelings about it in particular. Years of tagging and bagging men all over the world had kept him honest with himself. Emotion had no place on the battlefield and, with this being a battlefield of a personal nature, it was always crucial for him to remain calm and in control. It wasn't an easy task given the loss he'd suffered, memories of his wife and daughter dancing in his head behind the screens of his eyes like a movie almost constantly, coupled with the rage fueling his odyssey of vengeance. He saw Vlademir as another piece on the chess board — a pawn. Vlademir himself was of no importance, but what he represented, and what could be done with him, was.

The large man knelt down over Vlademir. The influence of outside illumination cast enough secondary light into the dark allowing the two men to see each other through a veil of gray well enough to escape intimate details. Ghost did not pay attention to the blood seeping from Vlademir's wounds. He used an organic foam filling to help stop the bleeding, but all it did was slow it down. Whoever showed the home would need to have the carpets replaced. Ghost stared down into Vlademir's eyes, looking past the surface, searching beyond for more than the anger the cub displayed. He wondered if Vlademir had any idea what his father had done, but he knew there was no way for him to know anything. It was almost a certainty Yuri had forgotten about the retaliation he'd taken against Ghost's family, which begged to deliver another betrayal leading to his true identity, or at least the cover he'd created a life under. No, Vlademir, as a man, was useless. There was nothing behind the fire in his eyes; no soul, no semblance of a leader, only a dogged follower who cared only for himself, and his father.

Vlademir's efforts gave him the appearance of having a seizure. He tossed and turned epileptically as much as the ropes would allow, but his fury never died. Thick, angry veins rose across his forehead as he continually attempted to yell beneath the duct tape. It was just dark enough to keep Ghost from seeing whether Vlademir's face had turned red from his efforts, but it was highly likely. Ghost patted him on the head in a reassured manner, his gloved hand soft against Vlademir's face.

"Shhhhhhh," Ghost hushed.

He continued to pat Vlademir's face, pausing as he rested his hand on the man's cheek. This seemed to enrage the Russian even more, which was an impressive feat for a bound man who was already overly excited. A thought crossed Ghost's mind, recalling different psychological reasoning he'd learned throughout his career, settling on one he felt suited the moment. Perhaps Vlademir had it right, as he was known for being a hot head, and it really was healthy to just let his anger out. Maybe Ghost needed to do the same. He balled his hand into a fist, still resting it on Vlademir's face. He aggressively rubbed the hard, knuckled glove sheathing his tightly formed fist into Vlademir's face. He no longer looked at Vlademir in a manner of searching. He saw him as though he were nothing. The grim appearance came with a heavy release and Ghost felt a burning sensation overwhelm him as his rage rose to the surface.

Vlademir's fury faded away as he witnessed an unexplainable change in his captor, sensing the shift rather than seeing it.

Ghost leaned in close to the wolf cub, pressing his fist into Vlademir's cheek, in turn crushing his head into the soft surface of the empty home's carpet. He felt the disruption of flesh beneath his fist accentuated by a cracking and popping sound that echoed in the silent room. Vlademir's jaw slowly misaligned from the pressure, snapping out of place, altering its placement beneath the skin, and creating a slack appearance from where the bone seemed to swing freely out of the joint. His teeth seemed to cave and slip away from their home within his gums. A guttural scream forced its way from the confines of the gag like the primal sound of pain incarnate. Vlademir struggled to get away as Ghost continued to apply more pressure, forcing him to close his eyes to escape the man's soulless gaze.

"Remember," Ghost growled through gritted teeth, fighting the urge to let his words roar their way into existence. His control began to whither as the rage violently trembled through him. "When you see your father in hell…" Ghost turned his head to one side, his pause cueing Vlademir to blink his eyes open for a moment. "He is the one responsible for *everything* that comes next."

Chapter 12
A Conversation with the Devil

Men of power rarely felt the anxiety inducing grip of being worried. They were in a position to control what happened, dictating situations and their outcomes. Yuri Kurikova felt that grip slipping away from him in the twilight of his time as the *pakhan* of his illustrious *bratva.* He'd never been so devastated by any event. When his father, Viktor, stepped down as *pakhan* fifteen years ago and Yuri became the patriarch, the Italians and the Irish attempted to make a power play against his syndicate. But it was in times of violence that the Wolf thrived. Kurikova, now able to act with unbridled fury, launched a war campaign against the rival families so fierce there was no choice but to submit. Trails of blood were all that led back to their homes. The level of brutality employed left the Kurikova syndicate unrivaled, and the criminal underworld was put on notice of just who had taken power.

Yuri remembered how his father had been proud of his actions. Viktor never questioned any of his son's decisions. He had resigned. He did not even offer any guidance. Viktor Kurikova knew his son was a leader; passionate and strong and fearless. Yuri was prepared to do anything for the family, and his first act solidified his legacy as a great leader of the Russian syndicate. He never faltered from day one.

But now, for the first time in the Wolf's life, he questioned the happenings of where the organization stood. The *bratva* had thrived for so long all he knew was success. Sure, there were speed bumps along the way; skirmishes with those who felt they could stand against them, prison sentences handed out for those willing to take the necessary falls for the family, and then there was the loss of his father within the recent years. But there was no room for failure. The current Kurikova *pakhan* sat stunned in the darkness of his den, statuesque in his position with the artistic lines of madness sculpted into his features. His large oak desk acted as a barrier between him and the world beyond. His wild eyes stared out towards the balcony where Vlademir had last stood overlooking the celebration earlier in the evening, yet he truly peered deeply into nothingness.

The septic titillation of fury and sadness blanketed Kurikova. Losses were inevitable. The discovery at the warehouse early in the day merely scratched the surface of his operations. Monetarily it was significant, but Kurikova could not dwell on that. His overall wealth trumped this transgression. Operations would move forward and continue in every order of business without fail. But the loss that haunted him in this moment left him in a form of purgatory he could not explain. When he'd lost his father in a high-profile government exchange, he'd known who to retaliate against. There was swift and immediate justice for the *bratva*. This was not the case now.

Only an hour had passed when he'd received the phone call that would change everything. His son's name and number flashed across the screen of the smart phone, and after three rings Kurikova slid the green icon to the right to answer.

"It is done?" he'd asked, his Russian accent heavy, but clear in speaking the English words.

His solemn expression shifted to confusion as he received no reply, wrinkling his brow into a thousand lines implanted by years of governing extreme stress and anger. Kurikova was on his balcony at the time overlooking his estate, lost in thought regarding the manner in which he was going to address this threat. He'd made arrangements capable of acting quickly and efficiently, but there was no way to determine the outcome, so he still couldn't help calculating and recalculating what measures to take. He trusted the situation would be handled professionally and cleanly. However, the silence filling the call thrust a sharp pain in his gut. Something had gone terribly wrong. Vlademir would never hold his tongue when spoken to by his father.

"Vlad?" Kurikova asked. The seconds had ticked away as though they never existed.

Kurikova had to admit to himself that Vlademir had failed. There was no other alternative. His thoughts immediately jumped to the dangerous man imagined to have killed nearly forty of his *boyeviks* in one fell swoop. Given the circumstances, what reasoning could possibly make any sense? But he was not one to be intimidated, and responded with the heat of boiling acid burning in his guts.

"*Who are you*?" Kurikova snarled. His lips curled as he forced the words from his mouth sounding more like a threat than a question.

"Now you're on track," replied a deep, gravelly voice.

The Wolf snapped and snarled more, unchaining the beast that truly held sway over his heart. "I will fucking slaughter *everything* you hold dear! I will eat your fucking heart!"

Kurikova seethed with indignation, and pounded his free fist down on the marble railing of the balcony. His temperature quickly rose, and even in the briskness of the evening he tore his suit jacket off and tossed it over the balcony. He ventured into a rabid pace back and forth, huffing and puffing. More curses escaped his mouth. His Russian was much smoother and more refined than his English. And then the clutch of fear gripped his heart. Kurikova froze in his tracks, paralyzed by chilling sounds blaring through the receiver of his cell phone. Few sounds could stop a man of Yuri Kurikova's stature and make him question everything he'd done. Suddenly he was no longer the Wolf, but a father aching to take away the pain of his son.

Vlademir screamed agonizingly through the phone, taking no breaths as his voice went up and down in octaves, singing a song of torture his father was intimately familiar with. There were brief instances of Vlademir's resistance; attempts to curse his captor cut short by the employment of increasing pain. Kurikova felt his son's strength as he fought whatever method his captor utilized. He hated that he understood, from a professional standpoint, that the man who had Vlademir was also an experienced professional.

"Stop!" Kurikova yelled into the phone. "Stop it now! What do you want?"

He was heaving to catch his breath. Tears ran down his face fueled by anger and pain and sadness for the position he'd placed his son in. Only he could be blamed for this — for this life. This was the only instance in his life he had ever felt guilty for what he'd been born into, and dragged his family into with him. There was nothing to be done now. He had not heard Vlademir scream in any such way since the day he was born and, even as a new baby, Vlademir had had a grand disdain for crying.

"STOP!" Kurikova pleaded, dropping to his knees. "PLEASE!"

"I'd barely warmed up at that point," the man stated coldly.

Kurikova looked around anxiously, his mind reeling as he tried to make sense of the man's words. Past tense. Was it a recording? "Where is Vlademir? What do you want? Name it, it's yours. Anything!"

There was no reply.

"Answer me!" Kurikova roared, desperation tainting his voice, and accentuating his accent.

"Your son is a very strong man," the man complimented. "He's lasted quite some time."

Kurikova's rage began to boil, his face taking on a flushed complexion, eyes narrow with the heavy scowl of his brow. But he needed it to remain tamed. He'd been on the other end of these circumstances before. The man wanted something, and Vlademir was his leverage. The mistake would be to think the situation was complicated when it really was quite simple.

"My son has always had an incomparable strength," Kurikova admitted, seething as he let the words remind him of his position.

"Like father, like son," Ghost replied.

"Indeed. He is my first born."

There was a brief pause, and then Ghost calmly and confidently said, "Yes. And then came Vitali, followed by Svetlana. I believe Vlademir's niece had a birthday today." He stopped long enough for his knowledge of Kurikova's family to set in. Ghost continued his next phrase mocking the stereotypical Russian accent. "*Katyana, yes*?"

Kurikova closed his eyes, fighting back his rage. How could this be? This man had intimate knowledge of his family; of his dearest, innocent Katyana. He took a series of deep breaths as he stood and entered his den. Kurikova sat at his desk and pressed a button installed beneath its overhanging lift. The device paged his security staff, and two men entered the den instantly. They appeared as though they were uncomfortable in the fashionable suits they wore, likely better suited in camouflage BDU's and armed with heavy automatic weapons. Regardless, they were incredibly professional and calm, silenced pistols drawn and clearing the room. The *pakhan* waved them off, and his security staff quickly holstered their weapons and stood at attention.

The line continued to emanate the white noise of the open phone line. The caller remained silent, and patient

While Kurikova made the man on the phone wait, he quickly wrote a note on a pad in his Russian language. His security, while elite trained soldiers, spoke multiple languages, but would only respond to Russian in any manner. It was a strict stipulation that ensured their loyalty and silence. Both guards read the note expressionlessly, and then exited the den urgently. Kurikova wrote a code word which instructed them to place heavy security on the entire family. It was a protocol he'd implemented when he'd become the head of the syndicate, and he hoped it wasn't too late.

"Yes," Kurikova finally responded. "Katyana's birthday was today."

"How old?"

"You tell me," Kurikova felt as though this was his chance to regain some control in the conversation.

"By now, I figure she is ten."

Kurikova shook as he continued to control his anger, looking all around the expanse of his den as if to search for an explanation for how this mysterious entity knew so much about his family.

"Yuri?" Ghost asked.

Kurikova braced himself with his free hand against the bookshelf. He stared into the titles he'd instructed Vlademir to read throughout his life, filling him with wisdom and philosophies of some of the greatest minds offered to the world. The memory burned in his heart as it turned his thoughts to what his son may have endured.

"Yes," Kurikova said.

"I'm going to give you your son back." The words were cold and empty.

"When? How?" The words came as emergently as Kurikova could speak them. Even then he felt it was too slow.

"Soon."

"What do you want?"

"There's nothing you can give me, Yuri. You can't return what you already took. You can't take back all the pain you've caused."

Ghost's words were weighted with anguish. Kurikova could feel the man's pain in his gritty tone, causing the hair to stand up on the back of his neck, sending a slight chill creeping its way up his spine. He couldn't imagine what he'd done specifically to anyone capable of what this man had accomplished sabotaging his operations. Granted, it was evident it had something to do with the sex trafficking aspect of his syndicate. In every city Kurikova's reach extended to it was only his trafficking operations that had been targeted. Had someone close to him been swept up into the business? That must be it. Someone this man cared for had fallen victim to the billion-dollar sex trade Kurikova marketed across the world. But where, when, or how?

A calm feeling washed over Kurikova unexpectedly. The man on the phone had given him the power he needed that he so cowardly tossed away as soon as he learned of Vlademir's captivity. His fatherly essence slipped away just as quickly as it had taken over, taking with it any remaining parental compassion and empathy. The two traits were worthless in combatting a merciless enemy. Kurikova straightened his posture to stand tall, confident and stoic in the moment as the Wolf returned to its rightful place in his mind and heart.

"If there's nothing I can give you in exchange," Kurikova said, "then you're wasting my time. You haven't killed Vlademir, yet. Otherwise, why would you call? You are weak. My son is strong. Whatever happens, know this: I will see to it you know every form of pain before you die. Mercy is not my strong suit."

Vlademir's agonizing screams blared through the phone. A reminder. The soundtrack of his torture escalated to a higher intensity. Kurikova suddenly felt nauseous, feeling the involuntary gut reaction it caused, but fought the urge to vomit. He closed his eyes and removed the phone from his ear. The screams were still easily heard, but Kurikova ignored them now.

The phone went quiet. Any sounds Vlademir made were lost in the digital world of cell phone transmissions, although they echoed within Kurikova's mind. A piece of him felt helpless, killing him inside, and tarnishing his wonderfully black soul. This was unacceptable to the Wolf. He could not give in to any transgressions against his family, and his family meant more to him than his own life. This was the moment to be strong. Emotions had no place in negotiations, and that was clearly what this man was counting on. Kurikova rebounded from the sympathetic moment he entertained in Vlademir's name. An energetic resurgence flowed through him as he returned to form.

"Is that all?" Kurikova asked coldly, ignoring the tears streaming down his bitter face. "Because you bore me."

"Papa?" asked a familiar voice in Russian. It was nearly indistinguishable as the words came in a mumbling diction. "Papa?"

Kurikova's heart wanted to sink with the helpless sound of Vlademir calling to him. What good was a father if he couldn't protect his son? No, there was no room to give in again, and no place to be weak of mind and heart.

"Do what you will with my son," Kurikova said. "You are not fooling me this time."

"Papa, it's Vlad," a man said.

Kurikova listened closely, thinking this was simply a hoax. When Vlademir repeated himself Kurikova could not keep from feeling an overwhelming sense of compassion. But no, it was not Vlademir. Not anymore, if at all. Vlademir had to be dead in his mind. The father had to accept this was his son's fate. It was the only way to protect the family, and the business.

"I am here."

"Papa?" Vlademir gasped, struggling to put words together.

"Yes."

Vlademir did not answer directly. Wet, gurgling sounds preceded a coughing fit followed by a series of attempts to clear his throat. Kurikova imagined Vlademir in a dark room where he spewed up thick strands of blood, restrained to a chair or table, beaten and bruised, likely unrecognizable. It was not something he was certain of, but a piece he extracted from his own memories of when he'd executed such a task. He did not realize it at first, but he held his breath until he heard his son's strained voice once more.

"Find him," Vlademir growled, "and kill him."

Kurikova smiled. These were undoubtedly going to be the last words he would hear his son speak, and Vlademir's words made him proud as he fought to the end, never surrendering.

“I will, my boy,” Kurikova snarled. “He will pay.”

“Will I, Yuri?” the man asked.

“You will. I swear it on my life.”

“I hope you’re ready to make good on your word.”

The tension hung heavily in the air as the silence between the men mounted. Kurikova wondered what the man’s next move would be, and what he would say. His professionalism was clearly on a level beyond anything he’d personally encountered. The man was driven, merciless, and skilled. A plan was certainly in play. There was no way this man could have accomplished so much without one, which spoke to his intelligence of strategy and tactical operation. It was safe to believe this man was specially trained for a singular purpose. He was doing what he was best at; the kind of man whose mere footsteps on the floor in the morning made the devil feel a chill up his spine.

Ghost broke the silence with a question, one Kurikova would not have expected. “What do you think my little girl’s last words were before you had her and my wife killed?” he asked.

Kurikova had no idea what the man’s question referred to. Was it a ploy to shake his nerves once more, or was he asking a serious question? The latter seemed to be likely given the passion behind his efforts. But Kurikova considered the possibilities as he’d had plenty of families killed over the years for infractions committed against his organization for many reasons. He never gave them a second thought. Business was business. He then considered how many people this man had extinguished in his own right, and wondered which of them was the true devil?

“You want to know what I think were her last words?” Kurikova asked. “I will tell you.”

The *pakhan* walked to a small bar next to his large bookshelf. He took hold of a bottle of Scotch and filled a crystal tumbler with the equivalent to two shots of alcohol. The liquid went down all at once in a smooth, heated swallow. He released a refreshing breath as he replaced the tumbler on the granite countertop of the bar with the utmost control.

“Well,” Kurikova continued, “I think she called out for her father. I think she was crying and scared and screaming your name. ‘Daddy, help me!’ She screamed it over and over, but you were nowhere to be found.

You let her down. You left her helpless and abandoned." Kurikova's volume raised as his words came quicker and more aggressively. "She was frightened, and you couldn't save her. She wet herself when the gun was drawn, and shook her head with tears sprinkling from her eyes hoping to wake up from a nightmare. And they were such beautiful eyes, too. So innocent until they turned black when she was shot in the head."

A white froth formed around Kurikova's mouth, coating the edges of his trimmed beard like rabid foam. His control was once again on the brink of displacement, but he maintained his hold on his emotions. A primal feeling originated from within him, pulsating from the nucleus of his core in such an animalistic way he had never felt before. His moniker finally felt real to him.

"I thought something along the same lines," the man replied calmly. There wasn't a single ounce of emotion behind his words.

Kurikova remained silent, and listened intently. His instincts told him the man had more to say.

"Yuri?" Ghost spoke evenly.

"Yes," Kurikova answered.

"I wish I could be as merciful as your story was." And the line went dead.

Now, an hour since that devastating phone call, Kurikova felt empty. Everything he'd said to the man about his child was exactly what he imagined for Vlademir. He knew better, but the essence of a parent could never be fully drowned out. Kurikova knew his son was gone, making peace with the idea earlier. And since the man offered nothing to be exchanged for Vlademir, with the exception of the return of his own family, he began to grieve. It was necessary to cycle through the emotion of mourning to regain clear thoughts. War had been declared on the Kurikova syndicate, and the battlefront had brazenly come to his doorstep. Battles had already been lost, but the Wolf did not intend on losing the war.

The phone rang once more, vibrating modestly inside of the right pocket of his slacks. He wanted to ignore it. He had nothing to say to anyone in this moment, yet his gut told him otherwise. Reluctantly Kurikova removed the phone from the pocket and read the screen: Unknown Caller. Again, he debated with himself whether to answer as the phone continued to vibrate. He slid the green icon to the right on the touch screen as he placed the phone to his ear.

"Hello, Yuri," said a familiar voice, always so energetic and charismatic. "I hear things are not going well for you. Perk up. We've got some mutual business to attend to, my old friend."

Chapter 13
There's Always Something

There was no conversation on the drive over to Anthony DeMarte's residence. Both Stone and McCrary had no need to speak any words as their minds both wandered through the possibilities of what could have happened. Stone's perception of DeMarte being dirty was an instinctual thought. During the course of his cat and mouse chase with the vigilante there had been many corrupt officials unveiled. It was a go-to hypothesis. A second thought allowed him to consider McCrary may have been hinting at something linking the massacre with DeMarte's resignation, followed by his home being reported for residential disturbance involving a gunshot. Suicide was a likely consideration. Stone hoped there would be clear evidence as to why DeMarte would kill himself, or try. Maybe there was a note, or not. Or maybe the vigilante had come for him, for whatever reason, and executed him. The last thought seemed unlikely. His history of violence had never involved killing anyone who worked in law enforcement.

The variables were staggering when looking through the lens of speculation so Stone let it go. They would learn the truth soon enough, especially with how fast they were going. McCrary drove like a bat out of hell. Stone noticed the color of his right hand was pale as he squeezed the 'Oh shit!' handle at the top of the door every time McCrary took a corner. He didn't feel overly anxious about the manner of driving, but he tended to hide those details well, even from himself. The hasty ride did get Stone's blood pumping after the call that saved them from the monotonous search through the Kurikova files. They learned the ins and outs of what was known about the syndicate's involvement in human trafficking, which didn't amount to much overall. Kurikova and his *bratva* were skilled at covering their tracks. Most of the information outlined known associates and case histories. These were important details as they could point to potential leads, but at the speed they were going, Stone couldn't stay focused on any information that seemed pertinent.

"Hold on," McCrary said courteously for the umpteenth time.

The detective braked slightly as he rounded another corner, simultaneously revving the RPMs back up by slamming down the accelerator and maneuvering the steering wheel in the direction the ass end of the car slid. This technique corrected the cars direction skillfully. The unmarked grey Dodge Charger drifted around the corner with a sense of precision Stone had not expected from the veteran detective. The engine roared like an untamed urban lion while its wheels squealed and smoked as the rubber died away. McCrary's correction was consistently flawless, and they rocketed down the road in a seamless transition.

"Remind me to hire you as my getaway driver when I decide to actually rob a bank and get out of the good guy business," Stone said, laughing as they took another corner.

McCrary chuckled at the thought. "You ain't foolin' no one, Stone. You ain't in the good guy business."

The G-man couldn't help but laugh. And there was no room to argue. He knew he'd told McCrary enough about himself for the man to know he was not a good guy. Being called a *boy scout* was more sarcasm than realism. Hell, McCrary probably knew that when he first met him. The man hid his capabilities well, and he'd read Stone as soon as they'd met. McCrary was a good detective and it would only be natural for him to play along without revealing anything he needed to keep to himself. He reminded Stone of the quiet man who saw everything, but said very little.

A ten-minute ride was cut nearly in half with McCrary at the wheel. The scene was already cordoned off, and it seemed as though a large portion of the Boston PD had come to DeMarte's aid. It was not a surprise to Stone. Soldiers always rushed to the aid of their commanders regardless of their likeability. It was the job that mattered first and foremost. The bond of law enforcement was no different than the military. You watched the back of every man who marched with you, or walked a beat, from top to bottom. There were those who could be excluded, but it was rare. And without knowing what had transpired at DeMarte's home, Stone couldn't jump to any conclusions as to how the man would be supported, or not.

They parked nearly a block away due to the perimeter set by the first responders. Residents were asked to remain in their homes, or at least in their yards, and not approach DeMarte's home. Patrolmen were already conducting interviews. Midnight was almost upon them, and the probability of anyone seeing anything was slim. As he and McCrary walked down the sidewalk to Demarte's house a neighbor was overheard explaining they'd seen a black SUV leave the front of the house only to pull around the back.

"Whoever drove it was going way too fast for this area," the elderly man had said. "They were in some kind of hurry, I'll tell ya' that."

McCrary held the police tape up for Stone as they entered the immediate perimeter. Stone ducked under and passed by the detective, who quickly broke into a speed walk. The agent fell behind as he took in the scene outside of the home looking for anything that might need their attention. He stopped in front of the home for a moment to look harder. McCrary slowed his walk and came back, asking what Stone was doing. Stone didn't answer immediately as he looked around to the surrounding homes. An uneasy feeling crept over him in the way he knew they were being watched, but couldn't tell who was watching. It was an eerie sensation, one he occasionally received at the messes left behind by the vigilante. Stone hadn't originally suspected the man to be a watcher, yet that same idea was countered by the fact he had to watch whoever he was researching in some capacity to learn about them. And there were too many eyes on them to get a good read on the area.

"Come on, let's go," McCrary urged. "What are ya' doin?"

Stone looked up through the darkness between the two houses across the street where a house on the back side of the adjacent block sat quiet and empty. A large window on the second floor faced DeMarte's home, but there was only blackness beyond the glass pane.

"Just looking," Stone replied, his words trailing off into thin air.

McCrary led the way into DeMarte's home. It was impossible to not take in the number of collectibles and knickknacks crammed into the space of the dwelling. They overwhelmed the immediate area of the living room where it opened into, and bled into other parts of the home. The detective ignored the nostalgic décor and walked straight up the stairway slightly misaligned to the right of the front door. Stone played catch up once more, following McCrary to the second floor. The concentration of crime scene agents and other police officers guided them to their destination.

"Hey, Lieutenant," greeted a junior detective. "It's bad, man."

McCrary and Stone shook hands with the detective, who presented himself as Andrew Carter. Stone learned he was in McCrary's division and in charge while the lieutenant was on special assignment as the FBI liaison. Carter came across as intelligent and sure of himself. Stone liked him right away.

"It's hard to say what exactly happened," Carter said. They were in the hallway outside of DeMarte's den. "There was definitely a struggle." He presented the appearance of the room as if he were displaying a prize on The Price Is Right. "That speaks for itself. But the additional bodies don't fit in, laid out on either side of the room, likely ambushed and executed; the burning garbage can, and the commish in his desk chair with his head blown back." Nothing but the facts with this man, and the facts were staggering.

Stone entered the room, careful not to step in an area littered with evidence markers. He squatted down to look closer at two dispensed bullet casings. Remembering there was a marker just outside the door he looked there too; two more bullet casings. His focus returned to the den as he stood and entered further. A heavy blood stain satiated the center of the floor directly in front of the desk, and indicated to him a body was missing. Two other bodies occupied the room: one to the left of the desk and one to the right. Both were laid out as if they'd fallen face forward towards the walls in front of them where their brains and skull fragments painted and textured the turn of the century wallpaper. Stone moved back through the doorway and looked at where the bullet casings outside of the room had landed. One was farther outside the doorway while the other was nearly in the room. The two casings inside the room had ejected in a closer proximity, distinguishing their usage and suggesting they were fired within the singular area of the den.

"Were either of these men armed?" Stoned asked a CSI agent.

A young black man replied, "They both had Glock 22's. Unsilenced. Nothing special about them."

"Were they holding them, or were they holstered?"

The CSI agent tilted his head as he considered the question, finding it to be curious. "They were holstered. Both men were carrying concealed. Very professional."

Stone smiled and nodded to himself as he considered the layout of the crime scene. "You sneaky, sonofabitch."

"What's that?" McCrary chimed in, assessing the scene in his own way while Carter stepped away writing notes.

"It was definitely him," Stone said.

"You sound incredibly sure of that assumption."

"I am." Stone moved around the area, careful of where he stepped as he backed out of the room until he was just outside of the door. "Both men have Spetznaz tattoos. You can see them at the base of their necks just under the collar." Stone moved around to the body on the right and pulled the collar down. The ink wasn't fully visible, but it was an emblem of a parachute with a roaring tiger head suspended by the canopy cords. Branded lettering was centered belong the animal head in Russian dialect. "They likely have other tattoos linking them to the Russian crime syndicate. These are highly trained men. You can bet they searched the house before they arrived here." He emphasized his words with his hands, patting them towards the floor twice. Then he pointed to the center of the room. "And as you can imagine there was a third man there. That couldn't have come from either of these guys, or DeMarte."

"I noticed," McCrary said blandly. "Clearly a fourth person was in the room. Could be from our guy, too. Or, they were wounded here and were lucky enough to get out in time on their own? Or taken hostage?"

"Maybe, but…" Stone pointed to the set of bullet casings in the hall. "These two were shot from outside of the room." He mocked shooting the man on the right side, pointing to the bullet casing farthest in the hall with his opposite hand, changed his angle towards the man on the left, and pointed to the casing slightly closer to the doorway. Stone moved forward, barely entering the room, and then mocked two more gun shots with his hands. "He shot the third one in the center last, but didn't kill him. This one was more important. It wouldn't make sense to drag away a dead body."

"If you say so, Sherlock," McCrary joked. "It's feasible. What about the commissioner? He clearly shot himself in the head. You wanna' mock that, too?"

Stone shook his head, ignoring the detective's offense. "I'm just piecing it together. And these two here are elite trained. Getting behind them would be nearly impossible without alarming them. They were distracted with something, the fire maybe, especially with their guns holstered. It's safe to assume the shooter was likely to be of equal skill set." Stone pointed to the center of the room where he believed a missing body should have been. "Whoever he is, he has rank. These guys aren't players, they're bodyguards."

McCrary cast a cynical eye towards the dead man on the left. "And what do you make of those?"

Stone looked near the right shoulder of the dead man on the left side of the room. Two other shell casings were marked on the floor. A CSI agent was still taking pictures while another outlined the bodies. Stone thought they were sure to have gotten close ups of the three sets of bullet casings.

"You've gotten these already?" Stone asked pointing to all the casings.

The agent nodded and presented the camera. The man scrolled through the pictures on the camera's digital screen.

"These two sets are forty-five caliber," the CSI agent explained, pointing to the casings in the hall and just inside the doorway. He scrolled further until he came to the set near the dead men. "These two are forties. I guess they were fired from a Glock twenty-two as well, but we only recovered the two off of each guy on the floor."

Stone thanked the man as he looked to McCrary. "It's possible our shooter might have taken a few rounds. These two had to be fired closer to the desk, deeper into the room. I can't picture him coming in any farther than just inside the door."

McCrary conceded silently with a nod. He casually looked up and down the doorway, inside and out. "Yeah. No bullet holes in the door jamb. Anything found down the hall?" The CSI agent shook his head. "That don't explain DeMarte then, either. That was by his hand, forced or otherwise."

The CSI agent chimed in before Stone could speak. "We recovered a three-fifty-seven revolver from his hand. He definitely shot himself. Bruising and contusions can be seen on what's left of his facial spectrum." The agent paused as the words he chose sounded far too insensitive. "Anyway, there is no suicide note, and given that he was beaten beforehand, he could have been forced, or coerced."

"Which would suggest a fifth person," McCrary concluded.

"Which would be our guy," Stone said. "Has to be."

McCrary pointed to the dead men. "Russians? In his house… Why?"

"Can only be one reason." Stone didn't want to be the one to say what they were both thinking.

"I don't want to believe it, but it's all that makes sense. Why else would he, or they, come here?" The detective thought for a moment. "Fuck, I don't like where this is going. Has he ever killed any other law enforcement before?"

Stone nodded once more, hesitating to explain. He exhaled deeply knowing what he had to say would cut deeply. "Yes, he has. All proven to be involved in illegal activity. I'll bet DeMarte's got an offshore bank account somewhere. We can find that pretty easily with a phone call to the bureau. And I'll bet he has a hefty amount of cash on hand." Stone considered his knowledge of the vigilante. "Or did."

"Or did?" McCrary sounded confused.

It was an odd thought to have, but when considered logically over the time he'd been pursuing the vigilante, Stone made good sense of what he was about to say. "Well, launching an assault on a high-powered criminal organization needs funding of some kind. Kurikova has been funding *his* vendetta. He takes whatever cash he comes across."

McCrary laughed mildly, wiping his mouth as if he were removing something unseen. He was thinking about what Stone had said. The G-man could see the wheels of thought spinning behind McCrary's sharp eyes.

"That's hilarious," the detective chuckled. "Blood money funding a blood feud. This just keeps getting betta' and betta'."

"The next question is this," said Stone. "Where did he hide to get by these guys?"

Stone turned his attention to another room being worked over by other CSI agents. He stepped down the hall a few feet and entered what was the master bedroom. McCrary walked with him. The room was being tossed, much like the remainder of the house, and it led the special agent into the large walk-in closet. Finely built wood shelving spanned the closet, clearly custom designed. An island occupied the center making the space awkward to maneuver around, but served its purpose as a usable center piece. One agent meticulously logged everything while she searched. She had the appearance of someone who did not like her space invaded, and had a specific way of doing her job efficiently.

The female CSI agent glared at Stone as he slowly made his way around the island. "Can I help you?"

Stone craned his neck from one direction to the next, searching for anything he thought stood out as suspicious. He made eye contact with the woman, but only for a brief moment. There was a heavy gaze of discontent already burning behind her thick glasses.

"I'm curious if you've found anything out of place," Stone said. "Anything odd?"

"I haven't been through everything. Just this side so far." She gestured towards the right side of the room.

Stone pointed to the left. "May I?"

McCrary entered the walk-in closet behind Stone, interrupting the uncomfortable exchange. "Hi, Katie," he greeted.

"Hello, lieutenant," Katie replied. Her eyes never left Stone, watching him like a hawk as he went deeper into the closet.

"She's our senior CSI," McCrary explained. "Everyone stays out of her way."

"I'm following my gut," Stone explained, ignoring the warning.

And he was. Stone immediately began searching the opposite side of the closet. It would be incredibly unnatural if there wasn't some sign of a hiding place where DeMarte could stow a shoe box of money, or even a safe. He'd found too many to believe there wasn't something. There was always a chance he was wrong, but he doubted that. Finding any form of a cache of hidden money would give them further purpose to pursue the financial angle of the investigation and attempt to link DeMarte to Kurikova.

"You can help, detective," Stone said, moving his hands over the frames of the shelving in search of any form of button or lever. "Looking for a hidden compartment of any kind."

"DeMarte was single," Katie said. "A widower. There's no reason to think he would need to hide any kind of secret stash in a house he occupied on his own."

McCrary was hesitant to help, but he followed Stone's example. For some reason it felt like the right thing to do. "Your logic makes sense, Katie, but there is one reason why he would hide any money, like the *very* special agent suggests."

Stone and Katie waited for McCrary's explanation as they both searched.

"If the commissioner was dirty while his wife was still alive there's no way he'd let her find out," McCrary said. "That woman was close with my wife. Saints these women are. He'd hide it for that reason alone. Trust me, even angels dance with devils on occasion."

Stone cleared a section of clothes hanging between sections of the custom shelving. He pulled the clothing away in large groups, searching the wall behind and the floor beneath. He froze for a moment as he studied the wall, ensuring he was seeing what he thought was there. A thin line in the wall caught Stone's eye. The line could have been misconstrued at a glance if it weren't for the slight displacement of the sectional piece, giving the wall the appearance of being set inside itself. Stone used his foot to dislodge the section. The space moved under the soft pressure he applied, and the corner of the section popped outwards.

"Got it!" Stone shouted, ripping the remaining clothes off of the hanging rod and tossing them to the floor.

McCrary and Katie surged into the corner where Stone searched, clearing away the clothes tossed by Stone. The G-man dropped to his knees on the hardwood floor and pointed to where the section of the wall was pulled cleanly away and set to the side. In a hidden alcove deeply set into the wall was an unlocked safe. The door to the safe was ajar and appeared to have been keeping the secret section of the wall from fully seating in its designated space.

Stone reached into the safe and tossed three bundles of cash wrapped in ten thousand-dollar bands. Katie scooped the money up off of the floor and placed them on the island center piece.

"I'll be damned," McCrary said. "You're full of all sorts of surprises, Stone."

The special agent knelt quietly on the floor looking at a single piece of paper in his hand. He read the writing on it more than once as it penetrated his mind and was repeated by his subconscious. The note wasn't long, but it delivered a powerful message.

"What's that?" the detective asked.

Stone exhaled loudly, reluctantly reaching a hand back to McCrary and handing him the message. The paper crumpled in Stone's hand. McCrary took the small piece of lined paper and unfolded it until he could see what was written on it. His expression hardened upon reading the message. Katie backed away from the detective feeling the grave intensity emanating from him.

"What the fuck does this mean?" McCrary barked, crumpling the paper in his fist.

Stone shook his head, looking up at McCrary. He wasn't sure what to say. How could he explain what was written on the paper? He couldn't, not without being misleading, and McCrary wasn't falling for any bullshit. If there were a corner to be backed into, Stone now occupied it. He'd have to think fast.

The G-man stood abruptly and pushed passed the detective.

"It's been a long day," Stone said. "I'm going to my hotel."

McCrary reached out and took Stone by an arm. The special agent half turned to face him but couldn't look him in the eye.

"Don't forget this," McCrary said, his tone laced with malice.

McCrary forced the crumpled paper into the agent's hand. Stone crushed the note in his fist, squeezing it tightly until his knuckles turned white. His frustration was on display, forcing him into a position where the entirety of the investigation was going to have to be unclassified. It was inevitable now. He wasn't making anything any easier on Stone.

"Nothing?" the detective asked. "No explanation?"

Stone said nothing. He thought about the words he'd read:

Stone—Honor comes before duty. We're almost done. You die last.

McCrary leaned in closer to Stone, looking into the special agent with fierce intensity, as if he were trying to summon an answer out of the man. Stone looked away from McCrary in an ill attempt at hiding his disappointment.

"*Who the fuck are you*, Stone?" McCrary asked.

Chapter 14
Getting Personal

There's a seemingly distinct sound to bone when it is traumatized. Even the slightest break can produce a thunderous crack. A fracture can snap like a whip. The audio tone of bone can vary, and Ghost thought he'd heard them all. Once he broke a man's kneecap with a mildly powered sidekick to the fragile joint, and the soundtrack played out as though a wet towel had been slapped against a brick wall. It was as though the dislocation of the joint ripped through the tendons and the connective tissue cried out in pain. Spiral and compound fractures varied between snaps and rolling crunches, but what remained, regardless of the type of break, was the memory of what was heard. Nails scratching on chalkboard came close to the cringe worthy sound.

Vlademir Kurikova's head played out to the same effect of an eggshell cracking against cement.

Ghost carelessly pulled the brawny Russian by an ankle from the back of the Escalade he commandeered. Vlademir smacked against the ground, his dead weight echoing a resemblance to a slab of beef hitting a butcher's floor. The report of his head hitting the pavement forced Ghost to look Vlademir over. He didn't want the wolf cub to die before he could finish with him. Lifting the head, Ghost examined the back of Vlademir's skull. The tissue was soft, definitely damaged, but not too severely. The faint rise and fall of Vlademir's chest reassured Ghost he was still with the living.

The alleyway where Ghost parked placed him in position behind a restaurant owned by Yuri Kurikova. A security light lit up the back of the red brick building high over the entrance. Ghost knew there was a security camera nearby; one was nearly everywhere these days, but he was not concerned. A device worn around his neck resembling a black band cast off a coded signal that electronically scrambled his face from digital reference, much like a blurred-out face commonly seen on television. He came here because Vlademir once oversaw the management of the establishment, *The Mother Land*, as his first opportunity to show his leadership skills to his father. Beyond managing the business, Vlademir also oversaw the laundering of money and exports of illegal goods that were syphoned through the restaurant. The quick success Vlademir gained, legal and otherwise, earned the wolf cub great praise from his father, and he'd quickly ventured into the darker aspects of the family business. Ghost held a set of keys taken from Vlademir's pocket, and tried each one in the back entrance until the right one unlocked the deadbolt. There was a security alarm which gave the entrant thirty seconds to deactivate the system. Ghost entered and quickly found the panel. He produced a small set of necessary tools to reroute the ground wire, cut what was appropriate, and deactivated the alarm. It was a simple task he'd performed more times than he could remember.

The next step was to get Vlademir into the kitchen. As quiet as the night was at the moment there was no need to take any unnecessary risk of being seen by any passersby. Ghost took long, urgent steps, grabbed Vlademir by the collar of his shirt, turned, and hefted the dense body inside of the restaurant. Even as he was close to five inches taller than Vlademir, and nearly thirty pounds of muscle heavier, Ghost felt a slight strain of dragging the dead weight of a 230-pound man. The only aspect in his favor was that he did not have to be gentle with his victim.

Once inside Ghost slammed the backdoor shut, pausing for a moment to assess the situation. He let his eyes adjust to the darkness to precisely locate the light switch, which was to his left. Its initiation illuminated the professional kitchen. Stainless steel gleamed throughout the expansive floor plan. Ghost's eyes moved directly to what he had come for; an island counter topped with an industrial grade cutting board floating individually near the center of a red tiled sea. He dragged Vlademir to the counter and, despite the heavy bulk the unconscious man embodied, easily lifted the Russian onto the island. He then squared the body on the counter in a four-point position. Ghost removed a roll of black duct tape from inside a pouch on his tactical vest, and proceeded to tape around Vlademir's wrists and ankles before securing the strong tape to each leg of the table. The Russian's limbs were stretched out so that, should he wake, there was no room for him to move. Ghost positioned Vlademir as though he were to be quartered.

The idea of chopping Vlademir into pieces crossed Ghost's mind, but he was not voluntarily a butcher. He cringed at the thought passing through his mind, disregarding it just as quickly as it had occurred, and returned to his purpose: *sending Yuri a message*.

Ghost looked over the body before him, studying it, committing it to memory. He remembered every significant target he'd ever retired. A long line of faces was stored in his memory of past assassinations. High valued targets were the governments terminology used to describe them. They were men of influence and power, typically, or individuals capable of committing horrible acts against humanity. Ghost remembered them because their deaths marked the movement of something important, like a cleansing of a world doomed to be forever dirty. But Vlademir Kurikova, as similar as he was to any other target Ghost pursued, was in fact much more significant. While operating on duty it was one thing to take lives in the name of his country, for the free world, to protect the security of others. Now it was a much more selfish condition in which Ghost operated, and he would never forget the part Vlademir would play in his mission. This was personal.

Continually scanning Vlademir left Ghost lost in thought. What he was about to do would likely produce the most significant loss Yuri Kurikova would ever suffer. And it would only be the beginning. Each step afterwards would continue to dismantle and expose the Russian syndicate. It would also direct law enforcement to the network of organized crime deeply established within the billion-dollar industry of sex trafficking. Kurikova was connected worldwide to other syndicates, and to government officials. The fallout would be devastatingly beautiful for the world to see.

Ghost raised a hand to his tactical vest, never looking away from Vlademir, and removed a knife sheathed behind another pocket. It was not his, and it had no real place in his gear load out. However, it was significant. The blade belonged to Vlademir, given to him as a gift from his father. It was a custom-made tool, eight inches in overall length, double edged, no guard, with a black textured handle engraved with a red wolf; the Kurikova crest. The balance of the blade was perfect. Were it not the tool of his enemy, Ghost would keep it. It was a good knife. But the plan was to leave it behind for the purpose he'd come here for. He had a message for Yuri.

The stillness of the kitchen was not absent of noise. A humming emanated from the industrial sized refrigerators and freezers lining the wall behind the vigilante. The overhead lights buzzed with electrical life overhead. Ghost felt the chill of the room set in as his body heat lowered, his pulse slowing from his calm demeanor. The sweat beneath his heavy gear began to run cold as his thoughts waivered for a moment from the task at hand. He found himself retracting from his violent path of vengeance, and softening to conjure the memory of his own child. She was the spark of life a man in his profession never expected to experience. Her mother, Veronica, had initially breathed new life into Ghost's world, a dark and violent universe where a family was never meant to exist. Yet even after Ghost had met Veronica his world remained dark. The exception came when Chloe arrived, and he finally experienced a sense of light and normalcy. From that point on he learned to separate the worlds he lived in. On one hand he was a professional operator whose essential purpose was to eliminate threats throughout the world. It was violent and bloody and he enjoyed his work in a fulfilling way. Ghost also fell in love with his new home life, a world he'd gone to great lengths to keep protected. Veronica understood. Her love was unique and genuine. Chloe had not been old enough to know the difference.

The gleeful laugh of her innocence was music to Ghost's ears. He saw Chloe running around the yard of the farmhouse he'd acquired for his family. She clutched a worn-out teddy bear missing a single eye to her chest as he chased her, cutting her off as she clumsily switched directions, continuing to giggle with endless energy as though she could not be caught. Her dark hair bounced with every step. A light breeze blew through the thick locks she honestly came by from her mother, and her Sunday dress ruffled as she ran against the wind. Green patches marked the white tights Veronica had dressed Chloe in when the child had stumbled and fallen, but her resilience had her ready to continue the game. She showed no signs of stopping.

Ghost remembered reaching out for her, taking her in his large hands and tossing her high into the air. Chloe's laugh exploded with excitement when she soared higher and higher followed by a stretch of suppressed surprise as the fall took her breath away each time. Once safely in her father's hands the child's blissful laugh returned with a renewed energy. Then Ghost twirled her around and around. Chloe cried out with joy. When the detriment of the turning caught up with his equilibrium and the spinning continued when he stopped, Ghost squeezed Chloe tightly to his chest, smashing the bear between them.

"More, daddy!" Chloe commanded happily. "Spin me a'wound!"

Dizzy or not, her father did as she wanted. Anything to make her happy. Anything to keep her happy. Anything to see her smile. *Anything to bring her justice*.

The memory went dark, melting away the veil of happiness Ghost held onto as he remembered she was gone. Her laugh echoed within his mind as though she were next to him now. That, too, faded away. What replaced it was the imaginings of a nightmare that kept Ghost awake most nights; that fueled his vengeful efforts. Chloe's tiny voice screamed. Her cries continued, frightened beyond description, balling uncontrollably until a word finally formed.

"Daddy!" the crying child called out. There was desperation in the tone that froze Ghost's blood. All he could hear was, "Daddy! Daddy!"

Her cry reverberated through Ghost's mind, a plea of helplessness no longer in his ears, and poisoned his memories. She was just a baby. His baby. His heart. His soul. And she was gone.

GONE!

The word roared within his head; *GONE*! Ghost lashed out with the Kurikova knife. His movement was not careless. It was swift and precise. The sharp blade sliced through Vlademir's shirt from the collar to the belly. He tore the loose cloth aside to expose Vlademir's naked torso, and then traced the tip of the blade down the center of the body. He stopped just underneath the ribcage, and left of the sternum.

"Where to begin?" Ghost asked himself.

Chapter 15
Puppet

Stone — Honor comes before duty. We're almost done. You die last.

The message kept him from sleeping soundly, as did all the previous messages left behind after each grisly slaughter. Stone couldn't help but envision everyone, in succession from each scene as the crime spree persisted through every city and across the country. He couldn't believe how much blood was on his hands now from the mistake he'd made, and how high its cost was. The worst part was all of the loss, but over time a piece of him felt it was overshadowed by the deaths involved. He wasn't concerned with the type of people who died. No, it was more like the significant number. It weighed on him how much the toll to hell would truly cost the world when he was a part of the devil's game.

Rays of sun eked through the edges of the pulled curtains. Stone had not set an alarm to wake up, and hadn't for nearly a year. It had become unnecessary since his insomnia was at an all-time high. The nightmares had become more sporadic and less vivid for some reason. Perhaps it was because he'd seen and been through enough now his mind was developing a sense of numbness to the violence? He didn't have an answer, and didn't seek one out. In the time he'd begun this special assignment, or rather, the assignment had chosen him, nearly two years had passed. It seemed like an eternity with the body count he'd been chasing. Even still, it's what motivated him to get up and put on the suit every day. He was working double duty, and he couldn't fail again.

The time on his phone read 06:45. Stone walked to the bathroom and showered. He turned the water on hot to get a good steam rolling, make him sweat and help loosen his muscles. The hotel soap was decent enough, and he lathered up. Habitually he scrubbed the scars littering his abdomen as if they could be removed with enough pressure. The spread of tiny holes decorated the left wall of his trimmed waistline and around the side of his rib cage. Stone had been lucky enough that when the twelve-gauge slug and buckshot hit him, he was far enough away that it hadn't cut him in half. The buckshot peppered his torso, and the slug miraculously lodged in his ribs, breaking them, but doing no further damage. Every time he touched the scars, he knew he shouldn't be alive, which only fortified the feeling he had for what had been done to earn them.

After his shower Stone air dried in his room. The heat was on high so it didn't take long. In the meantime, he meticulously made the bed, a habit from his days in the Corps, and laid out his suit for the day. By the time he'd put on his blue slacks, socks and tactically soled dress shoes there was a knock at his door. Stone looked at his watch, a plain black Timex from Target. It read 07:30. His gut told him it was his liaison. It was correct.

The surly detective stood in the hall looking just as tired as he had when Stone first met him, and he held two cups of Joe in his hands all the same. Stone opened the door and invited McCrary in as he walked away.

"I'm almost ready," said Stone. He stopped at the end of the bed where the remainder of his clothes and accessories lay. A neatly ironed white dress shirt with a blue tie waited to be put to use as the G-man wove a black belt through the loops of his slacks.

"Didn't mean to impose too early," McCrary said, ushering the door shut with an elbow. "Brought some pick me up to try to start the day on the right foot."

Stone thanked the detective. As he laced his right arm through the sleeve of his shirt and swung it around to put it on, he felt McCrary's eyes on him. It was like an extra sense. The scars always got attention because they told a story. McCrary didn't take long before he asked about them.

"That has to be a shotgun blast," the detective said. "Glancing shot?"

Stone tucked in the shirt, buttoned the cuffs, and finished the dressing process. He shook his head indecisively. "Yes and no. I was directly in the way of the shot, just at a good enough distance, I guess you could say."

"Hurts like a bitch."

"It did." Stone chuckled, thinking: *To say the least.*

McCrary nodded. "Mine still does."

The G-man's head snapped to attention, his eyes weighing heavy on the seasoned detective. "Yeah?"

"Happens when you get old. You'll see." McCrary laughed.

Stone donned his blue blazer, and then accepted the proffered cup of coffee from McCrary.

"Let's you know you're still alive, right?" Stone said with a smile.

"Yeah, and pain is just weakness leaving the body. I'll tell ya', if that's the case I'm getting weaker and weaker every damn day."

"Great," said Stone, interrupting his comment with a sip of coffee. "I've got a lot to look forward to."

They shared a laugh, and McCrary gestured for them to get moving. Stone set the coffee down to seat his holster and Glock on his right hip. He then attached a dual magazine pouch to his left side, snatched up the coffee, and followed McCrary out the door. Before the door shut, he patted himself down to make sure he had everything.

"So, this thing has been going on for what, two years?" McCrary asked.

Stone shut the hotel room door courteously, ensuring not to slam it so early in the morning, unlike any typical, noisy traveler. "Yeah. Closer to three. Seems like forever."

"I bet. Does it get to you at all? Seeing all the killing this guy does?"

McCrary's question had the essence of being legit, but Stone felt he was prying. He was sure the message that was left behind at DeMarte's home had made a significant impression. It made him wonder whether the detective had been up all night because of it as well.

"I've learned to cope," Stone replied. "It's definitely a lot to deal with, especially since I'm running this case alone. I can only imagine the nightmares the guy doing all the killing is having."

As soon as he said the words Stone didn't believe himself. A deeper part of him knew better than to believe the vigilante would be having nightmares about the lives he'd taken. He knew better than to believe the man responsible for nearly two hundred deaths over the expanse of nearly thirty-six months wasn't dreaming about his next move, tactical positions, strategic strikes, entrances, exits, and having a plan to kill every motherfucker who got in his way, if necessary. But it was beyond what he more than likely dreamed of, in some capacity that set him on this path of destruction. Stone hated knowing too much, and he couldn't talk about half of what he knew.

McCrary nodded as he took a sip of coffee. "I remember the first time I pulled the trigger and took a life. It was on a deployment of the hush-hush nature as a sniper-over-watch assisting some Rangers on an op. I had always wanted that sight picture to be filled with a real target. Not paper, or steel, but the enemy."

The detective's words faded off as he left his story untold. Stone could see his eyes had wandered off as he recalled the mission. McCrary was reliving it in this very moment.

"Took its toll on you, did it?" Stone asked.

McCrary shrugged his shoulders. "I didn't enjoy it as much as I thought. Didn't feel as patriotic as I anticipated. But I kept our boys safe, so I focused on what mattered." He paused, took another sip as they stood before the elevator doors. A thick, index finger punched the down arrow. "It still keeps me up sometimes. Just not nearly as much."

Stone said nothing in return. The moment was becoming too personal. He could feel McCrary's method of digging up information beginning to work. The urge to sympathize was difficult not to give into, especially being a fellow jarhead. As a member of a Marine Recon unit Stone had been in similar situations; dealt with similar repercussions. Not everything that kept him up at night had to do with this case. It just happened to occupy an overwhelming percentage of his subconscious.

The two men drank their coffee and entered the elevator once it landed. As the doors shut McCrary turned to Stone and asked, "So, how is it you got placed on this case as a one-man investigation army? Seems like the kind of thing that happens to men who have become expendable, and are expected to fail."

McCrary had a point. Stone was expected to fail, and do so miserably. Knowing what he was up against and, with what that meant to him personally, failure was an expected outcome. No one wanted to be within a thousand feet of this mess, or have their names tagged in the headlines of its aftermath. Unless, of course, the outcome came out positively, which Stone also knew would not include him. When multiple

United States intelligence agencies didn't want to touch an operation, deeming it impossible, they still needed to act as if it held some precedence to maintaining order and justice. They would also attach a scapegoat to run it; someone who was complete cannon fodder if it went further south. And who better to do so than the man responsible to take the lead? The only issue was that Stone did not intend to fail. That was not an option, and as for Stone's involvement the governing agencies were the least of his problems. "You die last," is what the message had read. And Stone had no doubt he'd pay that price by the time the dust settled, if it ever did.

Stone smirked as he contemplated McCrary's perspective. "You're not wrong, detective. You're not wrong."

He could tell his vague response did not sit well with McCrary. Those squinting eyes of his seemed to be trying to look at him with a deeper purpose. Not in a way to search his soul, but to find the truth. There was an obvious manner in which Stone was dodging the detective's introspective outlook, and he knew it. Stone wasn't hiding it. There were details he didn't want to reveal, particularly how deep down the rabbit hole he had ventured. However, the G-man's gut told him McCrary wasn't going to let up, and he could only resist for so long. It was like keeping a secret that needed to be told.

"Interesting," said McCrary.

They felt the drop of the elevator as its hum filled the sudden silence between them. The controlled descent made no stops, but seemed to go on for far longer than it should have. Stone could feel the awkward tension between him and the detective. Seeing the latest message was definitely a powerful tool to implicate Stone, or at least suggest his involvement in some capacity. A seasoned investigator such as McCrary would not let go of this detail, much like a hungry dog would not give up his bone.

"Why was the message directed at you?" McCrary asked, sipping the coffee, and bracing his questionable knees as the elevator finally slowed to a smooth stop on the ground floor.

And here it is. The direct question Stone had been waiting for. All in all, he thought McCrary had taken his sweet time in asking. It couldn't be avoided though having the message personally directed at him by the man they were hunting. The variables of what it suggested were mind numbing. What it came down to was how it suggested Stone's death. That detail was likely what fueled McCrary's curiosity. Stone would have felt the same.

The men exited the elevator and trekked across the generic lobby of the hotel. The smell of the complimentary continental breakfast wafted from down the hall to their right. Stone briefly considered grabbing a croissant, or a jelly filled scone but disregarded the craving. He didn't truly have an appetite in the morning, and hadn't for some time.

"It's his way of fucking with my head," Stone answered, sounding annoyed to hide the truth. "That's the only thing I can come up with. He enjoys this. All sides of it. Coming into a city undetected, making some noise, being pursued, and then vanishing like a ghost. It's his game because he knows he's being hunted."

They reached the lobby doors and McCrary opened the door for them. Stone passed through thankfully and the detective followed. "You know, Stone, I would think that a man of such lethality would garner more of a response. All the trimmings, you know? If you're gonna' feed on a family sized turkey you don't skip out on all the sides. What gives?"

Stone enjoyed McCrary's metaphor, except for one thing. Now it made him hungry.

"I told you, it's a special assignment. National security."

McCrary scoffed. "Bullshit. That's an even better reason to have a full team working on this. None of this sits right with me."

"Good, it shouldn't. Should make you want to help me finish this once and for all. Get this guy off the streets."

"It does," McCrary said, removing his vibrating phone from his pocket. "You're gonna' tell me more though, later." A gnarled sausage sized index finger pointed at Stone over the top of the car from the driver's side to emphasize his point. McCrary transitioned to answering the cell phone. "McCrary."

The clear morning felt cool and crisp, but it was certainly going to warm up. The springtime sun was burning bright already. McCrary's unmarked Charger was parked close in a handicapped spot. Seeing the car in a restricted parking place somehow seemed like something McCrary would do. Stone saw the man as a 'by the book' kind of guy, in a way like himself, but with just enough fuck you and pride in his authority to suggest his badge granted him such an amenity to park closer to his destination.

Stone opened the passenger door and maneuvered to slide into the cushion of the black leather seat. He paused halfway in as he witnessed the dark mood overcome McCrary's expression. The detective didn't reply to what he heard, and never moved once the words from the call touched his ears. Something was seriously wrong.

"Get in!" McCrary ended the call and dropped the phone into a pocket of his jacket. He spryly swung open the door and slid behind the wheel. "Your guy just keeps the hits coming."

Stone dropped into the passenger seat and shut the door. The Charger came to life with a hungry mechanical growl as its power rumbled through the seats, and reverberated up into their spines. The agent suspected they were about to repeat last night's interpretation of a scene from the movie *Fast and the Furious*.

"What happened?" asked Stone, securing the clip of the seatbelt in the buckle well.

McCrary backed the car away from the curb and whipped it into a quarter turn. His foot stomped on the accelerator, surging the car forward with an urgent purpose. Within seconds the detective had them weaving into traffic, sirens and lights announcing their emergent presence.

"The connection to Yuri was made," McCrary said, his head turning and eyes quickly looking one way and then the next as his well-honed driving abilities rocketed them towards downtown. "Vlademir Kurikova was found this morning at The Mother Land, Yuri's restaurant, butchered in the kitchen."

Chapter 16
The Twins

The hustle and bustle of Boston Logan International Airport was in full swing even in the early hours of the day. It was nearly eight in the morning, and Terminal E received its first arrival of the day for international flights. A Boeing 737-800 unloaded at gate E-7 after having arrived from a direct flight from Panama City, Panama through Copa Airlines. Most of the passengers were dressed for warm weather having departed from their sultry destination as Boston's spring season kicked off. Those who were natives to the city were well aware to have a jacket on hand for the typically recurrent moisture in the air. Luckily there were no signs of precipitation as blue ruled the skies, and the sun shone down upon the earthly residents, its rays gleaming through large windows in the viewing area. It was going to be a beautiful day in Boston.

As the passengers of flight 807 herded their way through the terminal, two men maneuvered their way smoothly around slower walking individuals. Their pace was not incredibly fast, but their intention displayed a lack of patience for the overwhelming pack of wondering and lackadaisical minded travelers populating the airport. Both men were tall with long athletic builds like seasoned swimmers with lengths of muscle packed upon muscle, and both wore their hair closely cropped with more length on the top to style. Were it not for the contrast in their garb and facial hair the two men could not be differentiated easily.

Richter was older by ten minutes, clean shaven, and carried himself with an authoritarian demeanor. He wore a black polo shirt with all three buttons wide open, exposing the tanned thickness of his upper chest, and fitted khaki colored slacks with casual black tactical boots. He walked slightly ahead of his brother, Simon. It had always been this way since they were children, but it wasn't because Simon was a follower. Richter oozed leadership in a charismatic way that assisted his brother in maintaining his composure more naturally in the general area of life, while Simon took the lead on many of their assignments that fell under some of his unique expertise. It was a give and take relationship that molded their professional status into nothing short of uncommonly elite.

Both wore dark shades of a fashionable brand, Gucci or Louis Vuitton, and Simon stood out more than his brother. His dark facial hair was intricately designed, which was a miracle in the fact he could barely sit still most of the time. He strutted in a tight green camouflage tank top that put his identical physical features on display, and garnered attention from the opposite sex. Fashionably designed black cargo shorts with dangling zipper extensions and bright orange highlights around the pockets extended just beyond his knees. He enjoyed showing off his well-exercised calves and small, bare ankles descending into a pair of white, low top shoes to round out his outfit. Fitness was a key ingredient to their professional success, and Simon loved to flaunt it when he could. His eyes wandered behind his sunglasses, flashing a model-like smile to every pretty woman, both young and old, who admired the results of he and his brother's shared discipline. He wasn't capable of remaining stoic as Richter always had. That meant remaining calm and patient, and it was boring. However, he needed Richter to keep him in line when they were working, an aspect that worked in favor of their dynamic. Manic energy constantly flowed through Simon, fueling a wildly predatory characteristic of his personality, not unlike Richter's, but more chaotic. Knowing they were in town for another business trip multiplied his excitement for travel, but learning who they were here for was the incentive to remain socially agreeable.

At the turntable of the baggage claim Richter stood as still as a sentry, unmoving in his patience for the retrieval of their belongings. Simon fidgeted in the manner of a hyperactive toddler. The distinction in their demeanors seemed far too contradictory for them to be identical twins, yet they would not have had it any other way. Richter enjoyed his brother's energy, and knew how to put it to good use. Simon admired his brother's firmness. Together they covered a broad spectrum between their skillsets and characteristics.

Once their luggage arrived Simon found his way through a group of assholes who stood at the rails when their baggage wasn't ready. His overzealous efforts bumped a couple to the side, and garnered the husband's objection as Simon easily hefted the large cases off of the carousel. His muscles seemed to strain, but he purposely added in some extra flex for what he could only imagine was an unsatisfied, homely wife. The younger brother looked down on the husband, entering his personal space, nose to nose, as he passed by, and snapped his teeth at the matrimonial slave. The husband backed away, quickly realizing he was not in the company of a man worth risking physical harm.

Richter walked away once his brother removed the baggage, disregarding his need for attention, and Simon swiftly caught up with him carrying both bags. They walked towards the arrival exit in the midst of other travelers being picked up by friends and family beyond the spinning sectional gateway. The brothers stopped short as they exited the building where they saw a wiry, rat faced man in a sleek black suit that looked far too expensive for the scars he wore on his face. A sign occupied the man's hands that read: Panama X. He and Richter exchanged a series of words, giving each other a piece of a phrase and, once it was correctly completed, rat face handed him a set of keys to a black Toyota 4Runner. As soon as the keys changed hands Richter and Simon approached the vehicle and rat face walked away raising a cell phone to a gnarled right ear.

"They've arrived," rat face said, and then quickly ended the call. He disposed of the phone in a nearby trash can and never looked back.

The rear gate lifted with the touch of a button, and Simon loaded the baggage while Richter got in behind the wheel. By the time the gate shut the SUV had been brought to life. Simon climbed into the passenger seat, rolled down the window, and smacked his hand on the door eager to get moving. A cell phone within the cabin of the vehicle began ringing, already connected to the 4Runner's Bluetooth, and signaling the call over the speakers and radio display. While he was still unfamiliar with the control layout, Richter followed the vibrations emanating from the center console where he found the cell phone. He removed it and swiped his finger over the screen to answer.

"Hello, gentleman," spoke a distressed voice in a heavy Russian accent.

Richter pulled away from the curb and entered traffic. Neither brother said a word and Simon rolled up the window to prevent the call being disrupted by any outside noise. Richter hated interruptions.

"Thank you for being so prompt in your arrival," the Russian said.

"The assignment sounded too good to be true," Richter replied flatly.

"Well, you come highly recommended by our mutual partner."

Richter noted a sense of disdain in the pronunciation of *partner*, causing him to smile. "He keeps us busy and pays us when we have nothing better to do."

The Russian cleared his throat. When he spoke his voice was clearer, but held on to an animalistic growl. His tone was angry and sullen. There was a definitive hint of grief as the voice strained to maintain some form of control. The brothers both noticed, but gave no indication of caring.

"You will find all the information you need in the glove box," said the Russian. "The flash drive contains all the information you will need. It cannot be copied."

Richter didn't care about keeping any of the information. It wasn't their standard of practice. He remembered asking their mutual partner to get them access to the contractor's business information. Locations, partners, members, subcontractors, and anyone else the syndicate was involved with in the greater Boston area. They needed to scout the locations as potential targets, and who was important enough to be targeted. Hunting a ghost was never easy, but an ace had been placed up their sleeves with the lengths the *pakhan*, Yuri Kurikova, was willing to go.

"I would like you to go to a location immediately," the Wolf suggested. "A recent development."

There was a pause in the call, and deep breaths could be heard over the line. The Russian seemed as though he was barely holding himself together. It was clear Kurikova was not himself. His reputation as a hardened leader was not being represented accordingly.

"Location?" Richter questioned.

"Yes," Kurikova said, "it is a place of business belonging to me. The Mother Land. It is my restaurant."

The destination seemed out of the ordinary to the twins. Richter asked, "And what are we looking for here?"

"I have been told there is an FBI agent named Stone, who has been pursuing these vigilante attacks against my organization. I've been assured Stone and the Boston detective assisting him will be there. There is a tie between these men and the one you're after."

Richter and Simon looked to each other. Interesting. It was a moment they shared where, despite any differences they had in appearance, their prominent facial features mirrored one another. Learning of this aesthetic quickly put them at a distinct advantage. In a manner it was disappointing as it took away from the thrill of the hunt, but the real excitement came from the confrontation. Having the target in sight, or within reach, and initiating the last confrontation of a man's life. That's where the true thrill was in the kill of the ultimate game. And if the mutual partner the twins shared with Kurikova was anything, he was efficient and accurate. They knew little of Kurikova's dealings with him, but he'd employed them numerous times, and his intel held an impeccable, guaranteed standard.

"Sounds like another quickie," Simon said, his smile taking on a predatory flare.

Richter recognized the shadow of Simon's psychosis taking shape with his excitement. It was now pertinent that the situation would evolve into some form of confrontation, otherwise Richter would have to manufacture a way for Simon to feed the urge swelling within him. His brother *needed* to kill.

"Make no mistake," Kurikova barked, a tone of concern in his voice, "this man is formidable. The death toll in my organization has been daunting."

The advisement from Kurikova was uncalled for, and Richter quickly raised a hand to instruct Simon to remain silent. They had agreed that Richter would strictly handle the business negotiations, but not without consulting his brother before coming to a full agreement. In this instance Simon promised not to interfere in conversations addressing details once a job had been fully commissioned. Kurikova's warning was insulting, but the man was not himself. Simon didn't care, and Richter could tell. He didn't care either. However, he was not about to let his little brother return the insult to their temporary employer. It was a point of professionalism with Richter to never bite the hand that fed them. Unless, of course, it was deserved.

"You will go?" Kurikova asked. His tone sounded doubtful, and further exhibited a major change in who, and what, he represented.

"Of course, Mr. Kurikova," Richter answered. "We're confident we'll have your current challenge fully addressed within twenty-four hours."

"I expected quick results with you again."

Now Richter needed to bite his tongue. Simon enjoyed the annoyance featured on his brother's face, taunting him with a malevolent grin and a turn of his head, silently suggesting the shoe was now on the other foot with their reactions.

"We will keep you apprised of our progress, Mr. Kurikova," Richter said, maintaining his professional impression.

The older brother wasted no time ending the call. A major irritant of his was to have their skillset called into question. They were highly sought after for a reason, and their reputation spoke for itself. Richter feigned his collectiveness as he secured the phone in the center console. Simon never took his eyes off of his brother, waiting for his full acceptance of the situation as his twin had a knack for discontinuing a job due to lack of professionalism. This usually led to a change in targets, and redemption for any transgression against them. *Which would it be*? Simon wondered.

Richter looked out the window, and then casually looked back to his brother with a satisfied grin. "We're going hunting, brother."

Simon jumped around in his seat and punched the ceiling of the cab repeatedly. His fists echoed off the steel and padding that made up the interior roof. He then rolled down the window to let the cool breeze wash through the cabin and take away the tension. It was time to have fun, let go of those social inhibitions, and take a life for good measure. He shouted out hysterically with joy.

A sense of pride filled Richter to see his brother's happiness. The child-like expressions Simon rendered so emphatically truly brought him joy. He knew it was one of the most manic displays the younger twin had, which was a completely opposing aspect to the lethal nature they shared, but it had its place in their relationship. Simon was his best friend, and when he was happy the hunt was always a good one.

Chapter 17
I See You

His keystrokes came quickly and accurately for the size of the appendages pounding down on the keys. A password was entered, prompting another firewall where an additional code was needed for access, but not the typical login for a phone app or email. This was a much more sophisticated system than anything the internet gave citizens access to. The code was nearly twenty-five characters in length mixed between a series of letters, numbers, and non-denominational keys. The program forced the computer to hum as it worked through the back door portal of the desired system he needed to access. Computer work was not Ghost's most prominent skillset, but he could hack the cities CC television system with relative ease. A few minutes passed, fingers busily pounding on the keys harshly as though the keyboard was under attack, and then a series of live video footage popped up on the screen in a series of quadrants. He located the video footage he needed, and linked the neighborhood security cams outside of The Mother Land with the micro cam he'd strategically placed inside the kitchen of the restaurant. With the click of a single key he could switch between screens to survey the entire area, inside and out.

A click of the mouse pad brought up the camera in the kitchen, enlarging the video, and the computer screen filled with the organized chaos of the crime scene he'd left behind. Forensics worked busily collecting evidence and documenting the horror left before them with the monotonous consistency of a television procedural drama. Vlademir Kurikova's body was covered on the island cutting table at the center of the kitchen. A dark blood stain soaked through the white sheet. The crimson fluid spilled from the cavity of the Russian's body, and cascaded over the left side of the table creating a pool of blood near the industrial sized refrigerators and freezers. When it was fresh it had oozed its way across the floor, but stopped short of reaching the cold steel barriers as it thickened and dried darker.

Despite the murder it wasn't the most interesting evidence in the room. Ghost stared at the wall adjacent to the direction of Vlademir's head and he read the message left behind continuously in his mind. The angle of the micro camera faced it specifically. His intention in watching was to wait for Stone to arrive. The agent and his new partner, a Lieutenant Detective Randal McCrary, were surely on their way. Primarily, Ghost's actions were to kill Vlademir Kurikova. Beyond that was to witness their arrival.

You took mine. Now I took yours.

The message was for Yuri this time. Ghost purposely placed it in the open versus the hidden ones' he'd left for Stone. Those were of a separate, personal nature to keep Stone motivated. As long as he played his part they would be discarded as the ramblings of a psychotic killer taunting his pursuer in a dangerous game of cat and mouse. However, Ghost's plan was to put them to use in his own way until he could appropriately handle the situation in person. The evidence would then ruin Stone's career, revealing a position of coercion and acting as an accomplice ultimately leading him to a deep, dark prison cell in a location unknown to the general public. Stone would die either way.

Contemplating the potential risk for Stone stirred up the memories of the black site prison Ghost had escaped from. When he was placed there, he'd accepted his fate without a struggle. Very few times had he ever turned the other cheek, but it meant protecting his family and, even though they would not have understood, they were safer without him. That was, until Stone fucked everything up by trying to help him.

The greatest mistake Ghost had ever made was involving Stone. He'd considered it to be a step up for the agent, letting him in on the excitement of being a CIA liaison to a splinter cell operative conducting an investigation on US soil. It was the only way Ghost could have followed the evidence of his mission at the time, at least within the statutes of the law, which was otherwise forbidden. Why he'd considered playing by the rules proved to be his second greatest mistake. It wasn't a standard of practice for him on cases beyond target elimination. He'd overthrown governments with fewer problems than what Stone had brought him.

As a Special Agent of the FBI, Stone stood out. He had a reputation of a boy scout yet he exuded the will of a man wanting to do more than go by the book. As an investigator the agent was impressive, relentless, and skilled. Overall, his intelligence soared. Objectively Ghost had reached out to him because the success of his mission greatly counted on Stone's involvement, even though it was quite limited. He simply needed to be a part of the team and his career would have been fast tracked to wherever he wanted to take it, no questions asked. It was too bad that Stone made a bad call on what would have generally been a good decision. He just didn't have all the information he should have had before acting, and the currency paid for his transgression came in the form of family.

The feed from the kitchen finally picked up new movement. Stone and McCrary made their way into the kitchen from the front of the restaurant. The entrance led them in from the foot end of the island table at the end of the row of refrigerators and freezers. Both men stopped abruptly. McCrary didn't seem to react. The man was older and taller than Stone, standing as straight up as he could with the slight hunch he held in his shoulders. McCrary cocked his head to one side, clearly considering the grisly scene before him, and then returned to his default posture with his shoulders curling up to his ears and rolling forward. Stone, on the other hand, turned away throwing his hands up to his mouth as his body began heaving to vomit. The agent released nothing. It took him a moment to regain his control. McCrary appeared to be pitching Stone shit as he laughed, mocking the agent while shrugging his shoulders.

It was morbid to believe a man could find some form of joy in such a tragic moment where a life was taken. Ghost understood though. He hadn't smiled in a long time, but the dark humor possessed by those placed in highly stressful and traumatic situations worked as a coping mechanism. McCrary was a seasoned veteran far beyond that of Stone, and it was safe to say he'd seen things Stone never would. Today Ghost would change that for both of them, and show them something they could never forget.

Ghost reached for a phone sitting in the center console of Vlademir's

SUV he continued to use for the time being. He opened the screen, dialed the number he needed, and watched the display screen light up with the contact name: Stone.

****

Stone stood tall as he recovered from dry heaving. He covered his mouth and nose with his left hand in an attempt to soften the repugnant smell hanging in the air. The heat in the kitchen had been turned up high creating a sweltering atmosphere in The Mother Land's kitchen, and drenching it in the lingering scent of death much like a slaughterhouse. He looked to McCrary, who returned a derisive expression, and seemed to be unaffected.

"You're losing it," Stone said, uncovering his mouth briefly so he could be heard.

"What do you mean by that?" asked McCrary, a smirk still apparent on his weathered face.

"This is funny to you?" Stone coughed to clear his throat. He couldn't help but laugh at himself, too.

A long smile replaced the smirk, and the detective pointed to his nose. "Hasn't worked consistently for years."

Stone turned his attention to a forensic agent and pointed to his face, gesturing for a mask to cover his face. The agent obliged, and Stone could see a wry smile form when the agent's cheeks grew rounder.

"Whadda' ya' make of that?" McCray pointed to the message written on the wall.

You took mine. Now I took yours.

It was written in a macabre fashion, in thick, broad strokes with trails of blood that ran down the white wall. Portions of the letters had blank spaces in them as the ink of choice smeared with the careless strokes as though it had been applied with a mop, or uneven tool. The bleeding words gave it the appearance of a vintage horror movie poster come to life. As grisly as it appeared the message was stamped with the most unlikely of endings, which doubled as the writing tool. Just after the final letter of the message was a human heart impaled to the wall by a custom-made knife emblazoned with a red wolf on the handle.

Stone stared at the wall and ran the words through his head over and over. He shook his head.

"This is Kurikova's son?" the G-man asked, his eyes drifting to the body on the island table.

McCrary spoke with another detective, and his sour scowl returned. "Vlademir Kurikova. No question."

"Ah, fuck." Stone was not entirely surprised. The death was certainly high profile being the son of Yuri 'the Wolf' Kurikova. But it also gave them cause for what they needed. "Well, that makes the connection we suspected. And it couldn't be more personal now."

"Except it doesn't give us anything to go on as evidence against Yuri."

The grim truth was staggering to Stone. "Yeah, I know."

A heavy vibration resounded from inside the G-man's pocket. He removed his cell phone to see Unknown Caller on the screen. A quick swipe of the red phone icon killed the ring. As he replaced the cell in his pocket it vibrated again. A text message had been received. Stone opened the message. *When I call, you answer, Connor*. He quizzically stared at the phone, uncertain of how to react.

McCrary saw Stone freeze up, staring at his phone. "You get bad news, or something?"

Stone shook his head, remaining silent. Then again, maybe it was bad news. The phone rang again, vibrating, and the screen again read Unknown Caller.

****

The image of Stone answering his cell phone held Ghost's focus on the screen of the laptop. The agent appeared to be frightened, or maybe just uncertain of what was going to happen next. Direct contact was never discussed, but there was a lot Stone didn't know for good reason. And improvising always kept things interesting.

"You should know better than not to answer," Ghost said, watching Stone squirm on the screen. "You're an FBI agent. Every call is important."

A moment passed before Stone found his voice, but when he spoke, he regained his resolve. "I had no idea it would be you."

"Expect the unexpected, Agent Stone. That is how this game is played. How do you think I've managed to get as far as I have?"

There was no way for Stone to have a correct answer. He knew very little about the details of Ghost's extensive training and experience in the field of espionage. His exposure was limited and controlled when he was brought in as a liaison for a domestic operation involving Ghost, and it worked to the man's advantage.

"My guess is you're intelligent, skilled, driven, and you have the tools to do what you need to do."

"Flattering. But, you're not wrong."

In the background Ghost heard McCrary ask, "Who the fuck are you talking to?"

On the screen Stone began gesturing to his phone in an attempt to inform McCrary of who the caller was. The detective then removed his own phone, dialed a number likely to place a trace on Stone's cell phone, and appeared to be giving information within seconds. Ghost anticipated this already.

"You might as well tell him who you're talking to," Ghost invited. "It's not going to make a difference."

He watched Stone look around the room. It became obvious they were being watched.

"So, you like to watch now?" Stone asked, removing the mask from his mouth to speak clearly.

"Not for enjoyment. I need to make sure you do what I want you to do today. I've upped the timetable."

"Was this your plan all along? To kill a Russian gangster's son?"

"Don't pretend as if you don't know what the end game is. You're partially responsible."

Ghost noticed Stone had turned the phone outward so McCrary could hear. An uneasy, suspicious expression contorted McCrary's face, and it was one Ghost recognized: the epiphany of betrayal. The veteran detective no longer saw Stone as a brother in law enforcement, but as a possible suspect.

"Hello, detective," Ghost greeted.

"Who the fuck are you?" McCrary barked. "What are you doin' to my city?"

Ghost nodded to himself as he mildly enjoyed the detective's surly nature. Under different circumstances he might have liked to work with the man. He pulled no punches, and had no time for bullshit. Detective McCrary, always right to the point.

"Who I am doesn't matter right now. What I'm doing, aside from cleaning up your city, does. I'm finishing a mission from some time ago. I'm sure Agent Stone can fill you in later. Until then, we've got work to do gentlemen."

Stone used hand signals learned in the Marines to let McCrary know that they were being watched and should leave the building. Ghost recognized them from the many times he'd worked with Marines. The two men then rushed out of the kitchen's back door and into the alley. McCrary, who was also a former Marine, like Stone, but came from a different generation. Many of the principles and traditions had been passed down, yet McCrary's was from a harder corps. Ghost had read his jacket the night before. Their dysfunctional partnership seemed to be working out well even with the older jarhead being mostly in the dark. Ghost was not surprised, however, and he liked that Stone had a veteran on his side. The agent was going to need someone with darkly tested resolve. The day was about to get much worse for them both. And it was going to happen very quickly.

The video feed picked up the maladjusted pair as they made their way around the building to the main street entrance of the restaurant. Ghost clicked his way through the available cameras to keep them in sight. They stepped out from beneath the restaurant's awning and into the street barricaded off at both ends of the block. The final camera Ghost selected looked down the street at an angle, putting the two men at a distance, but they were in view. They were even facing the right direction.

"What do you want?" Stone asked.

"You know what I want," Ghost replied. "And don't play dumb now."

Stone shook his head. "Why the call? You want to get all warm and fuzzy now?"

The special agent's frustration was clearly getting the best of him.

Ghost decided to throw him a bone. He was done wasting time. "Keep me on the line. I'm sure your trace will come back around soon enough. Unless I covered my tracks better than I wanted."

"If you wanna' be found, asshole, you can just march your ass on down here and I'll be happy to slap some cuffs on ya'!" McCrary growled. "Heh?"

Ghost growled to himself. Maybe he wouldn't like McCrary so much after all.

"Your cuffs won't be big enough for me, detective," Ghost said, his tone taking on a menacing rasp. "But you're going to get part of your wish. We're going to meet soon enough."

Chapter 18
Now We're Getting Somewhere

The Toyota 4Runner came to a quiet stop curbside a little over a block away from the destination Kurikova had given the twins. It was maddening for them to try to understand why they were directed to a location swarming with the Boston police. Richter ignored Simon's air drum solo as he attempted to scan the crowd of people from their distant placement. It was impossible to see, really, but it was also incomprehensible as to the 'why' of being here. Two snaps of his fingers caught Simon's attention, and the younger brother paused instantly in mid-play while directing his attention to Richter. It never got old for Richter as he laughed internally, seeing the look on Simon's face as he ceased all activity like a dog being given a command. The curiosity on Simon's face was priceless with absolute wonderment in his eyes, and a bleeding determination to be called to action.

Richter would never let Simon know how funny it was to him. Simon would be insulted. "Would you mind fetching me the eyes, please, brother?" Richter asked politely.

Simon opened his door and continued his drum solo as he walked to the rear of the vehicle. When the gate lifted and he needed to use both hands to search through their gear for the binoculars, Simon's drum interpretation became auditory. His version of the drums was quite accurate, and it wasn't too long ago that Simon had discovered Beat Box challenges, which he took an instant liking to. He'd even entered some competitions in particular cities when they took some down time to rest and recharge after an operation. He'd never won, but the experience was fun for him. Simon saw Richter smile in the rear-view mirror. He knew Richter enjoyed the simple pleasures of his silliness, which were comforting to the older sibling, especially in such a potentially stressful profession.

“Boom!” Simon called out. “Got ‘em!”

The drum solo returned to a silent performance, binoculars waiving in one hand as Simon closed the gate and returned to the passenger seat where he handed them off to Richter. He continued jamming to himself to pass the time.

As Richter began to raise the binoculars to his eyes a buzzing emanated from within the center console, catching Richter’s attention. He removed the burner phone and saw a picture message had been received. Using his thumb Richter swiped across the screen and opened the message. The image was of a Caucasian man, blond, fairly handsome, grimacing as though he stressed far too much, and he wore a nicely tailored suit. A second message arrived stating:

FBI investigator, Stone. Leading case searching for killer. Best lead we have. More details on flash drive.

Richter studied the image for a moment longer, committing Stone to memory, and then turned the picture to Simon. The twin continued to drum while he stared blankly at the image and read the message. Oddly enough, with Simon’s misguided attention span, he had an amazing memory. It wasn’t eidetic, but close. There was very little that he forgot.

“Got it,” said Simon once he was finished.

Richter erased the messages and set the phone down in the change tray near the shifter. His professional reading of the situation told him they were going to have to use it again in a short amount of time as the day unfolded variably. Simon had gone through the flash drive while he drove and Richter’s gut told him there was plenty of information missing, but there was no way Kurikova could know everything, especially what might develop in an unknown situation. Richter raised the binoculars while swiping his shades up to his forehead so he could appropriately fit the device to his eyes. The binoculars were military grade and came with a number of bells and whistles. Operating on a lithium battery source they could also be set to two other modes: night vision and infrared. They had an incredible zooming capacity, which Richter immediately took advantage of, and, although they were lensed, they provided high definition picture quality.

Life was far too easy sometimes, and in the world of assassins and espionage it was a rare token to be dealt. In less than five seconds Richter located the FBI agent specified in the picture message. He was on the phone and in the middle of the road between the blockaded streets. The man named Stone appeared to be agitated, possibly yelling, and there was an older man next to him who didn't appear too happy, either. The visual of the two men reminded Richter of every buddy cop movie ever created. Always two opposites placed together in such a cliché manner. It was entertaining, and a genre favorite.

"What are we up to, gentlemen?" Richter asked himself, pursing his lips as he let his thoughts wander to solve the mystery.

Out of his peripheral vision Richter noticed Simon had stopped drumming and looked to him with the same earlier curiosity. Nonchalantly he passed the binoculars to his twin and said, "In the middle of the road."

Simon raised his shades, looked through the binoculars briefly, and then returned them to Richter. "Got it." The drum solo continued.

Richter shook his head and grinned at Simon's swift retention. He knew the younger brother would not forget the faces of either man. He was also glad that Simon hadn't broken out into his mock air guitar playing. Getting his attention during that was much more difficult. Again, Richter smiled. Perhaps the most amusing aspect of Simon's air instrument fascination was that he'd never played an instrument in his entire life. They hadn't been afforded the proper instruction where they'd been raised, groomed, and trained. And, oddly enough for Simon, given his random fascination with music, he had not cared for it. But the younger brother could key his way beyond the NSA server firewalls without a single computer training course. The irony was amusing.

****

Stone knew they were being watched even after they'd left the kitchen, and now, as they stood in the middle of the street, he and McCrary felt the vigilante's eyes on them. Their conversation had diminished slightly once McCrary was told his cuffs wouldn't fit. Unbeknownst to Stone he hadn't noticed the detective was toying with a hinged pair of them while he paced next to him, ratcheting one side around in an endless circle. That's how they knew he could see them. The vigilante could see

McCrary and his cuffs. He wouldn't be too close. He couldn't be too close. Some distance was needed to make a getaway. If the vigilante were spotted it would take next to nothing to have the Boston police force come down on him like a crumbling building. However, ever the strategist, if he were nearby, he had a plan. And he had told them, "I need to make sure you do what I want you to do today."

"So, are we gonna' get on with the show, or what?" Stone spoke into the phone. His agitation was growing by the second. He hated being in the dark.

"Calm down princess," the vigilante said.

The reply sounded loudly over the cell phone's speaker, and McCrary couldn't help but chuckle. Stone shot him a dirty look and had to smile, too. Then he gave the surly detective the bird.

"How close are you? We can meet." Stone tried to come across as casual and coerce the vigilante to make a mistake knowing his proposal was futile.

"It's almost time," came the reply.

"What is it we're doing?" McCrary chimed in, looking directly to Stone. "The trace is bouncing all over the place, and he just decides to call in and fuck with us? I don't get it."

"Detective," the vigilante said, pausing briefly to ensure he had McCrary's attention. "The goal for today is to open up your senses. Smell what's happening right underneath your noses. I'm going to change your life."

"Hurry the fuck up, would ya'? I ain't no spring chicken anymore, asshole!" McCrary yelled into the phone.

Stone turned to the crowds of people on either end of the block, lowering the phone so he couldn't be heard. "Look through that side and I'll look over here. Maybe he is close."

The theory was improbable, but the vigilante was full of surprises. Stone felt it wouldn't hurt to look, or make an effort. Except there was one thing, and McCrary nailed it.

"We don't know who we're looking for, Stone." McCrary admitted.

"All I know is he's big, muscular. Could fill a doorway. Never seen his face, though," Stone stated.

McCrary took a few steps towards his designated area, looking at the onlookers. "Black, white?"

"White."

The crowd on McCrary's side was a melting pot of cultures. The majority of them were of Caucasian descent, some other ethnicities, but none of them large enough to fit the bill. "I got nothing ova' here."

Stone scanned his side and came up with the same results.

"Sometimes you have to look a little closer to what's right in front of you, Agent Stone," the vigilante said coldly.

Stone was ready to yell out in frustration. He knew he was not being given a chance at succeeding, and in one way or another it meant his death, but he had to try. He hated how easily the vigilante could screw with his head. The world spun for a moment as Stone checked all directions, straining his eyes for anything that struck him as a possible nesting place. And then it hit him when he faced west as though he'd just walked out of the restaurant. He looked hard into the distance, maybe four long blocks, nestled right in between two other buildings. Could that be it?

"Look," Stone said to McCrary, pointing in the direction he faced. "What is that?"

McCrary turned close to Stone and followed the aim of his extended arm. The detective squinted deeper than usual as he made out what Stone was indicating.

"Ya' mean the parking garage?" McCrary asked.

That's when the light bulb switched on. The two men simultaneously felt the realization drop on top of them like an Acme anvil. The vigilante was close enough to watch the events of the morning unfold, yet remain at a tactical distance to be able to evade capture. Stone assumed he had to be using a pair of binoculars or scope of some kind to see them now, but he had to be there. It made too much sense now.

"There you are," Stone spoke into the phone through gritted teeth, standing upright, confident and reassured.

The line went dead.

Stone and McCrary wasted no words or time getting to their vehicle. McCrary took the wheel, as usual, and burned off down the street as though he'd seen the starter light turn green on a drag strip. Smoke whirled around the tires until they caught the appropriate traction and shot the Charger off like a bullet.

****

Richter watched Stone and McCrary suddenly stop and stare hard in one direction. They exchanged a brief amount of words, and the FBI agent tucked the phone in his pocket as both men set off at a dead run to a vehicle. When the car spun off down a side street Richter's level of curiosity went through the roof. It could only mean one thing: they knew where this vigilante was.

"Oooh, interesting," Richter commented, his tone gaining Simon's attention.

Richter handed Simon the binoculars, and then shifted the 4Runner into drive.

"Eyes on, brother," Richter said with a sharp smile. "The chase is afoot!"

Chapter 19
Follow Me

Leaving the Escalade behind in the parking garage would not have typically been an ideal way to make a getaway, but Ghost's plan rested on the fact that Stone and his buddy cop would be able to keep up with him. For him there was no dispute as to whether he could keep from being apprehended. Hell, using a vehicle would make it outright unfair. Watching the agent and detective jump in the Charger and burn off through the side street once his location was discovered showed the detective could clearly drive, which would make a car chase unnecessarily entertaining. The idea was to show them a side of their job they would never forget by giving them insight into the savage industry that had taken everything from Ghost. It was time to bring some true justice back into this world.

He cleared the vehicle without taking any of the computer equipment. With what was about to play out, he had no leeway to carry around extra baggage — only the essentials. On his person, Ghost carried what tools he'd need for the morning. The double stitched inner lining was stronger and modified to attach inside pockets like the interlaced straps of a MOLLE carrying system underneath his black military fatigue jacket. A dual shoulder holster held two Glock 22's with hollow point rounds, and two extra magazines for each pistol. A mini three round Serbu Super Shorty twelve-gauge shotgun, plus one already chambered slug round, was holstered to his left thigh. The Shorty was sixteen inches in total length and modeled after the full-sized Mossberg 500 platform. It looked a lot like a child's toy, minus the orange barrel cap and the fact that it was easily concealable. Ghost stood outside of the Escalade and reached into the right interior of his jacket. He removed an explosive cylindrical device and pulled the ignition pin. Once the driver's door shut, he tossed the incendiary grenade through the open window where it landed on the still opened laptop computer. The thermite bomb would take nearly ten seconds to ignite, but once it had, the pyrophoric compound would destroy the computer entirely, set the vehicle on fire, and quite possibly burn its way down through the floor board. The Escalade would be utterly destroyed within minutes, leaving no trace of any of the work contained on the computer.

As he walked away, Ghost checked the cheap watch he'd purchased in cash from a local drug store. In his mind he calculated the timeframe needed to descend the three tiers of the parking garage and still ensure Stone and the detective kept up. The cab of the SUV exploded into flames behind him, blowing out the windows, and turning the interior into a vehicular bonfire. Ghost ducked slightly as he felt shards of glass pepper his back, some nicking the back of his head, but none of the debris threatened any harm from the distance he'd already put between himself and the vehicle. The concussion wave washed over him slightly as well, which only seemed to add a hurried step or two as he continued to walk away. His final calculation of time came to forty-five seconds, in which time he'd descend the levels at the center of the structure, and make his way to the southwest exit.

The levels of the parking garage were bi-lateral, rising at gradual angles rather than being flat and level, and at its core were one-inch steel cables strewn through and between the supporting pillars. Each level of cable was separated by about five inches, seven cables in total measuring up to five feet high, or just over chest high to the average sized person. They acted as a safety barrier to prevent any vehicles from crossing over the edge when parking and falling to the lower level. Ghost traversed the cable barrier, crouched down to grab the lowest cable, and then dropped to the lower level, which was only about five feet due to the slanted angle of the parking platform. He repeated this until he was on the ground floor. He touched down right on time.

Tires screeched and slid over the pavement near the parking structure, and Ghost figured his dynamic duo would be right on time. Police sirens came to life in the short distance between the parking garage and the crime scene. McCrary, or Stone, must have put out the radio call of his location and requested additional units. Ghost, of course, had planned for this. It would make no difference. They didn't have far to go and the scene he was about to create was an illusion of a hostage situation, which would prevent the locals from breaching the entrance to his destination. This did not include Stone because the agent was like a hunting dog on the scent of its prey, and he would go wherever Ghost led him.

The Charger roared into the parking garage through the eastern entrance. From Ghost's position he could see the unmarked police car from the opposite lane of the garage that began the mild ascension to the next angled parking level. He checked his watch. Thirty-eight seconds. They were ahead of schedule.

Ghost removed the Glock from under his right arm using his left hand and aimed blindly ahead of the Charger. Two gunshots exploded the windshield of a blue sedan. Two more blew holes in the car's grill, which had the desired effect of persuading the Charger to stop before it got too close.

McCrary angled the car behind a concrete support pillar that truly did nothing to help create cover as they came to a screeching halt. Ghost watched as the doors flung open and the occupants exited the car, guns drawn and using the doors as shields. The sight seemed overly standard and overzealous. Ghost knew his, or any, bullet would tear through the sheet metal just as easily as if the doors were not there. They provided less than adequate cover, and completely insignificant protection. The agent and detective should have retreated to the rear of the car if they wanted to keep from being riddled with bullets. Lucky for them Ghost had no intention of killing them.

"Don't fucking move!" yelled McCrary, aiming his pistol in Ghost's general direction.

Ghost paid him no attention since there was no clear shot, and holstered his own pistol.

Police sirens closed in from around the corner. They would approach from the same direction as Stone and McCrary had come. On the west side of the structure where Ghost stood there was an alley too narrow for any vehicle to drive through. This was also part of the plan, and the alley ended nearly three blocks south in the direction Ghost intended to lead his quarry.

Stone retreated from his cover and ran out into the open, gun in hand, making a break for the end of the lane to get closer to the vigilante. Just as expected. Time to move.

Follow me.

Ghost turned to the exit and broke out into a run. He cleared the structure, fleeing down the narrow alley, and disappeared from any direct line of sight. For being close to six foot five and two hundred sixty pounds, he was incredibly quick. His natural athleticism was a gift he never took for granted and he had always trained incredibly hard to improve himself in every facet. Since he'd begun this vendetta there had been no time to train, but his confidence in his cardiovascular system and strength remained high. He also took into consideration the added weight of the gear he carried, which always included a plated bullet proof vest intertwined with soft Kevlar body armor. Overall, he was likely close to two hundred seventy-five pounds. Nonetheless, he was quick and light footed in his steps rather than a lumbering sloth one would expect from such a hulking mass. Ghost's build was also a sculpted symmetrical build of thick, dense muscle, equally powerful from top to bottom, but he was not restricted to being stiff and inflexible. He'd always opted instead to be better conditioned and pliable while remaining predatorily strong for the tactical functions of his dangerous profession. Even on foot he knew Stone could not keep up with him. As speed is measured Ghost could run a forty-yard dash in 4.53 seconds, which was virtually unheard of for a man of his size. And, he could pace out two miles in well under twelve minutes. He knew Stone was fit and capable, but he was always going to be left behind.

****

Stone was already in a dead run when he watched the vigilante charge out of the parking garage. He was quick and agile for such a large man. Functionally Stone saw him as if he were some hybrid machine, the prototype of a mad scientist's machination marrying the strength and durability of a tank with the speed and maneuverability of a Ferrari. Still, the agent was undeterred. He had to keep up as best he could, follow the lead, and do his job to some extent.

He raced down the narrow alley littered with dumpsters, abandoned furniture pieces, and the occasional deserted vehicle. It quickly became clear that there was an imaginary boundary being crossed where the more upscale neighborhood transitioned into its less than favorable underprivileged sibling. As Stone pumped his legs, he hoped McCrary was paying attention enough to see the direction he was heading. The alley appeared to stretch beyond two blocks, likely three, behind any number of businesses fronted on the opposite side of the structures. If they went into any one of the structures it would be difficult for McCrary to keep tabs on Stone, even if he radioed in where he was as best as he could with not knowing the area.

I need to make sure you do what I want you to do today.

The words stuck in Stone's head as he sprinted. They were being led somewhere, to see something.

I'm going to change your life.

That's what he'd said to McCrary. But it was meant for them both. That was obvious. They were working together and there was virtually no way to separate them now. Where Stone went McCrary was sure to be there as well.

Running all out was mildly difficult for Stone as he tried to watch for any possible obstructions up ahead, and to keep his eyes on the vigilante, which forced him to raise his caution awareness. He slowed his pace slightly while still streaking his way through the alley in a blur. The vigilante was still visible. Given *his* pace he was ensuring that Stone kept him in view to some extent, toying with the agent per the usual. Stone hated the feeling of being led along, but there was no other choice at this point. It didn't help either that his dogged determination to get to the man face-to-face first drove his motivation at the moment. A part of him believed he could somehow bring the vigilante down on his own. It was truly irrational considering the vigilante's elite skillset, and it went against the ulterior role he was playing. But if Stone could get the vigilante it would ultimately keep him alive, too. There was no guarantee as to whether he'd gain the answers to the questions he had if he could capture the vigilante. In his heart Stone would rather die trying to do that than assisting a mad man, regardless of the reason.

McCrary's voice suddenly interjected into the heat of the moment, squawking over the radio he'd given Stone. "Requesting additional units south of the Parkland Parking Garage. Agent is in pursuit of suspect on foot. Large white male dressed all in black. Armed and very dangerous. Do not approach or confront individually."

Good man, Stone thought. The additional assistance would be needed. He couldn't fool himself that there would be any kind of apprehension today. They were being led to a location where the vigilante would have the advantage, and that meant an escape route. It didn't matter what Stone hoped or thought he could do. It wasn't going to happen. Unless he could get there before everyone else.

Stone watched as the vigilante rounded the end of the alley, turning right. Nearly ten seconds later he did the same and saw the flash of black clothing disappear around an adjacent block down another alley. He lifted the radio McCrary had given him in the car from his belt line and shouted his location into it. "Three blocks south of the parking garage. Crossing the street to another alley still heading south."

McCrary replied, "Copy that. We're coming!"

The second alley was shorter by half the distance. As Stone entered the alley, he saw the same blur of black clothing turn right around the corners end. He thought of radioing in his location again, but for the moment there was nothing to tell.

Stone's pounding feet quickly slowed to a moderate trot as he neared the end of the alley, clipping the radio back to his waistline to free his hand. The alley opened up to a quiet street in an older part of the neighborhood where the negligence of the sidewalks and the gutters lacked the more spectacular preservation of downtown Boston, or even that of the area five blocks away where *The Mother Land* was located. Stone saw it as a seedy area, littered and plain dirtier. The surrounding blocks were filled with more brick structures, decades old, cracking at the foundation, and weathered enough to impress upon anyone that demolition was needed to improve the area's appearance. Some were apartment buildings; others were run down businesses. Many were either abandoned, or appeared to be. The area definitely belonged to the lower middle-class. The street was mostly vacated except for the scattered human vessels of the homeless and a corner pusher just west of the alley. Even the drug dealers started early in the morning. Most of their clientele were nocturnal, yet the streets still needed to be worked.

The FBI agent emerged from the alley looking determined with his gun in a low ready position close to his chest. Everyone who saw him scattered. Just like the townspeople did in an old western movie. It must not have been enough to see a huge man dressed in all black come barreling out of the alley like a bat out of hell, but an armed man in a suit screamed *get inside* without even trying.

Stone huffed and puffed as he caught his breath while scanning the street, feeling his adrenaline trying to outwork his lungs, driving him to continue moving. Here was where the real need for caution came into play. Stone didn't have eyes on the vigilante anymore, and with the police sirens sounding around the corner and units searching down every street in the area, combined with the rhythmic thunder of his blood pounding inside his head, he couldn't take any unnecessary risks until he knew where the dangerous man had gone.

He searched the area for anything that could have suggested where the vigilante had gone. *Scattered papers. An open door to a building. Something.* Immediately to his right was a dilapidated business: Lucky Pawn. It didn't look so lucky. The inside was dark, and the cloudy windows were difficult to see through beyond the large, peeling stenciled letters covered in a dirty film. Either way the red neon OPEN sign was lit making it an option that needed to be searched. It was nearing 9 a.m. The interior appeared to be cluttered from what could be seen, which wasn't surprising for a pawn shop. Stone couldn't see through the large front windows well enough because of the dirt and glare of the morning sun, and there was no apparent movement inside from what he could tell.

Stone removed the radio from his hip once more and depressed the button to speak. "McCrary this is Stone. I'm out front of Lucky Pawn on…" He squinted to see the street name at the corner. "…Belvedere. I lost him."

Timing was everything and Stone felt as though it had happened just as planned, although he could never be certain. As he let go of the mic button on the radio a thunderous boom erupted from within the not-so Lucky Pawn shop, filling the morning with the unmistakable sound of a shotgun blast. Stone dropped the radio, turned on his heels to face the windows, pistol close to his chest but aimed at the business, and he began backpedaling away from the gunfire. As he cleared the edge of the alley,

Stone kept his eye on the business front where there was now definite movement inside hurtling towards the window.

The large pane window crashed outward, snapping and screaming in a chaotic shower of large, sharp blades of glass which shattered against the concrete sidewalk. Stone focused on the projectile used to break the glass barrier. A medium built man overdressed in a black-on-black designer suit with long black hair braided into a ponytail and a dark, well-trimmed beard slammed to the ground in the lake of glass shards. The man's body smacked to the ground with a wet thud, rolling backwards until the feet flung over the head and outward at legs length until it slid to a halt nearly a foot from where it landed. A gaping exit wound rivaling the circumference of a cantaloupe exposed the eviscerated bowels torn apart as a result of the shotgun round. Stone thought he could see part of the man's spine glaringly white amidst the gore. Blood flowed heavily from beneath the prone corpse, pooling out into the openness of the cracked and tilted sidewalk, winding its way through its broken contours. Stone moved around the flood of crimson, standing only five feet away from the body. It was hard not to focus on the fatal wound, aside from the expensive suit that was so out of place. The discrepant feature was quickly explained by a fine detail that found the agent's center of attention. A neck tattoo, identical to that of the men found dead in DeMarte's home, inched its way beyond the collar of the man's shirt.

Spetznaz.

This meant the man worked for Kurikova. Stone aimed his pistol forward and moved towards the pawn shop's entrance, diligent in checking the interior of the business through the empty, gaping rectangular portal vacated by the window. As he passed by, he moved fluidly and tactically with his knees bent, ready to spring. Screeching tires drew nearer, telling Stone back up was close. He needed to move quickly, yet he paused before he opened the door and looked back at the bleeding corpse. Lucky Pawn wasn't a lucky place after all and if this was any indication, Stone knew he was about to learn just how unlucky he really was.

Chapter 20
Abyss

Richter pulled away from the curb and nonchalantly drove in the same direction as the detective and agent Stone. Within seconds he pulled the 4Runner to the side of the road as a number of patrol units came roaring away from the restaurant crime scene. The sirens broke Simon's concentration on his air drum solo spectacular prompting Richter to ask him to quickly retrieve the police scanner from their gear in the back of the vehicle. The younger brother happily obliged and returned to the passenger seat. Once the convoy of patrol units had passed, Richter eased back onto the street. He passed the street where the police made their turn, drove on to the next corner of the block, and then turned right onto the parallel street. Just then Simon found the local police channel.

The 4Runner cruised at a moderate speed so Richter could peer down the adjoining streets to see where the police were heading. He couldn't see the exact location where the entourage converged, prompting him to stop. Here he and Simon could see that at the intersection of the second block heading south it appeared as though the police were in front of a parking structure. Something had convinced them to stop on the street just outside of the main entrance. Richter tapped Simon on the shoulder, and then pointed to his own ear, silently advising him to listen closely. He moved on at a crawl, unconcerned about any traffic at the early hour of the morning, especially in that descending economical location. The police sirens were blaring from only a block away making it difficult to hear anything else. Simon turned up the volume on the scanner to be sure they didn't miss any pertinent calls. From what Richter could tell the parking garage was the main focus of the police for the moment. He thought it was a foolish location considering the capabilities of their target. Tactically it seemed as though their target would be cornered like an animal if he'd remained in the multi-leveled parking lot, and there would certainly be a standoff. That wasn't his style. This man clearly knew his ins and outs, and given the information Kurikova had provided on the target, whose accolades spoke volumes to an elite tier one type of operative, Richter had to believe this location was a bust.

Suddenly a burst of breathy radio traffic squawked over the scanner in a mildly static mess. "Three blocks south of the parking garage. Crossing the street to another alley still heading south."

Richter liked being right. It was not certain to him, but he guessed the radio traffic belonged to the FBI agent, Connor Stone. More importantly, this also told him that Stone and their target were no longer at the parking garage, which meant only one thing. "Oooh, a foot chase, brother!"

Simon smiled. "They're the best. We haven't had one in so long."

There was something special about chasing down the world's most dangerous game. Man had been at the top of the food chain for so long that it made going against one, or more, a rush like no other. The profession of it had provided Richter and Simon an exciting life for nearly fifteen years. To chase someone down though, pitting yourself against them through sheer physicality and skill was the ultimate thrill. And then there was the kill, raising the stakes of the game, seeing who really belonged. But the chase as a whole couldn't be beat. It made the entire effort of stalking and killing a man, or woman, exciting for Richter and Simon. The hefty fee they demanded for their work didn't hurt either.

"I know." Richter sounded slightly disappointed. "I'm sorry for that. But we are professionals."

"I know." Simon's reply sounded like a whine, but his spirits quickly lifted. "It's okay, though. I like how we work, brother."

Richter agreed. They chose to work smarter rather than harder, hunting their targets, and then ambushing them in a manner they could completely control. This methodology was profoundly more professional and took into consideration the many variables involved – mainly location and witnesses. Would it be an accident? Or were there multiple targets? It was also safe and subtle, which for Simon, meant less exciting. However, it was the preferred way to go, prolonging the career they were raised to perform.

A reply to the prior radio traffic filtered through the scanner, but they paid no attention to it. Richter accelerated to get ahead of the police units while they were immobile, reaching over to affectionately pat Simon on the head. His brother smiled and quickly ran his fingers through his hair to fix the playful mess Richter caused.

"We are a good team," Richter stated. "Today will be a good day."

Simon nodded in agreement, staring at the scanner, giving it his full attention.

The elder brother slowed at the next intersection to scan down the side street, seeing nothing of interest. He accelerated to the next street, slowing again, expecting to see more of the same. It wasn't until he'd nearly crossed the intersection that he caught movement in his peripheral. The 4Runner jolted to a halt, and Richter immediately backed it up a few feet. On the parallel block emerging from the mouth of an alleyway was a blond man wearing a dark blue suit holding a radio and a pistol in a tactically low ready position.

"There!" Richter barked.

Simon turned to look. The man in the suit, Stone, scanned the street. His presence disrupted a few neighborhood residents, causing them to flee. The agent appeared to be lost in the moment, looking up and down the street intently. He quickly turned his attention to the nearest business. The only possibility Simon could think of was that the agent had lost the target, nullifying his interest. Simon looked back to the scanner.

Richter continued to watch Stone. The store front's sign before the agent said Lucky Pawn. Richter found the title to be oxymoronic given that it was an establishment where people sold their belongings for an undervalued price and, by the looks of the area, it was probably to pay for their next fix. Stone moved towards the nearest front window, his steps cautious in nature. His positioning displayed a high level of skill and awareness. Richter was impressed, but deep in his mind he considered the FBI agent as an inadequate rival. He'd lost count of how many agents he and Simon had killed throughout their career.

"McCrary this is Stone. I'm in front of the Lucky Pawn on…" Stone called over the scanner. Richter watched the agent look to the corner and call out a street name, and then he said, "I lost him."

The agent displayed some quick reflexes in the next instant. A resounding boom echoed from within the pawn shop, although its location dulled the sound from Richter's distance. Seconds later Richter was shocked as Stone retreated from the window, and with good reason. A body burst through the store front display onto the sidewalk, rolling over backwards, and sliding to a stop.

"Interesting," Richter said to himself, shaking his head from one side to the other. Simon remained transfixed on the scanner.

Agent Stone then maneuvered around the body. From here he could see a river of blood snaking its way down the sidewalk. Richter found the display of violence to be incredibly impressive. Their target was surely inside the pawn shop, and he held no prejudices against extreme actions. For Richter, killing the man and then launching him through the front window was a bit dramatic though.

A thought occurred to Richter as he watched Stone cautiously approach the Lucky Pawn entrance. *What if this is a set up*? *Was it a trap or a lure for the agent*? Richter analyzed the information at hand. He dismissed Stone for the time being; he was inconsequential. The target was in the pawn shop, which begged the question, *why here*? The police were close by and they would have the building surrounded within minutes. This was a tactical mistake. Gigantic, in fact. Unless, as before, the target had a way out.

Something else was off. It was a minor detail, but sometimes the tiniest details gave way to the most significant breakthroughs. The dead man on the sidewalk was wearing a suit. Men in suits do not work in pawn shops, so Richter believed. His mind worked quickly, thinking again of what he knew because there was nothing else to go on. In a particular manner it seemed that coming to a firm conclusion would be complicated, but that was a façade shrouded in simplicity. Their target had been going after anything and everything having to do with Yuri Kurikova, which meant this pawn shop must belong to the Wolf. As legit as it appeared to be, Lucky Pawn was likely a front of some kind, and his target knew this. The final piece was that there was definitely a way out for his target, although it had to be a way he could get around the police. The target would have planned for this. He was too efficient to be foolishly spontaneous. It was quite the conundrum. Richter could not underestimate this man after everything he'd been able to do to

Kurikova's syndicate. There was only one way to find out.

Richter drove on south, ignoring what Stone was doing now, and turned right at the next intersection. He wanted to approach the pawn shop from the west, opposite from the direction of the police, to get a different view. He retrieved the burner phone from the center console, opened the screen, and pulled up the number Kurikova had contacted him from. His thumb depressed the green phone button to initiate the call. As it rang Richter glanced over to his brother, who was still focusing on the police scanner.

"They're not saying anything important," Simon said, sensing his brother's eyes on him. "The Lucky Pawn." He laughed at the idiotic name.

"Thank you," Richter replied, making sure he didn't ignore his twin.

"I'm getting bored, brother." Simon's laugh disappeared in a flash. His expression became strained, irritated.

Richter nodded. It was only a matter of time. "Don't worry. I think we'll be going green here shortly. Within the hour."

Simon scoffed at the scanner, tossing it on the dashboard. "Good. I need to do something."

Richter heard the line open as his call was answered. "We will, brother. We're going to kill today."

And they both smiled.

****

Killing the man in the black suit was done at close range. Ghost walked into the Lucky Pawn and appeared to look over some of the merchandise laid out on large fold out tables, the same as anyone would have used for a yard sale. He purposely angled himself to conceal the Super Shorty twelve gauge strapped to his left thigh. Two men stood behind the glass display counter ahead of him. One was heavy set, greasy, wearing casual clothing one would expect in this kind of establishment. He chewed on a toothpick, was balding, and watched the world with a dark look in his eyes that would make most people uneasy. The other seemed out of place, but Ghost expected a *bratva* soldier to be on guard here. He was clean with a well-trimmed beard, slicked back dark hair dressed in a black designer suit splashed with a light scent of expensive cologne, and observed with predatory eyes. The man in the suit was a killer.

Ghost observed them from the corner of his eye as he made a quick stop at a table piled high with an assortment of tools. A worn pair of orange and blue bolt cutters found their way into his right hand. Ghost examined the tool, putting on a show of interest, although he could actually use them. He sidestepped his way closer to the counter, calculating the time in his head as Stone wouldn't be too far behind. A slight turn to his left worked as a distraction and Ghost un-holstered the Super Short, keeping it low to his side.

"Can I help you with anything, friend?" the greasy fat man asked.

"Actually, you can," Ghost said.

He took two large, quick steps towards the counter and threw the bolt cutters at the greasy fat man. The tool spun end over end until the cutting end slammed into the fat man's bowling ball shaped head, knocking him back into a partition wall behind him. His face fileted open immediately, splitting him from his right cheek up to the center of his unibrow and rendering him unconscious.

Ghost was too close and too fast to be stopped now. He had the Super Shorty raised up and extended forward before the fat man hit the wall. The man in the suit made a futile attempt to reach inside his jacket for his sidearm. A modified twelve-gauge slug ripped through his chest cavity before he could draw his weapon. Ghost had made two cuts around the lower circumference on either side of the shells, careful not to make a full circle cut and to not damage the innards of the shell. The remaining connecting material held the shell together, but would still separate when the round was fired. This cut shell method essentially turned the slug into a larger round and amplified the damage of any soft tissue. The projectile blew out the back of the man in the suit, penetrating the partition behind him as his blood decorated the wall. His body quickly followed from the concussive force of the shot, cracking the wall as he hit. A crimson streak littered with chunks of gore followed the man's body as he sank to the floor.

The shotgun blast would surely get Stone's attention, as planned, but it would also put him in a more cautious state and buy Ghost some more time. He holstered the Super Shorty, stepped around the edge of the display counter, and grabbed the man in the suit by his left ankle. Ghost dragged him around the counter, heading for the store front where he stopped long enough to grab the lapels of the man's suit. He squatted down and pulled the body close. When Ghost stood, he rotated towards the window, lifting the man's body with little effort. His strength proved to be more than enough as he ragdolled the man through the left side of the large, dirty display windows.

Ghost walked away as the glass exploded outward, hurrying back to the fat greasy man behind the counter.

Meaty hands struggled to pull the fat man off his own ass, slipping on the glass, and falling back against the partition wall. He persistently tried over again.

Ghost reached the fat man in less than five seconds, hauled him off the floor by the back of his shirt, and slammed him down on the countertop. The fat man groaned, swearing something, but his words meant nothing. Ghost searched his pockets, pulling them out to look like rabbit ears hanging off of each side of his jeans. A bundle of keys fell into his hand during the search. He let go of the fat man, disregarding the rotund body when it fell to the floor. Men like him were weak and talked easily. Leaving the man alive was a token for the police who would gain a wealth of information from the man, not that it was going to be needed by the time Ghost finished.

Ghost grabbed the bolt cutters and moved to round the partition wall, stopping short when the man spoke a little louder. He turned back and looked into dazed eyes.

The fat man repeated himself when he saw Ghost return his attention. His words came in a semi-slurred fashion, delirious from the blow to the head, but he was clear enough. "Stay away from my girls, motherfucker."

A number of thoughts passed through Ghost's mind in the moment, none of which disputed killing the fat man now. Before another thought manifested, he decided the fat man would never talk to the police. He drew the Super Shorty one more time, like a quick draw at high noon, shooting from the hip without aiming. There was no need — not from this close proximity. The cut-shell-slug blew the man's head wide open, splattering his skull and what brains he had across the floor like a watermelon at a Gallagher show. Ghost moved on as though nothing had happened.

Behind the partition wall was an old wooden portal leading to a short hallway. Ghost followed the hall to the end where two more doors waited on either side of the hall. They were both dead bolted with additional padlocks on them, and had the aged appearance of the first door with one distinct difference. The door to Ghost's right was made of wood while the other to his left was painted to have a timber disguise. Ghost rapped two knuckles on the door to his left. It called back with a steel echo, cold and unforgiving.

Ghost reached inside his jacket removing a flat, half inch wide rolled substance resembling dough. A black strip coated the back side of it and was six inches in total length. Ghost removed the black strip, pressed the dough along the edge of the door in front of the deadbolt lining the doorframe side. He pressed a small peg shaped pin into the center of the strip, and then took three steps back down the hallway. The strip was a breaching explosive designed for security doors such as this one, and the peg was an electronic blasting cap. A remote taken from the inside pocket of Ghost's jacket would detonate the explosive. He switched the remote on, which also activated the blasting cap displayed by a red light, and it was ready to go. He turned away from the door, blocking one ear with the wall, and the other with his hand holding the detonator remote as he set off the explosive.

The roar of the explosive was magnified in the small hallway. It blasted the deadbolt through the door and with it, steel shards of shrapnel shot into what was beyond. Ghost immediately returned to the door, held shut by the padlock and the hinged device it was attached to. A heavy boot kicked the lock free of the doorframe, slamming the steel door against the interior wall with a reverberating clap between wood and steel. A gateway to utter darkness stared back at him, deep and blank. In a manner of speaking, he felt as though the oily blackness looked into him, through him into the depths of what made him whole. He wondered if it saw anything there, if there was anything left worth seeing. Beyond the passage was more than darkness. It was an abyss — a familiar place Ghost did not enjoy visiting regardless of how necessary it was that he did.

When you stare into the abyss, the abyss stares back...

While Ghost did not have the immediate ability to see beyond the doorway it did not mean there wasn't anything to learn. In such dynamic scenarios, as the adrenaline pumps through the human body, it also assists in heightening the senses. While the eyes were rendered useless for the moment, so to speak, the other four became more aware. The most sensitive was Ghost's sense of smell, which became overwhelmed in the moment.

One of the most important lessons Ghost learned in recent years was that hell was very much a disturbing image like *Dante's Inferno*, or anything described in a biblical sense. It was more than just these horrific elements. It had its own entity given life through one's own traumatic experiences. Ghost's current version exuded the odor of fermenting rot, waste, bodily fluids. It was an audible stew of suffering, peppered with cries of fear and screams of pain — all the main ingredients. What set Ghost's apart was that he encountered these elements while among the living. This made his version of hell all too real, alive, and never any easier to deal with than the time before.

He never knew exactly what he'd encounter when he found stash houses such as this — holding areas for the victims of trafficking, not unlike the warehouse from the day before. As similar as these encounters were, they were never the same. The faces made all the difference. The loss of hope could be seen in darkened eyes that would have otherwise been full of life and light. Expressions were robbed of happiness, and weighed down by unforgiving sadness. And in many cases the innocence of the young, and even the old, was stripped from all areas of life. The conditions were always dismal and bestial. The victims were always broken vessels clinging on to their souls. That is, if they weren't already deprived of them. Ghost refused to grow accustomed to such discoveries. He knew, that as difficult as it was when he stared at the abyss, and it stared back, there *was* still some light left inside of him.

Ghost reached inside the door frame to a light switch mounted on the wooden frame of the unfinished wall, and flipped the toggle up. A series of faded yellow bulbs descended into the blackness of a steep stairwell. The sight added a sense of nostalgia as the aged steps were covered in dirt and dust. A sudden awareness of an earthy scent intertwined with the hellish aroma filtering up from what awaited him below. He stepped forward, entering the stairwell, pausing to listen towards the store area. Hearing nothing alarming, he continued downward. Each step creaked beneath his weight, yet they were sturdy. Periodically he reached up and removed a light bulb, smashed it on the stairs, and continued on. The broken glass would act as a warning system when Stone finally came along, giving Ghost more of a tactical advantage than he already had.

A small landing angled left three-quarters of the way down, leading to a final descent to the bottom. Ghost felt his nerves twist his stomach into knots. The sensation did not stem from any form of fear of what he'd find. He'd seen this before. Fear became irrational because what he feared most had already happened. No, it was a burning sense of anxiety as he imagined the fear of his wife and child must have felt; how he was not there to protect them. The feeling amplified with each step, radiating through his body as though a giant reached into his bowels, toying with them, fondling his guts just to tear them out. He paused when he reached the bottom step, waiting to move on to the ground floor. The anxious feeling evaporated. Anger took its place. His thoughts transitioned to envisioning his family enduring the horrors set before his eyes. A tear cast itself free from each eye, cascading down his stern, chiseled features until they dropped from the edge of his square jaw into nothingness. What he found, as always, justified in his heart and soul the methods he used to create the piles of bodies he'd stacked in the name of vengeance and justice.

Chapter 21
Closing In

The Dodge Charger fishtailed around the corner in a surgically executed drift, rear tires spinning and screeching like a banshee call signaling the urgency of arrival. As the back end spun out to the left McCrary quickly corrected the wheel into the turn, feathering the gas and brake together as he brought the vehicle back into line. A convoy of police cruisers was on McCrary's tail, sirens blaring, tires squealing and smoking as they tried to keep up with his skillful handling of the Charger. The detective saw Stone near the entrance of the Lucky Pawn preparing to enter, cursing at himself for not being with him the entire time.

A body of a man was laid out on the sidewalk before the business, a river of blood easily visible from a distance. He was surely dead. *Shit, had Stone dropped someone*? He hadn't radioed out about shots fired, but the broken window and the way his body laid told McCrary the trajectory of the man's origin had been from inside. He braked hard and turned the car so it was angled horizontally in the street acting as a roadblock. The following cruisers followed his lead, one of them turning to face his vehicle as a secondary blockade while the four others stopped head on to their sides.

McCrary swung open the car door and launched himself towards the pawn shop. Stone had ducked and backed away from the entrance, his pistol aimed forward into the business. The detective shouted out orders to set up a barrier at the opposite end of the block, and to set up a perimeter around the Lucky Pawn. Two of the cruisers backed away and sped around the Charger to the end of the block, turning out in the same manner McCrary had to cordon the street. Two other officers removed an M4 carbine rifle from the trunk, and a Mossberg 500 shotgun from the gun rack in the center console. Both officers followed McCrary's order of setting up a perimeter and ran to the rear of the building to cover the exit. The remaining two officers also took up arms with rifles and shotguns to guard the front of the store. McCrary removed his radio and called in their location, informing dispatch of the dead man on the sidewalk, and calling for shift supervisors and SWAT to his location.

"We have the suspect cornered," he growled, feeling a sense of early accomplishment. "A perimeter is being set around Lucky Pawn. We have reason to believe the killer from the warehouse massacre is inside."

Seconds later a dispatch operator responded. "Confirmed. Advised to not enter the premises until further notice."

McCrary ignored the dispatcher knowing full well he and Stone were going in. To assist in concealing their entry he turned the volume knob down to one. He didn't want any radio traffic to announce their presence any more than was expected. They were here for a reason, not just to bring down this vigilante, but with any luck some firm evidence connecting Yuri Kurikova to the case. Whatever the vigilante wanted to show them would have to be secondary as far as he was concerned. He replaced the radio on his belt and drew his sidearm as he moved to join Stone at the front of the store. When McCrary crossed the storefront, he faced the interior and aimed inside the shop as a safety precaution to cover his ass against any possible threat. He closed in on Stone, stepping to his left in a low crouch, knees bent and walking in the desired direction while aiming inward. An intense scowl masked his leathery face.

"What the fuck?" McCrary barked, looking closer at the dead man on the sidewalk as he passed by. The grisly sight of the man's body laid amongst entrails spilling from the torso, nearly blown in half, reminded of McCrary of an image out of his nightmares.

Stone shook his head. "Not mine. Our guy blew him away and tossed him out the window." He nodded towards the supplementary entrance, lowering his pistol to the low ready position, and maneuvered to the left side of the entrance. McCrary stood on the right, in front of the broken window aiming his pistol inside. Stone continued explaining, "He just killed someone else behind the counter as you rolled up."

"Well, like I said before, he doesn't waste any time." McCrary shook his head, uncertain to himself if it was out of disgust, natural reaction, some form of amazement at the guy's dedication to a body count, or all of the above.

Stone began to speak, but McCrary cut him off. The detective felt the cliché moment where the more invested partner made a speech about doing things alone, and blah fucking blah. "Shut up. I'm going with you."

The G-man chuckled, but didn't argue. He waved his free hand in a bladed motion towards the interior of the Lucky Pawn signaling to move in. Stone threw open the door and McCrary passed through the large opening where the window had been. He saw no reason to be so formal, which also allowed him to maintain a direct line of sight on the pawn shops crap laden display area.

Once inside, they moved in tandem with pistols aimed down range towards the front desk. McCrary signaled with his support hand to his eyes and then, raising his index finger as a single count, signing that he saw one person. It was easy to determine this was the second person the vigilante had dusted given the lack of any lively presence. Stone nodded in acknowledgement of the information. As they drew nearer to the front counter the detective stopped, and Stone ceased all motion as well. McCrary's view was farther to the right than Stone's, and the aisle he walked down led directly to the opening allowing access behind the counter. Laying belly up in the transitional space was a fat man, his rotund stomach resembling a protruding mass of trash with his arms and legs limp against the floor, and a fraction of what remained of his head. The second victim's face had been blown off revealing a razed skull. Only the mere leftovers of his brains could be seen with one side of his jawline hanging off the remains by barely attached skin.

Stone gave McCrary a quizzical look, but the detective didn't answer in any way. He stared at the dead man for what seemed like forever. The ghastly visual made him angry, not so much that the man was dead; McCrary settled in his soul the man likely deserved to be put down. It reminded him of the brutality of war, unsettling things he'd seen during his deployment in the Marines, and now that form of hyper violence had come to his town. The entire situation was deeply unsettling to him. He was a homegrown boy, born and raised in Boston, and with that came a tremendous sense of pride. The feeling was heightened by the fact that he'd maneuvered himself into a position where he was on the front line of Boston's defense, and this shit was happening right under his nose. It stung in his heart, burned in his essence, and provided a fiery motivation to bring this motherfucker to justice.

"You okay?" Stone said. His voice was a meager whisper in the heavy silence.

McCrary nodded, shooting the agent a stern look, steeling his nerves to keep from moving forward with such heavy emotion. Controlling his anger was a key factor. He'd learned this long ago in the early years of being on patrol, and knew he'd go too far out of his way if he didn't keep his emotions in check. The greatest help he'd ever received for this came from meeting his wife, Audrey. After being full of piss and vinegar for so long, hitting first and asking questions later in the manner of how things were done twenty-five years ago, she seemed to help settle him into a more professional way. Not everything was solved with fists first once she entered his life. Audrey was a soft-hearted schoolteacher, yet she knew how to put him in his place. *Must have been that teacher mentality*, he always figured. In a way McCrary had become a student of Audrey's as she guided him through his bleak world of arresting drug pushers, prostitutes, murderers and rapists like a beacon on a dark night. She gave him a reason to come home safe. Audrey was always at his side, keeping him on a higher path. He became a better man, smarter even, and kicked in the doors to every promotion he earned. He hated that such violence occupied the world of a woman who cared so much, loved so hard, and gave it all to him. If not for the city, McCrary wanted to keep the streets safe for the angel who likely saved him when he didn't know he needed saving.

"Let's go," McCrary said, motioning forward with his raised pistol.

Stone walked parallel to the detective, cutting over to his right once he'd rounded the last table in his aisle. As he approached McCrary, Stone watched the detective remove a brown tarp from an adjacent aisle and spread it over the corpse.

"Good idea," Stone said, seeing the dead man's blood pooling out into the display area from behind the counter.

"I don't want you puking on me, kid," McCrary snarled, grinning slyly.

Stone flipped him the bird, returning his amusement with a sarcastic smile.

The detective led the way around the counter, stepping on the tarp, which saved them from planting their shoes in a crimson pond before traversing the fat man's gut. Stone followed closely in a tactical line up, placing his support hand on the shoulder opposite to McCrary's gun hand. The agent canted his own pistol to one side so his barrel didn't sweep across his partner.

McCrary stepped as close to the counter as he could, opposite the partition wall painted with blood, and slowly turned to move in a circular angle to clear the area. There was no reason to move too fast, which allowed him to use the wall as cover if need be, and safely ensure he and Stone wouldn't be caught off guard by any possible threat on the other side. They had no idea where their suspect was so there was a definitive need to be extremely vigilant. As he turned the corner, methodically inching his way to the other side, his pistol only slightly extended forward as a way to prevent a possible disarmament. It was an old habit that had saved his life more than once. Rounding the partition became anticlimactic as the area behind it was clear. It took a whole five seconds, but felt like an eternity. Adrenaline had that effect on a person in a highly stressful dynamic situation. It wasn't until McCrary worked his way around the partition wall that he really felt the adrenaline pumping through him, and the sweat rolling down the sides of his face. It meant there was much more to be come.

There was every reason to be nervous. There was every reason to be scared. The suspect they were after was dangerous, lethal, nearly a one-man army. But Russell McCrary had a duty to perform. Keeping the community safe was the number one objective, especially for Audrey. He'd do anything for her. It wasn't like there was anything wrong with being nervous, or scared, either. Sometimes that heightened state of awareness was what kept a man alive. He'd certainly experienced it during the Gulf War, bringing him home then, and from many shifts on the streets of Boston. In a manner of speaking it was one of the most useful tools to be utilized, the same as his pistol or radio, just different. He'd always thought of himself as a *nerves of steel* kind of guy, and this moment changed nothing. The nerves naturally built up, roared in your guts to let you know something was definitely wrong. *Thanks for the warning*. Fear on the other hand, now that was a choice. At least it was to him, but it didn't make him weak. Sometimes being afraid was the smart choice. If nothing else it pissed him off in a way that made him want to face the challenge ahead intelligently, and that was the whole point here. This guy, this killer, had to go down, and today was as good a day as any.

On the other side of the partition wall was an old wooden door. It had been left wide open, maybe as a habit, or maybe as a lead. McCrary felt Stone tap him on the shoulder, signaling he was going to disengage. The agent stepped around McCrary to take point, moving to the doorway and rounding it in the same fashion McCrary had cleared the partition. Stone inched his way through the doorway leading into a hall, which took less than two seconds.

When the agent waved McCrary through, they stood shoulder to shoulder facing down a forty-foot hallway. At the end were two doors on either side. The door on the right was old and wooden just like the one they passed through; padlocked shut for sure and possibly dead bolted. Another locking mechanism could be seen jutting out from the door just above the doorknob. However, the most notable characteristic was the damage it had sustained, which also affected the neighboring wall. A dark area coated the door and white wall, coloring it black from some kind of burn. McCrary had seen this most recently on a raid with SWAT, and Stone was certain to have recognized the damage, too. The first and only idea that came to mind was it originated from the blowback of a breaching charge used on the opposite door. As evidence goes, it all' added up to the door on the left being steel rather than wood. Had it been a timber product the vigilante could have kicked it in without much effort. And it could be seen the passage was fully ajar. A faded yellow light bled into the hallway, its piss stained tone offsetting the natural daylight filtering in thru a murky window nearly ten feet high at the hallways end.

"Here we go," McCrary said. His gritty tone foreshadowed their destination. "He's gotta' be down there."

"Not gonna' call it in?" Stone asked.

Stone's words struck McCrary as insulting, as though he questioned his resolve, and possibly betrayed his own. "You fuckin' kiddin' me?"

"Just checking." Stone sounded shameful, regretting he'd asked. "You don't have to go down there with me. I already know he's going to try and kill me."

McCrary chuckled, thinking of the body count their suspect had accumulated. "Try?"

Stone shook his head and rolled his eyes in a manner suggesting he knew all too well there would be no trying, only doing. "Fuck you." He turned to face McCrary, shaking off the dust of sarcasm. "Seriously though…"

The remainder of what Stone meant to say hung in the air, a silent whisper floating along with the dust telling him to stay behind. McCrary could almost hear the words without them being spoken. He'd always backed up his partners no matter what. There had not been many instances in his career where doing so would have violated an order to stand down, but he knew this moment was coming. Stone had this sense to finish things on his own. McCrary sensed it stemmed from why the G-man was involved in the first place. Yet, despite the vigilante's chilling words about changing their lives, McCrary could not let Stone go it alone. The truth was that anything beyond that doorway held no guarantees for either of them, and anything that happened couldn't be predicted. There was a duty and an unspoken code to watch a partner's back in law enforcement, and as former Marines. McCrary considered the repercussions of following Stone into the devil's backyard, looked beyond his morals to the bigger picture, and accepted the risk. After all, if worst came to worst, he wouldn't have to worry about any consequences in his career because they would be dead. Audrey would certainly kill him again in the afterlife, but that's only because she loved him so much. However, to be successful, he couldn't think about dying. Dying meant he and Stone would lose, and McCrary wasn't ready to lose just yet.

Together McCrary and Stone made their way down the hallway to the open door. The nearer they got, the more their sinuses were violated from an odor emanating from beyond the steel portal. It reminded McCrary of the basement room below the warehouse where the women and children were found yesterday. It was the most pungent of odors laced with the acridity of human musk and waste, lost innocence and suffering. Unforgettable. They fought back a sense of nausea, distorting their expressions into an appearance of sour disgust, forcing them to cover their mouths and noses. He wished his sinuses would stop smelling again the way they did in the Mother Land.

"Oh, fuck!" McCrary coughed. His words trailed off, fighting back the sickness invoked by the stench. It was stronger than the holding area in the warehouse, which he didn't think should have made a difference, unless the situation was far worse.

"Whatever is down there is what he wants us to see," Stone said, breathing in the tainted air.

McCrary shook his head. "I saw this shit the other day. Somethings you can't forget. I don't need to see it again." Stone nodded, and surged towards the open doorway. McCrary reached out and took him by the arm, not to stop him, be to reaffirm his position. "Doesn't mean I ain't going."

Looking beyond the doorway showed them a steep descending staircase with bare wood framing lining the wall. The staircase was lit by naked bulbs sporadically suspended on raw wires at two-foot intervals from the angled ceiling. The orbs cast dreary yellow pockets of light into the abyss of the stairwell, which provided little illumination as every third bulb had been broken and the space in between was robbed of any clear light, leaving a veil of dust particles floating within the sections of yellow radiance. The darkness gave off a thick, oily countenance leaving the impression it would blanket whoever crossed its path in an inescapable defilement.

Stone reached into his jacket and removed a small, yet powerful, flashlight. He powered on the device producing a white LED beam, and shone it down the stairwell. The bright beam cut through the blackness, showcasing a landing fifty steps deep and a sharp left turn where the stairs continued to descend. He looked to McCrary, whose steely eyes were hyper focused and determined.

"On me," Stone said, breaching the passageway with his first step into hell.

The wooden step creaked as the agent slowly moved forward. McCrary turned with his Glock pistol and covered their backs as they disembarked. He briefly watched Stone move down the stairs, seeing where he stepped around the broken bulbs set up as an early warning system by the suspect. McCrary followed after the agent, who was four steps ahead of him. He trained his weapon towards the stairway entrance and slowly descended, looking to his destination, stepping down with his back foot, and then stepping down with the other to bring them together one by one. After a few steps the crunch of glass echoed from beneath McCrary's feet causing him to pause with a sense of aloofness. He tried desperately to avoid this moment. In the stillness of the instant the sound seemed amplified a thousand times. He looked to Stone, who'd also paused, returning the detective's harassed gaze.

Stone shook his head. "He knows we're coming," he said. "It doesn't matter that much. Whatever he's doing, he's ready."

McCrary thought about Stone's words for a moment. They couldn't have been truer, so why were they trying to be so quiet?

"Fuck it then," McCrary snapped, turning down the stairs with a pressing sensibility.

Stone saw the detective's big frame move quicker down the stairs and turned to the side to let him by. He smiled as he followed suit. There was no reason to sneak around. They had no advantage, and deep down they knew this. A dangerous man waited for them in the bowels of this decrepit pawn shop amidst what smelled of death and rot, and the best they could do was to go in with their guns ready, eyes wide open, and their heads on a swivel.

More glass was ground beneath their quick steps as McCrary and Stone rushed to the bottom of the stairs. The sound no longer permeated the silence as the pounding of their every step and the groaning of the stairs intermingled into the bleak atmosphere. When they reached the landing Stone quickly scanned around the corner holding his flashlight with his support hand and crossing it underneath the extended arm holding his pistol. The stairs descended at a steeper grade about a quarter of the distance they'd already plunged beneath the Lucky Pawn. They paused for a moment, watching and listening. Nothing alerted them as being out of the ordinary, which was a completely fluid concept at this point. McCrary patted Stone on the shoulder signaling him to continue.

Stone moved with more caution as the steepness of the stairwell increased. He stepped down at a sideways angle, bracing his back against the dirt wall where wood framing no longer existed. McCrary did the same, but on the opposite side. The detective felt his heart begin to pound harder with a resounding and violent rhythm. He wondered if Stone was experiencing the same feeling. It could have been fear, excitement, nervousness, or everything simply rolled into a stress laden response of fight or flight. Thinking in a non-linear manner would go out the window at first. Training and experience would ultimately help calm the nerves as the moment progressed. Things needed to be simple and consistent. Complex motor skills would become nonexistent, too. Knowing these details, thinking of them, helped McCrary regain some form of calm as he and Stone continued.

When they reached the room at the bottom of the stairs, completely unaware of the environment with their lethal suspect somewhere in the midst, McCrary expected everything to happen quickly. He felt it in his gut, which he trusted profoundly. What they discovered was unlike anything he'd ever come across. Something like this couldn't be unseen. It would never be forgotten as a whole; not the sight, not the smell, not the sound of the movement that suddenly came with their presence. What they saw struck them in the chest like a lightning bolt of regret. Both McCrary and Stone stepped back as though something metaphysical forced them to move and the overload of revulsion sapped away the rush of adrenaline.

The subterranean cavern was impressively vast considering its urban location, and it was lit slightly better than the stairway. But what could be seen, especially only a dozen feet away, was a vison of hell on earth. McCrary thought it was too much. He felt it stab his soul. His guard dropped, and he fell to his knees. Shock overcame him, shaking him to his core and leaving him helpless. He didn't want to see such a thing, but he was so entranced by the tragedy sprawling before him he couldn't look away.

Stone turned back towards the stairs, shielding his eyes, cursing emphatically. The agent bent forward at the waist as he resisted a powerful, involuntary assault of nausea. "Oh, God!" he cried out. "No, no, no..."

McCrary rested on his knees, revolted and full of apprehension. The madness he witnessed somehow coaxed him to look around, drowning him in the grandiose spectacle of abhorrence. He heard Stone finally vomit behind him, smelled it, and felt it rising within himself. His mouth gaped open, his spirit unsettled, and as he attempted to find his words there was no way for him to speak. His jaw bobbed up and down in a stuttering motion, locked in a repetitive loop of quivering silence. Tears welled up in his eyes and poured over the dam of his lower eyelids. The beads of lamentation streamed down his tormented expression, unrelenting in their escape. It was then, just as predicted, the realization hit him that he and Stone truly never would be the same.

Chapter 22
Revelations

The twins watched from the Toyota 4Runner on the opposite end of the block from where they first spotted Special Agent Connor Stone. Richter decided to park on the adjacent block at the corner beyond the side street. From this perspective Stone had his back to them. Simon periodically looked up from the police scanner while his older brother observed vigilantly. The blaring police sirens grew closer. Simon did not find these theatrics as interesting as his brother did. Richter fawned over the details of every job they took on; which Simon was fine with this. One of them had to be meticulous about such things. He on the other hand enjoyed the actual task of killing. The buildup of all the tension leading to the kill was exhausting. The suspense did provide a certain amount of entertainment for Simon, depending on how events unfolded, but mostly it was *boring*! There were perks to the hunt when they had eyes on the target, but what they were doing now didn't count yet. All of this cloak and dagger shit got Richter hard. It was his bread and butter organizing things, watching and planning. Sure, Simon felt they matched each other in similar skillsets, but his attention issues waivered frequently giving Richter the edge. Simon simply remained focused on the radio traffic, keeping his mind clear, and shutting up all the other voices.

"Oh, look, brother. The partner has arrived," Richter said.

Simon looked up to see a Dodge Charger drift around the corner at the end of the block, wheels burning rubber, smoke show and all. When the car came to a stop sideways in the middle of the road the driver launched himself out of the Charger like in one of those action movies. The maneuver was quite skillful and perked Simon's interest for a moment. He was a big man in a suit. It was Stone's detective buddy. This certainly was not the detective's first rodeo. The way he moved was smooth. His actions seemed almost choreographed. He didn't break stride as he appeared to shout orders to the four other police cars that arrived hot on his tail. Two of the police cruisers backed up and sped towards he and Richter's position. They stopped short at the end of the block, parking in the road to cordon the area. The intersection was all that separated them from coming face to face with Boston's finest. Then Simon watched the detective raise the radio to his lips as he moved towards the pawn shop.

Yay! Radio traffic!

"Dispatch, this is McCrary," the detective shouted. "We're on Belvedere at the Lucky Pawn. We've got one body, presumed dead from GSW. I need shift supervisors and SWAT ASAP!" McCrary appeared to take a breath, and then continued. "We have the suspect cornered. A perimeter is being set around Lucky Pawn. We have reason to believe the killer from the warehouse massacre is inside."

Dispatch confirmed the transmission and advised McCrary not to enter the premises.

Simon enjoyed Detective McCrary's commentary. His tone was rushed, excited, and overly confident. The younger brother became more interested in watching now, wondering if this McCrary felt as though they had the upper hand. Clearly, he had no idea what he and the agent were getting into.

"He's like a cowboy," Simon said condescendingly. "All sorts of yippi kay yay."

"The detective?" Richter clarified.

Simon nodded.

"Indeed, brother."

"And overconfident."

Richter nodded in agreement. "Do you suppose they think they have the tactical advantage now? Their perimeter is weak. And SWAT? Come on! They'll take at least ten to fifteen minutes to mobilize and arrive on scene. This will all be over by then." He shook his head in disappointment.

Simon enjoyed breaking down the faults of the situation with his brother. Their interactions were always so judgmental and playful at the same time. *God, we must sound like psychopaths.*

"Oooh, oooh!" Simon pointed towards the Lucky Pawn like a child witnessing something for the first time. Things were getting even more interesting. The detective joined Stone at the front of the building, moving quite well and tactically sound for an older man, and then… "Oh, my, brother! They're going in!"

Richter and Simon turned towards each other and shared a hardy laugh. The moment seemed surreal, but in Simon's mind it was justifiable. Superior training was on their side, giving them a superior set of skills, which in turn gave them a superior perspective. *Did that also equal out to a superiority complex?* It didn't matter. Simon could see the consequences the police would be facing, or at least McCrary and Stone.

"They have a death wish," Simon stated.

Richter bobbed his head in agreement. "You know how dogs are when on the hunt, brother."

Simon did. "Do you think this is going to end in some kind of siege where our job is done for us? Or does our target have an escape plan?"

He had gone through the dossier Kurikova had given them. Their target's skillset was impressive. Beyond impressive, really. Simon gawked at it as the scale of this man's destruction was something he could only think of as *epic*. A body count upwards of two hundred? In just over two to three years! *Seriously?* If it weren't for the fact that he and Richter were going to kill him, Simon entertained the idea of having an old school trading card made of the man and having him sign it before his violent end came. *Or maybe I could at least shake his hand before he dies?*

Simon noticed Richter was now staring at him, looking stern, yet impressed. He didn't like to be stared at. Not like this. Richter made him uncomfortable, and he knew his staring made Simon uncomfortable.

"You're going to make me mad, brother," Simon warned.

Richter shook his head. "Please, forgive me. But you are a *fucking* genius. I was far too enthralled that I'd forgotten."

"What?" Simon missed something.

Richter disheveled Simon's hair once again in his annoying manner of praise, prompting Simon to fix it immediately. Then he reached for the burner phone.

"Genius, brother. Pure genius." Richter echoed as he dialed a number. "We are one in the same."

Simon turned his attention to the front of the Lucky Pawn. He didn't care what he'd come up with as long as Richter stopped staring. More radio traffic blared over the scanner, and he shifted his attention back to the black electronic box sitting on his lap. Richter patted the air in a downward motion, silently asking for the volume to be lowered. Simon turned the volume tab counterclockwise. The dispatcher radioed the confirmation of the SWAT team being en route. Ambulances were also en route, as well as shift supervisors. Everything McCrary had asked for. Yet the detective did not respond.

"Idiot," Simon said to himself. It was clear after seeing the detective and the FBI agent go into the pawn shop, they were going to be all gung-ho, likely leading them to their deaths in an attempt to be heroes, which apparently meant going radio silent, also. With Stone and McCrary discontinuing the use of their radios Simon lost interest. He turned his attention to the pawn shop and listened to Richter's phone call sparked by his enlightened moment of thought.

"Yes, let me speak to, Yuri," Richter said. He sounded demanding and urgent. "No, now. It's imperative for the moment. We have a possible window of opportunity."

Richter turned to Simon and grinned genuinely. Simon could tell Richter was proud of him. He grinned back as assurance he understood. His elder brother likely knew he had no clue.

"Yuri," Richter greeted. "Yes, this is important. I know you're grieving, but I have two important questions." There was a pause. Simon could hear Yuri answering, sounding annoyed. "Sooner than expected if you answer my questions." Another pause. "The Lucky Pawn is a front of yours, yes?" Richter nodded, smiling. "Perfect. Most important, once someone is inside the establishment, Yuri, is there a secret way out?"

Richter waited longer this time, and Simon could not hear an answer. This perked Simon's interest again as he put the pieces to the puzzle together. Yuri's pause must have struck home. *Could I have figured out how to acquire the target?*

"Oh, really?" Richter's tone was curious. "Well, clear it out now, and we'll be there momentarily." He turned to Simon, smiling brighter. "Brother, I need you to remember this address and this code."

Simon smiled, listening intently.

Chapter 23
The Evil That Men Do

The expanse of the subterranean chamber was appropriately dank among the weak light bleeding into the thick pockets of shadows. An eerie chill felt alive and all consuming, uninviting in essence, yet welcoming in a powerfully luring fashion to the broken beings within its clutches. It had been all they'd known for as long as could be remembered. Their presence confirmed that life was surely present, but nothing truly *lived.* The notion to simply exist was the sole purpose of the chamber's occupants as its bleakness stole away their hope, and raped them of their innocence. These virtues faded away without necessary sustenance, tirelessly starving them of life's essentials until darkness consumed them. What secretly lived and breathed here, bred and grew here, could only thrive in such an environment. It enveloped its victims in a depravity forged from man's inhumanity. This was not just a chamber of forbidden indulgences, but a melting pot of lurid nightmares providing a peculiar sanctity to the evil in men's hearts.

Two men, one definitively older than the other, disrupted the atmosphere with their unexpected presence. Their attendance came to an immediate and emotional standstill. The chamber worked its dark magic on them instantly as the wicked indifference brought one to their knees, and involuntarily obligated the other to vomit in response. Futile words of denial were spoken as they immediately expressed their disapproval, yet the chamber left them obscurely captivated.

Rows of four-foot-by-four-foot cages, all six feet in height, filled the belly of the room. Each cell congregated in pairs of six, three rows deep with eight rows spanning the length of the chamber separated by a dozen feet providing an ample walkway. The totality of the holding area made up twenty-four island-like cages, 144 individual cells in all. Each one had individual gates chained and padlocked shut. The mass of each cage was made up of steel bars welded and banded together at six-inch intervals on the top and every side. The bottoms were all set in one large steel drain pan, interconnecting the six cell clusters. This made the floor of each cage slick and cold. It also made it possible for the captors to hose the cells clean to a centralized drain on each captive island.

Held within most of the cages were the shattered remains of misappropriated souls, young and old, boy and girl, mostly women. They did not speak, or call out when the two men entered the chamber. Whimpers and gasps and painful moans bellowed about like spirits of the damned left behind from unfulfilled destinies. Some pressed their faces to the confines of the steel bars, curiously looking towards the two men, frighteningly wondering what terrible things they would do, while some conspired of the pleasures they would bring them. Others retreated futilely in one corner, slipping and sitting in what waste had not been cleaned away. Then there were those who did not care to react, paying no attention to the visitors at all, aspiring to feel nothing; they had become numb to the realities forced upon them. After all, they were at the beck and call of their captors, or *else*. If a cell was not empty then some certainly gave this impression as there were plenty of those who had lost all awareness to the world around them. Their lives faded away from the brutal conditions suffered over time, making the lives of the other captives harsher as payment would be made up in one way or another.

A Cambodian woman nearest to the stairway and, slightly cleaner than the majority, began to expose herself to the men. She smiled a mouth full of broken teeth and bleeding gums from a recent beating she'd sustained for not appropriately pleasing a client. One eye was forced shut, purple and swollen where her orbital bone had been shattered. Her injuries did not keep her from retreating to the years of grooming she'd endured in the interchanging hands of those who paid to control her. A bloody tongue flicked beyond her thick lips like a serpent in a lurid gesture towards the two men. Time had taught her to be proactive in receiving potential suitors as her foreign language hissed a sultry invitation to the men. Fingertips with broken nails, and some broken fingers, roughly touched the soft curves of her body in an attempt to gain their attention. Her small hands squeezed her breasts as she hissed more unknown phrases, selling the product of her body as best she could. In her seductive attempt her hands continued to move over her belly before finally diving below her waistline. She desperately wanted to show those in control of her she'd learned her lesson. They were always watching. Despite the conditions and abuse she had not yet faded into a void where her life held no meaning. She embraced this grisly fate as her own, altering her nature to that of a woman reprogrammed to please beyond any doubt, and under any circumstances. She'd accepted it as her life's purpose. Experience had taught her that was how she survived, and how she would continue to do so.

Beyond the Cambodian sex slave lay a young woman, weeping in one corner of her cell. She clutched a small body to her bosom, running her fingers through tangled and knotted blond hair. A tiny girl shuffled in her mother's arms, no more than five years of age. The mother constantly whispered to her child. The words were not audible enough for the two men to hear, yet these words carried a weight of reassurance to be kept from harm. "I won't let them take you, baby," she repeated, rocking back and forth against the unforgiving steel bars. Her eyes sharpened to a hate filled glare, and her lips tightened into a determined thin line, instantly reducing her to an instinctual and primal state of protection.

The child shifted in her mother's arms, turning around to face outward, exposing her innocent features to the openness of the chamber and displaying her bruised jaw line and neck. She fiddled with a small, headless doll, holding it to her chest as she mocked her mother's actions with the toy. The child froze when she noticed the two men at the chamber's entrance. She couldn't tell if they had seen her, but their presence delivered an instant chill to her body she did not understand. A blank stare cast out through the borders of the cell as fear clouded her once blue eyes, tinged now with a sharp redness. Her tiny lower lip began to quiver, accompanying the sudden buildup of tears in her eyes, flooding the boundary of her eyelids until a steady stream contoured to the roundness of her pale cheeks, and dripped from her chin. She was a smart little girl, and it had not taken but one time to learn not to cry out when she was afraid.

Three cages away to the left of the men the overhead lights shone purposely into a pair of cells, one of which was on the corner of the celled island. Two children occupied these confines, one boy and one girl, roughly around the ages of seven or eight. They sat adjacent to one another, separated by the bars of the cell. They were Caucasian, possibly of European descent, maybe American. The boy sat upright with a small arm woven through the bars and wrapped around the shoulders of the girl — his sister. Big dark eyes lacking any color of life blankly stared at the men in the doorway, or beyond them. It was not certain. The boy wore only a pair of red swim shorts streaked with dirt and waste, no shirt, and no shoes. Grime of some sort streaked his face and discolored his short blond hair. Periodically a shiver rocked his frail body, and each time he squeezed his sister through the bars. She leaned against the steel rods separating them, enveloped in a torn, oversized black shirt. Her knees were drawn up into the lengthy fabric in an attempt to keep warm, and her face was buried into her chest. There was no response from the girl each time her brother squeezed her. It appeared as though he'd stopped checking on her, always looking past the bars, transfixed on the space beyond the cage, numb inside and out. Aside from the movement his trembling hug transferred to his sister, she did not move. There were no indications she even breathed in the position she held. There were no signs of life. It could only be assumed her soul had been rescued and at peace, maybe with her spirit hovering overhead while her brother insisted on remaining behind in a living purgatory. What wouldn't be learned until much later was that the boy had given his sister the shirt to keep her warm, but the effort only helped to hide her lifeless body from his undying gaze.

"I can't believe this," the older man said, wiping tears from his leathery face while rising off of his knees one by one. "This is a fucking nightmare…" His words drifted off with disbelief while reality dropped him back to one knee, shaking his head defiantly.

The other man, more youthful in appearance, was still dry heaving over the final steps that had led them into such a visceral hell. In between each empty retch he continued to say, "No… No… Oh, God!"

They were grown men — hardened men. Survivors of life's difficulties near and abroad, but they knew they would not survive this without the mental scars such trauma imbued. They were instantly changed. The chamber's greatest power was that no one ever left the same, not in mind, body, or spirit. It thrived on their disgust, and grew with their pain. The evil it demonstrated was not only put on display by its victims, secreting its way into their visual senses as it simultaneously saturated the air, heavy and thick, slowly suffocating everyone who breathed in its decaying essence. There was no telling what residual torment their souls would suffer.

The fragmented shells of flesh caged throughout the chamber suddenly began to stir. Something was waking the dead, intensifying the bleak atmosphere with an unfamiliar electric energy. The victims shuffled and moved with new motivation. Cells were shaken and pounded upon by open palms while unsettling moans disguising a single word slowly grew from whispers to drawn out shouts. Had they begun to realize these men were not customers, associates of their abusers, or anything else as remotely vile possessing the core of a man? The demeanor of the two men displayed their pain, empathy, and sorrow. No one else had ever shown such emotion. After far too long the chamber's desolation was shaken by these lost attributes that had been withheld from anyone trapped within its borders. The foreign infiltration broke the perverse hold that gave the chamber its power by introducing something human into its depths.

"Help," is what they said. The word carried from one end to the other, broken and lisped as fractured voices united into a single chant.

"Help!"

Some versions of the beckoning phrase came across mispronounced, or unintelligible. But overall, the message could be understood.

"H-E-L-P…"

The combined call of the confined bellowed like a banshee's wail. Arms extended beyond the restriction of their cages in an attempt to reach for salvation, crying to be saved. Their livelihood and will stubbornly failed to die as they abruptly clung to a new sliver of hope.

Each man looked to the other, shocked at what they witnessed. Pleasure replaced their pained expressions as they watched these people reanimate from the darkness of despair. Both men swept their jackets back to open up a clear channel to holster their firearms. Eyes wide with amazement looked on as they witnessed a near-resurrection. Were they the saviors to these displaced beings uprooted from their lives to be sold into lurid acts of carnal satisfaction? Was that unforeseen consciousness what gave these victims such a powerful surge of life?

In the moment that passed the two men were far too overwhelmed with the depravity of the chamber's secrets causing them to overlook the subtlety of what was to come. The sign was there in front of them, but they did not recognize it until it was too late.

The call for help was not directed at the men. They'd missed the obvious. For those who moved and banged and found a way to fight again, they looked past them. They called beyond them. And it was then that the men remembered that, as they were changed as promised, they had also come here for a specific purpose lost to the appalling discovery they'd found within the bowels of *Lucky Pawn*. Their mistake, however, was another's benefit, and the advantage was not wasted by the entity moving in the shadows.

Chapter 24
Focus

Ghost paid no attention to the cries for help. He did not wonder what could spur life into such mummified personas, nor did he let his thoughts waiver to such frivolous ideas even though it pleased him to see them rally back from being beaten down so hard. He already knew the answer, and had seen it before. It was a miracle of sorts to witness, warming the chill of his heart knowing there was some form of true goodness he could invoke on his bloody crusade. Upon entering the chamber earlier he'd announced they would soon be safe upon his return. In the end it was inevitable that he would not be there to physically free them, but bringing those who would was just as important.

The first task Ghost needed to handle waited for him deeper within the chamber. Towards the northeastern corner he had business to attend to before his guests arrived. And, as he'd felt the first time he'd witnessed such a detestable state of humanity, he knew the shock and awe of the chamber would slow down Stone and McCrary's progress just enough for him to do what he needed to. Seeing people in a chained and tormented circumstance had an effect not unlike driving a car into a concrete barrier; it was horrifying to see, but nearly impossible to look away from.

Now the vigilante moved with a hasty purpose as time was short. Above ground the police were likely mobilized by now to make entry into the premises, or close to it. He wanted, more than needed, to have a face to face with Stone before making his great escape. Ghost kept to the shadows within the area as he maneuvered his way along the wall towards the stairs. It was fortunate for him that the cries for help sang out as soon as he'd reentered the chamber. The disruption gave him the element of surprise, again throwing off the situational awareness of the detective and special agent. Their disheveled mental state led to his advantage, which was unfortunate for them as he'd have to make a special impression to legitimize their paths crossing.

Stone was the first to come into view as Ghost quickly traveled along the wall connecting to the stairway entrance. He approached from the north and could see the agent holstering his service pistol, slack jawed in awe as the overwhelming call for help left him unfocused. As Ghost grew nearer, he observed a realization wash over Stone, hitting him like a jolt and altering the man's expression from awe to that of something deliberate. But the light bulb had turned on too late.

First contact pinned Stone's hand to the grip of his pistol, and his momentum slammed into the agent with the impact of a human freight train. Ghost did not want him to retrieve the firearm while he was so close and force the vigilante to kill him so soon. Instead, Ghost used his momentum and drove Stone forward, knocking him into the detective, and immobilizing him against the wall. All he needed was a second to deal with the off balanced detective in the same instant. By all accounts and research, Ghost had learned Randal McCrary was a good man, and a good detective. Unfortunately for the veteran of the Boston police, he was not privy to Ghost's objective, and was immediately rendered unconscious with a swift boot to the side of his head. McCrary's skull bounced off of the wooden beam constructing the portal to the chamber before falling limp to the concrete floor.

Ghost's attention quickly returned to Stone, holding him against the dirt wall just long enough to deliver a mind-numbing elbow strike to the agent's jaw. He made sure not to overpower the blow so Stone would remain conscious, using it to drastically disrupt his thought process and motor skills. Ghost used the upward arc of his elbow strike to transition to a powerful hip toss, launching Stone just over five feet away into the openness of the walkway along the wall. The impact of the concrete floor knocked the wind out of Stone even in spite of the fact that Ghost ensured he didn't use his full strength and the agent didn't land with the full driving force of the maneuver. Had he done so the results could have been fully debilitating. The throw did loosen Stone's hand from the grip of his pistol as he gasped for air, involuntarily sitting up and clutching at his chest. Ghost swooped in and quickly removed the Glock from the agent's possession.

As Ghost stood over Stone, he kicked the downed agent in the side, provoking a painful roll across the floor to move him farther away from McCrary. The vigilante then turned to the downed detective and disarmed him as well. Within seconds both firearms were stripped of their magazines, relieved of their chambered rounds, and tossed nearly ten yards in either direction along the open space between the islands of cells.

Ghost returned to Stone, who was groaning and coughing from the blast of pain inflicted upon him as he sucked rancid air into his lungs. He lifted Stone off of the floor in a single, practiced movement from years of heavy lifting, and held him against the wall. Stone's bearings seemed to be slowly returning.

Focused and intense, Ghost watched Stone shake off the effects of the ambush in an attempt to present a stronger posture than he truly held in the moment. The effects from such a heavy strike to Stone's head had disoriented the man's motor skills in such a way that they functioned, but not in the proper state giving him the appearance of being intoxicated. Stone was trying hard to show he had recovered. Ghost knew better seeing the dilation in the agent's eyes and how he couldn't hold his head still from the dizzying effect of his off-balanced equilibrium. Nearly thirty seconds passed before Stone rested his head against the wall to steady himself. Once Stone could hold his head up without his eyes rolling into the back of his head, Ghost lightly slapped him on the face to gain his attention.

Stone stared forward with a glazed look in his eyes, likely seeing multiple versions of the man before him. It was good enough for Ghost.

"Focus," Ghost said. "There isn't much time."

Stone was silent, leaning back against the dirt wall as Ghost let him go. Standing under his own power was a chore at first. The room dipped and dived from one side to the other, then whirled one way only to quickly switch directions. His displaced equilibrium forced him to hold his head in his hands and close his eyes. Any memory of being knocked senseless escaped the agent. Altercations were something he'd dealt with fairly regularly, but he'd never felt such a devastating strike. He hoped it was because he'd been caught off guard, but considering the source he doubted that excuse. It was all he could do to remain on his feet even with the support of the wall.

"Do you understand now?" Ghost asked watching Stone still trying to find his baseline. Perhaps he'd hit him harder than he meant to, but that was inconsequential. "Come on, boy scout. Get your shit together." His words carried a heavy tone of disdain and disappointment at Stone's inability to control how quick he recovered.

Stone shook his head and stared at the floor for a moment, adjusting his jaw and neck from the whip-like motion induced by the hit he'd taken. "I understood a long time ago, asshole." The words came angrily with a stunned warble to their pronunciation.

Ghost said nothing.

The agent stood tall, posting his hands on the wall to steady himself. "You're not the only one who lost everything. If I'd only known…"

"You were told what was necessary," Ghost interrupted. His growl indicated restraint in his words, as though they'd been spoken before. "It was your mistake that landed us here."

Stone shook his head. "I had no idea things would turn out this way. There was no way to know. Once I learned the truth…"

"The truth was withheld from you so you wouldn't do anything." Ghost closed the short distance between him and Stone. He ducked down to look into the agent's still dilated eyes. He made the connection for the first time, never before being this close to Stone, and he saw the familial resemblance that escaped him in digital prose. A stir of emotion quaked in his chest for a moment as a flood of memories involuntary surfaced within his mind linking Stone to his Veronica. He compelled himself to back away. This was not the time to remember.

Focus.

Stone adjusted his feet to stand up fully, brushing against the dirt wall as it dusted his jacket. He gritted his teeth in an act to control his own anger and suppress his emotions.

"This is where they went, Connor," Ghost said, using the agent's name for the first time. The words were softer than before, compassionate, yet maintained the man's gravelly tone. He looked down shamefully. "They were caged and abused and likely sold numerous times. Probably separated. Frightened. Hurt." He paused, breathing heavily with each word as the descriptions boiled the anger within that he worked tirelessly to control. "Probably dead."

Every assumption caused him more pain just to speak them into reality. It was necessary to speak the truth. It needed to be heard, by him and by Stone. What Ghost's wife and child had endured was ultimately unspeakable. The devil truly was in the details even though the evil could be felt in the words Ghost spoke. There was plenty of evidence around him that filled in the rest.

Tears filled Stone's eyes as he fought back a swell of emotion stabbing him in the chest. "You think I don't think about them *every* day? *Every* minute? With *every* breath I take?"

Ghost raised his head to witness the grief washing over Stone. He said nothing in return.

"I lost, too, goddammit!" Stone roared, unleashing the repressed anger he harbored. "They weren't just yours, you selfish sonofabitch! They were a part of me, too!"

Stone surged forward, spittle catapulting from his roaring mouth and gritted teeth. He stabbed an index finger into his own chest like a knife he'd wanted to bury into his heart so many times. He pushed Ghost back with the opposite hand with no fear of retaliation from the much larger and skilled man. His rage and adrenaline sapped all rational thought from him.

Ghost remained silent, allowing Stone to express his subdued hatred. After all, who could Special Agent Connor Stone confide in about his personal connection to a vigilante mass murderer? He knew all too well there were entities in the shadows pulling Stone's strings for his 'special assignment,' but they couldn't be bothered with any emotional aspect of the situation. They were only concerned with keeping as tight of a lid on the truth as possible, which meant Stone was allowed the opportunity to fix his biggest mistake pertaining to *their* interests. Ghost knew these people saw everyone as expendable, and if Stone failed them, he'd be lost to the untimely winds of change people of power tended to control in the world of covert operations. He would not let that happen as Stone provided him with support at designated times, and he wanted to take the man's life himself. So, knowing that those who thought they were in control of Stone's professional direction did not care about how the agent felt, neither did Ghost.

"It doesn't matter!" Ghost snarled back. He launched an arm forward and sent Stone reeling into the wall again. "All you had to do was listen. All you had to do was forget about me. They would have been fine. Protected." He prodded Stone in the head with his right index finger. "But the boy scout suddenly felt he'd grown into the big leagues, and you proved you couldn't get the job done."

Stone did not back down. "You don't know everything! You don't know why I acted! I did what I thought was right! You didn't belong behind bars! I almost died trying to save you!"

A condescending laugh was briefly expressed by the vigilante. It had been too long since he'd laughed at anything. He shook his head with condemnation as his expression became hard and cold. "It wasn't your place to worry about me. I wasn't important. I made a deal for *them*." He pointed out to nothing as a representation of Veronica and Chloe. "For no retaliation. That's what happens in my world. No one knew better than I did that that was always a possibility."

"And what about Veronica?" Stone shot back. "Did she know she'd never see her husband again? Huh?" Stone surged forward again looking directly at the vigilante, returning the stone-cold glare, his adrenaline granting him the full recovery of his balance. "What about Chloe? Did she know her father was a killer? That her daddy would never come home while she was told some government lie as he rotted in prison?"

Ghost had thought about all of these things when he'd made the deal with the mysteriously high ranking operative in charge. Was life in a black site prison worth keeping his family protected from the wrath of a vicious Russian syndicate? He'd scoffed at the offer. There had been nothing to think about. He'd rot for a million lifetimes if it would keep his wife and daughter safe for a single moment.

"They would have been safe, Connor," Ghost said plainly. "They would have mourned and healed and moved on. I could have lived with that and been happy in the darkest hole in the world as long as they were safe." He looked away, mulling over the thought of what had transpired; how they'd gotten here. "You took that from me."

Stone shook his head. "This isn't my fault, asshole! You blame me, but *they* did this!" Stone pointed to the ceiling, thinking of the Lucky Pawn representing the despicable men responsible for taking two of the most important people in his life away from him.

"Your actions forced their play."

"I didn't know. I did what I had to."

"And you didn't need to." Ghost stopped speaking abruptly and listened intently. He thought there might be movement above ground in the Lucky Pawn. It had been long enough for the police to get mobile for an entry. SWAT was likely on the move. It was time to go.

A quick disorienting slap tossed Stone to one side, disrupting his balance as Ghost swept the agent's feet out from under him. Ghost dropped down close to Stone and he said, "The bottom line is this: now you can see what we're dealing with. *Now you feel it.* Save these people. That's the most important thing now. I'll take care of the rest."

Ghost swiftly rose and walked away from where he came. He stopped for a moment and turned back. The thought of warning Stone not to follow him crossed his mind. A heavy blanket of guilt and anger weighed on him, and he wasn't going anywhere now. Stone righted himself from being tossed to the floor and sat up against the wall, pulling his knees up to his chest, showing no signs of pursuit, devastated.

With that the vigilante ran into the dark.

The faint sound of boots and hollering upstairs drifted down the stairwell. SWAT was clearing the pawn shop as they methodically made their way closer to the passage leading to the underground chamber. The cavalry was on the way. Stone sat quietly, seething with anger inside while appearing to be calm above the surface. He noticed the cries for help had died out, probably minutes ago. Despite the rattling his brain and vision suffered, he found he had recovered enough to process his thoughts. Little had changed from his initial shock. This was by far the worst scene he'd encountered since he'd been assigned to this human trafficking fiasco, yet it remained completely beyond his understanding at what would drive someone to commit such horrendous acts against innocent people. Deep down he knew the psychology and could rationalize it scientifically, possibly even profile them to give any rationalization more depth, but witnessing such barbarism could never be justified. Nothing could appropriately explain this extreme ruthlessness. Most would label those responsible as monsters in an attempt to substantiate their cruel actions. Stone knew that was a mistake waiting to happen. Identifying them as monsters gave them a mythical status for all the wrong reasons. It had to be remembered that this was a heinous act committed by men, and men alone.

A sharp rumble snapped Stone out of his preoccupied thoughts and then a small explosion roared through the chamber. Debris and dirt rocked free from the walls and ceiling, blasting through the room like a sandstorm. Stone instinctively dove away from the direction of the blast and covered his head from any possible projectiles. The caged victims screamed in response, most balling to protect themselves from the unknown.

Stone coughed as he lifted himself off the ground, trying not to breath in as much dust as possible along with the foul air he'd somehow become accustomed to. The dust hung throughout the chamber like a clouded veil, then settled enough so he could look around to see the imprisoned captives. He called out to them in an attempt to see if anyone was harmed but received nothing in return. Then Stone remembered he had not come alone.

All of Stone's energy urged him to move towards the opening of the stairwell, or at least where he thought it was. He needed to check on McCrary to make sure he was okay. He knew the man was tough, but the boot to the head McCrary had taken was quick and brutal. Stone futilely fanned the dust away from his face as he moved, clearing nothing; but he was still able to find his destination, and with it the surly Boston detective. McCrary sat up against the beam the vigilante had bounced his head off of while covering his face with the lapel of his jacket. It relieved Stone to see the old man conscious.

"Randal," Stone called, "are you okay?" He knelt down in front of McCrary seeing a gash along the upper left side of his forehead. The blood ran down the side of his face, but the wound appeared to have already begun to clot and fill with dust.

McCrary put up a hand, patting the air in a gesture to suggest he was fine. He coughed into his jacket, squinting in his usual manner even as the dust hung in the air obstructing his vision. Both he and Stone turned their attention to the thumping of boots rapidly closing in from above as the tactical line of SWAT operators neared the stairway entrance. McCrary clapped Stone on the shoulder, and dropped the jacket away from his face. An obscure expression looked up at Special Agent Stone, in a serious way that presented a questionable disappointment.

"You know something," McCrary said. "As interesting as things are becoming, I'm gettin' tired of repeating myself."

Stone didn't understand the statement. "What?"

The agent's mind reeled in the moment. McCrary's vagueness carried a heavy weight of suspicion. Stone feared that with the detective being conscious so soon he may have absorbed more details than Stone cared for him to know, and the last thing he needed was McCrary talking about things he didn't understand. The memory of his sister and niece would not be tarnished by the misappropriation of facts.

McCrary pulled Stone close to him, talking right into the agent's ear. "I heard everything, boy. Now you really got some fucking explaining to do."

Chapter 25
Lying in Wait

An eerie silence weighed heavily in the air where Richter and Simon found themselves. The destination supplied by Yuri Kurikova was nearly six city blocks south from the Lucky Pawn, where the lower middle-class neighborhood exuded the lost despair of a wild west ghost town at the intersection of industrial progression. Even with the recent years of restoration Boston had been undergoing, this seemed to be the tail end of South Boston still awaiting resurgence. Given the emphasis on the nearby industrial area of the harbor, Richter assumed businesses were taking precedence over renovating the remaining triple story homes broken down from age and neglect. The skeletal wood-built structures gave the appearance of saddened animated characters, waiting to be given attention from artists who could skillfully make them shine and smile again. This image also reminded Richter he needed to limit Simon's morning cartoon fetish. It was clearly having a dramatic effect on his own imagination he didn't care for.

The twins exited the 4Runner and surveyed the area. One of many intrinsic qualities Richter and Simon shared, through training or something twins instinctually were instilled with, told them they would need to use suppressors on their firearms. They nodded to each other as though the thought occurred simultaneously. Given the natural quietness of the neighborhood it would ensure they didn't garner any unwanted attention. There would also have to be consideration to the resistance their target may provide, but they could not control his actions or the noise level he resisted with. Unless, of course, they ideally put him down before he could give them any trouble.

Simon went about opening the rear hatch and unloaded their baggage. A rear storage compartment lifted and folded backwards toward the rear seat. Stored within the hidden cargo space was an assortment of specifically ordered munitions contractually obligated to be provided by Kurikova. Every item was fitted into secure black foam padding. Naturally the brothers couldn't travel openly with an arsenal of munitions so it only made sense for their employer to provide the necessities. Simon had procured the list of essentials this time, which was questionable given his aptitude for being unpredictable, but Richter stood impressed by the selection. There was an assortment of light carbine rifles, heavy armor piercing machine guns, two sniper caliber rifles fitted with optics, four selections of pistols, ammunition for everything provided, and a number of tactical blades. Off to the right side, fixed into their own secure positions, were options to carry each weapon and other optic selections for the rifles. To the left were suppressor options designated for their respective firearms. Everything was neatly configured in the storage space, and professionally presented.

Standing shoulder to shoulder the twins looked upon their weapon selection beaming with pride and sharing wolfish grins defining their incarnation of underlying troublesome behavior. They began to take up arms, decidedly selecting their preference in weaponry.

"Well done, brother," Richter complimented.

"I appreciate that," Simon replied.

Richter nodded in response, entranced by the tools of their violent trade.

Behind the brothers stood a long and wide sheet metal structure painted a deep red with a black roof. Extending along the face of the building were half a dozen steel bay doors intermittently spaced in the northern direction away from the small office space where Richter had parked. An expansive parking lot extended along the length of the building and was nearly as wide. On the far end the last two bays encompassed a larger portion of the structure where a loading dock was fabricated with a long concrete ramp highlighted by a yellow chipped guardrail. The blue-collar scent of oil and diesel, rubber and steel sifted out into the open air like a mechanical vapor shielding it from the rest of the world. Near the road a large sign read: Red House Trucking and Distributing. It was a small operation with only three semi-trucks and trailers parked in the lot. However, it was perfect as a front for any one, or all, of Kurikova's nefarious enterprises. Richter applauded the Russian for his many innovations in business. He could see how Kurikova had stayed on top for so long. Ruthlessness was nothing without intelligence, and the elder twin respected that kind of self-awareness.

"Shall we, brother," Richter said, presenting Simon with taking the lead to enter the trucking facility.

Simon rubbed his hands together in anticipation of the day. "We shall."

The twins closed the rear hatch on the 4Runner and turned to approach a steel entrance fixed into the structure adjacent to the nearest bay door. Simon held the access code in his busy brain and moved forward to enter the numbers to gain unalarmed entry to the garage. While Simon did this, Richter scanned the parking lot one more time. He noticed a lone vehicle curiously parked between two cargo trailers as though it was meant to be hidden. Being parked with such an obstructed view raised Richter's suspicions. *A getaway car?* The thought also crossed his mind that the vehicle, which appeared to be a late model Jeep of some sort, could possibly belong to a patron of the business. Or even a driver who could be on a haul. Regardless, he felt something needed to be done about the vehicle in case its presence colluded with their targets retreat. After all, this location was highly anticipated to facilitate their target's exit strategy. Richter had no intention of letting the mystery man make it out of the trucking garage alive, but he was also a respectably skilled target. *Better safe than sorry*.

Richter raised the M4 rifle he'd selected to carry. He adjusted the tactical sling wrapped over one shoulder and under the opposite side, and shouldered the weapon to fire. Two clicks later and the top rail mounted scope revealed a simple red dot site, which he trained on the front tires of the Jeep nearly seventy yards away. He adjusted his shot immediately for the distance and squeezed off two consecutive shots as soon as he was ready. The suppressor provided a significant noise reduction, and 5.56 caliber rounds spat out the barrel with a metallic hiss. Simon paid no attention to the discharge of the firearm as he entered the correct security code giving them access to the massive garage.

"Getaway vehicle?" Simon asked, breaching the entrance as the front tires of the Jeep popped and hissed with Richter's expert marksmanship.

"Possibly," Richter replied, lowering the rifle as he followed Simon into the building.

"Good shot."

Richter smiled. "Thank you, brother."

For a moment, while Simon searched for a light switch, Richter pondered their mutual respect for one another, as well as their politeness. The idiosyncrasy provided him a mild laugh. *We must be the politest killers in the world*, Richter thought. *How ironic.*

Simon noticed his brother's chuckle as he found the light switch near another door leading into the office. He gave life to the lights with a flip of his finger while musing over the possibility of Richter laughing at him. Richter knew how Simon hated it, but the younger twin dismissed it almost immediately. His brother got nearly as giddy over the execution of a target as he did, and Simon knew Richter was excited.

In retrospect, their target held a nearly mythical status within the vastness of the deep web. Chatter about the 'ultimate killer' and 'Ares Incarnate' were just a few of the geektastic aphorisms given to the man. These keyboard cowboys had a way of over selling nerdy monikers for warrior-like entities they likely had nothing in common with, let alone the Greek God of War. Nevertheless, Simon's considerable time spent in the encrypted network had led him to private message boards talking about the Russian massacres occurring across the country. Such a fete was difficult not to debate or dispute, especially amongst the digitally depraved. To assist the conjecture of the subject crime scene photos had been uploaded from Seattle and Austin. Both Simon and Richter had been impressed with what they'd seen. It wasn't the blood and guts that garnered their respect, but the man's vast execution. He was tactically sound, strategic, and brutal. In the course of his three-year crusade he'd accumulated a body count somewhere over two hundred, respectively, and confirmed. Simon teased that he and his brother had a rival in the game, but Richter ousted the idea.

"No, brother," Richter had said. "This is big game for us. The ultimate hunt. You'll see."

And so, it came to be.

The illumination was scarce at first as some lights immediately flashed on and others needed to warm up. Richter had instructed

Kurikova to have every worker clear out of the building immediately. They did not hesitate to do as they were told. Each bay seemed to have some kind of project underway, anywhere from semis with their hoods folded out to expose massive diesel engines to stripped tires and brake jobs. Toolboxes occupied each area, many with tools scattered about on benches, or dropped on the floor. The striking odor of grease and steel mixed with every other mechanical fluid hung in the air. For Simon it was a sweet scent, oddly attractive like his affinity for the smell of gasoline.

"This way," Richter said, maneuvering around equipment and parts strewn about on the concrete floor.

Simon followed his brother, nose sniffing the air, breathing in the mechanical ecstasy.

Richter navigated his way through the garage past two semi bays to a location he considered to be the center of the shop. "Here," he said, shouldering his rifle and pointing to the ground. A cast iron plate, roughly thirty-six inches by thirty-six inches, was embedded into the floor. A stainless-steel handle stood out on one end, folded down into the body of the plate where an exact space had been molded. This was the tunnel exit Kurikova had told him about.

"I have to admit, brother, this is a pretty clever idea," Simon said, eyeing the iron portal.

"Agreed," Richter stated. "He is well researched, that is for sure."

Simon turned his back to the iron plate to take in the space surrounding it. They needed to find the appropriate places to conceal themselves. Tactically setting up an ambush on such short notice was cumbersome, yet the garage provided an assortment of advantages if used properly.

"Damn!" Richter gasped.

Simon turned to his brother urgently. The elder twin was bent over halfway with the handle to the iron plate in his hand, straining to lift it. "Locked from the inside?"

Richter released the handle gently, laying it to rest quietly to keep from projecting any noise into the tunnel below. He rubbed his right shoulder to assist in distributing the burn he felt from attempting to lift the plate. "I hope so. It didn't budge, and I know I am not weak."

"That's a ridiculous idea," Simon chastised. He switched his tone to appropriately compliment his brother. "Oxen are jealous of your strength."

Richter smiled. "You're too kind, brother. We rival them together."

Simon nodded. "Speaking of which, I've been meaning to change up our routine. It's becoming too monotonous."

"By all means, please do. Variety is the spice of life."

The twins turned away from the steel plate, both setting their eyes upon the arena where they would confront their target. A silent conversation took place between them consisting of directional looks, nods, and hesitant expressions about considerations. The telepathic language of twins. Once a decision was made Richter took the lead.

"Comms?" the elder twin requested, speaking of the electronically enhanced ear buds Simon carried.

Simon removed a hard, plastic box from one of his cargo short pockets. He flipped open the lid as he presented it to Richter. Inside rested two earbuds set to the same frequency. A miniature, pliable antennae was exposed on the outer portion of the transmitting device, doubling as the power activation toggle with a light squeeze. They both inserted the buds into their desired ears.

"Check, check," Richter said.

Simon nodded in response.

"Here we go, brother," Richter announced, rotating his neck to loosen the building tension.

Simon took a long, deep breath, and held it for nearly ten seconds. He repeated this three times, releasing the air in long extensions. Afterwards he turned to Richter, a deadly gleam shining in his eyes to match the maniacal smile that accompanied it. Richter knew Simon was working tirelessly within himself to refrain from setting his excitement free. He was proud of his younger brother's restraint, but he'd be damned if he didn't enjoy seeing Simon completely let go.

They shared a determined look, and then split off to their respective positions. There was no telling when their target would arrive. Richter questioned how the man would exit the steel portal, but he also knew better to think that the man wasn't prepared for the heavy weight. Many things ran through Richter's mind, thinking of any possibilities with such a short time to plan, even though he and Simon had accumulatively made all considerations. He didn't want to overthink the situation. Killing was simple as an act, yet complicated as a whole. Time and experience had made it easier, even with as natural as it had come to them. Simon was never swayed by the intricacies of the process. He did it, and enjoyed it. Richter, however, being far more cerebral, liked having his bases covered. He was certain of their advantage, which almost guaranteed their success, but could not discount the abilities their target had displayed numerous times in difficult scenarios. It was then a revelation hit the elder brother:

I'm nervous.

The realization was refreshing, and Richter felt a perk in his energy levels. His excitement grew as his forehead lightly perspired from the increase in body temperature at the idea of being nervous. How could this be? But he knew the answer. It had been far too long since he and Simon had been contracted to actually bring down a dangerous man; someone who could fight back, even if he wouldn't win. The day was just getting better and better.

Chapter 26
No More

Over the course of a long career in law enforcement Lieutenant Detective Randal McCrary had taken his share of bumps and bruises with the occasional ass kicking. He'd also given just as many, if not more. It was an expectation of the job. There was no way to act as a protector of society and not be faced with physical confrontation. This profession was inherently dangerous; lethal even. That was no secret. McCrary accepted this simple fact. Today, however, might have been the first time he felt as though some sense had been beaten into him.

In the midst of the chaotic scene, the detective sat on the rear bumper of an ambulance. The paramedics had wanted to take him to Massachusetts General Hospital off of Fruit Street, but McCrary had no desire to leave the scene yet, and a bump on the head wasn't anything he was worried about. The gash on his forehead had been bandaged with gauze and tape, which was already soaking through. It probably required stitches, but he didn't care. There were more pressing matters at hand. First there was the discovery of Vlademir Kurikova's butchered body in his father's restaurant, quickly followed by the terror that the Lucky Pawn had to offer. That added two more dead bodies into the mix stacked on top of DeMarte's killing the night before. Not to mention the looming question of how many victims he and Stone just discovered in the bowels of the pawn shop. All in all, it was one hell of a start to the day, and it wasn't even noon yet.

McCrary had more important things on his mind that extended beyond the scene. His piercing gaze scanned the mob of first responders for Special Agent Stone. The government title flashed in his mind and he thought, *He's special alright.* As if his head didn't hurt enough from being kicked by a giant, it began to pound more violently thinking about the words exchanged between Stone and the suspect. What was it the FBI called him? Un-sub? McCrary scoffed at the abbreviation. *Unknown subject my ass*!

And then McCrary saw Stone walking briskly in his direction.

The agent still had a light coating of dust and dirt covering him, disheveled with his dress shirt pulled loose from his belt line looking like he'd slept in an alley. He had his phone pinned to his ear and appeared to be speaking only two familiar words McCrary recognized from his years of service to his country: Yes, sir. Stone's head nodded every time he spoke, likely unconsciously, and it was accompanied with the expected scowl of a Marine's war face. The expression intensified as Stone stopped briefly. Something was said that didn't sit well with the G-man. McCrary's eyes followed Stone as though he were pulling the agent in his direction. Soon Stone placed the phone into a pocket and continued forward to greet the detective with open arms of frustration.

"Well, shit's about to get crazy," Stone said.

McCrary couldn't believe what he'd just heard. "Oh, now it's going to get crazy? Great. I thought we'd been missin' out on all the fuckin' fun."

"Are you alright?" The agent's words were sincere. "You went down hard. Should we get you to the hospital at all?"

The detective shook his head. "Don't worry about me, kid. I can take a beatin'. I've had more than I can count, an' this ain't keeping me down."

"I took my share of licks, too."

Stone spoke as if this consideration mattered to McCrary. It didn't. McCrary had questions, but he didn't know where to begin at the moment. He simply dismissed Stone's declaration by shaking his head.

"What?" Stone asked, throwing his arms out to either side.

"I must have missed that part, boy scout," McCrary snarled, thinking of what he'd heard. "Wish I hadn't."

"Look, if you're pissed because you're working with me and what we've found, then I can have you reassigned. We didn't get this far by chance. He planned this, and it worked. He's got an end game, and it's happening soon. He. Does. Not. Waste. Time."

The detective stood from his seat on the ambulance bumper and closed the distance between himself and Stone. "Oh, you're not getting shit reassigned. I'm getting this motha'fucka'. With or without you."

Stone took a step back and lifted his shirt. A large bruise had already formed on his left side, wrapping around his torso to the back and climbing his ribs. The sight knocked McCrary back a step as well. The G-man really had taken a beating, too. But what difference did that make? He still heard what he heard.

"So fuckin' what?" McCrary snapped. "We both got our asses kicked. You want a fuckin' merit badge or somethin'?"

"I want to get this sonofabitch!" Stone yelled back. "I've got more reason to than anyone!"

McCrary snapped. Not just emotionally, but his right cross did as well. He knew he was quick and, being that it wasn't expected, the sucker punch came even quicker. His meaty fist landed square on the right side of Stone's jaw, driving the agent backwards and down on his ass. Stone instantly put a hand to his jaw, stunned, but not injured. He moved as though he were going to leap up to his feet. McCrary moved in, still moving quickly for an older man, and poised himself over Stone with his fists clenched and a daring scowl contorting his expression.

"More reason than anyone?" the detective growled. "If I heard correctly, you are the reason for this. I told you, you got some explaining to do. And I mean that, motha'fucka'. Every damn bit of it."

Stone looked around the scene seeing how everyone had stopped to watch. No one had dared to get in McCrary's way, and given the heat of the moment it was a wise decision. There was no other choice for the agent but to come clean.

"Okay," Stone said, pursing his lips as he gauged the level of damage McCrary's lunchbox of a fist had done. "Not here, though."

McCrary stepped back extending a hand to Stone. The agent accepted it, feeling the strength of the man as he effortlessly assisted in pulling him to his feet. "No more bullshit, Stone. This shit is gonna' get us killed if you keep hiding the truth from me."

The scene continued on as though nothing happened, recognizing the minor altercation as nothing more than a school yard mishap. Life went on that way, and sometimes it took a good punch to set things straight.

"No more bullshit," Stone repeated. His eyes wandered as though he'd find the words he needed outside of this moment.

McCrary stepped closer. "I said before. I heard everythin'. And if not everythin', enough to know this ain't ya' typical manhunt. This is something different, an' it's getting covered up." He pointed beyond Stone to the Lucky Pawn. "People are dyin', and you wanna' keep secrets. Not anymore."

Stone nodded understandably. "Later. Let's meet up. I'll get what clearance I can."

McCrary scoffed at the thought.

"I'm serious. I have to." Stone paused, thinking of his friend Mason Jones, a seasoned hard ass with the United States Marshals Services, and the line he'd had to give him to get him to back off. "If I bring you in, as in *in*, on this there's no going back. Life will never be the same. The job will never be the same. Secrets and lies will dictate whether we get the job done, or get killed."

McCrary thought for a moment, believing Stone was exaggerating and being dramatic. *I'd tell you, but then I'd have to kill you.* He questioned the disclaimer. Could it really be that bad? But he already knew it would be. There was evidence of it written in blood on the sidewalk of the Lucky Pawn storefront, as well as behind its counter. Even more preceded this from earlier this morning back to the previous day. And to add to that there were the victims in the cavern, and how that horrific sight still clawed at his heart. Life already wasn't the same. It wasn't just the circumstances that did this, it was the job. That was its nature. As a law enforcement officer, he did what others wouldn't, or couldn't. He braved the terrible things that went bump in the night for a thankless position at the forefront of a war on crime that sometimes kept him up at night, and reminded him again six months later after he thought he'd gotten passed it. Change was inevitable.

"What's the worst that can happen?" McCrary asked. "I'll have a few more nightmares than I usually do?"

Stone grinned, recognizing the sarcasm, needing it in the moment, but he couldn't sustain the expression. A veil of sadness enveloped him, sifting the life from his eyes, reversing the momentary jovial expression, and draining him of color. Death warmed over his energy, and McCrary could feel it.

"Much worse, Randal," Stone said, and he meant it. "This is incredibly serious. Beyond the trafficking. Beyond the Russian mob suspicions. Beyond the rules. There are people pulling strings here that can change the projection of our government with a phone call."

McCrary doubled back, flipping his suit jacket open, casting dust into the air as he put his hands on his hips while he paced. He knew then he couldn't just walk away from this. Not now. Not after his city was being turned upside down with corruption and death. Men like him didn't tuck tail and run. He was a fighter. He was a guardian to his wife, Boston and its citizens, and to his brothers in blue. What good would he be doing if he turned the other cheek? The consideration of what Stone told him had to be taken seriously. He also had to ask himself, what harm would it do if he continued working with Stone?

"There's no shame in walking away," Stone said. "Why do you think it's just me doing this?"

McCrary wanted to say why, but he knew now was not the time. "Oh, I know why, pal." He made sure his words hit hard with condemnation. Stone looked away, and McCrary got what he wanted. "And walking away isn't that easy." He paused again and shot a finger in the direction of the pawn shop. "Walking away from *that* isn't easy."

Solemn and exhausted, Stone simply nodded in agreement. He knew McCrary was referring to the trafficking victims. Still, he said nothing.

The detective continued to stew, his thoughts tossing and turning. He faced away from Stone, his head bobbing from one side to the other like a mad man, figuring out what course of action he needed to take. Learning what Stone knew carried a lofty price. But what was the cost of doing nothing? What kind of man would he be then? McCrary performed an aggressive about face and stalked towards Stone. He stopped inches away from the agent, looking him square in the eyes. The agent stood unresponsive, nearly cathartic, defeated. There was a sense about him that he hated being in the position he was in, but Stone had started something he couldn't stop. And at this point McCrary couldn't let him do it alone.

"I'll text you later with a time and an address," McCrary snarled, his squinting eyes beaming through Stone like lasers. "We're going to finish this if it kills us."

Stone gave a nonverbal confirmation, and life seemed to return to his expression. Deep down no one wanted to fight alone. "You're sure?"

McCrary spit to the side. "I am. I have to be if what you say is true. If we can end it here then the way you say life will change means dick. And I intend on making that happen. 'Cause I want you outta' my city. Got it?"

Stone nodded.

The detective stepped back and began wiping the dust off of his suit in an attempt to hide his annoyance. Satisfied, he straightened himself, adjusting his collar and tie, and then buttoned his jacket. He cast an icy stare over Stone as though he was sizing up the agent.

"Now," McCrary barked, "get the fuck away from my crime scene. You're done here for now." He pushed past Stone, never looking back. "Look for my message. And don't be fuckin' late."

Chapter 27
Mr. X

Wolves inherently held sway over expansive territories, and Yuri 'the Wolf' Kurikova was no different. His operations spanned the United States in key locations, as well as breaking borders into Canada, Europe, and a mostly turbulent relationship with the more powerful Mexican cartels that recently came to an end. As a pack leader he'd made good on expanding and guarding what was his throughout his entire criminal career, especially after taking the role of *pakhan* of the Russian mafia. His syndicate enveloped others with less stature, creating coinciding business relationships with fruitful rewards. For more than twenty years Yuri had cultivated an empire constructed by the evils of man. Until today he had no regrets.

The loss of his eldest child was never a consideration. Vlademir had been such an exceptional son, student, and soldier. Yuri always kept his children at a slight distance, or rather kept his emotional attachment at a distance. He was hard on them because the world would always be harder, and he knew he could only protect them for so long. But Vlademir was different. He'd always shown such promise in wanting to please his father. His temper was beyond manageable until Yuri set him into training to be his future brigadier; a position much like a captain, but more professionally referred to as *avtoriyet*, the Russian word for authority. The goal to becoming his father's second in command gave Vlademir the discipline to do everything needed of him. Yuri had never been prouder.

Yet, in the blink of an eye, an adversary presented themselves to Yuri's syndicate, and took the one person he held so dear. It was difficult for the Kurikova patriarch to think of the business decisions needing his attention after learning of his son's death. And to be butchered was just further insult. It made Yuri look weak to his associates being so vulnerable.

When he thought about his vulnerabilities Yuri had to go back to the beginning of the attacks nearly three years prior. His operations in Seattle had been devastated in a single night. It was a message to him, which came with a personal flare. Thriving as a mob boss for so long came with its share of enemies, outside of the law, and he spared no expense to make sure every possible threat he *knew of* remembered that the Kurikova name was not to be fucked with. A number of small, violent gangland style wars had broken out, but these skirmishes were short lived. Ultimately the way of the Wolf was understood.

San Francisco came next. Shipments of Chinese nationals were to be imported for the Triad, one of many Chinese transnational criminal organizations. It was a special deal Yuri brokered after a Triad family stateside had gained sudden attention from a conjoined task force made up of the FBI and the Department of Justice. The shipments docking for the Triad family were raided with empty results. Every container came up clean with legally imported merchandise. A week later a Russian freighter docked with three extra containers storing three dozen men, women and children. Traveling for a two-week voyage across the sea was incredibly difficult in scope, let alone making it with limited supplies and space, costing anywhere from fifty to sixty thousand dollars per person. On average two to three people, per container, would not survive. It was a hell of a business the Triad ran. Most of the illegal immigrants would be forced into slave labor to pay off their debt before they could get a real taste for the land of the free. Yuri thought of the situation as an opportunity to create a bridge into the Orient.

On an early Saturday morning the freighter arrived at port, passed the customs inspection, and was allowed to unload. Yuri's end of the deal was to load the containers on to tractor trailers and deliver them to a location farther down the California coastline. His men were brutally gunned down on the docks, and in turn a whorehouse run by a local Chinese boss was exposed. Every man within the China Town establishment, gangster and client, was murdered while the women forced into the sex trade were set free. Yuri lost two dozen men that day, and a trade deal worth nearly fifty million dollars.

Austin was a blood bath. The Mexicans, who Yuri did not

particularly care for, were a greedy species. He likened the cartels to cockroaches, but their operations in the Lone Star State were mutually beneficial. If anything, Yuri respected their loyalty to one another. The way they did business did not sit well as they always wanted to renegotiate the terms of ongoing imports of weapons, drugs, and sales of human product. Either way, when the business in Austin went to hell nearly seventy-five men, Russian and Mexican alike, were killed. A series of small stash houses were hit. Somewhere around fifteen working girls were released and ten *boyeviks* were killed. An escalation of the killings ensued the following day at a landmark hotel. Initial reports from the scene, before it was covered up, stated the Russian soldiers were fighting side-by-side with the cartel against a mutual target. An FBI agent was nearly killed as well, but he survived with superficial injuries. In the end Yuri severed all business ties with the cartels, and suspended all operations in the southwest as a way to keep a larger scale war from erupting between the Russian and Mexican syndicates.

By this time Yuri's leadership was under massive scrutiny. He was forced to make a statement of control. A meeting of associates was held, and he cut every throat in the room with his own hand. With this act he absorbed every outside faction as his own, displaying the severed heads before the respective organizations to prove his point. Operations continued without failure.

In the grand scheme of life, it hadn't taken the fight long before it landed on his doorstep, rendering him helpless and weaker than before. It was a position he had never held having always forced his way upon others, taking what he wanted. Now he was confined to his estate for security purposes, and one of his children was taken from him. He had other children, but they didn't mean nearly as much to him as Vlademir. Still, Yuri had his family placed under strict, heavily armed guard. By the end of the day they would be touching down in Mother Russia where their safety could be assured. Meanwhile, he had lost everything that he held dear.

For himself, Yuri kept only the best of his men for protection. Nearly two dozen SPETZNAZ trained men were stationed throughout the estate. At the moment they were outfitted in tailored suits, much like they would be as if they were executive protection agents. Yuri did not care for anything less than professionalism from his security detail. Every man was skilled and deadly, loyal to a fault, and prepared to die. They were of course appropriately compensated for providing his protection, knowing their absolute sacrifice may be required. Even before his syndicate came under siege, maintaining his safety was of the highest priority. Two men were stationed near him at all times, directly in his presence, and two more guarded any immediate exit or entrance. These four were the best of the best — his personal guard. Vlademir, with his penchant for reading, referred to these men as his father's own *Knights of the Round Table*. It was one of the few novels of fantasy Yuri allowed his son to entertain. It upheld the disciplined and loyal aspects that he expected from the boy.

Yuri allowed an arrogant thought to briefly eclipse his memory of Vlademir and the retrospective events leading him to his place of mourning. For an instance Yuri imagined this dangerous man besieging his empire stood before him, like the climax of an action film where the hero faces the final boss. And in that foggy daydream Yuri watched this man contend with his personal guard, four of the hardest and brutally equipped killers the Russian military had ever spawned. It was a comforting thought for the Kurikova family patriarch, envisioning his enemy's demise.

The thought did not last long.

Ringing at his side was his cell phone, resting on the glass end table next to the chair on his expansive patio. It was ironic to think that only twenty-four hours prior a celebration of life had taken place here, Vlademir was alive, and now it was all gone. Yuri deeply wanted to ignore the call. There was no one he really wanted to speak to at this time. In the meantime, he had delegated duties to capable men to handle everything to do with procuring Vlademir's body once the police had finished with it, and his lawyers were already up in arms and barricading him from any inquiries. Despite his reluctance to answer the phone there was one call he was expecting. He did not believe this was the call he wanted, but his heart pounded anxiously for the good news he hoped to be provided, twisting his insides nervously. Wolves were not meant to feel this way.

He picked up the phone and let the phone ring twice more, feeling a tinge of hesitation. 'Unknown' registered on the screen. The late morning sun shone on him, warming his skin and forcing him to squint in the light. He hated sunglasses, and the moment reminded him of the eccentric pair Vlademir always wore. It was a fashion statement the boy had always joked; one of the few he shared with his father. Yuri shook the memory loose and answered the call.

Customarily Yuri said nothing into the phone. He was the important one on the call, so the silence should be broken by whoever sought him out. When the caller spoke, it wasn't a voice he wanted to hear.

"You know, Yuri," said the energetic voice, "it's rude not to speak when you answer the phone. Proper social etiquette suggests you say hello, especially with old friends."

Old friends, was not the manner in which Yuri thought of this man. The admonishment he felt towards him nearly rivaled that of the man who killed his son. The caller's charisma oozed through the phone, oily with a con man's expertise, capable of drawing in even the steeliest of minds. The Wolf could see this man smiling as he spoke, and it ignited an alternate form of anger within him, something hateful. Every word the caller spoke seemed to hiss with the serpentine tongue of a snake. Yuri held no misconceptions that he was considered an evil man for the enterprises he wrought and prospered from. This man, mysteriously referred to as Mr. X in their dealings, was something else entirely; too bad for heaven, and too evil for hell.

"Well, you must be wondering why I've called again, Yuri," Mr. X said, his tone more questioning than stating. "After all, when I called you yesterday you assured me you had the situation under control. Am I wrong?"

Yuri mulled over his response, pushing his irritation deep down inside. It would do him no good to upset this man. A long breath and a quick snap adjustment of his neck allowed Yuri to find some semblance of relief to maintain his temper.

"Given the change in circumstances," Yuri grumbled, "I wondered if I'd hear from you."

"Interesting. Given the circumstances I suppose I should have contacted you earlier, dear friend. But I trusted your declaration to handle things, and frankly, I had more pressing matters to attend to." Mr. X paused, ever a fan of the dramatic. "Or, so I thought."

Yuri grimaced as he continued speaking. "I can only imagine the CIA has better things to do than protect their subsidized funding." His words were meant to be insulting.

Mr. X laughed condescendingly, forced, and for effect. "That's cute, Yuri. You know damn well our business relationship lends itself to the many side enterprises that I entertain." He hummed as he considered his next words, wittily explaining, "They just happen to intersect with special operations I oversee for the agency, is all."

Yuri imagined Mr. X smiling again. He always smiled, not particularly out of joy, but to accentuate his smart-ass quips. The Wolf did not reply.

"Aaaanyway," Mr. X overstated, "I thought it time to interject myself into your situation. This, hmmm, challenge you're experiencing has gotten too far out of hand."

"No shit! My son is dead!" Yuri screamed, veins in his neck and forehead bulged through his skin like a biological roadway on a map. His accent grew thicker when his anger erupted. "Dead! Do not tell me how far it has gotten out of hand!"

Yuri thought to throw the phone into the concrete stamped patio, or snap it in two and release it into the thick forest border of his property. Somehow, he found the will to continue holding it to his ear, seething with every breath.

"My apologies, Yuri," Mr. X proffered, his silver tongue developing a sincere pitch to his words. "How insensitive of me. I'm deeply sorry for your loss."

Silence cinched the tension to a taught standstill, confusing Yuri to the point he wasn't sure whether to continue screaming at his untrusted caller, or accept what appeared to be a genuine apology. Either way he didn't like his options. Moments of weakness were foreign to him and, like a frightened child, he wanted to react out of that fear with a fury that would ultimately lead him nowhere.

"Truly, Yuri, I am sorry," pleaded Mr. X. The Wolf remained silent. "Okay, that's fine. You have every reason to be upset. However, despite the grim mood, I believe I can help bring some justice to your situation."

Yuri disagreed, squeezing his eyes closed, and shaking his head.

"Why do *you* care?"

A scoffing laugh preceded Mr. X's words. "Come now, Yuri. We're business partners. What hurts you… hurts me."

And the lies return. Yuri checked his watch, a gleaming silver and gold Tag Hauer. It read 11:54 a.m. "My situation should be handled here shortly. Interjecting is not necessary."

"Of course, I almost forgot about your hired assassins. Tell me what you think of them, Yuri." There was a momentary pause to let the revelation set in. "The Twins are a rather *particular* taste, aren't they?"

Yuri remained silent, chastising himself for not expecting this underhanded serpent to somehow know he contracted two of the world's deadliest assassins.

"I know this, Yuri, because I know everything. Nothing happens without me knowing. I always have someone somewhere. How do you think I have such impeccable resources?"

Mr. X laughed heartily, enjoying the upper hand he held over Yuri. It rang in his voice flagrantly. Yuri detested how he overlooked this possibility, but the information was out so there was no hiding from it.

"Yes, I outsourced some wet work," the Wolf admitted.

"On a target you know nothing about?" asked Mr. X. His question carried its own sense of uncertainty.

"The Twins are good at what they do. Hunting trophies is what they do best."

"Hmmm… Yuri, I'm slightly disappointed. On one hand, you did hire the best. The cost you've… I mean, *we've*, paid in the losses sustained to our endeavors warrants such a worthy response. However, there is one detail you're unaware of."

Yuri hated these games, but they had to be entertained. It was a part of Mr. X's con; the mastery behind his technique. "Indulge me then."

"It is very likely that you have also signed their death warrants, which is a shame, I'm afraid. They are a couple of delightful psychopaths if I've ever met any." He laughed at the oxymoron of his description, always amusing himself.

"Do not underestimate them. I have used them before in Moscow." Yuri waited for his caller to attempt to speak again, and interrupted him immediately. "Before you continue to ramble, can you get to the point?

You called for a reason. Justice to my situation, I believe?"

"Ah, yes! Thank you, friend! I do fall off track from time to time. We don't talk anymore." A sarcastic element was interjected into the delivery, but there was no expected response. Mr. X continued. "Oh, and by the way, they probably are going to be killed. First-hand knowledge. I'm calling it now. Anyway, justice for you. Here we go:

"I know who is coming after you."

It was Yuri's turn to laugh, and despite the grief and anger swelling inside of him the release served him well. His expression came from deep within, beyond his belly, and possibly straight out of his soul. He laughed long and hard, so much so that tears welled up in his eyes.

"Hmm… that wasn't meant to be funny, Yuri," Mr. X commented.

Yuri continued until the exasperation forced him to cough and catch his breath. When he gained control of himself, clearing his throat and spitting into the bushes, Yuri sat back in the deck chair to entertain the remainder of Mr. X's bullshit.

"I'm sorry, *friend*," he laughed. "Go on."

"Well, as funny as it's not, my Russian comrade, I assure you this next part won't elicit your laughter again," Mr. X proclaimed, his voice taking on a gravely serious tone. "The thing is, considering our relationship, Yuri, if I know him with your regard, you know him."

A stoic poise immediately transformed the *pakhan*. Such an accusation lit another fire within him, and his anger again boiled. He said nothing.

"Ah, thought that would get your attention. It gets better, though. Are you ready, Yuri? This is where I deliver your justice."

Yuri simply growled in response. The idea of actually knowing who was destroying his operations, but having no clue as to who they were, was insulting. How could that possibly happen? Could it be in the same vein as Mr. X saying he had someone somewhere, suggesting a member of his *bratva* reported to the rogue CIA operative? His disdain for the man managed to grow deeper and deeper as time ticked on.

"I'll take your silence as confirmation for your preparedness," advised the charismatic caller. "If your world is upside down, Yuri, allow me to right its bearings. The man destroying everything you've built, with my help, is the man who was to be traded for your father's release from the Gulag almost three years ago." Mr. X let that dab of information set in before he continued. "But it gets better for you. The FBI agent assigned to track this vigilante and bring him to justice, Special Agent Connor Stone..." Another pause thickened the dramatic effect Mr. X relished in his deliveries. "...is the man responsible for your father's death."

There were no words for the Wolf to say. His anger even diminished for a fleeting moment and in that space and time, regardless of his villainous ways, karma had come around in his favor. He was being served an opportunity for revenge. The conversation continued on for some time as Mr. X indulged himself with his dramatic effect and overstated mannerisms. There was assurance of a way to end this predicament, which the charismatic caller intended to assist with, and there was more critical information to drink in. Yuri simply sat back in the deck chair, his weight flexing against the meshed fabric of its backing. When Mr. X abruptly ended the call, Yuri was overwhelmed by what he'd learned, yet in the very moment he simply focused on the positive. He now knew who was responsible for his father's death, a wrong he could right. It would also bring him the man responsible for devastating his business and killing his dearest son.

Yuri laid back in the chair and let the mesh of the fabric press against his skin, bearing his fangs with a smile while he thought of all the harm he would soon do.

Chapter 28
Killer Composure

Patience, as it were, was considered a virtue. And such a virtue was considered, by definition, a good or admirable quality. But for Richter and Simon it had become more than a quality of excellence in their profession. It was a necessity. Beyond the innate eccentricities they were both well aware of, and going so far as to discuss the diagnosis of being psychotic at times, patience was a staple in their toolbox of abilities. The life of an assassin required it, so much in fact, on the list of capabilities needed to become a professional killer patience was right up there with having the capacity to take another human's life. One who was careless in their execution of duty did not last long as a killer in one of the oldest professions of mankind's existence. This quality contributed to the twins' flawless success rate. The buildup was painstaking, but the fulfillment was second to none.

They were both set up within the Red House Trucking and Distributing garage, choosing positions with an elevated advantage. Parked in the bays on either side of the iron plate framed into the concrete floor were two conventional, engine forward tractors with sleeping berths featuring wind deflector covers that arced over the top of the cabs. Richter chose to position himself in the orange/black semi on the north side of the plate, climbing up the backside of the cab and crouching in the hollow space beneath the wind deflector. He faced the iron plate where they suspected their target would emerge, relying on the dimness of light and depth provided by the shell of the deflector for concealment. Simon found a similarly higher perch on a deep blue semi with the exception of lying prone on the top of a short cargo trailer still connected to the truck's fifth wheel coupling. The younger twin found better stability here, taking up a proper sniper position, sighting his scope on the iron plate. Richter enjoyed the freedom of being able to quickly move if the situation called for it. At times he'd found he was much more adaptable to remaining mobile, an advantage for him now with the unusual amount of nerves and excitement he felt.

Simon seemed to be oddly calmer than he was known to be. It was amusing to Richter how their typical roles somehow altered for today's assignment. He remained confident in their ability to achieve success. Richter held himself in high esteem, but he had also witnessed Simon's aptitude for excelling when needed. The nerves and the excitement surging through the elder twin made him believe that this anomaly of Simon's characteristics would be put to good use very shortly.

"Ready for action," Simon said, settling in his position at the edge of the trailer. He adjusted his rifle in his shoulder, laid out flat, legs extended with each foot turned outward so the inside of his shoes rested on the roof of the trailer. His body configured into a position similar to a Y.

"Should be anytime, brother," Richter responded, crouched with his left leg folded underneath him like one half of sitting cross-legged, while his right leg was posted up, foot flat on the cab, and knee bent perpendicular in front of him. He used the inside of his right thigh to rest his elbow against, to support the position of his rifle.

"May I make a quick observation?" Simon asked. His tone was uncertain.

"Of course."

"This seems like it will be too easy for such a valued target. I almost wish there would be more of a confrontation…" Simon took a deep breath, allowing his thoughts to settle in before he continued. "… *Like a test*!"

Richter smiled, allowing a calm feeling to re-associate itself with his body. *And the roles return to normal.* He felt Simon's growing excitement in the words he spoke. "Oh, I understand, brother. But we wouldn't try to wrestle a bear when we could bring it down unscathed, would we?"

There was hesitation in Simon's reply. "Well, maybe *you* wouldn't."

They shared a hushed laugh. The joyous sound echoed in either brother's ear bud, effectively clear and without static. It was as though they were standing shoulder to shoulder. And then a whining screech stopped them both cold. They listened intently, instantly focused, something they'd mastered over the course of their profession. The sound came again, old and rusty, forced and stubborn, and it emanated from the center of the floor.

"It's time, brother," Richter whispered. He grinned slyly, knowing Simon was doing the same.

Their target had arrived.

The iron plate at the center of the Twins' attention continued to screech and whine from within. Their focused attention zoomed in with the powerful optics mounted on their rifles, sighted in from their perches that virtually lined up with the two corners of the portal that faced their respective positions. Once the target managed to raise the heavy plate and emerge from the tunnel he would be caught in their crosshairs, or red dot sights to be more exact, and each round they fired would be aimed at such an angle Richter and Simon would not be subjected to the dangers of crossfire.

More whining and screeching came from below the surface, slow and high pitched. Richter wondered just how the target would manage to open the hinged plate, which had to arc upwards thirty-six inches and with enough forced pressure for the hinges to roll back over to fully open the tunnel exit. That was when they would fire upon him. He would no doubt have to rise out of the hole in the floor while pushing the plate upwards, giving them the perfect opportunity to execute him. Richter was incredibly fit, and stronger than his 185-pound frame would have one to believe. Simon, just as their biological title as twins suggested, was the same. Both brothers were capable of lifting nearly twice their weight for repetitions well into the mid-twenties. Their athleticism had been a gift, and they were groomed through life not to rest on their laurels. And given that Richter could not budge the iron plate beforehand told him its density added to its heft, and was likely latched from within. It would take a powerful man and a miracle for that iron plate to be opened without an extreme amount of effort.

As a professional and prideful man, with ambiguously designed morals, Richter was also humble to some degree. His natural arrogance would suggest otherwise, as he found he was simply better than others at most things, with Simon being his most significant rival. But Richter could pass the torch when needed, and it gladly went to his brother in every case. Today, however, neither he nor Simon could take home the blue ribbon for strength. They were on the losing end of what Richter felt could only be a God-given miracle.

The iron plate rattled, shaking the elements of dirt and grease and silt carried in from past trucks, and mechanical repairs. As it settled, the pressure of impending danger uncannily emitted through the garage, like static electricity, suggesting the proverbial calm before the storm. And then it happened; the plate shot up from its resting place with the effort of a balloon being tossed into the air. There was a brief flash of an arm rising out of the tunnel exit, cloaked in all black, but it quickly retreated out of sight. The Twins had no chance of taking a shot, let alone fully seeing their target. The iron plate formed to its naturally hinged motion rising up, arcing backwards over itself, and crashing down in a deafening collision with the concrete floor. A cloud of dirt swept outwards from the iron plate, reminiscent of a skyscraper toppling to the earth. The dull clang echoed throughout the garage, filling the expansive space with a single chord of cringe worthy music set in a pitch somewhere between nails scratching down a chalkboard and the beating of a gong.

The Twins reacted simultaneously, shocked and impressed. They shot each other wide eyed looks with gaping mouths. How could that have just happened? The portal was opened with ease and, not only in a display of little effort, but extreme strength. Richter released his support hand from his rifle and flexed, followed by him signing to Simon, "Holy shit!"

Simon agreed, replying in sign language, "So strong!"

Richter agreed. He then pointed to his eyes and directed his fingers back to the portal. Each brother returned to their sniper positions, focusing on where their target would emerge. Hearts beat with tremendous force, adrenaline flowing through their veins, excitement and nerves tangled in their thoughts as they took in deliberately slow breaths to settle themselves and remain on target. Their patience set in as they waited. Calmness eclipsed the anxiety. Still, no one rose out of the tunnel.

A thought occurred to Richter as the hands of his watch ticked away. He wondered if Simon would be thinking along the same lines as he was, but the younger brother had a tendency to clear his mind as the moment of execution came nearer. For Richter, however, he could remain focused and multitask mentally with free thought. What sparked within his mind was the idea of their target being such an elite tactician that he sensed something was wrong and would not continue without caution. Richter wondered what could inspire such reluctance, and in that thought process he found he had been humbled a second time within seconds of each occurrence. Their target was not proceeding because he knew that on a Wednesday morning the Red House Trucking and Distributing garage would be busy with work, and upon his planned escape he discovered that there was no work being done.

"Brother," Richter whispered.

"Yes?" replied Simon, his hushed words returned.

"I fucked up."

Hesitation in reply gave Richter the sense that Simon was now taking details into consideration.

"Ah, no one's working," Simon said.

"Exactly," Richter agreed. "I apologize, brother."

Simon shook his head. "It's no matter, brother." He looked over to Richter, smiling in his sinister way. "Where's he going to go?"

Richter needed that reassurance, and in the moment, he loved his brother even more if it were possible. Simon was correct. Their target was cornered. He certainly couldn't retreat into the tunnel. The police waited for him on the other end, and research showed that, unless they were corrupt, he had never harmed law enforcement. His only way out was to continue forward.

"We're going to get our fight, brother," Simon said. The joy could be heard in his voice.

"Yes, we are, brother," Richter agreed. "Yes, we are."

****

In many people there is an innate feeling that resonates from deep within; it's a sense of knowing that cannot be explained, and in that inexplicable process there is a warning, or awareness, that is raised. It comes from the gut, and more often than not, much like the voice in a person's head, a gut feeling is more accurate than the narration of the conscious. Ghost knew this feeling well, and he listened to it when it came every time. It had saved his life more times than he could count, and he felt it immediately. This time it came with a number of precursors grounded in reality, and they registered within him instantly.

First, the garage was quiet. No garage was ever quiet during business hours. Air tools should be whining, steel tools should be clanging (most likely from being tossed across the floor in frustration), and engines should be running. An exorbitant amount of cussing typically went hand in hand when working on motorized vehicles, and given the ownership of the establishment, it would be done in Russian not English.

Second, the motion sensor Ghost had attached to the inside of the iron plate had been activated. It was a cheat, in a sense, as to knowing something was wrong. The sensor was regulated to go off if the lid was lifted, or attempted. In his reconnaissance Ghost had learned the bay where the tunnel entered the garage was never compromised, which meant it was never tampered with. Since the sensor had been tripped, it meant someone had tried to open the hatch. They were lucky Ghost had decided against arming it with an explosive.

What Ghost was feeling could only be explained as a sixth sense — a warning system. He felt a heavy sense of tension in the atmosphere that raised the hairs on the back of his neck, and the crushing weight of a confrontation. His experience gained from an extensive amount of combat missions contributed to the overall sensation delivered to him. It was never wrong, and it was never falsely activated. It was Ghost's fail safe whenever he walked into an anomaly in his plans.

The question now was this: how many people am I going to be dealing with? His best guess told him they would be professionals, if they weren't *just* anyone. A group of mercenaries would be too extreme, and Kurikova would send his own men anyway. They were elite trained military operators, or at least the majority of them were. The Wolf favored former, or easily paid off, Spetznaz soldiers. Professionals were assassins; people who could be discreet and leave no trace of their existence once they'd finished the job. Ghost came to the conclusion he was going up against no more than three men, but likely less. Killers for hire rarely worked in small groups, but he knew of a handful from his days as a splinter cell operator. Being a few years removed from the profession, Ghost decided the time span could have easily birthed more divergent elitists from the world of violence he'd walked through for so long. He looked up to the opening, seeing beyond into the garage, knowing there was only one way to find out.

Ghost took into consideration, given the environment above ground, there were any number of positions of concealment. Every position from the garage floor up fit this description, but beyond that generality the best would be a more elevated spot such as on top of a trailer, or the cab of a semi. Next would be beneath a truck or trailer for concealment. And then behind any number of toolboxes that could also act as protective barricades. No matter how Ghost looked at the scenario he was at the ultimate disadvantage.

On a good note, he did have the advantage of knowing the layout of the building, which did him no good in a hole in the ground. Experience was also on his side in the sense that he had a habit of planning contingency plans well in advance. In the case of any resistance within the Red House Trucking garage, Ghost planned to disorientate and blind anyone who got in his way with the tools at his disposal. There were three flash bang grenades and three smoke grenades in his arsenal, along with another incendiary explosive. He came to the decision that the blue-collar occupation of mechanics was not a deep enough involvement with Kurikova to warrant taking their lives. These men were likely just your typical employees. Red House Trucking and Distribution was a legitimate business, and he had not found any information suggesting their employment extended beyond working in the shop. The mechanics were just that, and working on Kurikova's trucks wasn't a good enough reason for Ghost to kill any of them.

Strategically speaking those who were lying in wait would take their shot at the first sight of him. He was quick, but not as quick as a bullet. His only hope to get out alive in this moment was in timing and distraction. The double padded bullet proof vest he wore with front and back trauma plates would help. They would protect him fairly well, but there was no telling what type of rounds those hunting him would be using. Ghost had to think quickly and call on the depths of his extensive skillset, as well as the tactics he could use to aid what little advantage he had. At least six of the seven grenades he had were going to be made useful. And he only had one chance to get it right.

Chapter 29
Bad Meets Worse

Waiting was always the most strenuous aspect of the profession, pushing the boundaries of one's patience, especially when the payoff was right there for the taking. It weighed heavier when time was extended, naturally effecting self and situational awareness. The major downfall was that tunnel vision was known to slither its way into the equation, and this debilitating characteristic had the capability of instilling hesitation when it was most critical.

It worked.

The first sign of movement was quick and brief. It was followed by a series of metallic pings skating across the concrete floor.

"Movement," Simon spoke, blunt and matter-of-factly.

"Copy," Richter replied.

Each brother adjusted their position in their own way, ignoring the numbness of remaining still as they focused, fighting off the excitement of their anticipation. They had held out for much longer in previous times, but this moment was similar to having a carrot dangled in front of their faces. It had been nearly ten minutes since the iron plate had been thrown open with gorilla-like strength. Since then Richter and Simon's attention never faltered. The plan was simple: when their target tried to come out of the tunnel, they would put him down.

But he never came.

Another sound followed within a matter of seconds, something vaguely familiar to the twins. A secondary *ping* of metal hit the concrete in the silence of the garage resounding in the same vein as the proverbial pin dropping. Quickly afterwards a rushing aerosol soundtrack sang out within the garage, *poof*!

"Smoke," Simon said.

"Copy," Richter replied.

But it wasn't just a mist of white smoke. They could have dealt with that to some degree. White smoke, although thick at first, would not provide a perfect veil of concealment. When their target decided to escape from the tunnel, they would be able to see his silhouette move within the fog, and follow it. A blue and green haze quickly filtered into the garage, filling the empty space of the bay with thick smoke. It spread out where the iron plate teased the twins with the opportunity of fulfilling their contract knowing their target was right there. A third smoke grenade turned end over end as it was gently tossed out of the tunnels opening. It landed in the iron plate with a *clang*, and was quickly followed by the ejection of a metal cap and the rush of more heavy green smoke.

"Fuck! More smoke!" Simon growled.

"Copy, brother," Richter replied. "You may very well get your fight with the bear."

The green and blue smoke swirled and mixed together creating a dense mist that completely obstructed the twins' vision. Within seconds the opening to the tunnel had been swallowed into the smoke's cloud, still expanding and drifting farther out from the immediate area, and filling the nearest three bays with its ominous presence.

"I welcome it," Simon replied. He rose from lying prone to a kneeling position. He shouldered the rifle once again and took aim in the direction of the tunnel's entrance. "Firing."

Richter did not reply. He understood Simon's tactic. In this moment where the smoke was thickest their target would, or already had, escaped from his pinned down position. Their best chance was to lay down cover fire in the general direction while watching to see if the smoke was influenced by any internal movement. In the moment it was very heavy, as the grenades were in close proximity of each other, and it made any visual identification nearly impossible.

But Simon fired, as he'd stated, keeping his aim directed in the crossing pattern he and Richter had set up. Richter followed suit. Each shot was singular, firing from the suppressor with the hush of a metallic whisper, and ricocheting off the concrete erratically. Thumps and bangs of dull impacts sounded at random within the garage. The ricochets could be equally as dangerous as any purposely placed bullet, but a streak of luck seemed to be in play as they lodged into toolboxes, wooden workbenches, and sheet metal. It wasn't a factor either brother took into consideration for the moment, but the bouncing bullets could always find a home within their target by chance as well.

A gust in the smoke caught Richter's eye. He noticed a rolling swirl in the void of green and blue, which made him look away from the red dot optic mounted on his rifle. The hunted man had moved out of the tunnel, disrupting the aerosol colored spray meant to disrupt their vision.

"I've got movement your way," the elder brother said. "Moving."

"Copy," Simon replied, standing and keeping his rifle trained to the left of the semi cab where he was positioned.

Richter dropped down from the cab of the semi he occupied. His agile movements gave him the appearance of a specter floating down to the coupling of the truck, and then bounding seamlessly to the floor. When he landed his feet moved quickly. Within seconds he crossed the empty bay, slid beneath the trailer on his backside, and emerged on the opposite side in a kneeling position with his rifle trained to the front of the blue semi. He could feel Simon directly above him, mimicking his position, but it wouldn't last.

"Moving," Simon advised.

"Moving," Richter repeated.

Each brother moved forward, slowly, and methodically. Richter took each purposeful step with his knees bent to support him carrying his weapon, thus allowing him the ability to remain stabilized in a shooting position. Simon nimbly leapt to the top of the blue semi's wind deflector like a cat, landing with balletic grace, and immediately dropped one leg down to slide over the deflectors arcing curve to the flat surface of the cab. He maintained his balance by guiding his motion with one arm while single handedly keeping his rifle aimed forward. His elevated position gave him an advantage to view far more than being on the ground, but the long nose of the conventional tractor was also a disadvantage for him as it stretched out far enough to provide cover for their target.

Richter and Simon moved in tandem as though they had choreographed every step. When Simon reached the edge of the cab he paused. Richter did so as well and, when this synchronicity occurred, he sidestepped to approach the front of the semi from an angled position, which gave him the advantage of opening up his range of vision. As

Richter reached a point that set him up for a forty-five-degree angled approach to the driver's side corner, he paused again. In this beat was where he and Simon would symbiotically reconnect and move forward together.

They weren't allowed this opportunity.

Ping, ping…

Two metal posted rings bounced across the floor. The silence of the garage in combination with the density of the concrete floor caused these tiny pieces to echo within the vast space. Their sound hit with a resounding impact, allowed only by the heightened senses of the adrenaline-fueled killers in the room. Instincts and experience intermixed immediately, bending the context of time, connecting thoughts and reactions all at once.

Richter turned to Simon.

Simon turned to Richter.

The twins' connection proved to be as innate as anyone's imagination could predict, and they both retreated for cover as their thoughts came to the same conclusion: grenades.

One came up over the top of the blue semi's cab, floating and twirling in the air end over end as its tube-shaped shell drew nearer to Simon. The younger twin leapt up to the wind deflector's edge, landing on one foot while his next step continued forward to lead the drop down to the fifth wheel's coupler.

The second grenade skipped sideways across the floor in Richter's direction. He dropped down to one knee, knowing time was against him, and spun around one end of a tall, rusted toolbox for cover.

Boom!

Boom!

The grenades exploded in sequence, one directly after the other, producing an intensely loud bang and a blinding flash of light. The flash was meant to activate the photoreceptor cells in the eyes and cause blindness for nearly five seconds, which could also create an afterimage that would impair its victim's ability to aim precisely. Coupled with a blast of nearly 170 decibels, the grenade was created to disrupt the fluid in the ear, causing loss of balance, and temporary loss of hearing. A third factor included its concussive element of the explosive, not made to inflict damage, but they were more than capable of doing so.

The cab of the semi blew out, shattering the glass, and raining chunks and slivers of it across the garage floor. A wave of force impacted the sheet metal, bending it to its will, rocking the cab of the truck. The flash mimicked a synthetic sun, burning bright within the building, and disappearing just as quickly.

The second detonation shot its light and concussion across the floor, scattering loose tools like shrapnel, and creating a second sun within the garage. Richter was shaken by the toolbox as the force slammed it into his back. The force of the grenades rolled outward and partially cleared the green and blue smoke that was filtering underneath the blue semi.

Richter and Simon had both closed their eyes and covered their ears. This assisted in prohibiting the effects of the flash bang grenades. Neither brother was blinded or fully exposed to the deafening blast, but the stunning factor of the explosive impact did have a slight effect.

Simon slipped to his backside when the grenades went off, losing his balance in the semi-cramped space between the cab and the trailer. He shook off what little of the effects he'd sustained, pulling on air hoses to assist in getting back to his feet. As he regained his balance and looked up, he'd nearly wished he'd been struck by the stun grenade. The first sight he took in was the furious black flash rushing towards him in the confined space he occupied, quickly followed by the powerful impact of what he could only imagine was a knee strike aimed at his chest. There was nowhere to go but backwards, and Simon was forcefully knocked from the space between the cab and trailer. He landed flat on his back, his chest burning and aching instantly, followed by the rush of air hammered from his lungs.

A heavy gasp made Simon involuntarily lurch up off of his back, clutching at his chest as though he'd briefly joined the dead and then came back to life. Between the sudden pain in his chest and the lack of air, he had been quickly debilitated and was out of the fight for the moment.

Following the blast of the flash bangs, Richter kept his eyes closed and ears covered. He came around the toolbox to spring into action when he was certain it was safe to avoid any residual effects of the explosions. Richter turned from his backside and rose up on to his feet. By the time he maneuvered around the tool box he caught sight of Simon lying on the floor of the garage, gasping for air, clawing at his chest and at the air as though he were scooping air back into his lungs. The sight of his brother distracted him from the immediate threat that moved with brutal intention.

The man before him, clearly their target, moved incredibly fast. He kicked the toolbox Richter used for cover, knocking the twin backwards into another tractor trailer in the adjacent bay. The toolbox pinned him in place, and the man followed up with a lunch box sized fist to Richter's face. A daze came over the elder twin as his brain was rattled by the massive fist and compounded by bouncing off the metal trailer. The dual impact sent Richter's mind reeling, losing his focus, and stealing away his motor skills. Richter couldn't even raise his hands up to defend himself. Immediately following the punch, he felt the toolbox easily moved away from pinning him against the trailer, and two hands took hold of him by his shirt. Suddenly Richter defied gravity by levitating off the ground. The next thing he knew he was flying towards Simon's distressed position.

The brothers collided on the garage floor as Richter came crashing down from a powerful throw technique. He landed on Simon, knocking what wind he'd regained out of him once more, and then toppled into a roll. The man had managed to get the upper hand, and he wasted no time putting it to good use.

Richter leapt up to his feet, feeling the pain through his back after slamming into the concrete. He was forced to pause in a hunched position, and strained to surge forward to counterattack, realizing he'd somehow lost his rifle. In the rare moment of hesitation that set in, Richter watched as their target, a large man, clad in black tactical gear from head to toe, continued his assault. A vicious kick to Simon's midsection nearly lifted his younger twin off the ground. Simon howled in pain, rolling to one side onto his knees, arms hugging his abdomen with his head pressed against the floor. It had appeared that somewhere in the melee Simon had also lost his rifle. The only sense of relief Richter had in noticing this detail was that their target had not taken up the arms they'd lost.

The man moved towards Richter with purpose. Not one step was wasted. The elder brother saw a big black boot launch in his direction, but he was not there to receive it.

Richter sidestepped the attack, using his hands to deflect the missile-like offense, and then circled around to stand between Simon and their target.

The man quickly rerouted his efforts back towards Richter, closing the distance between them with incredible power and speed. But Richter was faster.

A flurry of punches blurred back and forth as their combative skillsets collided. Richter landed clean body shots, but he felt the padding of body armor worn by the target. He wasn't sure the strikes would have done any good in the first place. The man walked through everything, surging forward with an uncanny amount of power, and setting a furious fight pace for his size. Richter deflected a number of strikes to keep himself between Simon and the man, hoping his brother would recover quickly to get in on the fight he'd wanted so badly.

Richter's prayers were answered.

Simon had a knack for enjoying pain. Laughter was his way of dealing with it in every form. His howling had turned to grunts and moans, but the finality of what he felt managed to reach a stuttering giggle, which in turn escalated into a full-on psychotic cackle.

Richter smiled as he continued to fight, blocking and parrying, side-stepping crushing kicks and knees, while gaining ground and delivering his own. Nothing seemed to slow the man down. He needed to cause an injury of some kind, and force the man to slow. If he could show the man he was vulnerable it would turn the tide in Richter's favor. And once Simon joined him there would be no stopping them.

****

Ghost had not experienced such a challenge in hand to hand combat in far too long. As serious as the situation could be with the results meaning life or death, he was enjoying this little sparring match. The man who'd been putting up the fight was quite skilled; elite even. He showed no fear, and the wild look in his eyes gave him the appearance of a feral animal. His protective instinct kept him between Ghost and the other man. A brief pause gave Ghost the opportunity to see that the two men looked nearly identical, which also allowed him to realize he was in the presence of the famed twin assassins, whose reputation preceded them within the circles they ran.

The twins were well known in the underbelly of the criminal world for being extremely dangerous and skilled and crazy. There was virtually nothing they wouldn't do for the right price. And they weren't cheap, either. In the days he worked as a splinter cell operator, Ghost had come across a job the twins had done. He knew he'd never forget it. He was in Istanbul at the time, and a European ambassador was visiting a private school on a goodwill tour. The twins had been tasked with his assassination. They could have easily taken the ambassador's life since the diplomat's security detail was half-assed at best. But the twins liked making statements. Instead they blew up half the school yard with a car bomb they'd planted. Ghost took in a small sense of pride that Yuri Kurikova had not wasted any expense at coming after him. And Ghost also knew he was going to enjoy killing them.

****

Simon stood holding his stomach with one hand and wiped away the tears streaking his face. He wasn't a crier by any means, but there were just certain things the body couldn't help reacting to where pain was concerned. The sensation made him feel more alive to some degree, but the hits he'd taken nearly made him wish he were dead, too. Richter stood between him and their target as a slight lull in their fight gave him time to enter the bout.

"You," Simon snickered, standing at Richter's side and pointing a finger at the man in black. "You are a strong sonofabitch." Simon lifted his shirt to reveal his tightly trimmed midsection, and a bruise below his sternum that had already begun to form.

Richter looked to the wound, and then back to the man. His fury showed instantly on his face, forcing his muscles to tighten and strain. He fought the urge to carelessly lunge at the man in a protective manner as the older brother, knowing the emotional overload would only hinder his abilities. Simon reminded him to relax, and that he didn't need to stick up for his little brother. The younger twin lightly patted Richter on the shoulder, squeezing it on the final tap to let his brother know he was alright.

"It's okay," Simon said. "We're gonna' kill this fucker."

The wicked smile Simon produced somehow calmed Richter. And maybe it wasn't just the smile, but the twinkle in his eye that accompanied the far-off look Simon had that matched his own, if not surpassing it. The gleam there was predatorily focused, and slightly insane.

Simon reached behind his back and produced two four-inch ceramic blades sheathed in a custom belt holster. His lanky, muscular arms stretched out as he circled to one side, away from Richter, and closer to their target.

"Let's fight the bear, brother," Simon said, grinning wildly and baring his teeth.

Richter removed a steel blade he'd strapped on before entering the building, and began circling to the opposite direction of his brother.

The man in black took a step back, and it was the first time he'd given any ground during the struggle. Typically, Richter would have seen it as a display of weakness, but the man was simply angling his position for the fight and hiding the quick reach into his jacket. He produced a pair of brass knuckles, and stepped back once more to distance himself from the twins' advance. He again reached into his jacket, on the opposite side, and produced a talon shaped blade, double edged and with a retention ring he wove his index finger through. Richter knew the blade well as a Filipino fighting knife, or *karambit*. It was a favored tool amongst many elite trained operators and assassins, but any killer worth their fee could handle any knife. The real question was who was more skilled with the blade?

Once the man was equally armed, he did not give any more ground, and he did not wait to be attacked. He lunged towards Richter, which made sense to the brother as he was already familiar with his fighting style, and slashed with the karambit. Richter avoided the attack, slashing back in his own right, but both missed. It was a calculated distraction as it gave Simon an opportunity to move in, yet the man expected the twin to come forward, and caught him with a powerful push kick to his already damaged midsection. Simon lurched back a few steps, bent forward from the force of the kick. He came right back, unencumbered, fighting through the gut-wrenching strike. His awareness and adrenaline fueled the fury swelling within him, and he began a berserker-like onslaught even Richter needed to be wary of.

Simon wielded the knives as they were meant to be, extensions of himself, slashing, stabbing, and lunging in with them with precise movements. The man avoided every effort Simon made while returning with his own. Simon blocked everything that was thrown at him, increasing the pressure of his offense with his speed and personal drive to win. The men became a blur of limbs and blades, blocking, dodging, counterstriking and parrying each other. And so, the dance of death was performed.

Richter circled around the melee, watching his brother intently. It was difficult for the untrained eye to keep up with what Simon was capable of, but Richter knew his brother all too well. What was impressive was the skillset of their target. Richter had alluded to believing the man's capabilities were incredibly high with what he'd been able to accomplish, but he was becoming more and more impressive as the clock ticked on. He heard the tearing of fabric as he watched the fight continue relentlessly. Simon was making his cuts, and those cuts would eventually slow the man down. Knife fights were of the most brutal form of combat. Injuries sustained by a well-trained blades man could easily result in death, and at the very least maim. The body armor the man wore was meant to stop bullets, not blades, and in the end, they would see who the real winner would be.

Simon and the target never let up, attacking back and forth. The younger twin transitioned from one movement to the next seamlessly, and he was matched with equal skill by the man. Simon's anger boiled, unable to get the upper hand. And then it briefly fell apart.

****

They were strategically approaching him with the utmost intelligence, fighting one at a time, wearing him down so they could then attack simultaneously and finish the job. Ghost was growing tired, but he couldn't let it show. The twin he was fighting came with nearly twice as much energy as the one before him. He had to do something to gain the advantage. This brother was slightly faster than the other, but it was likely because he was more careless and unbridled. Each twin showed no signs of fear or caution, but Ghost believed the one stalking him and waiting to tag back into the fight was the most controlled of the two. He had to use what little knowledge he had to turn the table in his favor.

The moment came as the twin moved to slash at Ghost's lower extremities in an attempt to disable his mobility. Ghost lifted his left leg as the blade swept underneath him, missing, and launched his foot outward. The kick landed, but not flush with the twin's head as he'd intended. Instead it disrupted the spinning motion the twin employed and knocked him forward. Ghost followed up with another thrust kick, landing cleanly between the shoulder blades of the twin. The blow forced the twin forward, yet he displayed his agility as he tucked into a roll and fluidly leapt to his feet.

The twin turned back and came right in to continue the fight. Ghost saw the briefness of the opportunity he needed and took it. As the twin lunged forward Ghost sidestepped, letting a furious blade thrust pass by him. He hammered the twin's hand with the retention ring of the karambit, forcing him to drop the knife, and delivered a straight punch to his jaw with the brass knuckles. The success of his offense disoriented the twin, and allowed Ghost to quickly transition into a control hold that would do damage to the twin's arm while also tossing him out of the way. Ghost was successful once again, managing to use as much of his strength as he could to tie up the extended arm, twist it into a pretzel-like position, and throw the brother nearly five feet ass over tea kettle into a rolling toolbox. A resounding snap accompanied the throw along with a painful yelp. The twin slammed against the toolbox in a perpendicular position, and crashed down on his head.

Ghost began to move away from the crowded space near a work-bench, but was quickly blocked in. While putting his focus into disarming and debilitating the twin he fought, Ghost lost sight of the brother. He was quickly reminded of the assassin's lethal presence.

****

Opportunity gained is an opportunity earned, and the upper hand in the fight unfortunately came at Simon's expense. Richter made sure he didn't waste it. He swiftly moved in when their target tossed Simon through the air, nearly snapping the twin's arm in half with his power. Richter launched a roundhouse kick to the man's head as he turned to move away from the nearby workbench. The impact of the strike spun the man around to his right, dazing him and forcing him to stumble. A high velocity spin followed when Richter delivered a double aerial kick. One kick struck in the sternum, forcing the man to bend forward at the waist as the second kick, while still spinning in mid-air, quickly arrived against the side of his head. The force of the blow sent the target reeling to the floor where he slid another foot prone upon the concrete, unmoving.

Lions stalk their prey in a number of ways, and so did Richter. Wild eyed and anxious to lunge in with his razor-sharp blade, the elder twin steeled his primal urge with a professional caution. He could see the man was breathing, laid out on his belly like a beached Great White. But then the man moved, and Richter knew he was still very dangerous. Cold, black eyes looked up to him as the man slowly pushed himself off of the concrete floor. Death stared at Richter, but the twin simply laughed back.

"Got more than you bargained for today," Richter growled, wiping his chin as the thirst for the kill found him salivating like a hungry beast.

The man said nothing. In one quick movement his feet were beneath him, standing tall with his massive chest huffing and puffing. His lips became a taught, thin line, and beyond the blackness of his eyes Richter could see the fire of rage burning bright. He simply grinned at the man, flashing his eyes wider, rocking his head from side to side tauntingly.

Richter lunged forward, feinting a strike, but the man did not move. He quickly stepped back, minding his distance, and continued to circle. Simon moaned and groaned on the floor behind the man, struggling to move and regain consciousness. The man looked back over his shoulder at the incapacitated twin, and then glared back at Richter out of his peripheral. It was clear to Richter the man was going to use Simon to lure him in on his terms, but Richter couldn't allow that to happen. He knew Simon would understand. *Sorry, brother.*

A vicious kick to Simon's midsection slammed him back into the toolbox he'd collided with moments before. Simon was barely conscious enough to feel the pain, and nearly vomited from the brunt force. Another kick followed in succession; this time with more power behind it. The younger twin spewed stomach acid from his mouth in a milky white froth as he strained with the involuntary action. The target raised a heavy black boot to stomp on Simon, but Richter had seen enough.

The elder brother threw his knife with as much force as he could, screaming and roaring with anger at the pain inflicted upon his brother. He was willing to sacrifice Simon to a degree, but his brother was surely close to having his life snuffed out. The man was too large and too strong not to finish Simon quickly; although Richter got the aching feeling he would gladly prolong Simon's demise to make them both suffer. The blade embedded into the upper back of the man, near his swelling trapezius muscle giving him the appearance of a hulking Brahman bull and took away the notion he had a neck. Richter watched the man lurch forward, dropping his boot safely to the ground without hurting Simon further. He knew the man was wearing body armor, possibly two vests given the thickness he felt with his earlier punches. The bullet proof vests were not generally blade resistant. The design was entirely different and, from what Richter could tell, the knife had penetrated the armor.

The brief disruption in the man's tactics was all Richter needed. He moved as swiftly as he ever had, light on his feet with calculated steps. Within seconds of throwing the knife Richter closed the distance between he and the man. He scaled the man's body by methodically jumping to his right hip, grabbing the back of his jacket collar to pull himself up higher, and then he delivered a series of elbow strikes to the target's head.

The man quickly covered his head with an arm to protect himself. Richter anticipated this and, while still holding on to the bull of a man, took hold of the knife. He shimmied the blade back and forth, digging it in slightly more, and for the first time heard the man expel a guttural roar of pain. Richter felt the success of his efforts as the man flailed beneath him, unable to shake him off, and he continued to hold on for dear life like a cowboy in a rodeo. What he realized as he enjoyed hurting the man was that he'd lost his sense of focus. Instead he thrived on the pain he induced, and for a moment it was all he could stand to do. It was for himself, and for Simon. *Nobody hurts my brother*!

Richter felt more alive than he had in quite some time, and he relished the moment of conquering another human being. Yet, in the same instant, it was his deepest and darkest downfall to let go of his professional hold on reality. He reveled in the screams and the pain and the blood. But enjoying what he did too much was the biggest mistake he could have made.

The blade came free with all the turning and bucking the man did as Richter meant to drive it in deeper. The man's strength and rage made it difficult to hold on, but Richter managed for the time being. When the knife came loose there was a window of opportunity for the man to take advantage of Richter's slight imbalance, and he did. Although the man could not see Richter pull the knife from the right side of his bull neck, arcing high and backwards as though he were going to immediately stab him again, he could feel Richter's weight shift to his left side. As this displacement occurred, the man reached across his body with his right arm, turning at the same time in this direction, and grabbed hold of Richter's left wrist of the hand gripping his jacket. This swung Richter into an even more unbalanced position. The man then reached up with his left arm and quickly took hold of any part of Richter he could find. When this seemingly complex maneuver reached its fulfillment, Richter was tossed down to the floor with no more regard than a sack of potatoes.

The shocking amount of force Richter felt as he crashed into the floor washed over him in a level of degrees, forcing his hands open with his arms flailing. His knife went spinning and skipping across the concrete. He first felt the immediate pain. Bone and flesh did not mix well with an immovable substance, bluntly smashing and cracking cartilage, fracturing and bruising his body in ways he likely would never fully know. The air in his lungs seemed to have evaporated instantly, and he was gasping and moaning as though he'd suddenly been subjected to an atmosphere where oxygen did not exist. A throbbing sensation blanketed him all through his back, which quickly burned as though he'd been tossed into a fire. Next came the sense of helplessness that lodged in his chest, instilling a foreign concept he was not ready to accept: *Simon and I are going to die today*.

Death did not come.

Richter struggled to breathe in through his nose and exhale. Time seemed to work very slowly, and he felt like he would not regain the ability to breathe regularly. It had not been the first time he'd felt this way. He and Simon were raised specifically to be assassins, incorporating a lifestyle built on pain and discipline, and over twenty-nine years of existence they had been instilled and trained with the capability to return to a resting calm. This assisted in renewing their full lung capacity, which took less than a minute. Richter knew this all too well, and applied the training instinctually. He scrambled towards Simon, who was coming around. The younger brother was now sitting up against a support post of the workbench lining the wall. He appeared to be conscious, but barely.

Once Richter guarded Simon with his body he frantically looked around for their target. The man was nowhere to be seen, but Richter didn't trust that he was gone. A thin mist remaining from the smoke grenades drifted low across the garage floor. Richter noticed a disruption in it that swirled and twisted the smoke in the direction of the orange/black semi's cab where he had originally been perched. He dropped down to his belly and looked beneath the vehicle. His vision was obstructed by the smoke and he could not tell whether anyone stood at the front of the cab. It would have been more dangerous to assume the man was not waiting to finish him and Simon off for good. Perhaps the knife injury was enough to convince him to flee?

"If you don't kill us now," Richter said, "you'll be making a big mistake." He emphasized the words with his pronunciation, searching the immediate area like a feral predator.

His attention turned to Simon who was awake, but clearly battered. The younger sibling had the droopy eyed look of a child who resisted waking up, yet his lethargic appearance was accentuated by an unusually wicked smile. "Did you finish him, brother?"

Richter assumed Simon had not heard him call to their target given his line of questioning. "No, brother. I was not able to." He turned to Simon and looked into his eyes, seeing glazed evidence of what was likely, at best, a mild concussion. "I did hurt him. As did you, I'm sure." He smiled to show elation for his brother's accomplishment.

Simon's heavy eyelids slowly closed, and his smile altered to a thin line of joy. "I think I cut the shit out of him. I know I got him more than he got me." Richter agreed silently, and Simon looked himself over and giggled. "Or so I thought."

"You're okay, brother," assured Richter. "We've been through worse, yeah?"

Simon nodded. "That guy is very good, though. I want to kill him very badly."

Richter reached around to the back of Simon's head, pulled him near, and kissed him on his bruised forehead before resting their heads together. "Yes, brother. So do I."

The moment of brotherly adoration came to a brief pause. Richter's more heightened awareness heard the first *ping* come from his right, and it immediately jumpstarted his heart. He whipped his head around to scan the garage, having only turned away for a matter of seconds, but saw nothing. And then the heavier sound came, similar in nature, but clearly from a weightier device. Richter looked around madly, certain he knew what he'd heard, but he couldn't see it. There it was, about five maybe six feet away, just waiting to explode. The man was still present, and he'd issued another flash bang grenade into the equation.

Richter turned to Simon and screamed to cover his ears. He did the same as he shielded Simon from the blast. The twins clenched their eyes shut as tightly as possible, and when the grenade exploded their efforts slightly hindered the effects of the flash bang. Richter felt the concussion pound against his back, knocking him to one side past Simon, and under the workbench. The heat from the flash could be felt, but it did not burn. The brothers remained still for a matter of seconds, waiting for the grenades effects to fade away before opening their eyes and readying for another bout of combat.

Nothing happened. There was no follow-up to the explosive device — no assault. The twins quickly realized it was a distraction for the man to escape without being seen, and it worked. Neither brother had the energy nor cared to follow him. They were alive and that was all they needed to be successful with another chance at him. They would not fail again.

"Brother?" Simon said, turning to Richter, who now sat at his side.

"Yes," Richter replied.

"Do me a favor, please."

"Anything."

"Talk me out of fighting the bear next time."

Richter laughed, realizing that the look Simon gave him was one of absolute elation. He shook his head, saying, "Not a fucking chance in hell, brother."

Chapter 30
You Are Not Alone

Special Agent Connor Stone was not a man who could be swayed easily. His instincts and his natural drive told him to tell McCrary to go to hell when he'd ordered Stone to 'get the fuck away from (his) crime scene.' Except Stone did nothing of the sort. He conceded, even though the crime scene was not McCrary's at all. It was his. He had been brought in to pursue the vigilante, and the events surrounding the Lucky Pawn fell underneath that umbrella of his investigation. But Stone was exhausted, so he didn't give a shit. Let McCrary shoulder this one. If he wanted a taste of what Stone was involved in so badly, he could have it. With pleasure.

A double whiskey on the rocks had become Stone's partner for the day. Jack Daniels was his usual poison, but whatever this firewater was he didn't know, and it didn't matter. He holed up at a dive bar in Southie cloaked in the athletic hew of a sports pub that was sparingly occupied. The bartender didn't seem to be too friendly at first, but overpaying for his drinks with big tips brought the big man around. As the day pressed on, a flirty young waitress talked Stone into some food to abstain from becoming bumbling drunk. Stone accepted as he took up residence in a booth positioned so he could see the front entrance. He ordered a double quarter pounder with fries, and stared at the sixty-five-inch screen showing the Red Sox game. He paid little attention to the game's details. Baseball was not his favorite pastime, however the movement on the screen helped him organize his thoughts, disheveled by the buzz from the whiskey.

The trouble brewing within his mind stemmed from past revelations being in Boston brought to light. McCrary had certainly seen and heard too much. Typically, Stone could keep his municipal liaison in the dark for the length of his stay, but this investigation was rapidly unraveling.

Besides the details he'd kept under wraps for so long, outside of reporting back to the security council appointed to him as overwatch, Stone felt he was losing his grip on the situation with the detective getting so close. McCrary was very good at what he did, but Stone had allowed him the opportunity to be in the positions where he learned more than he should have. Playing both sides of the coin was catching up to the agent as he was clearly dropping his guard, and he was tired of having to be more than he was meant to be.

Throughout the day McCrary kept Stone updated on the forthcoming details of the case. A massive perimeter was set up just like at the Boston Massacre to keep back the media hounds. The Organized Crime Unit put in their two cents linking everything to Yuri Kurikova, but the evidence was thin. Their accusations alone created a media firestorm, but there were no answers to be had. The Lucky Pawn was owned by a trust funded by a series of shell companies that had nothing to do with Kurikova directly, maintaining that there was no way to garner enough probable cause to even question the Russian kingpin. Yuri's lawyers were earning their pay by keeping him as far away from the situation as possible, going so far as to threaten harassment charges if any calls were made to their client after the brazen accusations.

The victims in the cellar of the pawn shop were cleared medically and transported to a secure facility to be processed. This task took all day, according to a message from McCrary. A large tent was put together outside of the pawn shop to hide the trafficking victims from the media.

McCrary texted, "Taking great precautions to protect these people. Buses are being used from City Transit to move them out. Windows were blacked out for obvious reasons."

Stone never responded to any of McCrary's messages, although he read every one of them. Around 2 p.m. McCrary said they found the vigilante's vehicle in the parking garage. Or at least that was when he got word of what was found. SWAT suspected an incendiary grenade was used to destroy a computer in the front seat. Nothing could be recovered. The detective hinted at 'their guy' having incredible resources. Stone scoffed at the realization McCrary made. *You've got no idea, pal.*

Somewhere in the late afternoon McCrary reported there had been some kind of confrontation six blocks south in a trucking garage: *Red*

House Trucking and Distributing. The business was discovered once the entrance to the tunnel beneath the Lucky Pawn was cleared. Stone thought it possible to use the connecting tunnel as evidence to link Kurikova, but McCrary quickly sent a message saying how the tunnels were old and appeared to be unused otherwise. SWAT members followed it to the garage and found evidence that a number of smoke and stun grenades had been deployed. Some high-end rifles had been found scattered in the area as well. One of the semi cabs had been heavily damaged from the concussion of a flash bang, covering the floor in glass. Evidence of a fight was apparent where blood mixed in with the glass shards in numerous places. Near one area of the workbenches it appeared as though someone had vomited numerous times. No bodies were found.

Outside of the garage there was a Toyota 4Runner parked near the entrance. It had been fitted with a hidden compartment custom made to hold a variety of weapons, which was empty. An incendiary grenade was also used to burn out the front of the vehicle's cab. 'This has to be our guy,' McCrary wrote.

Stone's text message feed read like a book, and by the time night fall came he'd stopped receiving them. McCrary was getting into the dirt of the situation, putting everything together, and that meant he was too busy to keep Stone updated. He didn't care, though. At some point he was supposed to meet up with the detective and give him the low down on what was really happening. Stone suspected McCrary had a plan to make things more difficult for him if he didn't give up any information. What that could be was a mystery to him. And again, he didn't care.

What do I care about?

It was a loaded question, even to ask himself. He stared into the tumbler filled with small, circular ice chunks with a hint of watered-down whiskey settling at the bottom. By the looks of things, he was well passed being a glass half full or empty kind of guy, which withdrew him from being optimistic and pessimistic. The only thing left to be was a realist, and at the heart of the matter he was just like this glass; empty.

What do I care about?

Again, the question was far too complicated. Even the simplest answer begged to be explained wholly, but there was no short answer. To do that meant reliving everything he'd been through, and feeling everything he'd lost. His sister, Veronica, and his niece, Chloe, were the only family he'd had left in this world, and he'd never been able to grieve for them. It burned within his heart, tired of being squelched, but there had been no time to mourn them. His actions had thrust him into a world he had not been prepared for; a world he thought only existed as a 007 fantasy. Yet, here he was, drowning in his sorrows, and in the deep cover world of espionage.

Stone swirled the ice around in the tumbler, preparing to sip out the remaining liquor, and looked up to the big screen again. Another game was playing, but he was still uninterested. His thoughts wandered, and his mind went numb with remembrance as tears threatened to well up in his eyes. When the pain of the past continued to resonate in the present without finding closure, it had a way of luring a man back into its cruel grasp and bleeding him of his soul.

With every scream of the crowd's resounding and concussive celebration the audio waves pounded into the agent's mind with a tidal wave of force that stirred his memories, and altered his reality. When the baseball field erupted into a raucous roar, the jovial praise of adoring fans Stone heard blaring from the speakers of the television became something else; something worse. Perhaps it was the cause and effect of the whiskey and his imagination, but all he could hear were blood curdling cries for help, replacing the audience's chorus with sporadic glitches of a woman's voice. And then a child's. The audio synchronicity flashed from one to the other.

Screams.

The crowd roared.

More screams.

The interchanging cries continued back and forth, quickly amending one to the other seamlessly. And then Stone saw them: Veronica and Chloe. Their faces contorted into fear laden masks, fighting off mysterious hands grabbing at them, assaulting them to gain their compliance. Chloe was crying while Veronica shielded her from their assailants. The mother tried to fight them off; first for her child, then herself, but she didn't stand a chance.

The crowd roared again, and Stone looked to the television. He was sweating now, feeling tightness in his chest. His breathing became constricted and he wheezed in short bursts.

Veronica's dark hair was wrangled into fists that dragged her away from her daughter. She clawed and punched and screamed for help to no avail.

Dark figures swooped in and took Chloe in their arms. Even the child tried to fight back, hitting and yelling and scratching as she cried for her mother.

The television focused on a player happily jogging around the bases as the crowd again cheered him on. A fan raised an arm high into the air clutching the victimized orb launched outside the safety of the field's tall, green walls.

Stone closed his eyes in an effort to stop seeing anything. His visions took on their own motivation and were relentless, as they continued to play beyond the veil of his tightly closed eyelids.

"No!" he growled. Spit involuntarily sprayed beyond his lips as he smashed the tabletop with one fist. He used the other hand to massage his head, deeply rubbing into his temples, twisting his head as tension stiffened in his neck.

He could see Veronica knocked to the ground; her shirt ripped from her back as her assailants pulled at anything they could get their hands on. Frantically her feet kicked out, hitting some of the shadowy figures, but her actions only served her assailants' abilities to grab her by her limbs and drag her across the wooden floor of her home towards a dark portal filled with nothingness. Nails raked flesh, tore at anonymous clothing, all for nothing. She was struck again and again, surrounded with nowhere to go, and no way to win. Bruising set in quickly with the immense impact of the black clad fists, and blood ruptured from her sinuses and thick lips.

Chloe's cries suddenly diminished in the melee of Veronica's violent efforts. *Snap*. And just like that, as suddenly as the assault had begun, it was over. The child's silence halted everything as though a whip had been cracked to gain the attention of everyone involved, and it became a turning point in the imaginings of Stone's nightmare. He saw Veronica's focus turn from battling to save her life to lying perfectly still in that moment of tragic realization. Her hazel eyes went wide; her bloody mouth gaped in awe, seizing her voice instantly as she watched her baby drop to the floor. Chloe hit with an emphatic thud that echoed within Stone's mind as she lay there with her innocence snuffed from her tiny body.

The television boomed once more from the baseball games excited audience cheering and stomping in the stands.

Veronica's wail came in a muted roar as her pain twisted and rattled and vibrated the very boundaries of Stone's reality. Tears flooded from his eyes, and he pounded on the table again, this time with the tumbler cupped in one hand.

"Nooooo!" he cried, a gravelly rumble rolled through his lips as he clenched his teeth, fighting the urge to let loose the grief he'd been carrying for so long. "I'm sorry!"

The agent paid no attention to his surroundings, lost in submergence to the liquid depths of his drunken stupor. His vision was all too real, but he knew how much it wasn't. He hadn't witnessed Veronica and Chloe's abduction, or death. It was pointless to think he'd have died before any harm came to them because his life for theirs wasn't even a question, but he couldn't protect them from the fate his actions had ultimately dealt them. He didn't even know what had truly happened to his sister and niece. What he did know was that whatever horrible fate they met, he was responsible.

The audience went silent and, in that moment, Stone tried to shake the thoughts he drunkenly manifested from his mind. He covered his face with one hand to cloak the hurt distorting his typically chiseled features and to hide the cascading tears streaking his cheeks. As he began to cry, he fought back his self-loathing, feeling his anger boil from deep inside. He pounded the tumbler on the tabletop, again.

The visions wouldn't let up, and Veronica's cry still carried no sound. She clawed her way forward, pushing away hand after hand trying to control her, begging and fighting as she reached out for Chloe. And then it changed. He was there, in the hallucination, staring back at Veronica, witnessing her struggle. Stone simply watched. He was unable to react in any way, seemingly bound by invisible bonds even as his soul lit on fire to find a way to save his sister.

Stone felt some form of touch upon his hand, but had no idea how he could feel such a thing with his arms pinned to his body. There was comfort in the squeeze and, although he didn't understand how it could happen, Stone's nightmare froze, leaving him with a disturbing sense of ease. Veronica was left behind, reaching out screaming for Chloe amongst the mysterious shadows that made up her assailants. He unexpectedly forgot what her voice sounded like as it was trapped in some endless void where sound no longer existed. The stillness of what he saw was the last he envisioned of his sister and niece in this moment, rising above the false narrative of events he dreamed of so horribly. He then allowed himself to move towards the warmth of the firm grip squeezing his hand.

As the G-man wiped his face clean of the tears and snot from his painful and episodic relief, he found a familiar pair of eyes casting judgment upon him. McCrary stood over him, patting his hand with a rare sense of empathy. The detective didn't say anything at first. He just looked at Stone with his natural squint seemingly full of more life than was typically seen, yet clinging onto the hardened essence of who McCrary was at his core.

Stone said nothing, wounded and bleeding out from a place he seldom acknowledged.

"I got worried," McCrary explained. He looked to Stone's cell phone near the edge of the table. "You didn't answer my calls."

Stone looked to the phone and saw the screen was dimly lit with two notification bars listing a number of text messages and missed calls. Then he saw a cup of coffee in McCrary's free hand, and looked up at the detective. Still he said nothing.

McCrary removed his hand from where he'd stirred the agent back into reality, and offered Stone the warm cup.

"Tracked your phone here." He looked around the establishment, taking in the discontent from the big bartender as he watched on, clearly upset by the scene Stone had made. McCrary threw a scowl at the man, and the bartender returned to his less-disturbing patrons. His eyes returned to peer down at Stone, taking on a softer sensibility: sympathy. "I been here b'fore, drowning away my sorrows."

Stone accepted the coffee.

McCrary gestured for Stone to follow him with the nod of his head. "Come on. My wife is making dinner, an' you're the guest of hona' tonight."

Stone appeared to be confused and embarrassed, hesitating to respond or move.

"She's expecting you to come with me," McCrary said, emphasizing how the agent's presence was needed. "Move ya' ass, Stone. I ain't going home without ya'. She'll fuckin' kill me." McCrary shoveled his arms in the direction of the door. "An' I ain't dying for your sorry ass tonight. Come on."

The detective turned and walked across the bar, eyeing the bartender in a way that forced the big man to look away and mind his own business. He didn't turn and look for Stone to follow. He knew the agent would because he had nowhere else to go, and Stone wasn't the kind of guy to disappoint. Boy Scouts honor, and shit. McCrary held the door as his federal counterpart caught up to him, never saying a word, but kindly nodding to him thankfully for the cup of Joe.

Stone walked out into the cool night air, feeling his head spin and tumble from the effects of the countless whiskeys he drank. McCrary never said another word as they walked to the Charger. As men of action and former Marines, regardless of never serving together, they shared an unspoken bond. Brothers in arms could feel the pain of another and, although they may not know the details, they sympathized. They'd all been in that dark place where nothing made sense, and everything hurt for some reason or another. The cause didn't matter. They just knew, and a little quiet and a little understanding conveyed the most important message of all; you are not alone.

Chapter 31
Licking Wounds

Ghost sat motionless and statuesque with his right arm extended out to one side over the plastic covered chair where he sat. Blood dripped over the majority of the chair, oozing from the lacerations from both arms and numerous areas across his torso. The thick plastic covering was properly oversized and lengthened well beyond the chair and across the floor to make for easy clean up. An old, quiet Chinese man bent forward at Ghost's side skillfully weaving a stitching needle through his skin and hooking it through the parallel side to connect the silk sutures. Lu Pang received his instruction at Harvard University and graduated with honors in 1985. Upon his graduation, he immediately returned to his native Hong Kong where his skills were honed and sold to the Chinese Triad for the majority of his career in an effort to pay for the smuggling of nearly thirty family members to the United States. Lu Pang never operated under the legal standards of medical practice, but he did operate with surgical precision. Many years had passed since he'd last crossed paths with the man in front of him. Even then he had saved Ghost's life, patching him up from similar injuries, if not worse. Ghost had repaid Lu Pang by terminating the Triad boss holding the doctor's contract in Hong Kong. Not only was it a professional necessity for Lu Pang to be pulled out from underneath the crime syndicates thumb, it was also meant to fulfill a personal vendetta for the surgeon. After this bloody task had been resolved, Ghost set out to recruit the old surgeon into the black ops subdivision of the CIA that employed him.

It was in the moment that Ghost managed the sharp pain through concentrated breathing and focus: meditation. A discipline he learned early on in his days as a splinter cell operative that had ultimately become one of his greatest mental tools to rely upon.

Ghost stared forward into the darkness of the room while he sat beneath the bright white rays of a Welch Allyn medical LED lamp. All the windows had been covered in the safe house. Ghost knew that beyond the shades dusk was setting in, and within the hour the early evening would be shadowed over by the night. This would help him in returning to a newly acquired hotel room near the storage unit he'd secured to house his supplies. Under the cover of the dark he could better ensure he was not followed before he relocated to a new base of operations. The Twins weighed heavily on his mind, but he found it difficult to focus on them and manage the fiery pain radiating through his body at the same time.

The elderly Chinese surgeon said nothing as he diligently repaired the numerous lacerations Ghost had sustained. He never asked any questions, and rarely ever talked. There was always a calming energy around Lu Pang, and Ghost enjoyed his company despite the circumstances. Overall Ghost sustained a little more than a dozen cuts from the psychotic twin he'd engaged in the knife fight, half of which needed serious medical attention and hurt like hell. The scars would only add to the portrait of pain his muscular body put on display when bare and unclothed. When these new wounds healed, they would be forgotten among the old that littered his torso, chest, arms and back. Everything from gunshots, bullet grazes, shrapnel, burns and cuts had left their signature marks upon him, and each scar told a story he would never forget.

Lu Pang snipped the final strand of silk on the last of the wounds needing his attention. He remained accustomed to the older style of sutures rather than the naturally deteriorating stitches for no particular reason, except perhaps for his own sense of nostalgia. His movements were slow and deliberate, giving him the appearance of being frail and unsteady. This appearance, however, was an extreme contradiction to his strong grip in a handshake, and having the steadiest hands Ghost had ever been repaired by. Lu Pang applied an herbal rub over the wounds, making no attempt to be gentle, and proved how a seventy-five year old man could still carry a significant amount of strength. Ghost knew exactly what he would get with Lu Pang's rough touch considering he'd used the master surgeon a number of times through the course of his operations. It may not be the last either.

A thick wrap of gauze soon covered Ghost's forearms and his lower abdomen. Lu Pan went about packing his tools as Ghost shamelessly stripped out of his bloody clothing until he was naked. The doctor handed the patient antibacterial wipes to clean off the remaining blood stains greasing his body. As Ghost dressed, Lu Pang watched and waited while clutching a brown leather Gladstone doctor bag to his chest.

"*Xiexie*," Ghost said. His Chinese was rusty and flat, but his pronunciation was clear.

Thank you.

Lu Pang looked on dully, unimpressed. "*Ni de kouyin bian de geng zao*."

Your accent is worse.

Ghost grinned as the old man criticized his lackluster attempt at speaking to him in his native tongue. "*Jingya ma*?"

Surprised?

A gnarled and wrinkled finger pushed Lu Pang's bifocals higher up the bridge of his nose as he slowly turned his head from side to side. Ghost expected as much.

"*Ni duzi gongzuo*?" Lu Pang asked. He raised his eyebrows in a curious fashion, emphasizing his words with the non-verbal cue.

You work alone?

Ghost hesitated to respond. His relationship with Lu Pang could be easily mistaken as storied history culminating in the doctor's faked death, the death of a Triad boss, and converting the surgeon to a CIA asset within the States. The encounters they shared had formed a bond that would last a lifetime. Ghost knew this all too well as he'd saved Lu Pang's life from the Triad, and the favor had been returned tenfold.

"*Wo mei zai gongzuo*," Ghost said sharply, looking at the old man briefly, and then turning away.

I'm not working.

Lu Pang nodded as though he automatically understood. "*Geren*?"

Personal?

The grim look cast over the features of Ghost's hardened face told Lu Pang everything he needed to know.

"*Jiating*," the old man said to himself, nodding as he understood the violent mystery afflicting his patient.

Family.

Lu Pang fastened the buckle on his bag and slowly rose. He then shuffled his way to the edge of the plastic where he cautiously removed the rubber booties protecting his black Dockers Sinclair dress shoes. Each toe tip moved to each heel, peeling the rubber bootie away from the shoe, and then he slipped out of them onto the hardwood floor. The old surgeon then shuffled a little faster towards the door, which gave him a nearly robotic appearance, but it was just life's natural way of slowing a man down with stiffened muscles and arthritic joints. Lu Pang paused for a moment as he rested one hand on the doorknob, allowing for a long breath to escape his paling lips, passing a sigh as though it carried a heavy toll.

"What is it that you seek?" Lu Pang asked, his English pronunciation halting and dramatic.

Ghost looked at him from across the room, still standing on the opposite side of the bloody plastic draped across the chair and floor. It was rare to hear the old surgeon speak English, let alone speak in general. Tonight, had been the most Ghost had heard him say in a single session. He squeezed into a drab olive-green military jacket. His size and build seemed to threaten the seams of the worn fabric, but it simply fit snuggly. He did not answer Lu Pang.

"Revenge? Justice?" the old surgeon asked. He half turned, but never far enough to make eye contact. A boney finger adjusted his glasses again, pushing them higher up the bridge of his nose.

Ghost said nothing. He wondered if he answered the old man, would Lu Pang begin spouting off ancient Chinese proverbs meant to force him to question his actions.

Lu Pang turned more, but only slightly, barely looking over his left shoulder. "Nothing?"

Ghost looked away for a moment, searching his thoughts, but there was no hiding the truth. "I want my family back."

The old surgeon's head bobbed in agreement, understanding. "Is that possible?"

Ghost closed his eyes, knowing the answer, but he'd never said it out loud. The thought drove him every day and with every move, every action, and every life he took. It was his fuel, but he knew the answer.

Was it possible?

Not only did he know the answer, he knew he would never hear the sweet and innocent laughs of his little girl. He couldn't taste the addictive flavor of his wife's lips ever again. He couldn't see or hold the only people that ever gave a damn about who he wanted to be.

"No," Ghost growled, hating the word as he finally spat it from his mouth.

Lu Pang hesitated to respond, pondering the obvious question. "Then why?"

When the vigilante opened his eyes, his tears rolled freely down his face. He made no attempt to hide his pain, or to bury what he felt in the deepest and darkest place in his soul. There was no shame, and no fear of judgment. There was only a canvas of agony, and Ghost brought to bear these deeper, more damaging wounds to the surface and put them on display just as he had the rest of the scars he carried. His lower lip quivered slightly as he fought through the emotional toll that tore at him with every breath taken. Ghost gritted his teeth for a moment and turned his head away, struggling to compose himself well enough to answer what should have been a simple question.

He knew where Lu Pang was coming from as the old surgeon asked his questions. He knew they shared a form of loss, although the circumstances were quite different. He knew it was what truly solidified what could barely be called a friendship, although it was actually much more. He knew that the old man really cared, and it was devastating to him.

"Because it's what I do," Ghost said, uncertain if he made any sense, even to himself.

Silence filled the space between the old man and the vigilante for a moment, heavy and tense like the weight of the world rested on either man's shoulders. At the same time, it was light and calm. Lu Pang wiped a tear away from his cheek with the aggressive nudge of a bony finger, accompanying the gesture with a sneer. The old surgeon's head nodded in agreement because he knew Ghost spoke the truth, and he sympathized.

"Our families will always pay for our actions in this world," Lu Pang said. "Sooner or later." He turned his entire body towards Ghost and, even with his bifocals present and accounted for, squinted to focus on the man across the room. "My Ming would have been only two years older than your daughter. My great-great granddaughter." He smiled as another tear navigated the wrinkled landscape of his face, unobstructed until it fell off into nothingness. "You did this for me. I will never forget."

Ghost said nothing.

Lu Pang looked around the room without aim, gathering himself as his own horrific memories flooded his mind. They would never let him find peace knowing how he'd worked to give his family a greater life, and yet later on it somehow came back to take it all away. He remembered the massacre his family had endured, and the balance that was quickly delivered; precise and focused. Tremors shook the old surgeon as the painful thoughts overwhelmed him. He held on to the doorknob so that he would remain steady on his feet. Following a deep breath and a notable effort to stop shaking, Lu Pang said three words before he left the room that Ghost would never forget; "Kill them all."

And then Lu Pang was gone.

Ghost had decided this was the only outcome long ago, and he didn't need the old surgeon's reassurance or guidance to come to this conclusion. It did make him think of his next step, and it was only too obvious to him where he needed to begin.

****

If there was one thing Richter could say for Kurikova, it was that he employed an impeccable medical staff. He and Simon had been quickly picked up from Red House Trucking and Distributing and whisked away to an underground medical clinic in Roxbury. They entered through an alleyway entrance and were escorted below ground to an immaculate laboratory made up of multiple rooms. The entire area was completely sterilized and smelled of bleach. Entering the hidden laboratory required them to wear thick rubber booties before passing through a decontamination room. Beyond this sally port was a stainless-steel lined hallway that led to nearly a dozen fully equipped medical rooms, capable of anything from basic medical care to intensive operating procedures and recovery.

Richter and Simon were escorted by burly security guards dressed in neatly tailored suits. Richter couldn't help but notice the cut of the men's jackets. Typically, he'd see security professionals, or those who thought they were, dress to the nines but they forget the tactical positioning they needed to uphold. These men had not floundered this important decorum, and certainly didn't fall into the category of being typical. The professional aspect Richter noticed was that each man's side arm did not print against the fabric of their custom-made suits. He knew they had them, which was nothing special to take note of considering every man openly carried a suppressed Heckler and Koch MP7 submachine gun. The weapon only enhanced the professionalism of the men guarding the facility with respect to its uniqueness in being made adaptable to close quarter combat scenarios, and packing the kind of firepower that would penetrate body armor. Kurikova's *boyeviks* were, without a doubt, specially trained.

More importantly, at least from Simon's point of view, he'd noticed the custom-made combat boots each man wore. Ever the fashion aficionado of the two, he pointed them out for his own amusement as he leaned on his elder brother for support en route down the steel hallway. Simon walked two fingers in the air, and then pointed down. Richter nodded in reply, taking notice. Simon then patted Richter on the chest, leaving behind a pair of bloody handprints, and leaned closer to Richter's ear.

"Gucci," Simon chuckled lightly. His candor was nothing new, but in the moment, it was likely due to the amount of blood loss he'd sustained, giving him an almost euphorically drunken quality. And then he got louder with his observation. "Fuckin' Gucci, brother!"

The laugh told Richter his brother's actions were most definitely due to his blood loss, and the high amount of pain Simon was dealing with. After all, his little brother looked as though he'd survived a slasher film, although during the actual moment of combat he had not let on to any injury. Richter could only imagine that their target had sustained a good amount of pain as well, something he hoped to deliver again in a more potent dosage. Until then, the main goal was to get patched up. It was still early, and there was much to be done.

Richter had not sustained nearly as much damage as his younger brother. He allowed the medical staff, who mysteriously arrived from where Richter could not tell, to separate him and Simon to administer the appropriate amount of care. Within less than a minute Richter's dirty and bloody clothing was cut from his body by a team of nurses, both male and female, as they began their triage.

A female nurse, clearly unconcerned with his shameless nudity, walked him to a shower stall and immediately began rinsing the gore stains from Richter's body. He imagined Simon was undergoing the same experience, but with more assistance. The elder twin coldly stared forward, all business, as the nurse then guided him out of the wet stall. It occurred to him this was not likely normal practice, but, then again, this was not a normal situation. As he was examined, Richter learned he had no open wounds, but a healthy amount of discolored contusions unequally spread about his face, arms, and torso. The aching and burning sensation radiating through his body amplified the discomfort that let him know he was alive, yet he reveled in its capacity to be thankful for the brutal training he'd endured his entire life. Without any warning to his senses his nostrils were suddenly assaulted by a heavily minted liniment that also burned his eyes. A nurse applied the rub to his bruises, avoiding any facial application. Within seconds the affected areas grew slightly numb, and Richter could actually feel as though the swelling from his mild wounds were decreasing.

In the next moment Richter was escorted by a large male nurse, carrying extra weight and not because he was muscular, to a partitioned station with an enclosed X-ray machine. A lead apron was hung and adjusted to the height of Richter's waistline to protect his genitals from exposure. He heard the humming of the machine as it warmed up, and positioned himself as the nurse instructed. He silently noted to himself as a professional that this person must have doubled as an X-ray technician. The sound of a flash and the electronic whine that followed told him the first image had been taken. Instructions from behind the safety barrier were delivered by the male nurse, and Richter turned from one side to the other until three images had been taken.

The nurse then quickly shuffled him away from the X-ray station and back to the main examination area. Within ninety seconds he was dressed in a pair of black sweats, a white tee-shirt, and a pair of black crushed satin slippers sitting on the end of the examination table. Not thirty seconds later a tall man with a full head of dark hair styled like a money hungry wolf from Wall Street, sauntered into the room. It was the doctor. His overly baked brown skin screamed from its tightness stretching over what might have been attractive features thirty years ago. Deep, dark eyes surveyed Richter briefly, careful not to make direct eye contact, and then shot back to the tablet he carried in his hands. Long fingers danced over the touch screen, tapping and swiping, but he did so without saying a word. Richter first thought him to be rude, as many doctors typically were. This man struck the assassin as irregularly arrogant. He was likely a surgeon of some type, perhaps cardiothoracic, and with a god complex from all the lives he'd saved. Richter wondered if he'd taken more than the good doctor had preserved.

"What's up, doc?" Richter spoke, addressing the doctor with his most sinister Bugs Bunny impression. He even accompanied the phrase with a long grin, and the slight bow of his head forcing him to look up ever so slightly with a hint of menace only a real killer could produce.

The doctor froze for a moment as he took in the evil staring back at him. He hesitated to speak, uncertain of what to make of the look on his patient's face.

Richter sat up and smiled. "Loosen up, doc. I'm just playing with you."

Now I really want to kill you.

The doctor snickered marginally, just enough to make him appear as though he had a particular tick as his head twitched to one side like a short electric shock. "Of course," he laughed.

"What's the damage?"

"Nothing serious. No fractures. Obvious pain and swelling and bruising." The doctor's dark eyes finally met the wildness shining out of Richter's visionary orbs. "No worse for wear."

Richter figured as much, and cocked his head to one side as he spoke. "And my brother?"

A long sigh preceded his reply, and the doctor stood there looking at his tablet as he shook his head. "I'm afraid he'll need significant stitching from the numerous lacerations; X-rays as well." He paused and looked at Richter directly for the first time. There was no sign of fear as the doctor knew what kind of patients he would be caring for under Kurikova's employ. But he did show hasty signs of wanting to be over and done with. "The two of you will be here for the afternoon at the very least. My team is going to take very good care of you both."

"This set up is quite impressive, doctor…?" Richter turned his head to one side slightly, offering his ear for the man's name.

A sly grin stretched the surgeon's face. "We don't deal in names here. Only the best care possible."

"Apologies," the twin offered, bowing his head respectfully.

"No need. I understand. Trust me, you're in good hands. You're welcome to remain here until I finish with my other patient — your brother. Or staff can take you to the recovery room."

Richter mulled over the possibilities, but chose to remain in the exam room where he could be closer to Simon. He lay back on the table, finding it abnormally comfortable, and began pondering their next tactical pursuit. As far as he was concerned there was only one move to make, and it was to return to following the FBI agent. It made the most sense given how quickly their target presented himself to them, albeit unknowingly. The problem was this made it even more obvious as their target was clearly watching the agent as well. Richter needed to find where the agent or his Boston detective friend were. Either way, he knew this was the best course of action. Experience told him the simplest way is not always the best way, however, it is still the simplest. The remaining factor would be how to handle the target once they found him, given that he presented an incredibly dangerous opposition as a whole. Richter's ideas began swirling through his mind in a sinister tornado of violent actions when they were abruptly interrupted by one of the nursing staff; a thick little piece whose face was too pretty for the train wreck her body represented.

She smiled brightly as she extended one hand forward, saying, "Sir. Mr. Kurikova is on the line for you."

Richter sat up quickly, his lips nothing more than a thin line etched into his inscrutable face. He dismissed a sense of annoyance at the interruption to his thoughts, and then took the small cell phone the nurse offered with a grim smile. Once she'd relinquished the phone the nurse turned on the ball of one foot and was gone.

"Hello, Yuri," Richter said, "it's been one hell of a day so far."

"I have heard," replied the Wolf. There seemed to be a hint of pleasure in his rough voice. "I have information that is important."

Richter cocked his head to one side. "We both survived, not unscathed, I'm afraid. Thank you for asking." His discontent came through as he spoke, but he neither cared nor believed Kurikova did either. "But I must say, Yuri. This is a fantastic little clinic you have here. Best I've ever been in, I'm afraid."

Kurikova wasted no time getting to his point. "I know you and your brother have been injured. I know you are both fine. You are under my watch, in my city. I know. And I know where you need to go to lure out this man."

The idea perked Richter's interest. Kurikova was being overly informative, which seemed unusual over the phone given how short the crime lord typically operated. "Well, this must be good. Do tell."

Kurikova gave Richter an address, and then paused with an additional request. "Do not just watch this man. Bring him to me."

"Send your goons, Yuri. We kill people, not kidnap them." Richter thought about that statement for a moment. It wasn't entirely true. He and Simon had taken many people just to kill them elsewhere. It wasn't the point. "We're not you couriers."

"I'll double your fee."

Richter's interest heightened. "Well, I suppose a little grab and go won't hurt." Money certainly did talk. And what would it take to snatch the FBI man? Not much between he and Simon, who was certain to be up and running on a full tank of insanity soon enough. He knew how temperamental his sibling got after being bested, and evening the score was the only way to satisfy him.

Kurikova proceeded to relay more details, and it made the decision more appetizing to the twin assassin.

"As long as it doesn't have to be done cleanly," Richter said. "Simon is going to have to let loose after this morning."

"Kill everyone around," the Wolf snarled. "I don't care. It may even be better this way. Just bring him to me alive."

There was no real reason to refuse the request Kurikova proffered. It wasn't out of their way, and it gave them a necessary outlet. Finding some success in what they lived for only boosted morale. And, if lady luck flashed her smile upon them one more time, their target would present himself, as well. It was worth a shot; two birds and all that.

"Deal," Richter said, hanging up the phone.

There was a multitude of ways Richter could plan the secondary objective Kurikova presented. He didn't want to overthink it, and certainly not plan anything without his brother's consent. His mind did work quickly, and every scenario Richter imagined had an outcome that was beneficial to them. There would be blood and violence and a lot of satisfaction. Plan, or no plan, it didn't matter to Richter. Some fun just might come out of this day after all.

Simon is going to be so excited.

Chapter 32
Prepared for the End

Mourning for Vlademir was not going to happen today and, by the way the day continued to unfold with disappointment after disappointment, Yuri Kurikova had to accept the most difficult idea possible: the end was near. The campaign launched against his criminal enterprise was an astonishingly successful one. He could not have predicted anything like this would have ever happened, and now it was out of his control. At every turn he'd lost more and more, all while building around it and acting as though he'd lost nothing. In reality he'd lost too much. The worst aspect of it was that it put a target of vulnerability on his back, and there was no way to work around it anymore. His organization looked weak. However, even in the darkest moments of a man's life, Yuri also knew he could not simply give up. Men of his nature did not quit. He would rise above this challenge and reclaim his position within the world he ruled, or he would die trying. There would be no end without a fight.

To ensure the former option, Yuri's security was strengthened to having two dozen elite trained soldiers at his disposal. These were not Yuri's private guard, but in addition to them. These men were ruthless contracted mercenaries sent by the mysterious Mr. X. The spook had a particular investment in Kurikova's business, and he was not quite ready to see Yuri's legacy fade into insignificance while the Russian was still useful. At the very least the man wanted a return, and Yuri could not guarantee that unless he survived the night, which also meant he would have to take back the control he lost. Knowing such a critical detail, Mr. X, the all-knowing it seemed, had already planned ahead by sending an advancement of men for Yuri's security detail. They were rough, worldly men; skilled in the art of taking lives. The toll could be seen in their dark eyes. It was the look of men who had sold their souls. Yuri knew this all too well. He believed, for the right price, that anyone of them would not hesitate to kill a woman, child, kitten, or grandmother. They fit right in.

The Kurikova patriarch was unaccustomed to being a victim. It was a role that did not suit him. He hunted. He killed. He was the alpha. Mr. X's strong advisement to remain at home, essentially as bait for the vigilante, cast a shadow of doubt over the Wolf he did not care for. That the mysterious man suggested this was as though Yuri could not handle his business. What Mr. X did not understand was that the vigilante was on Yuri's turf now — his hunting grounds. There was no pack alive that would tolerate invasion of their territory and, maybe, after all this time Yuri was not given enough credit for allowing this killer to come to his doorstep. There was no better place to end things, one way or another, and Yuri felt as though his greatest advantage rested where he could control everything. After all, a plan that went unspoken was still a plan.

Mr. X had strongly disagreed.

The charismatic spy said boastfully, "Some men, Yuri, as you well know, are forces of nature. Through strength, discipline, training, and an ungodly amount of determination, these men exist as living myths. They're like demigods. I do my best to employ them. Pay them well. After all, they're world-breakers. It's what they're meant to do. Topple governments. Assassinate. Infiltrate. Hell, even bring other parties to power." He paused as he laughed. "They are extraordinary assets, Yuri. Unbelievably exceptionable. They could have been surgeons, lawyers, scientists, anything they desired." Mr. X paused again, creating a more dramatic effect, altering his tone as he became slightly more serious. "Except, Yuri, there is an inherent abnormality coded into their DNA that sets them apart, making them Tier One operators. Do you know what that is?"

The conversation at the time annoyed the Russian. This was not the kind of information he'd wanted, or thought he needed, to hear. "Do tell," he replied.

"I'm glad you're interested. This is the important part."

Yuri waited to be enlightened by Mr. X, feeling the tension build. He noticed his breathing became heavier as his chest lifted and fell harder with every deeper inhalation. His fist clenched with annoyance, putting up with this manipulative asshole's antics. Damn it if he was able to do anything about it.

"These men, my friend, like your Spetznaz, are born killers. They may not know it at first, or maybe they do, but they're unsure what to do about it. It's a question of morals, except it's a fluid question for them. They don't want to abide by these morals. Not simply to be criminal, but because there's a primal calling within them they don't understand; or, it goes against the grain of society's civil and ethical codes hammered into the minds of every living being walking the earth. These men, men like yours and mine, are elite, no-questions-asked killers, soldiers even. They are necessary in this world. And if they answer that true calling, beyond successes of money and fame and glamor, they are the ones who truly make this world a better place because they will do *anything* to protect it if given the appropriate target."

"You're becoming too long winded, *friend*," Yuri stated, sure to emphasize his discontent with the final word.

Mr. X had laughed. "Apologies, I just get so caught up sometimes in the intricacies of the moment."

"Can you skip to the point, please? After what you have told me I need to make preparations."

"Of course, Yuri. Here's the bottom line." Again Mr. X paused; old habits and such. "The man who is after you eats men like these for dinner. As a measure of nature, they may be a Category three hurricane, maybe fives, and he is a ten, Yuri."

The Wolf sat in disbelief, smirking to himself as Mr. X's metaphor logically fell apart. "Your system of measurement does not exist."

"Precisely."

A light click sounded, and a dial tone followed.

This had left Yuri in an uncomfortable state. It was not unlike Mr. X to make him, or anyone, feel as though they were insignificant. Yuri was well aware of this in the man's nature, which he felt was more for effect than anything, despite his continued success with the technique. What made him uncomfortable was the way Mr. X spoke; his tone became ominous. Goosebumps padded Yuri's skin as though a chill had blown in from the balcony of his den. In a moment of uncertainty Yuri had considered he was affected because he sensed something in Mr. X that the man could not help conveying, but perhaps he had not meant to. The more puzzling aspect of it was that Yuri would have never suspected Mr.

X to be the kind of man this revealed him to be capable of being. Mr. X, for all of Yuri's knowledge and business dealings with him, was a rogue spy and criminal mastermind with fingers in the pots of many organizations, making him insanely powerful. Yuri knew he was surrounded by the most dangerous men in the world. But Yuri had heard it in his voice, something profound and abnormal given his lethality, and Mr. X was afraid.

This revelation had all but convinced Yuri to remain at his estate for a cliché showdown with the enemy at the gate. There was no other way to deal with the matter. This vigilante, who Mr. X was afraid of, was truly a force of nature; a world-breaker, as the man said. He'd proven time and time again to not only be capable, but unstoppable. But what if two dozen hardened, elite trained military specialists waited for him, prepped for him, and coveted the opportunity to challenge him? Would he be unstoppable then? There's no way he could prepare for such a thing, could he? Yuri considered everything possible. The man was clearly informed, so he would expect a heavy guard, but not necessarily one of this caliber. It was likely he would consider his Spetznaz trained men, and then the *boyeviks* in heavy numbers. They were no push overs, but they were not elite trained.

Or, would the man's plans be overkill in general? Would he expect more than should be present, and more men with better training? Would he proceed to strike where he would have the tactical advantage? The variations were mind boggling. Yuri's thoughts were bordering paranoia with the number of scenarios his imagination came up with. He couldn't discount anything though.

Casually, he walked through his den and poured himself a shot of vodka. And then another. The warmth was comforting, but not as helpful as he'd wanted it to be. For the first time since he was a boy, he felt nervous. The sensation was irritating. Being angry was easy, yet he couldn't quite fully manage the emotion. Mr. X's words stuck in his head, 'The man who is after you eats men like these for dinner.' The compliment to the vigilante's capabilities, or a warning to Yuri, or both, was a matter of perspective. Either way the Wolf intended on having his revenge for Vladimir, even if it meant he would have to sacrifice himself.

Yuri strode out to the balcony, reflecting on the loss of his son, seeing him here in this doorway last. He paused to touch the doorframe where Vlad had stood before he'd left to bring in DeMarte. This is where his son's spirit would remain, watching over him as he always had. And if Yuri survived the night, he would forever believe Vlademir was with him, like a devil on his shoulder.

Chapter 33
Feels Like Home

A lot could be learned in a quiet car ride if there was nothing else to focus on but the scenery and time. The silence provided that for Stone despite the intoxicated feeling that consumed him. For instance, he learned McCrary lived within twenty minutes of the bar he'd holed up in for the day, which told him the detective was a resident of the Charlestown neighborhood of Boston. To his right was the flowing boundary of Mystic River, and among the mix of brick townhouses and triple decker homes they arrived at their destination of McCrary's residence. This compassionate invitation reminded Stone of something he failed to pay attention to, although he only acknowledged it subconsciously: Boston was McCrary's community, a historical landmark scarred by an unprecedented amount of violence that once again etched its place in history with blood. The idea of it was sad enough, let alone to experience such a tragedy. Even worse was the thought of ultimately being the catalyst that sparked it all.

Stone briefly thought back to every city he'd chased the vigilante to and wondered if he'd ever taken this deeply personal detail into consideration with the others who'd guided him through their terrorized streets. Had he cared that their home was being tarnished with brutality? Had he respected the people assigned to help him in the manner they deserved? It couldn't be helped to suddenly ask himself a slew of questions that unexpectedly overwhelmed him. And for what? Because of McCrary's kindness? The agent felt a resoundingly disturbing turn in his stomach at the thought that he had not, and here was one of Boston's finest taking pity on him to bring him into their life, their home, and treat him with more respect than he deserved. Stone felt sick, and it wasn't because of the whiskey.

As McCrary parked along the street, quiet and brooding in the haze of the dashboard lights, Stone turned to him, humbled by the detective's kindness and understanding. "Thank you," he said, looking at McCrary, unable to maintain eye contact, and then looking down to the darkness of the floorboard.

The detective surveyed the G-man like the wounded animal that he was. He'd been in Stone's shoes before; shameful of the pain he hid inside, grappling with the demons he thought no one else would understand. McCrary thought about it for a moment and realized he'd been there more than once, too many times, but there was no shame in it. It was a part of the job. It came with the culture of hunting monsters people didn't want to know existed, and seeing things that could never be unseen. Even more so, it was about having to make decisions a man never thought he would have to make. Life or death decisions, not just for themselves, but for others, too. He could see that Stone carried a heavy burden on his soul in the way it physically curled his normally confident stature into a slumped over shell of a man.

"Yah welcome," McCrary said, patting the agent on the shoulder, nodding in acknowledgment of his own empathy. "Now get the fuck outta' my car before dinner gets cold."

Laughter erupted from deep within both men, comprehending the shared darkness of the humor accepted within their profession. For Stone it eased the tension of the regret he felt, solidifying the natural comradery working so closely with another agent or officer provided in their line of work. It was unspoken, and the sarcastic dig in the inappropriate moment was like a rite of passage. McCrary clapped Stone on the shoulder once more, smiling and laughing harder than he had in far too long. He threw open the car door and hesitated to get out, considering the affirmation of the moment as an undying bond, not just because they were professionals in the same field and Devil Dogs in the fraternity of war veterans, but because it made them something far more than brothers in arms. Like the prideful attributes Boston was known for, McCrary felt a decisive closeness to Stone after what they'd endured and persevered through in the last forty-eight hours. Going through that kind of hell together made them family.

McCrary waited for Stone to balance every wavering step he took. The sight of a man who suddenly couldn't walk around the front of a car and was known for having his shit together made the detective laugh again. He watched Stone pause and cover his face with one hand in an ill attempt of hiding his own comical response.

"Come on, Agent Stone," McCrary cackled. "You walked outta' the bar just fine. What the fuck happened?" He bent forward as he laughed louder and harder, clapping a knee with a large hand. "Hurry up, Audrey's got coffee brewing strong, especially for you. That cup o' Joe clearly wasn't worth a shit."

Stone continued to laugh without taking a single step. McCrary reached out and guided the G-man towards the steps of his home, suggesting he use the railing to help with the steep ascent. At the entrance McCrary unlocked the door and threw it open to give Stone a wide birth. The agent couldn't control his laughter, which in turn further restricted his ability to walk straight. Once inside the home McCrary gently shut the door and locked it again. Despite the uproar of drunken and misguided humor, this detail caught Stone's attention and forced him to control himself to speak.

"What's the matter?" Stone asked, using the corner of an adjacent doorway to hold him up. "You don't feel safe at home?"

McCrary's amusement stymied for a moment, letting the diversion fade away into scrutiny. He cleared his throat as he removed his jacket, searching for the right words to explain even though he owed no one an explanation. It crossed his mind that it might seem odd for a police officer to be overly diligent in locking his front door, but memories of a violent youth told him that a locked door was his first line of defense against a wicked world.

"Always have," the detective stated, his gravelly voice filled with a nearly unnoticeable tinge of pain. "After the things we see day in and day out, we know we're never really safe anywhere."

The depth of McCrary's words prohibited any form of retort, and it effectively shut down any delight Stone had felt. The dark squint McCrary viewed the world through returned, and his solemn features became set in their default position. It was far too easy to sense the grim taste of tragedy laced in McCrary's words, so Stone said nothing and simply nodded. After all, the detective made a compelling argument.

"That you, Randal?" a voice called from within the depths of the

McCrary home. The sweet tone was clearly feminine, but with a sharp edge to it, and no hint of a Bostonian accent.

Stone had seen any number of transformations people were capable of, such as how McCrary recently went from upbeat to sorrowful in an instant, sparked by a single, indescribable thought. Rarely did these emotional highs and lows immediately reverse, but Stone witnessed just that. With the calling of his name McCrary answered the delicate chime of the woman's voice as though a blanket of warmth had been mysteriously wrapped around him. It didn't simply encompass his physical being, it radiated from within the hardened man's spirit, and it showed when he smiled softly. The agent couldn't help but feel some form of transference of McCrary's mood, and the dark weight they carried from the gloom of the moment unexpectedly became as light as a feather. McCrary's squint became less intense, and his eyes opened slightly wider. Light damn near sparkled from his entire being, and flush redness filled the fair finish of his cheeks. Stone knew what he saw as it occurred in real time; something he hadn't seen in far too long. He saw a man in love and, beyond the stupor of the whiskey he'd consumed, it was overwhelmingly intoxicating.

"It's me, hon'," McCrary called back, his happiness rang clearly in his heavy voice, and a grin remained after he spoke.

"I thought I was gonna' have to send out a search party for you!" the woman called, her playful banter forcing her to giggle.

Stone watched as McCrary melted and he knew that it was not only his wife Audrey speaking to him, but that she was the man's heart. He'd never seen anything quite like this before. It was certainly nothing he'd experienced, at least not in this way. For Stone the greatest love he'd felt was with what family he'd had left in this world, his sister and niece, Veronica and Chloe, and they were no more. The reflection was painful enough without the amplified stimulation the alcohol provided. Stone fought off a trembling lip as his breathing quickly stuttered against his efforts, and a tear escaped from the corner of his right eye. He turned away to hide it, masking its removal with a yawn and a quick swipe of his hand.

McCrary was too entranced to notice Stone's reaction, but he could feel it as he replied to his wife. "I brought a guest, hon'. No need to wrangle the boys to find me."

A stiff slap assaulted Stone's chest to gain his attention. When he turned to face McCrary, the detective waived for him to follow.

"Well, get your asses in here. Dinner's ready!" Audrey announced.

Stone couldn't help but smirk at the alteration in the woman's manners. He heard McCrary chuckle as he turned back to address him, and the G-man saw a spark of satisfaction in the detective's eyes. It wasn't just a star struck twinkle representation of the man's love for his audacious spouse. It went well beyond the basic emotion. Stone suddenly felt as though he were in the nostalgic presence of Carrie Grant or Frank Sinatra. McCrary was calm and collected, yet the look in his eye screamed, *That's my girl*! That singular moment displayed a sense of pride that opened up the armored heart McCrary carried, and Stone stood pleasantly envious of his Bostonian liaison. All he could do was smile.

"She's a schoolteacher, not a saint," McCrary said, dismissively shrugging his shoulders with a grin.

Stone walked by McCrary and patted him on the shoulder saying, "I beg to differ, my friend."

****

Dinner was simple, yet classy, as Audrey lovingly served up a mean steak with buttered red potatoes, brown sugar squash, and a sautéed medley of vegetables. The agent couldn't remember the last time he'd eaten so well, and the Saint of School Teachers was ready to pack him a to-go box before his plate was cleaned. McCrary seemed to relish the sight of his wife bossing around the sobering Stone left and right as she continued to fill a mug of atomic black coffee and a large glass of ice water.

"Drink up, baby face," she ordered, smiling at the sound of her demand. "This will flush that shit out of your system, I'll tell you!"

Amazingly Stone hadn't witnessed the woman sit still long enough to eat as time flew by, but she had as the conversation moved back and forth between the trio. Audrey had the habit of sitting, putting in her two cents, and then neurotically finding something else to do in the kitchen.

McCrary turned out to be good company. Or at least better company than he had been. Stone learned of the man's time in the Marine's, battles won and lost, not just in the field. They shared a number of service stories which consisted of bitching about commanding officers dissatisfied reprimands for multiple forms of comical insubordinations. Laughs roared into the evening, and Stone had a fleeting sense of what a home should feel like. Audrey continued to be the angel McCrary dismissed her for being, while his eyes told a completely different story.

In between sittings and chiming in, Audrey also worked on finishing a cake in the kitchen, constructing the triple layers of a chocolate caramel masterpiece worthy of gracing any number of baking cook off shows. Stone didn't think he could stomach eating anything else, but Audrey's insistence was irrefutable.

"This right here was my grandmother's recipe," Audrey said. Her short stature placed her about chest high to McCrary, but it was inconsequential in the moment. The woman was larger than life; outspoken, bold, direct, and eloquent all at the same time. "She taught me how to cook, bake, iron, and take no shit. She put all that attitude into her food, and I'll be damned if you'll ever love a chocolate cake like this ever again."

The sincerity and assuredness Audrey directed at Stone made him feel as though he were a student back in elementary school, and he was 'this close' from getting sent to the principal's office.

"Yes, ma'am," Stone replied, instantly feeling as sober as he could possibly be.

McCrary noticed the look on the G-man's face and couldn't help but comment. He'd worn the same look many times. "Careful now. You keep this up and she's gawna' break out the rula'."

Stone and McCrary shared a laugh.

"And you be careful, smart ass," Audrey chirped. "You weren't complaining about the ruler the other night." The amount of sass emitted from the tiny schoolteacher was reminiscent of liberated steam, and she'd just burned her husband with it.

Wide eyed and curious Stone turned to McCrary only to find the once surly detective red in the face with embarrassment. A witty rebuttal quickly followed.

"I didn't hear anyone else complain' eitha'," McCrary shot back.

Audrey winked as a devilish grin turned up one corner of her thin, red lips. "And you're not going to."

The little woman turned on her heels and disappeared into the kitchen once again. McCrary continued to engage in conversation with Stone as his wife exited the room. His eyes never averted from her petite figure, fully entranced until she vanished around the corner.

Amusement and relaxation were the theme of the night. There had been enough darkness over the past two days to warrant an eclipse, and Stone was glad to be able to forget it all for an evening. More war stories followed, both in service and from their law enforcement careers. McCrary was a much more compassionate man than Stone would have ever realized, even in the early years of his service, and it showed. He saw a man who'd been there and done that; a man who'd survived tragedy in Iraq during Operation Desert Storm, when an improvised explosive device decimated half of the squad he led; a man who'd talked down more suicidal people than Stone had ever heard of just by listening to them and sympathizing with the daily struggles he endured to protect the public; a man who's demons reared their ugly heads every time he heard a gunshot, or loud blast of any kind, and it forced him to grit his teeth and remind himself he was strong and okay. The experience in life that McCrary shared with him left Stone in awe.

As a boy Stone had grown up watching old westerns with his father. 'The Duke' was by far his favorite, with Clint Eastwood, typically the Man with No Name, being a close second. Stone had looked up to these characters as the mythical being they were, always doing what was right, sometimes doing what no one else could, and usually for the right reasons. Yet, before him now, as he listened to McCrary talk about his old days, the agent realized he was sitting with those men in a triple decker home smack dab in the middle of Boston's prideful city. McCrary was an urban cowboy, a gunslinger, and Stone was honored to know the detective in an entirely different light.

****

Audrey McCrary was a hustler and a bustler. She didn't waste a step, a breath, or a word. Her mind moved too quickly for her body to keep up, especially after nearly forty-seven years, but it wasn't for lack of trying.

She just kept moving. Had to. Life was too short not to. This evening provided her with a chance to enjoy and show off her Randal. Company in their home had been scarce anymore since Randal was investigated by Internal Affairs. Some of the old timers would still come by for barbecues and Patriots' games, but they weren't frequent visits. It was embedded in her heart to nurture, and she absolutely relished the opportunity to entertain.

When Audrey first learned of their guest, she nearly went overboard with planning dinner, and Randal had to reel her in a few notches to keep her from damn near planning a full-blown party. She couldn't help it. This was before he'd left the house this morning. As the day moved on, surging forward with her unbridled energy, she taught a fantastic series of middle school classes to children who somehow brightened her day even more. She and her husband communicated regularly via text message. Typically, it was just little messages here and there, checking in and filling each other on their day. It was a mutual component they agreed upon. She worried about him, and he didn't want her to feel that way. Randal held a high standard of integrity, which led him to be vague in the details about his day-to-day investigations, not that she wanted the grisly specifics. That all changed when Randal sent her a text late in the morning. And it continued with the next and every message after that.

Working with FBI Special Agent Stone was a subliminal repercussion from the force. It wasn't that Randal was hated for what he'd done; it was that he wasn't loved as much for what he didn't do. Audrey hated the Blue Brotherhood code. She hated everything it stood for, and when Randal did what was right, he was punished by them for it. He had no business working with this agent on a manhunt after riding the desk for six months. That was how Audrey saw it. The desk job and paper pushing kept Randal safe, which mattered to her the most, yet it was killing the man. She hated that and what it had done to their marriage. Ever the good wife, Audrey stood beside Randal, supporting him and keeping him as strong as she could, even as he slid into a darker version of himself no one could have imagined. In truth, Agent Stone's arrival saved her husband from a depression she never thought he'd bounce back from. Randal had literally returned to being the man she originally married, before the reprimand, with a single phone call.

The spark in their relationship returned immediately. Even after the first hard day Randal's rejuvenation made a triumphant return. Audrey was grateful for having her husband back even as she wondered what cost it would come with. Despite the horror of the case he worked and the motivation of the department for putting Randal on it with Stone, he somehow remained positive, at least in her presence. She adored that about him: making the best of things. They had been through more than their fair share of hard times with many of the cases he worked, and maybe more so with the cases he couldn't. It added to their strength facing down adversity as a team.

Today proved to test their strength again and Audrey insisted on having Stone over for dinner. Randal had protested it after the first day he had, but she wouldn't have it. He'd first come home after doing all he could for the poor victims they discovered, and informed her of the details involving Stone. Randal was angry with him and his secrets. He had said, "This guy's draggin' me into a rabbit hole, and it leads straight to hell." Audrey listened, as she always did, never truly understanding the conflict her husband struggled with. It was all she could do, really, and she was happy to do it. She held herself to the standard of being the consummate policeman's bride, slightly old school and traditional, but with some attitude. Randal was hurting again, all too soon for her taste, and there was no way she could stay quiet.

"We're doing dinner with this Stone," Audrey had told her husband. Randal had looked at her with an irritation he rarely displayed. She wasn't having it, though. "First, I went and started prepping dinner for three already." It was more like for ten, but these hard-working men needed to eat. "And second," Audrey crawled onto her husband's lap this morning at the very table he sat at now, "if you're hurting like this after just one day, I want you to ask yourself a question, babe."

Audrey lifted Randal's chin so she could look into him. In the moment his hazel eyes had lost the glow she'd seen them dawned with recently. That pained her deeply, and she felt she had to do something.

"What do I ask m'self, hon?" Randal asked apathetically.

"I want you to ask yourself, how does this guy feel? How has this affected him?"

Randal's face had scrunched into an expression of confusion.

"What?"

Audrey's sass turned on hot. "Look, you said he's been at this alone for a while, right?" Randal nodded. "So, imagine where he's at right now. Quit being so damn selfish. If you feel like this right now, after what you've told me, imagine how he's doing."

Randal had looked away, seemingly ashamed. It wasn't Audrey's desired effect, but she also knew it would make him think. He would know she was right, but she already had the solution.

"Hey," she yelped, playfully smacking Randal on the cheek. Her smile brought back the light in his eyes. "Bring him to dinner. We need some life back in this place, and I bet he could use the company." She sounded as though she had asked a question as she'd looked around the room, thinking of opening the drapes, letting the light back in, and how good it would feel. "Let's have him over for dinner. Everyone needs someplace to feel like home."

And that was that.

Audrey hummed to herself as she lathered the triple layered chocolate caramel cake in a thick, homemade icing. The look of it reminded her of something off of the show *Cake Wars*, and the thought crossed her mind once to submit an application to the show. It was a fleeting thought because Audrey enjoyed baking for herself and Randal. She lightly sprinkled powdered sugar over the top of the cake, and strategically placed cherries to add to its aesthetic.

"*Voila*!" Audrey said to herself.

Her little hands lifted the weighty dessert and shifted it to a clear space on her island counter. Immediately she began clearing and wiping down the counter, filling the dish sink and letting utensils and dishes soak, cleaning without fully cleaning. Laughter from the dining room warmed her heart. Audrey couldn't help but smile. Her home hadn't had this kind of energy in it in so long she couldn't help but cherish being able to think back on the memory of it and the night wasn't over yet.

Curvy hips swayed back and forth as Audrey naturally moved in hyper speed. Her short steps made her look faster than she likely was, moving in a manner that Randal lovingly described as a 'vixen's waddle.' It wasn't the most tasteful of compliments, but Randal's sometimes odd humor made it worthwhile. He even called in to see if she needed help, and she politely declined.

"No, thank you, hon'," Audrey chimed. "You'll just get in my way."

Audrey travelled back and forth through the kitchen, making room in the dishwasher for what was to be transferred from the sink. There was no hurry to finish cleaning up, with the exception of being able to gaze upon her husband as he finally enjoyed an evening. It was all she wanted tonight, to heal and love with some joy and laughter, and it was all coming together nicely.

Once the dishwasher was reloaded, Audrey moved to the cupboard and removed three plates. She had to stretch to reach them when the stack was full, ascending to her tippy toes, and masterfully guiding the dishes into the security of her tiny hands. The dishes clanked when Audrey briefly set them down to close the cupboard door, still humming through a bright smile, eyes nearly forced shut as her prominent cheeks and age reacted to the muscular reaction. As she lifted the plates and spun, a movement she had inherently done since she was a child, Audrey involuntarily paused; an instinctual reaction for her when confronted by a jolting fear. She froze. Her eyes went wide. The hesitation kept her from screaming when it was most critical. This left the frightened void of shock in her mind at a moment of absolute stillness. There were no forced thoughts. Audrey witnessed a short burst of white light she would never have to explain, drowning in what her brain finally registered as her final moment on earth. In the space and time of her last seconds she remembered her husband's smiling face, the glaze of satisfaction in his eyes when he looked upon her after the finality of their recent love making, and the safety in the way he held her.

In this moment Audrey wanted nothing more than to cry for help; to summon her knight in shining armor for protection. The thought took too long to register. Between her shock and fear there was no telling if she could have ever reacted in time to make any kind of difference for herself. She was supposed to be safe here in her home amongst the needed joy felt this evening, and the resounding laughter that had been absent before tonight. The last sound Audrey McCrary heard was the dual metallic whisper of a suppressed pistol.

Chapter 34
When Angels Fall

It was the spray of blood that caught McCrary's attention, flickering out of his peripheral to his right, splashing across the void of culinary space beyond the doorway.

It was the wet slap of Audrey's sanguine fluid impacting against the cabinets and walls around her that somehow echoed in McCrary's mind.

It was the immediate overwhelming melting pot of anguish that boiled over with sadness and anger, pain and rage, shock and numbness. These heavy substances planted him in his seat like a well rooted tree, weighing him down with an unpronounceable grief. He became lost in a moment of violence that could never be taken back, or forgotten.

Time halted for what would ultimately turn out to be the briefest of moments, as if an enigmatic force had taken control of reality, hitting the pause button, and then slowly allowing it to painfully inch forward. Within that prolonged juncture an inescapable tearing occurred within the heart of a husband as he bore witness to the crumbling of his entire world in an instant, watching the infrastructure of what his life meant to him, imploding into irreparable pieces, and being tossed out like everyday trash.

McCrary sat frozen. Stunned. He swore he felt his heart stop beating. There were no breaths to take. Oxygen held no importance. His eyes didn't blink. Every sense within him quickly became hyper-powered and, in the darkest moment he never could have imagined, he saw more clearly than he ever had before.

He couldn't help but watch, wide eyed and horrified, his soul twisting and turning in an evaporated storm of emotion guided by what he witnessed, and it drowned him in disbelief. McCrary had no choice but to accept that what he saw was real. The loving husband was well aware of his surroundings; of the conversation he and Stone were engaged in; of the cake's sweet scent wafting through the house that would now be tarnished with the stench of gunpowder and death.

As the tragedy played out Audrey's body dropped to the floor in intermittent pulses that coincided with the amplified beats of his heart threatening to explode within his chest.

1… Her body cascaded downward, nearly parallel to the floor.

2… McCrary saw the trio of plates separating in midair and following her descent.

3… Audrey first touched the floor, eyes suspended in terror, mouth gaped open in horrific bewilderment.

The impact of Audrey's body sent a reverberation through the shell she left behind with an elastic-like ripple. Her head thumped against the floor multiple times before she came to rest. Her beautiful locks of hair bounced and waived with the concussion of the fall, blood cascading from her skull as though a bottle of Pinot Noir had been broken wide open, desecrating her memories on the linoleum.

The crashing of the dessert plates Audrey held came next. A high-pitched banshee's cry of shattering dishware screeched its way into the atmosphere. Every fracture resounded throughout McCrary's home with an exaggerated effect, mimicking a fictitious scream Audrey never had the chance to exhale. The delusional outcry quickly registered the event in his mind at full speed, finally launching the detective into action.

****

In the midst of Audrey's assassination McCrary missed the sudden response from Stone. The FBI agent was already pushing away from the table, drawing his sidearm from his hip, yelling for the detective to move. Flashes of the event seemed to replay within McCrary's mind's eye a hundred times, quickly working into a rapid and repetitive vision of his wife's ruination. When he finally responded his roulette wheel of emotions landed on rage, and all he saw was red.

McCrary's home quickly exploded into a war zone.

Stone stumbled back from the table; his heavy inebriation not quite dissolved from the meal. He caught himself against the wall and kicked his chair out of the way. As he steadied himself, the G-man watched

McCrary maniacally flip the end of the dining table high into the air over his head, duck under it, and drive it towards the kitchen doorway. Before McCrary blocked the passageway, Stone caught a glimpse of a shadow quickly moving their direction. The detective moved in one continuous motion, slamming the table against the doorway and, as he held it there with one hand, McCrary skillfully drew his pistol. Rapid trigger pulls erupted as McCrary emptied the magazine through the table at chest height into the kitchen, wood splinters littering the air with every round as he fired at multiple angles. His rage was vocalized by a guttural roar that seemed to have no end, nearly as loud as each bullet the pistol dispensed.

The action was meant to catch Audrey's killer off guard, and contain them in the kitchen for the moment. It was unconventional, brazen and completely uncharacteristic of the calculated and organized detective Stone had come to know. McCrary spun to his right, away from the doorway, as he ejected the spent magazine. He was already retrieving a full replacement from his hip as he moved. The detective's timing couldn't have been more perfect as return fire burst through the table. The killer was still functional, and each shot they fired was suppressed. Stone dove to the floor to avoid taking any rounds, and answered back with his own shots.

McCrary was back in the fight within seconds. His free hand reached to the table, not to hold it in place, but to remove the barricade. He was ready to take the killer on face to face. Stone shot forward to the wall, opposite of McCrary, and rose into a kneeling position farther off to the left while he reloaded his firearm.

Glass shattered at the front of the house, and for another punishing moment time elapsed with a dazed effect. A bright white illumination flashed through the dining room with an ethereal and blinding effect coupled with a thunderous concussive force. Stone and McCrary had no choice but to turn away from the fire fight and protect their eyes and ears from the flash bang's powerful effects. The desired disorientation was achieved, reducing them to cowering fetuses on the floor.

The distraction device was immediately followed by multiple gunshots from heavy slugs that blew the hinges off the front door to McCrary's home. Wood splintered into the house's interior along with the scattering of the warped metal hinges violently stripped from the doorframe. A tall, lanky built man entered next, moving with tactical skill, and holding a KSG shotgun in a forward moving position. He wore nothing to protect his identity. Instead the man openly presented a face with intricately designed facial hair, an unstable glare in his eyes, and a scowl so angrily strained the devil would burn with envy.

McCrary tried to aim his pistol in the direction of the front door, unable to clearly see yet, but desperate to survive. His attempt was quickly thwarted as a strong hand twisted his Glock from his grip, and then skillfully twisted McCrary's wrist in a way that effortlessly rolled him head over heels. It was the killer who'd shot Audrey, a tall, black clad man who was clean shaven, and identical to the second arrival. Stone thrashed forward in a blind attempt to aid McCrary, however, he too was disarmed and tossed across the room. The killer turned to McCrary while delivering a heavy boot to the detective's face as he tried to rise, staying in the fight only to be sent reeling in pain.

"Put him down!" yelled the bearded assassin.

The first killer was calm, poised with an expression blank of all emotion, and hyper-focused. He aimed his suppressed pistol at McCrary, a black gloved finger moving to the trigger as the sights set on the detective. McCrary was far too dazed to realize he was under the gun as what he could see of the room spun in a tipping and turning circular motion. The house rocked once more from a jarring blast and a glaring light. Both killers reeled away from the center of the room. The shot meant to kill the detective went wide and missed him completely.

No one saw the cylindrical device tossed in from the kitchen that exploded almost immediately as it entered the room.

Painful screams, both physical and prideful, played like a horrific soundtrack. Senses were thrown off track, and the disorientation pummeled everyone with full effect. The bearded killer tried to shield his eyes and raise the shotgun for defense while he stumbled drunkenly, off balance from the distortion set upon his equilibrium. A short series of gunshots knocked him backwards, punching him square in the chest, and dropped him to the floor. Following this, another series of gunshots blasted the first killer from behind, driving him into the wall and to the floor beyond where Stone lay dazed and confused.

****

Among the mist of gun smoke and violence, a lion among wolves strode into the room from the kitchen to set order in the world. The hulking mass filled the doorway as he passed through, eyes vigilant and scanning, not wasting any movement. McCrary was to his right aimlessly searching the floor for his pistol, or just trying to get his bearings. The man grabbed him by the lapels of his shirt and hauled the detective to his feet, assisting him into the kitchen where he sat him on the floor, paying no attention to placing the husband in direct sight of his murdered wife.

The man moved back to the dining room with his pistol forward, again scanning as he entered. All threats were still down. He crouched near Stone and checked him for a pulse at his carotid artery. The agent was still alive. He made no attempt to wake Stone. Instead he scanned the two black clad men he knew to be the Twins, professional assassins, and looked for any sign of movement before he turned his attention to getting the agent the hell out of there. He slowly counted to five in his head before cautiously giving Stone the attention needed to get his dead weight moving.

It turned out the Twins were more patient than was expected, and they took the opportunity to turn the vigilante's caution in their favor. That's when they attacked.

Chapter 35
Pin Drop

Chaos was a familiarity that Simon had grown accustomed to throughout his life from the moment he was aware of the path he and Richter would pursue. Raised and groomed to be assassins was not a choice they had made as orphans, but a decision forced upon them by diabolical forces they had never faced. He would not take back the lessons taught through rigorous and, more often than not, violent instruction. Neither would his identical twin brother. Together they had risen through the ranks of achievement to become a razor-sharp team; doppelgangers of madness and death, and for the longest time they knew no equal.

Until now.

Their target had been easy enough to find thanks to information provided by Yuri 'the Wolf' Kurikova. Then Kurikova issued a new order that was sure to bring Simon and Richter face to face with the only rival they had ever known. The fantasy of the idea made Simon's mouth water with hunger for redemption. He had never lost a fight, or let one go unfinished, so the opportunity to finish what was started between them doubled his excitement. However, being dropped on his ass as soon as he entered the scene was not a part of the strategy. The detective's home was not the battleground he and Richter had hoped for, yet they had come prepared.

Simon took a practical approach in prepping for the assault on the Boston detective's home and wore a special type of body armor known as Dragon's Skin. The new age material was stab resistant as well as bulletproof. Richter had been so kind as to demonstrate its effectiveness with a point black shot from a twelve-gauge shotgun loaded with heavy birdshot. Simon preferred slugs with this type of weapon, but Richter knew the practicality of the armors defense, and a slug would definitely rip through the interwoven Kevlar based material. High-powered rifle rounds meant certain death. But the Dragon's Skin was also a soft armor fabric, and Simon was not a fan of wearing heavy trauma plates. Richter had always preached being light, quick, and functional, something that had always paid off. The advanced body armor could definitely stop large caliber pistol rounds, but they still hurt like a bitch.

Simon could attest to this fact as he slowly returned to consciousness on the living room floor of the detective's home. The target's rounds had knocked him backwards with such intensity that he had bounced his head off the hardwood floor, whipping his feet into the air over his head, and then fully rolling over once more until he lay on his back. It was a miracle the McCrary's didn't have a coffee table for him to crash through after his involuntary acrobatic demonstration. Nonetheless, Simon recovered quickly. He always did. Through numerous sparring sessions during training with Richter, both past and present, they had exchanged a number of blows that had rendered either of them unconscious. Simon remembered recovering faster than his brother, but it was not always a blessing. Richter had mentioned it as being a point where he thought too many strikes to the head may have caused Simon irreparable damage, resulting in his bouts of psychopathy. The younger brother reassured him the intense sparring had nothing to do with it, and that he had come by his madness honestly.

As Simon awoke, he raised his head slowly, fighting back the blistering ache in his chest where the bullets had struck him. The bruises that would follow would only add to what damage already existed. He squelched a painful grunt, scanning the room as best he could from his supine position. The detective was across the open room, parallel to Simon, where the living room bled into the dining room. McCrary was aimlessly crawling about the floor beyond the doorway of the kitchen reeling from the shock of the flash bang grenade. Richter was off to his right on this side, also down on the floor, unmoving. The elder brother appeared to be unconscious. Simon knew better. Their connection proved to be as strong as ever and, within seconds of staring at his brother, Simon witnessed Richter's eyes open, staring directly back at him. To Richter's left was the FBI agent they had come for, and over him was the black clad mass of their initial target. The man must have felt as though they were no longer a threat to turn his back on them.

Big mistake.

Without raising his hand to high, Simon signaled to his brother, communicating silently that he would cause a diversion so Richter could attack. The elder brother blinked twice to agree.

Simon cautiously rotated his head to locate the shotgun he had used to breach the front door. The weapon was just out of arms reach to his right. He felt he could have reached it swiftly if it were not for the injuries he already had sustained. Adrenalin usually masked the pain during dynamic and dangerous circumstances, alerting the instinctual reaction of fight or flight. Simon and Richter always fought, and left fleeing for their victims to die tired. In the moment, he figured going for the shotgun would be the perfect distraction to allow Richter to make his move. The detective still seemed to be worthless in the moment, disoriented and shocked by the death of his wife. Simon thought it set him and Richter up for exactly what they wanted, which was to kill the target and abduct Special Agent Stone in one fell swoop. Then they could get the hell out of Boston.

Using his fingers Simon counted down from three.

Richter made tiny movements to position himself so he could spring up off the floor and deliver a vicious onslaught to the vigilante before the man could counterattack. Simon watched his elder brother rotate his hands palm down to the floor in their respective positions; his right arm extended out above his head, while his left arm was tucked close to his body.

3… 2… 1…

Simon kicked his feet into the air and back, sending him into a reverse somersault, and rolled over his right shoulder. As Simon moved, their target reacted, instinctually stepping away from the perceived threat, and turning slightly in a bladed stance to minimize himself as a mark while he faced what was to come his way. Richter sprang off the floor with amazing agility, pulling his feet underneath his body until they were flat against the floor beneath him, and then leapt into the air, launching a spinning kick attack.

The fight was on.

****

When Simon rolled, he'd lost sight of his twin's immediate and violent actions. He missed the aerial assault launching the assassin into a helicopter spin with potentially lethal kicking maneuvers. Richter's speed and accuracy allowed him to use the element of surprise and land a swift series of strikes. The vigilante was knocked off his feet almost as quickly as he'd reacted to Simon's movement. Richter wasted no time in following up with an innate sense of urgency, overwhelming the vigilante in a way he suspected the man had never experienced. He also figured no one other than he and Simon had lived through an encounter with the man, and Richter intended on making sure they were the *only* ones who lived this time.

The elder twin leapt to the man's fallen body and rained down heavy fist after heavy fist, allowing the hard-knuckled, tactical gloves to rain down with maximum brutality. He grunted and roared with the effort he put forth, his eyes insanely wild, baring his teeth like a feral animal dominating its prey with a rage of spittle spraying from his mouth. The vigilante used his log sized forearms to block Richter's offensive as best he could, but the assassin's speed slipped through the cracks of the vigilante's defense.

Simon closed the distance between him and Stone with long, quick strides. The FBI agent was still unconscious, slumped up against the wall beneath a window only a few feet away from his brother's onslaught. Richter was too close for him to maneuver the limp body into a position to carry, so Simon instead dragged Stone's shell across the floor until he could manage the dead weight accordingly. He paused for a brief period of time to witness Richter's berserker rage, relishing his brother's deep capacity for violence, becoming slightly excited by it. Richter's body was positioned over the vigilante in manner that obstructed his view. Surely, by now, he imagined the vigilante's head was nearly caved in, and at the very least brain dead. He envied Richter's role in the moment, and the satisfaction he must be feeling by doling out their sweet, sweet revenge.

Focus, Simon.

The younger twin quickly wove his head through the tactical sling connected to the shotgun, positioning the nylon strap diagonally across his chest from left to right. Simon still held one of Stone's ankles in his left hand. He switched his grip so that he held Stone's leg closer to the knee, and then swiftly fell into a roll. His right arm scooped under Stone's leg, pulling it tight over his shoulder, rolled across the agent's body while using the leg as an anchor to pull the dead weight of the unconscious man into a cradled arrangement across his shoulders, or what is commonly considered a fireman's carry. Simon's momentum carried him over to where he paused in a kneeling posture, quickly positioning himself to place one foot firmly on the floor to begin standing with an explosive push. The maneuver was something he and Richter had trained countless times, and it took mere seconds to perform. It made hauling a limp body off of the ground nearly effortless.

Simon turned to his left, sweeping his eyes over the miserable shape of the bewildered detective, passing by his lost firearm, and crawling with a hesitant and stuttered disposition. The thought occurred to Simon to put McCrary out of his misery; tie up all the loose ends and such. A sliver of humanity crept into the assassin's heart for the brevity of the moment, considering the aching loss of someone so important, immediately disillusioned, broken, and left with nothing but a life of absolute devastation. There was only one person who meant anything to Simon that could cause him such pain and, in seeing his brother's success over their most dangerous target to date, he felt as though there was no reason to worry. The younger twin forgot about the useless thoughts of agonizing loss and continued with the main objective; retrieve Stone for the Wolf, and kill their prior target.

In the melee of his rage the elder twin heard, "Moving!" called out from his little brother. Richter continued to pummel the man beneath him. This meant Simon was in possession of Stone, and was continuing as planned.

Richter ceased his frenzy, maniacally twisting his head from one side to the other as he observed his work. Such expressions were typical trademarks for his brother's animalistic psychopathy, but given the opportunity to be placed in an advantageous position for vengeance, Richter could not help but to lose himself in this instant. The target's facial region was battered heavily, already showing facial edema and deep tissue injury. Blood streaked the man's face from lacerations. His nose, as well as his gaping mouth, leaked crimson. The right eye was turning black and blue, coupled with singular swelling along the lower ocular cavity. Richter admired the beating, reveling in his supremacy over such a dangerous man.

The thunderous clap of his heartbeat rhythmically pounded like a war drum in his chest, and in turn, the pulsation echoed within is ears. His hearing faded away while he admired the level of violence he'd inflicted, cherishing the accomplishment for too long. With his focus laid upon perceived success, Richter did not hear the snap of the pulled pin, or the sound it made when it was dropped against the hardwood floor, and he had not initially felt the explosive cylinder formerly attached to the pin slipped beneath his Dragon Skin vest. He had allowed his thirst to reconcile their earlier encounter in such a bloodthirsty manner that he'd nearly lost all consciousness of his surroundings, save for the familiar and ultra-trained aspect of communicating with his brother. It was in this hyper-focused state that Richter made the ultimate mistake, and he realized his target, the vigilante, had seized his own opportunity through personal and bodily sacrifice.

A tremendous amount of force launched Richter backwards, sending him into a half somersault roll. The agile assassin righted himself from the tumble, stopping on his hands and knees before jumping up to a full stance. Richter frantically began pulling at straps of his vest, releasing the ties that bound the body armor to him, and so stealthily hid the device that could lead to his demise.

"NOOOOOOO!" Richter cried a guttural roar laced with anger and desperation.

In his mind he could hear the clock ticking down to his final judgment, painfully slow, yet it became a futile attempt at becoming aware that there was not going to be enough time to live.

"God damn it!" the assassin screamed. "Come on!"

He felt the grenade beneath his vest, pressed tightly to his body, and so close to being released. The vest was nearly off, but it wouldn't be soon enough. Through his distress in this space and time Richter accepted that this was his grand finale. He didn't think of himself. He only thought of Simon, and wondered how his little brother would cope. And then, in the final millisecond of life that remained, Richter felt at ease. There was no need to worry about Simon. Simon would be alright. The question was how would the world cope with him? Richter's final look turned back towards the kitchen, seeing the vigilante yard the disoriented detective out of the path of the open doorway to take cover behind the wall. As a delicious smile stretched Richter's thin lips, expressing the malicious nature embedded within him since his early childhood, his thoughts turned to the vigilante and wondered, *Oh, what have you done…?*

The time delay of the grenade's firing mechanism was brought to life once the pin had been pulled and the internal striker level was released. This triggered the spring-loaded striker down against the percussion cap, creating a spark that ignited the slow burning fuse of the device. Within the first four seconds the delay material burned away where, at the end, the detonator capsule was lit. The remaining seconds burned through the combustible material within the capsule, igniting the grenade fully. It exploded outward with an incredible force filled with metal materials devised to shred and maim nearly anything in its path.

Richter laughed as the thunderous detonation ripped through his body in an effortless deconstruction of his anatomy. The flame of the explosion masked the shrapnel as it traveled into his flesh, but there was no hiding the devastation left behind by this instrument of death as his internal organs were exposed to the outside world. Hot metal shards flayed his throat and face, and his limbs seemed to separate from the shell of his humanity with ease. The assassin was instantly reduced to a grisly jigsaw puzzle of crimson chunks of meat, vaporized bone and brain matter. All that was left of the elder twin decorated the living space of the McCrary's home from the ceiling to the floor.

In his final moment Richter's life was reduced to six seconds, and as he was torn apart, he laughed that final laugh for two reasons; the wrath his brother would impart on his behalf, and that, with the extensive lifetime of training he'd endured, he died at the sound of a pin drop.

Chapter 36
No Time

The concussion from the grenade rocked the house in a way no home on the Eastern Seaboard was meant to endure. Loosed drywall dust shook free from the force of the explosion, cracking the walls of the home, scorching its immediate interior, and embedding it with the foreign metal substance meant to cause maximum damage in the worst possible way. Ghost stood from shielding McCrary's weary body, and immediately drew a pistol from his thigh holster in the same action. He moved to ensure there was no longer an immediate threat, filling the doorway with his bulk to scan the scorched living room and dining area. Beyond the smoke and dust, he could see that there was no one left alive. Thick mats of blood dripped from the ceiling and trailed its way down every adjacent wall where units of shrapnel had torn through the home. A small flame burned on a shredded section of the couch on the one side of the room, and the tattered curtains that covered the blown out front windows of the home smoldered.

Satisfied, Ghost holstered his pistol and looked to where Stone had been. The remaining assassin must have taken him. There was no other option. To what end he had no idea, but Ghost was certain Stone would be taken back to Kurikova's estate. Despite Ghost's personal vendetta, he knew why Yuri would want the FBI agent.

A painful groan sounded from the downed detective. Ghost turned his attention to the devastated man. He watched McCrary try to rise up to his knees, but he didn't have the balance. The bombardment sustained from multiple grenades discharged in the detective's home left him in utter shock beyond that of his wife's murder. McCrary fell backwards and to his side as he attempted to stand. He reached for the island counter to catch himself, but he was nowhere near it. Ghost did not try to catch him either.

"Audrey…" McCrary said. His voice was an aching stutter that was nearly indecipherable. He reached for her body, his arm trembling down to his fingers. "Nooooo…."

Ghost closed his eyes as the detective's voice trailed off like a ruined cartoon character falling to the bottom of a canyon. He felt a twinge of humanity in the moment, wanting to sympathize, knowing and understanding the sudden loss. But he couldn't give into it. This was not the time, which was a relative factor in the moment. The expanse of the entire fray had lasted less than five minutes from the time McCrary's wife was murdered to now. Blown out windows, gunshots, fires, and explosions tended to cause quite the disturbance and, right on que, Ghost heard the wail of police sirens slipping into the frantic soundtrack of chaos unleashed upon the night.

Time to go.

The vigilante grabbed McCrary by the collar of his shirt and lifted. Fabric tore under the pressure from Ghost's brute force and McCrary's sheer size. As Ghost lifted the big man, McCrary began to struggle, pushing and kicking with his legs, trying to move towards his wife's body. He didn't fight Ghost directly, instead falling limp as toddlers tended to do, turning to rubber. McCrary then slipped about as he tried to regain traction to move towards his heart's destination.

"We have to go!" Ghost yelled. Surely the detective wouldn't understand why he had to leave his demolished home, but there was also no time to explain that to the detective. "Let's go, Randal!"

Ghost picked McCrary up again, but the big man's flailing was too wild to contain with mild tactics. He slammed McCrary's head back down to the floor, stunning the detective briefly, and then yanked him up to his knees with little effort. McCrary's eyes were glassed over from the impact. His mouth gaped open, slack jawed and incapable of operating properly as his disheveled brain couldn't put the right commands together. Ghost looked right into the detective's eyes knowing there was very little of what happened, or what he was about to do, that McCrary would remember. A short right cross connected with the detective's jaw, whipping his head to his right, instantly shutting out his lights, and rendering him unconscious. Ghost stepped in and dropped to a knee, turning his broad shoulders so they caught the weight of McCrary's body as he slumped forward, and then rose to his feet with the detective draped across his back.

The first few steps Ghost took encompassed him adjusting McCrary's body in the fireman's carry position, and it forced him to pause over the corpse of the detective's wife. He knew he had no time to waste, but his thoughts raced a thousand miles a minute. Black, lifeless eyes stared up blankly, seeing nothing, and taking in nothing. Her soul had departed already. Perhaps there was a light to follow, or maybe there was nothing. Maybe it was just gone into some spectral realm where it would wait to be paired with another vessel in time. Ghost didn't know, but he wondered. He wondered what had come of his wife's essence, and that of his little Chloe. Was there a heaven where they would be waiting for him? Or was he a husband and father who had surely damned himself to the eternal flames of hell? The thoughts were irrelevant, yet he still wondered. Looking over the body of this poor woman, who had likely never maliciously hurt another human being, forced Ghost to consider the price his campaign of revenge now cost. First, his family suffered to start him on this path. Then many, many bad people deserving of his violence fell for their involvement. Now this innocent wife had been taken all too soon. Her death would ultimately change nothing for Ghost and what he had to finish. But it was regrettable, and Ghost hated himself for it.

Shamefully the behemoth hung his head, averting his eyes away from the woman's body as he drew in a heavy breath, and released it as he spoke. "You probably don't care and you wouldn't approve, but we'll make sure they pay for this." He half looked to her unconscious husband hanging over his shoulders. "I promise you that."

Never being much of a true believer, Ghost couldn't help but look upward, not to the ceiling but beyond it. Violence and loss had always played a prevalent role with many men in military service when considering their own beliefs; some found God while others lost Him. Ghost figured that, regardless of his personal convictions and confusions, giving a little for the sake of someone else could never hurt. He said softly, "Take care of her, please."

****

The McCrary's home had burst into flames and exploded outward in all directions, littering the immediate area of their yard and neighborhood with glass and fiery debris. Nearby car alarms sounded as they felt the concussion from the powerful blast. Simon had successfully dumped Stone's body in the back of a Cadillac Escalade provided by Kurikova, and had just finished securing the agent's wrists and ankles with zip ties to render him immobile should he wake before they reached their destination. The twin walked away from the vehicle and into the empty road nearly a block and a half up the street that ascended the beginning of a mildly pitched hill. This gave Simon an elevated view of the McCrary's home. It also provided him with the ability to see those immediately affected by the explosion; the ones brave enough to attempt to investigate. A series of porch lights came on, which added even more light to the area.

In the moment Simon did not react. He stared coldly at the home, seeing small flames burning in its interior, and thinking, oddly enough, how he felt the exact opposite of what the flames produced. It was surreal for him as he suddenly felt outside of himself, empty and uncertain if what he was witnessing was real, or if his mind was playing tricks on him. His head fell to one side as he pondered the possibilities of what the consequences from the explosion could be, although he couldn't help but realize there was only one explanation. He had to accept it, this final, last resort possibility was exactly what had occurred, and he felt a piece of himself die.

Richter.

A tear materialized at the inner corner of his left eye, forming into a bulbous shape until its size could no longer remain equally balanced on the shelf of Simon's lower eyelid, and was forced to cascade down his sharp features to the bristled dark hair bordering the corner of his thin lips. Simon blinked and nodded, knowing that he had just lost his brother and definitive guardian. What swelled up within him, the burning and the boiling, was something so intense he couldn't label it. There were no words for it. Hate, fury, rage, and anger all seemed inadequate. Yet, he endured it with an eerie calm, most of all surprising himself.

There was a job to finish. Richter always told him, "Always finish the job, Simon." So, Simon did as he'd always been told.

He moved stiffly, turning with a military like about face motion the trainers in their orphanage had once demanded, and returned to the storage area of the Escalade. His empty eyes searched over the shape of Special Agent Connor Stone, who now glared up at him from the floor of the compartment. Simon began nodding, uncertain as to why, but no longer able to contain the feeling that burned within him. His lower lip trembled slightly, and then the rest of his body followed suit as he unleashed a small portion of what overcame him. He struck Stone repeatedly in the body, growling between clenched teeth in a conscious effort not to draw attention to himself. Stone moaned and cried behind the gag keeping him quiet, wincing as the pain set in, lighting his torso on fire. Simon continued for what felt like an eternity, but was realistically a ferocious sixty seconds. He hit with every ounce of power he had, and he knew he had a lot. By the time he stopped, the assassin was gasping for breath as though he'd just sprinted two miles, something he and Richter did regularly to test one another. The lactic acid began to set into his muscles, hitting Simon with a wave of fatigue. He fought it off, shaking his head in a display of his refusal. His swift action led him to shutting the gate, remaining in control, and driving off calmly as police lights flashed in the distance.

As the former twin took the necessary actions to return to Kurikova's estate with the FBI agent, having memorized the directions for him and his brother, he lightly rocked back and forth in the driver's seat. Periodically, Simon screamed at the windshield and hit the steering wheel in a rage, but he immediately returned to his calm, rocking state. All the while, throughout the forty-five-minute drive, he spoke to himself under his breath, rhythmically syncing with each rock forward when he said each word in a seemingly individual patter. He continually repeated, "Always finish the job, Simon. Always finish. Kill the target, Simon. Kill the target."

Chapter 37
Involuntary Alliance

Nightmares were typically constrained to the mind as lengthy, terrifying dreams evoking fear, anxiety, and sadness. Detective Randal McCrary knew better than to believe such things could not manifest into reality. As his memories, rather than a disturbance in his imagination, replayed the murder of his wife over and over, he found his own life within the darkness of the haunting he was forced to relive. Even as he lay unconscious, he gasped for air as though he rose from the dead, clutching at his chest and face to ensure he was real, awaking to a reality based on the most horrific illusion he never thought possible.

McCrary sprang upwards into a full seated position, snapping to life like a sweat drenched Jack in the box. He found himself on an old, rag tag fold-out cot in a small, dank corner room where a claustrophobic sensation gave him the feeling he was not on the surface. The muffled echoes of footsteps, voices, and the clanging of dishes confirmed he was below ground. Mold and Chinese food permeated his sinuses with the slight infusion of dust. He spun and twisted inside his head, moving too quickly upon waking. He rubbed his temples, reliving the concussion grenades during the war waged in his home, and realizing he was suffering from the residual effects. McCrary kicked his feet over the edge of the cot in a frantic attempt to stand, unable to think clearly, and reacting out of confusion and fear. His balance faded as he fell back against the hollow framing of the room. A big hand wiped the sweat dripping down his face, uncertain as to where he was while equally unable to forget where he had been. He shook his head and closed his eyes, trying to regain his bearings and deduce whether he was in any danger. The image of Audrey falling to the kitchen floor waited for him behind closed eyes, showing him the blood and brain matter spilling from her skull as her body slowly arced downward. The mental trap forced him to snap open the windows to his soul, giving solace to the defeated man as his only way of retreat.

Quick, heavy breaths made him realize how frightened he was, not only from the reality of the night's experience, but also from the current situation. He was no longer at home, which was more than obvious, and he needed answers. *Where am I*? *Who took me*? A visual sweep of the room confirmed he was alone. *And where is Stone*?

McCrary heard some movement beyond the room. There were no windows framed into the cell sized cubicle, and a thinning black blanket was all that provided a semblance of privacy beyond the doorway. A quick survey of the room told him it was vacant of anything he could use as a weapon. McCrary searched over the bedding, above and below, and checked the metal framing for any loose clips or frayed spring wires. Still, he came up empty.

Rationally, it had to be thought, that if he were in danger he wouldn't have been left to wake up freely and move around. There would be a guard watching over him and, at the very least, a locked door to keep him confined. McCrary looked to the corners of the room for any video devices. Still, he found nothing, and was left just as confused.

The detective felt confident in his equilibriums rebalancing after a moment of rest. He stood and took a step forward. His brain was still a little rattled from the evening's tragedy, and the gentle throbbing he felt within his skull only added to the numerous facets that would not allow him to forget. The pulsation of the headache quickened when his thoughts turned to fiery anger over Audrey's assassination, but the quickening of the pain was nearly enough to bring him to his knees. McCrary launched an arm out to the doorway to stabilize himself while he stumbled forward. He concentrated on his breathing to help slow his heart rate, and began to focus on finding some answers. His attention turned to the blanket lightly fluttering in the open doorway, knowing he had to venture beyond its frail border into the unknown to learn anything. Before moving forward, the detective had to ask himself whether he was in any condition to face a possible threat. For all he knew the men who had raided his home had taken him and, in doing so, they were not threatened by him in any way. As a veteran detective, the scenarios his imagination came up with were overwhelming, which brought the truth crashing down on him like a ton of bricks: *You're in no condition to do anything right now. But you've also got nothing else to lose, either.*

McCrary took a deep breath and stood tall. What could charging beyond the veil possibly do to him that was any worse than what he'd already suffered? There was no reason to fear anything outside of this room. His worst-case scenario came down to his soul being reunited with the love of his life, and *that* gave him more courage than he'd ever felt before.

Brushing aside the thin blanket, McCrary burst out of the room with a youthful authority. His eyes focused intensely as he scanned his surroundings, his fists clenched and his chest full. For a moment the burning fire of anger warmed him, radiating upward until the flames danced behind his eyes and empowered him to surge forward. This time he ignored the pounding in his head, using its pain to fuel his actions. He'd exited the room into a dark, narrow hallway. There was only one direction to go, and that was left. Light filtered in his direction from the end of the corridor, accompanied by meager sounds McCrary could not identify.

He surged forward intent on confronting whatever he found. Every step took him closer, but the hallway was oddly longer than he initially thought. The extra distance allowed him to rethink his actions and lace his bold plan with a taste of caution. He placed one hand on the wall to his left as a stabilizing guide, and used it to gauge what he could see as it opened into the next room. McCrary angled his body to allow him to stealthily make his approach while slowly broadening his view from the shadows. What he found forced him to pause briefly, absorbing the absurdity of it. He quickly snuck another look and retracted back into the hall once he affirmed his vision had not played any tricks on him.

McCrary's heart was stimulated by the discovery, and he began to question what he should do next. This wasn't a room he wanted to barge into. He was not only incapable of taking on what he discovered, but he now felt a surge of fear interwoven with his adrenaline. Dying and joining Audrey became a thwarted idea and was something he realized he was not ready to do, yet. Had he found anything else beyond the hallway in this bleak situation, McCrary likely wouldn't have given his course of action a second thought. He'd been face to face with what waited for him beyond the hall, albeit only a brief encounter, but the experience was devastating, nonetheless. A number of considerations flooded his mind, and the pounding of his blood through his veins made his headache worse than ever. How could he lose courage so quickly? Was he really afraid? And for what, the possibility of dying? It certainly was a frightening thought, but did it really matter anymore? His decision quickly settled once again on the idea of having nothing to lose, and nothing to fear.

He grimaced and scowled as he forgot everything he was incapable of, and entertained the idea of a forward assault without caring about the consequences. Living and dying were concepts that no longer held any place within his reality. There were actions and re-actions. What would happen next would ultimately determine the course his life would take, whether it ended, or if he somehow managed to live through it. Either way, McCrary found the energy to wade into the fray and unleash his own version of hell.

The detective turned the corner at the end of the hall and pressed forward with an intensity reserved for the possessed. Anger and fury raged behind his eyes, and the snarl forming on his face displayed a hunger that quite possibly had no way of being satiated. His fists tightened to the point his big knuckles turned white, and his long strides carried him across the room at an immense pace. He didn't feel like himself in the moment, and when the beast inside him spoke he did not recognize his own voice.

"Hey, motha'fucka'! You killed my wife!"

****

Ghost had heard McCrary moving down the hallway, and anticipated an aggressive reaction. The man had suffered a terrible tragedy mixed with the residual effects from a number of explosives. The concussive results of the devices were enough to leave any man rattled for hours and, in McCrary's case, they had. The trauma the detective endured could carry any number of negatively effective symptoms, and one of them was displaced or confused aggression. Having predicted McCrary's response accurately, the experience of the former black ops operator equipped him with being all too prepared.

Fury contorted the detective's face as he approached, dividing his expression into something demonic and vengeful. Ghost could sympathize as he felt this way often. McCrary's fists were balled up tight pumping away at his sides, ready for a fight. Their knuckles shone white, and the lunch box sized paws could certainly do some damage. His red hair glowed like the inferno Ghost knew burned within him. He understood the anger better than the detective could ever imagine, and he also knew that it burned hottest in the beginning. There was a sense of regret that Ghost felt being fully aware he would have to stomp out McCrary's fire.

As McCrary swiftly approached, Ghost gave no reaction. His nonchalance was probably insulting, but he figured the detective to be a man who didn't forget easily, and he knew what an uphill challenge he faced. Ghost stood waiting, bare chested, displaying he was no less human with an abundance of bandages wrapped and taped to his scarred body. Older scars faded into the lines of his muscle tone like shadows of his past. Some even glowed when hit at the right angle of illumination. Others, more recent and fresher, blemished his body with their dark lines as though they couldn't wait to have their stories told.

Ghost's cold eyes watched McCrary's movement as his mind calculated when to take action and how. Experience on this level had a way of literally slowing time, and blessed the vigilante with the advantage of putting it to good use. He could do anything he wanted to, and played out any number of scenarios in his mind. Seeing McCrary's actions allowed him to select which variation he would pursue.

Any way it played out, Ghost had to make a statement, but not so much that he couldn't get what he wanted.

Once the detective was within range, he launched a very aggressive right cross, and immediately followed it up with a left uppercut. Ghost parried the initial strike, and was long gone before the secondary attempt was made. He wanted to avoid hitting McCrary in the head. Lord knew the detective didn't need any more damage than what he'd already suffered, and Ghost wanted him to be functional. Instead, Ghost stood offline to McCrary's second punch and, being more than one step ahead of the enraged widower, he twisted his body into delivering a crushing strike to the detective's solar plexis. He made sure not to put his full power into the punch, allowing for McCrary to recover more quickly, and not kill him. Ghost's accuracy was laser focused, and his own block sized fist collided with McCrary's stomach just below his sternum. He avoided hitting too hard so the physical trauma would not cause any number of cardiac contusions, or other forms of a deadly arrhythmia. Ghost was familiar with the capability of such a blow.

With the counterpunch landing precisely, its consequences came instantaneously. McCrary's feet were lifted off the concrete floor while his torso simultaneously folded in half at the waist. A gruff exhalation shot from the detective's suddenly wide-open mouth, nearly expunging the evening's meal along with it. The pain from the punch translated onto McCrary's face immediately, and was accompanied with the involuntary tears raining from his bulging eyes. The detective was reduced to a mountain of coughing flesh and bone, falling to his hands and knees as he desperately fought to regain his natural aspirations.

Ghost knelt down next to him and encouraged him to relax. It always amazed him how the face of pain seemed to drain the sense of a person's natural abilities to survive. Having the wind knocked out of you was a perfect example, which was all McCrary had experienced, and the panic it induced withdrew his ability to breath.

"Come on, through your nose, out your mouth," Ghost coached halfheartedly. He patted McCrary on the back, using the effort to assist him in standing. "Breathe, Randal."

Ghost walked away to a nearby stool. He slouched on the seat, and curiously watched the elder man regain his ability to breathe appropriately. McCrary remained on the floor, posted on all fours, breathing and coughing, waiting out the lingering effects until he could stand under his own strength. As he made the climb back to his feet Ghost kicked another stool in the detective's direction. McCrary used it and a roughly made metal table to pull himself off the floor, ultimately perching himself on the stool.

The detective sat hunched over huffing and puffing, paying no attention to how the position restricted his breathing. With his mouth gaping open and his eyes still watering, he shot a disdainful look to the vigilante sitting across from him. He had no words at the moment, but he knew there was plenty to be said. It was then that the parameters of the situation were laid out for him.

"Here's how this is gonna' work, Randal," Ghost said. "Tonight, we have a mutual goal in need of an involuntary alliance. Now, so you know, I don't necessarily need you to finish what I started, but there's a catch to all of this that is going to beneficially require your assistance."

McCrary's head shook from side to side, not so much out of dismissal, but out of this circumstantial irony. He found it within himself to summon a lengthy chuckle between gasps for air, although it could have been out of the insanity, he felt he was experiencing. *Was this guy serious*?

And McCrary quickly found out that Ghost was.

****

"I'm not a murderer like you are!" McCrary barked. Spittle sprayed from his mouth as he spoke aggressively, and brought the thicker diction expected from a Bostonian. "I'm a fawckin' cawp! I don't do that shit!"

Ghost stared blankly at the detective. "Killing Kurikova and his men is the only way out of this."

McCrary shook his head, this time on purpose. "No, it's not. I can cawl this in. If Stone's at Kurikova's I could have a war'awnt and the stayette police raid that fawcker's estate wit'in an hour."

The idea was put off by Ghost without hesitation. "And you'd get a lot of men killed who don't need to die tonight. You and I can end this, and get Stone back." He looked away, thinking of how the man just lost his wife. "And you can avenge your wife…"

Ghost let the idea hang in the air, showing no sign of emotion as he spoke.

McCrary came off of the stool yelling and jabbing an index finger at Ghost's chest, fearless of any retaliation. "Fawck you! Don't you tawlk abo't her! You gawt my wife killed, mawtha'fucka'! Yaw're responsible for that!"

"Maybe I am, in a long, roundabout way," Ghost admitted flatly. His eyes carried no doubt of the matter, or an apology. They remained cold and focused. "There's nothing I can do to change it, and nothing I can say to help you. No one can do either of those things. As a cop you assume those risks. The job doesn't affect just you, but the people you love as well, so don't lecture or place blame on me. I can help you get justice for her."

McCrary's anger seemed to involuntarily subside when he thought it should have increased. He laughed hard at the vigilante's statement, stepping away, but never taking his eyes off Ghost. A sense of calm came over the detective, and he felt like he was losing his marbles. "Are you serious with that bullshit? Justice? Is that what you call what you're doing?" He paused as the absurdity of the idea hit him full on, and the core of his diction returned to something more understandable. "What? You want *me* to kill the guy?"

Ghost watched as McCrary began to fidget as he struggled with the idea of it. An abundance of grief symptoms were setting in and the onset of it began to make McCrary twitch and stutter. Ghost recognized this behavior when the mind struggled with the confusion of a traumatic loss and what capabilities one had to ease the pain. The solution for it was likely different for everyone, but as cliché as it was, time was what it took. Ghost imparted his fury on the many people responsible for transgressions against him immediately, and even then, it wasn't enough. He needed the *one* responsible. It took him some time to be able to focus and gather the appropriate information needed to direct his final intentions, and then it took more time to research and plan. Once he'd resorted to a state where he could fully commit to the focal point he desired, he knew there would be no stopping him.

Right now was the part where McCrary struggled to rationalize between what he wanted and what he was willing to do to get it, and in that mental comparison Ghost knew the detective was questioning everything about himself. *Why*? Because what McCrary truly wanted conflicted with everything he stood for.

Confronting the detective wasn't a challenge, and Ghost met it with ease. He stood, barely taller than the veteran Marine, and closed the distance between them until they were only inches apart. McCrary continued to dismiss the idea Ghost presented, but the conflict between his desires and morals were not hidden. Anger and fear were all a part of the process. It would be unnatural for them not to be. Ghost saw them appropriately represented in McCrary's varying expressions, through the red eyes and tears. He'd experienced them himself almost as if there was an unnamed checklist the experience inherently provided. He was asking a lot from the detective, but at the same time he was also offering an opportunity.

Ghost stood face to face with McCrary, looking into his watering eyes, seeing more than just the heartache, anger, and distress overwhelming the man. The question posed by McCrary was a fair one, although it was not something Ghost had been burdened with deciding upon. He knew instantly what he would do after losing his family. A part of him knew that McCrary, despite the ethical direction of his moral compass, wanted to make the same decision too.

In a manner of encouragement, Ghost nodded his head ever so slightly, maybe a little more than a fraction of an inch. The gesture let the man know he understood how he felt, and suggested they agreed on the subject. Ghost reflected back to McCrary's question: *You want me to kill the guy*?

To which the vigilante asked nonsensically, "Don't you want to?"

Chapter 38
The Best Laid Plans

The best laid plans of mice and men often go awry.

Yuri Kurikova thought of this phrase derived from an old *Scots* poem by Robert Burns he'd read as a boy. The subject of the poem was irrelevant, yet the line was powerfully significant in the moment. Even as he listened to Mr. X's eccentric statements squawking from the phone receiver, learning of Special Agent Stone's role in this chaotic mess, Kurikova focused on the one line. It clearly defined the futility of creating detailed plans when it was uncertain to completely, or even partially, carry those plans out. At times it was next to impossible. Kurikova always kept this quotation in mind throughout his lifetime. He had experienced its inevitable place in the world many times, and was well aware of how it was teaching Special Agent Stone a valuable lesson now.

"I had no idea you had any role in that part of the operation," Yuri spoke into the phone. As he spoke, his predatory gaze was fixed upon the beaten mound of flesh of the captured FBI agent. "Yes, I knew of the transport, but that does not explain your betrayal."

Kurikova listened intently, applying the *Scots* line in his mind to Mr. X's explanation. It was circumstantially universal.

"You were playing both sides," Kurikova snarled. "This is not good business. I should have known better long ago."

Kurikova listened as Mr. X laughed off his comments. The rogue spy applied his enigmatic charm to explain how it was all 'business as usual' in the risqué criminal underworld. He had stakes in both claims, so to speak, and needed to see which was more valuable. His words were of no comfort, especially when he told Kurikova he had won in the end, which allowed their partnership to thrive.

"I would give all the money in the world to have my father back," said Kurikova. His grimace hardened, threatening to become permanent. "You manipulated the situation to get what you wanted. To kill him because you couldn't have it done otherwise without leaving a trail back to yourself, which let you manipulate me all of this time."

A "congratulations" from the other end of the call nearly sent the Wolf into a rage. Even as he fought to control himself, his bestial personality physically transformed him. Veins strained and corded up his exposed forearms, stringing their way up beneath rolled up sleeves to a blood-spattered white button up shirt. The fury in his eyes came with a crimson hue that washed over his face in the same fashion mercury rose in a thermostat, bringing on a biological increase in his temperature and causing sweat to bead across his high forehead and the deep recession of his hairline beyond a thick widow's peak. Kurikova lowered the phone to his side, growling and spitting as he fought to control his temper. To calm himself, the Wolf closed his eyes, and took a few deep breaths before returning the phone to his ear.

"You will pay for this," the Wolf stated coldly.

The statement hung in the air, resulting in a heavy silence where the unstoppable force of certainty collided with the immovable object of its polar opposite. The paradox was fittingly strange in the moment as Kurikova was sure of his resolve, and he could feel the tension of Mr. X's disapproval through the line.

Kurikova opened his eyes and looked over the shell of a man sitting before him. Agent Stone was slumped over in a steel chair, restrained by steel cuffs and anklets, four-pointed to the chair. His dress shirt was torn and bloody. Contusions and fist-laden lacerations marked the man's once handsome face. Blood washed over him from the abuse he'd endured already, and his disheveled mind was barely able to allow him to lift and control the movement of his head. Kurikova's fists were the tools responsible for the beating, lathered in blood, and swollen as evidence of the torturous session the agent was subjected to. The sight of the agent breathing gave Kurikova another idea, and it was intended to leave an impression with Mr. X.

The rogue spy was still on the line, which told Kurikova he had the man's typically divided attention. Mr. X had impeccable timing and, this time being no different, he released a light chuckle just before the mafia boss began to speak, further motivating Kurikova to speak his mind.

"You laugh now, fucker," Kurikova said, noting the spy's laughter ceased immediately. The tone of his voice delivered nothing less than malice, heightened only by his accent. "But I will show you that I can, *and will* find you. And when I do, you will witness my unrelenting savagery imparted by my own hands." He displayed his free hand in front of himself as he walked to Stone, grabbed a tuft of his blond hair, and lifted the agent's head so his dazed eyes stared up at him. "I am going to use your pawn here as an example."

Mr. X laughed at Kurikova again, but this time it was short lived, forced and fake. It was obvious the man did not care about Stone, but this was not the point. The point would be made when Mr. X received the Wolf's display of impending vengeance, and he knew the spy considered this as the example. The man was very smart and, while seemingly ten steps ahead of everyone at all times, he had to have some semblance of information knowing Kurikova could actually find him. Kurikova had his own secrets and resources, unbeknownst to the spy. Then Mr. X reminded him of what was most important. Yuri 'the Wolf' Kurikova had to survive the night first.

Kurikova let go of Stone's head, watching it fall without resistance. "This is true," he agreed. He weighed the possibilities of survival against his opposition. It was best to be prepared for the worst. "But, if I don't, I am not the one you will have to worry about."

And with that final message, Kurikova crushed the cell phone in his grip.

****

Simon had watched from the second floor of the mansion as Kurikova beat Stone to a bloody pulp, and then threw a fit on the phone with God knows who. It was inconsequential to him. For the time being it allowed him to disassociate himself from the evening's tragedy and concentrate on how he would move forward, not just for the night, but in life. A fit of rage seemed like it would be the appropriate way for him to respond to his brother's death, but something deep down wouldn't let him follow through with a grieving tantrum. He was alone now, and there was no doubt he would be completely misunderstood. Richter had been his compass and kept him on track. Often times he knew his impulses would have gotten them killed, yet there was Richter to keep him focused. The task of controlling himself would be all too difficult on his own now. However, while feeling quite conflicted for the moment, Simon seemed to be suddenly endowed with an eerie calm; assured of what he was capable of, as though gifted with a sense of mastery of self.

Kurikova tossed the cell phone across the marbled floor of the living area. One of his military clad Spetznaz cronies picked it up and set it nearby. Simon studied the men, all former operators, and brought in for the Wolf's personal protection. They all appeared to be disciplined and capable men. Being of the former Russian elite special forces was no joke, although for Simon, it was comical to be in the presence of so many of them considering he and Richter had killed quite a few of them over the years. They did not discriminate against any particular target if the price was right, which left them loved to a small degree, and hated enormously within the community of killers. Everyone had their 'codes' that dictated how they conducted themselves. Richter had always found this to be too limiting. But, over time, as their paths crossed with other operatives, former Russian operators being the main consideration for the moment, Simon couldn't help but enjoy the irony. If they only knew how many of their *comrades* he killed he would not be so welcomed. That being said, with their assignment being Kurikova's protective detail, the remainder of the night was expected to be a huge blow out, or so rumor had it. Simon was happy to be a part of the party. *Finish the job*. That was the first step forward. Simon had a target to kill, and it was in Kurikova's best interest to allow him to do so.

Looking around the vastness of the home told Simon there were more vulnerabilities than strengths to the landscape. On either side of him, even on an empty tier, there were two soldiers standing guard. He was certain there were plenty more he had not seen, or who were strategically placed. Kurikova's personal guards were distinguishable from the other men stationed here for the man's protection. The main forces varied in description, had individualized tactical kits, and were generally meaner looking than the rest. They didn't care about Simon when he approached or passed by. They had nothing to prove. The dozen or so others making up the cannon fodder for the night's impending event needed to eye him, and present themselves as a force to be reckoned with. Simon sensed they were experienced, and some of them may be dangerous. But tonight, they were a form of back up that was not meant to survive. At best they would take the aim off of the better skilled men on the grounds so that they could live a little longer, and try a little harder not to die.

If they only had a clue as to what they were up against.

Simon's mind wandered to what it would have taken for him and Richter to dispose of this ragtag group. The proposition was boring, and he quickly decided on *next to nothing*. They would have barely broken a sweat, and for Simon that was giving these men a healthy compliment. He considered the opposition these men would soon be up against. The man's ability was impressive, especially having fought Simon and Richter side by side, twice now, and he survived. Simon couldn't help but to think that the target wouldn't need to try very hard either. *Except, the man would do just that.* He'd be well prepared, heavily armed, strategical, and likely surgical in the execution of his plan. Simon wondered if he himself was taken into consideration for the festivities. Would the vigilante think of the twin assassin as a possible threat to his plans still? After all, and the vigilante knew all too well, he was the intended target. And, how professional would Simon be if he didn't *finish the job*?

The answer was obvious, but Simon needed to make sure he was involved. He needed Kurikova to know he was going to stick around and finish what he was hired for. And who wouldn't want the help of a professional killer in a circumstance like this?

An idea manifested within Simon's mind, and it quickly carried him down to the main living area. Kurikova had taken a seat with a drink in his hand by now, sitting across from the FBI agent. When he approached Kurikova did not acknowledge him. Simon did not like this. It reminded him of how Richter was always the negotiator for their contracts and, when meeting in person with anyone — a waitress or tenant of any kind — they always looked to his brother. Richter did carry himself as the one with a more authoritarian air about him, whereas Simon didn't pay much attention to the inconsequential things, other than the fact that he was not the person people made initial contact with. That would have to change immediately, but Simon knew he couldn't do it as diplomatically as Richter could have. He had to use his own methods.

Kurikova appeared to be in a trance, sipping on a short glass of vodka. Fury burned in his eyes. Simon actually sympathized with the old Wolf. He imagined having a similar gaze, although it may have appeared to be slightly off kilter. Something, perhaps a greater power he would never understand, allowed him to see beyond the rage. There was a time and place for it, and a way to manage it appropriately. *Who the fuck am I now, Richter*? Regardless, Simon needed to gain Kurikova's attention. So, he did.

A quick slap turned the FBI agent's head to the right, and as it made space Simon sat cross ways on his lap. He petted the blond man's head for moment, ignoring Kurikova's surprised acknowledgement of his attendance. Simon played with the agent's head like a puppet while he kicked his feet over back and forth, crossing and uncrossing, until he settled with kicking them up and down like a giddy child, but only briefly. He talked to the unconscious man, saying nothing of importance, speaking mere gibberish in the same fashion annoying people spoke to their beloved quadrupeds like tiny little babies. After a moment Simon caught Kurikova within the spectrum of his peripheral vision. The mafia boss looked annoyed. Simon was pleased.

When the timing seemed right Simon acted as though he'd been caught being naughty, going so far as to mime an 'oops' type of reaction, covering his mouth with a flat hand and all. His eyes acted the part, wide and surprised, but he generally didn't give a fuck. He chuckled as he returned Kurikova's acknowledgment, turning slightly to look at the angry Russian.

"Sorry, Yuri," Simon clowned. "Am I interrupting something?"

The Wolf provided a stern look, more irritated than he had been seconds ago, with no less fury. He said nothing.

Simon readjusted his seating arrangement so that he faced forward, propped up on the end of the agent's knees. Stone was no Santa Claus, but he'd do for now.

"What are you doing?" Kurikova finally asked. His right fist strained around the tumbler he held, and gave off the feeling he was close to breaking it in his grip.

"Yuri," Simon began, "I don't think you're taking me seriously in my role here." He leaned forward as he paused, uncertain as to where his zany sense of dramatization had come from.

Kurikova shook his head, looking into the glass of vodka as he stirred it. He was relaxing as he considered the assassin across from him. "It is not on purpose. I know you have now suffered a loss as well."

Simon nodded in agreement. "Yeah… Just a little bit. But I want in on the fun, Yuri. My brother always said, '*Finish the job, Simon.*' So, I have a professional obligation to finish." His words were matter-of-fact, as though he'd suddenly inherited Richter's no bullshit attitude. Simon looked over his right shoulder to where Stone's head dangled. "After all, Yuri, we want the same thing now. Don't we?"

"I have plenty of men to stand guard. Run offense."

Simon contorted his expression to show he was confused. "So, what? Am I chopped liver all of a sudden? Your men couldn't do shit to stop this guy, and no one's gotten closer to him than I have. Now, he's coming to you, and I'm your best bet at getting what you want tonight." Simon leaned closer and half covered his mouth. He spoke in a whisper as he continued to speak. "We both know *every one* of these fuckers are gonna' to die tonight. And don't tell me you think you're gonna' live through it?"

Kurikova scowled at the assassin, yet remained silent.

"I thought so, Yuri," Simon said.

"What role do you think you can play?" Kurikova asked. Considering Simon's skillset must have finally set in.

Simon leaned back against the agent until the man's head rested on his shoulder. He looked Kurikova in the eyes as he crossed his legs and brought his hand together at his chest. "If *you* want to live through tonight, and get this sonofabitch, we're going to have to play this right. Like the rules of a game."

Kurikova appeared annoyed, but he was tempted. "What game?"

Simon's hands opened wide as though taken by a sudden shock. He found a smile to offer as though the answer should have been obvious. "Oh, Yuri, Yuri, Yuri…" He leaned forward as the manufactured echo of his words faded away. "The game is an age-old favorite. It's Simon

Says."

Kurikova stirred his vodka again, watching it swirl around in the tumbler glass. His fury had not died any, but his logic had been altered. Simon could see that the wheels of his mind were spinning, scrutinizing the idea to let a psychopath take the helm in his protection.

The Russian slowly raised the vodka to his lips and finished off the glass. He closed his eyes as he savored the beverage, pursing his lips as he savored the flavor, and solidified his decision. When he opened his eyes there was less rage reflecting outward with no less predatory lethality.

"Why not?" Kurikova said. "I was planning on dying anyways."

Chapter 39
Eye to Eye

Stone's eyes fluttered, fighting to open, and remained that way. The fog within his mind was heavy, and finding the balance of his equilibrium seemed impossible. Consciousness feigned restoration numerous times before the agent was able to fully wake. Control over simple motor skills took more effort than Stone had ever had to put forth just to hold his head up. He groaned as his pain receptors were overloaded with the torturous acts that Kurikova forced upon him. The swelling in his face amplified gravity's natural weight, forcing him to hang his head for a long period of time. His mouth gaped open in conjunction with the inability to lift his head, making him more aware of his physical suffering with every second. Blood had dripped from his face to his shirt from various lacerations over and around his eyes, his nose, and lower lip. Stone tried to move his mouth as he fought the effects of mimicking a dashboard bobblehead. The rampant pulsation radiating through his face ached steadily with his heartbeat, so much so that when Stone could hold his head up, a numb sensation washed over him, and then slowly dissipated.

More groaning ensued. Sharp pangs shocked him each time he moved his jaw and blinked his eyes. The facial edema devastated his ability to concentrate. He still suffered the spinning brought on by the head trauma, likely as a result of a concussion. A clammy feeling blanketed him, and nausea stirred within his core. From second to second he wrestled with the displeasing quality of weakness and irritability. Stone gathered his thoughts and figured this would take some time to recover from if he lived long enough. First, he needed to identify his surroundings. The lighting was dim, and the air was cool. Dust particles floated in the obscured atmosphere. He was encircled by rows and stacks of objects he didn't recognize and couldn't define. His vision remained blurry, weaving in and out of clear images, and multiplying them in a kaleidoscope fashion.

Stone was able to control looking side to side, slightly dipping his chin when he turned from left to right, and then back. Slowly he became more aware, believing he saw a figure in front of him, and possibly one to either side. He wasn't certain. One became two, and two became more. What he was abruptly certain of was the cold bindings restricting his wrists and ankles. He tested their movement, finding them extremely limiting. The clanging of steel on steel defined his circumstances, and it brought back the memory of where he'd been taken. The stimuli of his position gave him the impression he was being closely watched, involuntarily persuading him to talk. Despite his dire circumstances he found it to be impossible to panic.

"Where am I?" the agent asked. His voice was groggy and slurred, imitating a drunken state. "I know someone's there." He laughed slightly, unsure as to why. It could have been the shock from the torturous assault and the following trauma, or the silly pronunciation of his words given his vulnerable capacity. But Stone had no idea. Assimilation to the situation seemed futile at the moment. His irritability quickly spiked as he was unable to figure out an answer. "Probably that fucking Russian, isn't it?"

A strong hand grabbed Stone by the hair from behind, yanking his head backwards with tremendous force. He heard the quick shuffle of footsteps from his left before the transgression took place. The pain would have been excruciating if it weren't for the fact that Stone already hurt to a mind-numbing degree.

A gruff voice barked from the shadows, issuing an order. Stone didn't understand what was said, but he was sure it wasn't English. It took a few seconds to resonate where the order came from. When the appropriate information reached its destination, Stone was able to pin-point that the person who spoke was in front of him. He strained to focus forward, seeing the silhouette of a man take shape before him, but he couldn't hold the image together for long before one became two and three, and then immediately following the man's voice, the grip on Stone's head was released.

It was then that it became clear who was in charge.

"Is that you?" Stone asked, continuing to manage his head

movement in a dazed fashion.

"Who do you think it is?" the voice asked.

Stone smirked, despite the pain. The accent confirmed his assumption, or rather, his hazy memory. "Oooh, Yuri. At last we meet."

"We met earlier, Mr. Stone," Kurikova stated. "I'm sure I left an impression."

Stone nodded. "Yeah, good work." He surveyed the room again, still not gaining any more information than he had before. "Where am I now?"

There was hesitation in response. Footsteps moved forward. Fine shoe soles slid lightly over concrete, never fully lifting off the floor with each step. Kurikova moved into the light hovering over Stone from a single cord. His hands were in his pockets, seemingly relaxed, except for the anger chiseled into his features. Stone couldn't make out every detail of the man, but his hostility was easily translatable.

"Not where you were," Kurikova said.

"Fuck you," Stone spat. Blood sprayed from his mouth, and a fire burned in his jaw. It was probably fractured. The defiant act created more pain for him, but it was quickly forgotten amongst the sea of agony that enveloped his body.

Kurikova smirked, only adding to the evil he already exuded. "Do you know why you are here, Agent Stone?"

The disorientation encompassing Stone made it difficult for him to come up with a probable response. He mindlessly stared at the mafia boss, still unable to focus the man into a singular being.

"You are here because of information I recently learned," Kurikova stated, stepping forward gradually, keeping a short distance between him and the agent. "I learned that you are the man responsible for the death of my father. I learned that the man who has targeted my syndicate, who was originally thought to be responsible for my father's murder, is attached to your antics in some way, furthering his *need* for vengeance against me." Kurikova dismissed the idea of revenge with a confused look of disgust, and waved the idea away. His words began to roll with his pronunciation, growling rather than speaking. "It turns out that having been lied to in the beginning, I targeted this man's family in my retaliation."

Stone felt a swell of anger as Kurikova openly confessed to him. The surge of his heartbeat increased the rapid frequency of the achiness through his body. Adrenaline masked the pain, yet seemed to amplify the throbbing of his injuries.

The Russian stepped forward, bending over at the waist, and supporting his body with his hands on both knees. Kurikova studied Stone, looking for something in the agent while displaying his loathing of the man. "It seems as though, in the chaos of the circumstances, I made a mistake. While I'm uncertain of your connection to this *vigilante* and the *spy*, I should have targeted your family, not his."

The searching gaze continued from the mafia boss, although he now seemed to be looking through Stone rather than at him. Stone's anger flashed in his eyes and, although he still couldn't focus clearly, he saw Kurikova as distinctly as he needed to. The agent leaned forward, trembling through every limb, chest heaving as his breathing came quickly and heavily, overcome with ferocity. He thought of his sister. He thought of his niece. He thought of the chain reaction his actions had created, and the results of his idiocy. And then how Kurikova's declaration closed the circle of lives taken from him.

Stone strained against his restraints while he and Kurikova stared through one another. The Russian maintained a calm disposition while his own fury burned beneath the surface, secretly matching, if not exceeding, that of Stone's. There was a secret war brewing between them; chess pieces marching across an emotional board only they could feel.

With only a few feet between them the two men engaged in an age-old demonstration of supremacy, facing off with neither man wanting to back down. Stone was in the most obvious disadvantage as the captive, but he didn't consider himself so in the heat of the moment. The revelation of Kurikova's admittance inspired an uncontrollable lucid awareness.

...I should have targeted your family, not his.

Stone spoke through gritted teeth, blood and spit spewing over his wounded lower lip, delivering a revelation of his own that took Kurikova by complete surprise. "You did."

Chapter 40
Who I am?

"*Don't you want to?*" Ghost had asked the detective.

McCrary had no answer to the burning question posed to him. This man wanted him to kill the other assassin who played a part in taking Audrey's life. It was a stupid question when he thought about it, but that was only after the man's retort sank in.

And the detective did want to. Maybe… No, it wasn't right to kill so flagrantly. But what was right anymore? Here and now, in the presence of a mass murderer dubbed '*America's Most Dangerous Man*' by the media, McCrary was overwhelmed and exhausted with disbelief. Yet, the question lingered, and he remained uncertain. The conflict warred within him between the righteousness of his moral code and his wanton desire of vengeance. Too many questions flooded his mind all together, and he found it difficult to process anything in the moment to manufacture an answer he could stand by. He looked to the vigilante, who instructed McCrary to call him Ghost, and watched the man quietly arrange an assortment of weapons on a plastic fold out table typically used for catering or barbecues.

"How do you do it?" McCrary asked, turning on the stool to face Ghost's direction. He clicked a few fingers against the mug of coffee sitting before him on the metal table where he sat. A cup of Joe had always been a good ice breaker, except for today.

Ghost looked to the detective, acknowledging him with an uncertain glare. "What?"

McCrary's arms spread wide, gesturing to the lengthy basement room converted into the headquarters of an elite killer. "This! Everything you've done! All the lives you've taken! How do you live with yourself?"

Ghost placed two large ammunition boxes on the table, dismissing McCrary's short rant. He took a moment before he gave the detective his attention. It seemed fair to give him some information considering what he'd been through so recently.

McCrary waited impatiently, tensing as the seconds passed by.

"Okay," Ghost said, "you want some answers. I get it." He turned to face McCrary and sat on the edge of the table where he worked. "This isn't a debate, though."

The detective shook his head. "Fill me in. I'm lost here. After everything I've learned about your case, from what Stone's told me, to what I've seen and heard and experienced for myself, I'm still at a loss."

Ghost nodded to himself, mulling over what knowledge McCrary was likely aware of. "Well, you asked two different questions, Randal. Or, rather, one is more general than specific, and vice versa."

"Now you're just being an asshole."

Ghost found the declaration amusing. The detective wasn't wrong.

"I can't process my wife being dead," McCrary stated. His jaw shuddered when he acknowledged Audrey's death. He tensed his jaw and remembered his anger to right his dejection. "I know she's gone, lying alone in my kitchen with her mind leaking out onto the floor…" He had to stop again as the image fluttered behind his eyes, choking him into a fleeting silence. He took a deep breath and regained his composure. "She's was taken right before my eyes, and I can't even fathom retaliation on this level."

Again, McCrary looked around to indicate the operation Ghost had set up in this subterranean workshop. On the far table to his left there were three separate computers hard wired to what appeared to be a score of independent servers, ten lining the top row and ten below, on a custom-made shelving system. The detective wasn't particularly too tech savvy, but from what he remembered from an FBI course on cyber-crimes it looked familiar. Near the computers were a set of white boards on wooden rolling frames with a slew of maps and pictures attached across them both. Beyond where Ghost glared at him, were stacks of wooden crates. Nearly a dozen of them were pried open with the wood packing fibers strewn about the floor, once securing Ghost's weaponry and tactical gear.

Black eyes stared back at the detective, burning through him like plasma through steel. Ghost fought back any sympathy he had for

McCrary, suppressing his emotions so that he could remain in control. He knew where this conversation was heading, and the darkness it was rooted in. McCrary wanted peace of mind; justification for what he truly wanted. Ghost could feel it and, whether he liked it or not, the detective needed to understand the issue to come to terms with the ultimate violation of his moral code.

"Okay, I'll bite," Ghost said. He shrugged himself off the table and closed the distance between he and McCrary until they sat across from one another. Their eyes locked for what seemed like an eternity, although it was only a few substantial seconds. Ghost waited to speak until he saw the detective's gaze harden. To him it signified McCrary was capable of pulling himself from the pool of fear and pain drowning him from the inside. This was important to Ghost because their similar circumstances dictated that the matter was more personal and intimate than he cared for, and controlling the emotions involved was difficult. It was a topic that could get out of hand all too easily.

The stillness of the silence made McCrary uneasy as he waited for Ghost to explain something, anything. His discomfort quickly became irritation as he began to fidget in his seat, unable to hide his displeasure. Ghost simply watched him, and it was then that the detective realized he was being tested. Once the realization set in McCrary nodded to acknowledge the unspoken understanding. Ghost let the time pass a little longer before he spoke just to be an asshole, but the detective held out and returned his blank stare.

"Here's the simplest fact about the two of us," Ghost stated. "We're completely different people. A paradox of sorts. In my line of work, I do many things that you do, albeit, on a much more dangerous level. It's something I don't expect you to grasp, or understand, and I'm not going to waste my breath explaining it to you in order for you to agree with me. Agreement is of no interest to me. Understand?"

McCrary nodded without speaking.

"I don't operate within the safety bubble you protect every day." Ghost sat up straight, and McCrary mirrored him. Their eyes never deviated from each other. "I am not a law-abiding citizen. Outside of the time I spent with my family, I virtually never have been. I don't even know if I'm an American citizen. As far as I know, beyond my cover identities, both professional and personal, I have no official identity."

The detective's brow wrinkled with confusion. "What does this have to do with anything?"

"Context, detective. You want to know how I do what I do. Revenge. Vengeance. A killing spree. Mass murder. Whatever you want to call it. It all boils down to who I am, and the only insight I can give you is to let you know there are very few men in existence who can relate to the objectivity I have lived by.

"In *my world* a family was not ideal. When you've reached the heights that I have, there is a point where being alone just doesn't cut it anymore. I wanted *more* life and *less* death."

McCrary shook his head. "This isn't helping."

Ghost folded his arms across his chest, and continued his explanation matter-of-factly. "It will. Imagine, or remember, your life before your wife. There were no limits were there?" An answer was not expected, but Ghost paused so the idea could sink in. "You were invincible, right? Full of piss and vinegar, ready, willing, and able to take on anything thrown your way?"

Another silent nod replied.

"Now, take in that moment when you met *her*. When the wilds of bachelorhood faded away. When you decided you wanted nothing else as badly as her. Your existence meant nothing without her."

McCrary looked away, acknowledging his discomfort as he tried to remain stoic, yet easily accessing the early memories of when Audrey came into his life. It started with them clumsily bumping into one another in a coffee shop, spilling her drink. *Cliché-ish* as it was. Her fiery personality exuded her displeasure immediately. She cussed him out; cussed herself out for not paying attention. He was nothing less than apologetic having been in a rush. But she'd stopped time once she spoke, and their eyes became fixed in some magnetic trance. In an instant McCrary just knew he had to get to know her. Everything shouted at him to release every ounce of charisma he possessed, but she stole it all away with that look, right along with his ability to breathe. For more than twenty years he would never look at a woman the same way he looked at Audrey, who comfortably, confidently, and lovingly became his wife. After revisiting the memory, McCrary resisted the involuntary need to let everything pour from his soul; to let go of the anger and pain and guilt. His attention faced off towards one of the basement walls, allowing the noise from the restaurant upstairs to interfere with the memories playing in his mind while Ghost continued.

"Yeah, you know what I mean," Ghost said. He remained expressionless. Cold. Yet, even his own sentimental fortitude betrayed the emotions his words invoked as a tear rolled down the lines of his face. "Now, as if that wasn't bad enough, add the innocence of a child. Inject the glowing wonder projected from her blue eyes culminating in an endless array of silly questions that can only have ridiculous answers."

Ghost paused as his voice trailed off, fighting his own demons, blinking away the swarm of tears shamelessly welling up in his eyes. The hard line of his jaw began to tremble with his efforts to suppress what he felt. *Maintaining control was paramount.*

"And then she laughs when you answer her. But it's not just an ordinary laugh. Oh no…" Ghost shook his head, continuing to repel his own agony, knowing the words had to be spoken. He'd come too far not to finish, and it didn't matter to him when his voice cracked and growled and trembled through his soliloquy. "Her laugh is nothing short of angelic. It's intoxicating to you. It's better than any sound you've ever heard in your entire life. It's inspiring, drives you and gives you warmth. And with it you learn that this tiny little person you're responsible for loving and teaching and protecting holds the key to who you are, and she has filled you with a purpose that is more important than anything you've ever done, or will do…"

McCrary listened casually, trying to focus more on the ambient noise from above to prevent Ghost's words from piercing the wall around his heart and accepting that this killer of men was not a blood thirsty criminal, but a grieving parent and husband. He refused to look at the vigilante, feeling the man's grief fill the room. It seemed to consume McCrary, adding to his own internal torment. A moment passed in silence. McCrary closed his eyes, preparing for the worst as he heard Ghost taking in long winded breaths, knowing that it was so the man could manage to continue speaking.

"…Couple these two beauties together and you've achieved something you never deserved to have. Something that should have been impossible to attain, but you have it — your Holy Grail. And now that you have it, you know you will do great and terrible things to keep it safe." Ghost's expression darkened as the focus of his narrative altered its course, and his lower lip quivered with the quaking of his jaw.

But it was not grief that fueled Ghost's momentum anymore.

A heated energy suddenly replaced the frigid mood, melting away the cold anguish invoked by the recollection of loved ones lost. McCrary felt the atmospheric change, snapping his eyes open, and involuntarily casting away any attention he focused on the noise from above. He impatiently waited for Ghost to continue, drawn to his story with a spiritual connection to an idea he couldn't explain to himself, unaware that what would come next was more important than anything spoken beforehand.

"Now, as you've experienced, it's all gone. Not with age. Not naturally, but maliciously. *Violently.*" A steely tone replaced the shaken word's Ghost emitted only seconds ago, lacing his voice with a growing fury. A deep blackness settled in his eyes like an empty space seemingly void of direction and all-encompassing at the same time. A rare firmness shaped his facial appearance with wicked intent. "That love is gone. Someone took it from you. Tore it from your embrace, and *murdered* it."

McCrary could feel the overwhelming heat of rage radiating from the vigilante. It was impossible not to imagine the discontent he would embody if he'd had his own child, but it also brought back the sharp indignation and disgust stemming from the discoveries he'd made with Stone. Ghost was so intense and focused McCrary knew he was a man on a mission, and *nothing* would stand in his way.

Ghost sat in a fixed position, wildly staring beyond everything in his path with his fists clenched so tightly before him that they shook with tremendous force. As the storm seemed to pass, the shaking stopped. Deep breaths followed, in through his nostrils and out through tightly sealed lips. The vigilante repeated this half a dozen times before he slowly lowered the bulging cords of muscle making up his arms. Veins threatened to pop through his skin, forking and spreading in all directions from the tension in his limbs. As he returned to a calmer state, Ghost acknowledged McCrary's eyes on him, feeling as though he'd transcended space and time to a place where he was familiarly alone when he truly was not. His chest rose and fell heavily with each exhalation until his breathing slowed to a regular pace of normalcy. When his shoulders relaxed and sloped forward slightly, Ghost retained his self-control, and finished his explanation.

"It makes you want to do something," Ghost said plainly. "The loss, for me, only enforced a primal sense of justice. Biblical. Old Testament. *Eye for an eye*. So often people look to Him for forgiveness, or guidance. Not me. If He's real — if He's watching. He's granting me vengeance. Either way, I'm taking it." He let the words sink in for a moment, sensing the understanding in the detective sitting across from him. "This is what I do, Randal. This..." Ghost spread his arms and looked around, mimicking McCrary's earlier actions. "... Is who I am."

McCrary's words spat forth unexpectedly and, in a way, he didn't want them to. They conflicted directly with the thoughts and desires that he felt compelled to follow through with. It was as though his words somehow overpowered his thoughts, told them to fuck off, and they came out anyway. "Revenge... Killing all those people for your family... It's wrong. It's not justice."

Ghost hung his head as he stood, and then rotated his neck as a way of filtering out the tension in his muscles. When he looked up his exhausted gaze projected a feeling of dismissal. "Again, I don't need you to agree with me, Randal. Deny it for yourself if you want. I don't care."

"When Kurikova is dead, will you stop and turn yourself in?"

"No." There was no hesitation in his response.

McCrary looked confused at first, but then he remembered the message left for Stone in the closet of DeMarte's den. *You die last*. Then he remembered the conversation he overheard in the cellar below the pawn shop. This man was related to Stone.

"You'll kill Stone?" the detective asked.

Ghost said nothing.

"Why?"

The vigilante shrugged nonchalantly. "He's also responsible. Having him help me has kept the feds off my ass, and out of my way. They're not my enemy, and I prefer to not have to kill anyone who had no part in my family's death."

"What about all the men who work for Kurikova you've killed along the way? Don't they count, too?" McCrary appeared to be angry as he spoke, in some manner trying to dignify those who had a hand in so much misery.

Ghost gestured a sign of dismissal with a quick turn of his head. "Collateral damage. And if I had to pin their deaths to something, it's for all of their other victims. None of those men are innocent in anyway."

McCrary wrestled with his thoughts, trying to make sense of it all. It was simple and straight forward, really, but his mind resisted the logic to take such violent action against so many. "And then what? In the end Stone dies and you stop?"

Ghost shook his head, relinquishing a condescending smirk. "I know this is hard for you to grasp, even though I know what your heart wants out of the matter. I see it in your eyes. But you also know the law is broken, otherwise guys like you would have stopped men like Kurikova a long time ago. Put a stop to it for good." He paused to consider if there was anything else to add, finding the right train of thought and emphasis. "No, I won't stop. I probably never will."

McCrary scoffed at the consideration. He didn't really want to ask, but something deep within compelled him to anyway. "Why?"

Ghost half turned away, lowering his chin to his chest, lost in thought. "Because the victims in that cellar and warehouse had families, too, and there's too much evil in the world to do nothing about it, Randal."

The detective had no words when he considered the images of the caged victims, tormented and abused, desperate for help. His thoughts drifted off to the prior victims from the warehouse, equally disparaged, and he remembered the depravity the scene anchored to his soul. And then there was the afterthought of how many other people out in the world were forced into slavery of some kind, trafficked across the globe for the malignant purposes of demonic men. Audrey sifted into these thoughts with her glowing smile, adding his personal heartache to the matter and, in a way, bringing the cycle full circle. It was then that McCrary decided his course of action, letting the bigger picture help him realize he had to do what he thought was right. That alone uncompromisingly lay at the heart of who he was.

Chapter 41
Puzzle Pieces

Boston had become a bloodbath over the course of the last seventy-two hours. It was the only way to paint the picture.

Jamal Laurence looked as weary as he'd ever been. The day was one he could easily mark up as the most difficult to keep up with, moving from one tragedy to another in devastating succession. Working the scene, following leads, following up on said leads when they don't pan out at first, and so on had him and Bill, his camera man, running non-stop. He sometimes wondered why he lived this gypsy life, chasing stories from one end of town to the other, sticking his nose into the darkest business Boston had to offer. Morbid intrigue came to mind, but it was truly a passion for the truth. His action news segment's success spoke volumes for his work, in which he cataloged his efforts reporting on the Boston Marathon Bombing, and wrote *3 Days of Infamy: The Taking of a Boston Tradition*. The nationally praised work of non-fiction garnered him a Pulitzer nomination, yet even after busting his ass reporting on the bombing of 2013, Laurence thought this story just might outdo his previous work once there was an ending to all the chaos.

He wondered if there was an ending in sight. Was this vigilante a proverbial one-man army? The idea seemed ridiculous for the amount of devastation Boston was enduring. It was clear this wasn't a random spree of violence, begging the question, was he truly working alone? And if there was an end in sight, how would it come to pass?

The body count brought on by this so-called vigilante was drastically high, and climbing. The idea forced Laurence to think about the rumored involvement across five separate crime scenes. For that to be true there had to be interconnecting pieces to the puzzle, which wasn't out of the question. Ever.

It all began with the Warehouse Massacre where nearly twenty women and children were found in a dismal, abused state as victims of human trafficking, and with them were an unprecedented amount of dead Russian *bratva boyeviks* numbering in the upper thirties to forty.

Next came the death of former police commissioner, Anthony DeMarte, who suffered a single shot to the head, and was found with two Russian *bratva* associates. Laurence only knew this secondary detail because of Redmont, the rookie officer he'd made friends with at the warehouse scene. The information was kept tightly under wraps from the media. The young officer had volunteered the details since he learned he would soon be forced to resign, and he didn't respect the idea of a cover up. Suicide had been openly released as DeMarte's cause of death, and the story was spun so that it appeared he was remorseful over his resignation.

"It's a bunch of bullshit," Redmont had stated. "The crime scene photos show two dead Russians in the guy's office, laid out on either side with bullets in their brains, man."

At the time of the conversation Redmont had paused, and Laurence heard a faint beep in the background of the phone call as he received a notification on his cell.

"I sent you the case file and the evidence report for the Commissioner's death, and the warehouse," Redmont said. "I'll be collecting what little I own and I'm blowin' town. Good luck, man."

And that was the last Laurence heard from the rookie cop. What had been delivered into the palms of his hands was the single most condemning evidence he could ever hope for. The files connected the previous events to the murder of Vlademir Kurikova, found in the kitchen of The Motherland with his heart speared into the wall. Murdering the son seemed to be a direct crime of retaliation, appearing deeply personal. It wasn't a standard form of mob execution, and it pointed to the Wolf, Yuri Kurikova, Boston's most brutal mobster. Yet, even though it was considered circumstantial in the manner it fit together, no one was going to confront a grieving father with such a notoriously violent legacy. Laurence was experienced in investigating and reporting on the criminal underworld imprinted in Boston's history. The vast majority of what he investigated could easily put a target on his back. That experience, however, had told him there was always a point where you had to consider the risks of the truth you were trying to uncover. He was not equipped in any fashion to put his life and career on the line by pointing a finger at a notoriously violent and untouchable figure such as Yuri Kurikova. However, the puzzle pieces expanded so deep into a darker place that Laurence had a hard time believing it was real. That made the entirety of this siege of violence gripping Boston all the more frightening.

As he stood in the blaring light of the camera these thoughts came quickly to Laurence, even as he began his monologue.

"The recent violent crimes involving a vigilante killer shrouded in mystery have washed the streets of Boston with blood in a short period of time. This wave has continued to flood through the neighborhoods that make up the heart of our city, as you can see behind me. So far, the violence has crisscrossed the greater Boston area, beginning yesterday morning, and relentlessly continuing over the last twenty-four hours into the heavy depth of the continuing night…"

Laurence stepped to one side, expressing a mask of slight shame and pain, waiving his free hand down the street to give the camera an unobscured view of the chaotic scene behind him. He attempted to speak, halting ever so briefly to recover from the cracking of his voice. For a moment he let the repetitive glow of flashing lights from first responders' vehicles do all the talking. Numerous personnel from Boston PD, fire, and paramedics were navigating their way through the street, some in and out of their homes, others settling and maintaining a perimeter. Altogether the public looked on in awe. It was easy to speculate who may have known the couple of the residence in question as they freely let tears stream down their weary faces. Hands mostly covered mouths as people gasped in awe and attempted to process what they were seeing.

The home now filled with first responders appeared to have mild interior fire damage resulting in the large front window having been blown out. Similar damage could be seen near the front and sides of the home as well. The traditional triple decker smoked ever so slightly, replacing its typically peaceful and well-kept demeanor with the remains of familial desecration. What pained those in attendance was not simply the appearance of the home, but the shock that derived from it. Just as Laurence stepped aside for the camera to zoom in down the block and beyond the police perimeter, two gurneys were carefully extracted from the scarred residence. The reaction sucked the life out of the air across the entire neighborhood as though some ethereal vacuum had been switched on. Within seconds the view caught bystanders reeling with a deeper sense of shock than before, some forced to turn away while others were knocked back a few paces. Hands rose to cover their disbelief, and others ran fingers through their hair and over balding domes. The speculation began as neighbor turned to neighbor.

Jamal Laurence did not speculate. He told the truth. He reported facts. It was then, with what seemed to be such a deliberate coincidence, that he delivered the remainder of his monologue.

"Here, as you can see behind me, the trail of chaos has struck with devastating results." Laurence looked into the camera with a steely eye, shaking off his personal feelings. He knew who lived in this home. He'd known them throughout his career and even before then. It was hard to tell the story he had to report without feeling something, but he tried. Tears be damned. "Earlier I reported on the pawn shop murder, which became another horrific discovery in human trafficking that put the warehouse slaughter to shame. Scores of people were found in cages beneath the storefront façade, and…"

Laurence trailed off again, veering his eyes away from the camera for a moment. He conceded to a deep breath as he regained his composure. His producer chirped into his earpiece, suggesting they cut away to the studio. Laurence shook his head and dismissed the idea. "No, I'm fine."

The hard look returned, although it appeared to be fractured and fragile. There were no apologies for his humanity shining through. And, not that it was much of a concern, but it would up the ratings, too. Laurence continued. "Beneath that storefront facade, a house of horrors lay just beyond the public's knowledge. The worst kind of evil lay beneath the feet of the men murdered there, who had caged and tortured women and children. These vile acts of inhumanity are performed in exchange for money for any number of vile reasons, all to displace the victims on a global scale."

Laurence paused as he turned back to the camera. It was for only a moment, and all about timing. The dramatic pause was slightly cliché, yet it was if done correctly it hammered the viewers with a devastating effect. It was a technique Laurence had mastered, pulling it off with ease and excellence every time while also allowing himself to take a much-needed breath to reset his emotions without being noticed. Simultaneously he looked deeply into the camera, imagining he was looking into the eyes of those watching.

"That was how the day began. Their salvation seemed to be the glimmer of hope, spotlighting the evils of man, yet overcoming them as their rescue became the object of a deeper conspiracy. We can't forget what brought these people to safety and, as obscure as it sounds, it was the only way it would have happened. That is, through one man's crusade of violence with a much deeper meaning than what has thus far appeared on the surface."

Laurence paused, staring hard into the camera. His eyes widened to the point of appearing to pop out of his head. The line of his lips flattened and became tight. Here he let the pain guide him. Here he let Jamal Laurence take over; not the reporter, but the friend of Randal and Audrey McCrary. Here is where he let the real truth speak to his audience.

"Now, as you see where I stand in this upstanding neighborhood, suddenly rocked by violence, its people are clearly shaken. The violence of this so-called crusade simply continues in devastating fashion, but in the same obscure manner.

"Some watching may recognize the home behind me. Some may have had the honor of knowing the lovely couple who lived here. Reports so far indicate this is the home of a well-respected couple within the community; one a teacher of more than twenty years, whose life was unfortunately claimed during the suspected home invasion. Her husband, a Boston PD homicide detective working in concurrence with the FBI investigating the Boston Vigilante case, is said to be missing. Police have placed a BOLO out for him, stating, 'He is not a suspect.' The other remains found within the home you now see being removed were those of an unknown person suspected to be an assailant of the home invasion."

He let that point sink in with the sight of two bodies being wheeled out of the home.

"Further details on this scene will be released at a later time once police have had an opportunity to properly investigate. What can be said of this is that it has all the makings of something far more sinister than what can be speculated. It has many in the area rightly concerned. We'll keep the viewers updated as the news from the scene develops.

"This is Jamal Laurence saying; hold your loved ones tight."

The light of the camera died out at the same time Bill gave Jamal the cue they were off air. The burly man lowered the camera off of his shoulder and cradled it in a ready position, similar to a soldier with his rifle. His backwards Red Sox hat, saturated with sweat from the days hustle and warmth, was adjusted so the curved bill faced forward and slightly to his left away from the camera. The worn fabric and design of the classic dual sock emblem dated back beyond the man's youth, but displayed the nostalgia of the undying loyalty to his team. Bill felt the same way about his professional and personal relationship with Jamal after having worked some crazy stories with him over the years. He could see the frayed similarity in his friend at the moment.

"Good run, man," Bill said, sighing to gauge Jamal's reaction. The reporter failed to react while standing before him in some kind of trance. Bill knew his mind wasn't in the moment. "Where you at, man?"

Laurence snapped to attention, looking to Bill, confused. "What? Huh?"

Bill closed the distance between he and his friend, looking him square in the eye. "I feel like I should already know what's going on in your head after all we've been through together. But, you're way smarter than I am, and way more creative, so I'm lost. You okay?"

The question was more rhetorical than direct. Bill knew something was wrong, but the question was 'what?'

Laurence hesitated to respond, still thinking, shaking his head as though the action would rattle something free. When it did, he said, "The woman in that home used to be a teacher of mine. And her husband, the cop, once caught me being bullied in an alley and helped me out." He turned and took in the sight of the flashing lights and the destruction of the home. It was more like the first time he really *saw* the scene for what it was, not professionally, but personally. It choked him up, shaking him to his core, but he overcame it to speak. "I've never known better people, Bill. I'd hate to be the one who has to pay for what happened there."

Chapter 42
Mission Capable

Randal McCrary stared at the cold steel encasing him in the back of a box van Ghost had procured and broke down who he was in three ways: a former Marine Scout Sniper, a veteran Boston Police Department detective, and newly made widower. Those were the aspects of his life that readily defined him. They were the apex of his memories at this point, not the molding of his youth, or anything before life fed him into the meat grinder of the military. For the moment these were the only thoughts he let filter through his mind, trying to remember the most important pieces of who he was that had shaped him into the man he'd become. As the van jolted over the roadways in a direction McCrary wasn't certain of, he focused on these events to ground his mind in reality so he wouldn't lose himself to the future of what the night held in store.

In the back of his mind he was boxing in the pain of losing Audrey only hours ago, and the guilt of leaving her alone on the kitchen floor. It was a constant battle. He applied layer after layer to encase it, wrapping it in chains to keep it from bursting open, and further weighing it down so it could sink to the darkest parts of his soul. It wasn't that he wanted to forget her, but he knew the grief of her loss could do him more harm than good right now. He was back in the field, deploying for battle so to speak, and that required a clear head. There was no doubt he'd dive in after the memory, retrieve it from the cold depths of his despair, and grieve later. It was important to put Audrey aside for the time being. McCrary had to be fully present to help save Stone, otherwise they would all suffer. Lack of focus led to hesitation, and hesitation would get them killed.

He turned his eyes to the front of the van, seeing the hulking mass of Ghost's silhouette overtake the captain's seat. Concern for the vigilante wasn't something McCrary held too closely to his heart in general, but he hoped and prayed the man was as good as he'd ever been after explaining to him what they would be up against.

"Kurikova employs only the most loyal soldiers," Ghost explained before they left the dank basement below the Chinese restaurant. "They'll die for him without question, and willingly fall under his wrath at the same time. I've wiped out a good portion of them already, but we'll need to play nasty regardless. At the peak of his security are former Spetznaz soldiers. They're brutal in their execution, and elite as most come."

McCrary had smirked at the phrasing Ghost used. *Way to pat yourself on the back*, he had thought.

"These men are likely being joined by mercenaries from an outside source," Ghost added. "I haven't taken the time to figure out who Kurikova's working with, or for, but additional support has been provided in the last twenty-four hours."

Ghost continued to explain his strategy and tactics. McCrary's initial placement would be nearly 700 yards back into the woods surrounding Kurikova's estate in an elevated position. He would maneuver his way in to 400 yards and act as overwatch while Ghost infiltrated the grounds, advising of any close contact movement, and removing any threats if necessary. McCrary would then follow once Ghost entered the home. The estimated time of moving into position would be immediate once they parked.

The layout of the home followed suit with the grounds of the estate being just as vast in its construction. Prior surveillance showed nearly two dozen men securing the grounds of the multi-storied home through satellite heat signature photos, both inside and out, as well as in various exterior locations. The display of these visuals continued to blow McCrary's mind. Even during his time in the Corps, it was hard pressed to get such detailed reconnaissance. Seeing the photos and 3-D blue-prints forced him to ask who Ghost *really* was, and how in the hell did he have such far reaching resources?

It was estimated to take nearly an hour to get to Kurikova's estate, and they had barely been on the road for twenty minutes. McCrary closed his eyes to rest them, and folded his arms across his lap. He let his legs extend freely where his boots nearly touched the opposite side of the van's enclosure. He felt the stiff fabric of the fresh BDUs, or battle dress uniform, Ghost provided. They reminded him of his deployments in the Marines. Everything they wore tonight was black, blending them into the night like lethal shadows. McCrary hadn't worn a tactical kit for nearly thirty years, and even when he had it was of a lesser fashion and quality than the ballistic carrier Ghost provided. The ride alone was enough to spark flashbacks of rough riding Humvee convoys tearing through the dessert of Iraq during the Gulf War, transporting him and other Scout team members into the urban terrain they oversaw. The biggest difference right now was the extreme temperature as well as an even more extreme lack of support.

Again, he looked to Ghost, taking in a deep breath while he made peace with the task at hand. He was here for Stone and Stone alone. The FBI agent was his main purpose in this mission, but to be successful he had to watch the back of a man with the most questionable history he'd ever come across. He stunk of CIA ties, yet McCrary felt Ghost was too sophisticated for the Agency. And any other three letter organization meddling in the business of espionage just didn't amount to much for what McCrary knew of him, if what he knew was even accurate. Regardless, the vigilante's resources were considerable to boot, giving the man access to classified information and military grade weaponry. Whoever Ghost knew that could provide this equipment, McCrary was thankful for them tonight.

Surrounding the detective was an assortment of cases. In preparation for the assault on Kurikova's home, Ghost introduced the detective to the contents of the many crates making up his impromptu headquarters. The man wasn't keen on giving details of where the product had come from, but he did let on to having many loyal resources in both the government and the criminal underworld. McCrary decided he would stop asking questions. When he learned the answers or even what little information was given to him, he'd wished he hadn't asked. Neatly stacked near his feet were two hard cases nearly three feet in length. In each one Ghost had outfitted two M4A1 carbine rifles with single point slings, tactical flashlights on the lower bottom rails coupled with forward vertical hand grips utilizing a pressure pad that activated the lights. A red dot optical scope on the upper picatinny rail rounded out the simple and complimentary additions to the rifles. The telescopic stocks made the M4A1 more compact than their predecessor, the M16, even though they were developed to be used for close quarters combat. That would be their main use tonight as they moved within the confines of the mansion, essentially returning the detective to his roots of urban combat.

McCrary liked the M4. He noticed Ghost had opted for the model with a firing selection of semi-automatic, or fully automatic, with the latter being better for clearing rooms. Ghost had also only provided armor piercing rounds, or 'black tips,' a nickname for the 5.56 mm rounds. Body armor was expected to be worn by Kurikova's security force, which would likely be soft armor. Ghost suspected many of the men may not even wear any at all, but he never took the chance of finding out the hard way.

"I know they won't be wearing double coverage," Ghost told McCrary. He tucked AR500 level three rated armor plates in the front and back of both their carrier vests, and then he tossed them to the side and looked at the bewildered policeman. "I don't take any chances."

McCrary had scoffed at the concept of the man not taking any chances. The whole damn plan was taking a chance and, on top of that, these plates added considerable weight. "That's because you're built like an ox!"

Ghost had shrugged off the comment. "Maybe so, but you'll thank me later."

McCrary had thanked Ghost, but it was before they had loaded up the equipment into the van. The vigilante's resources once again rang true with detailed information and weaponized provisions. While McCrary changed, Ghost placed a 'present' on the table for him. Propped on the table's surface in all of its glory was the intimidating framework of McCrary's rifle of choice; an American creation he'd always referred to as 'The Harbinger of Death' during his service years. McCrary stared at the spectacle of a Barret M107CQ fifty caliber sniper rifle, known as the 'Light Fifty' due to it being nine inches shorter than any preceding Barrett models, and five pounds lighter. A Nightforce NXS Tactical 5.5-22X50 mm Riflescope rested on the top rail of the big gun, and two brick-like magazines housed its massive rounds. He was captivated at the sight of the rifle, pausing and looking at it in awe as though it were some kind of lost treasure newly discovered. A suppressor was fitted over the muzzle break of the main barrel, nearly adding back the weight removed from the design while maintaining its reliability. The weapon was known for being an anti-material rifle, originally developed to take on military equipment. McCrary knew it well.

When the detective paused it wasn't just the sight of the rifle that had stunned him. Yes, he was happy to see the M107 variant, as he had used both an M82 and M107 model during the Gulf War, but it was the fact that Ghost knew he had. The idea of this being a 'present' is what really shocked him, which raised its own questions on top of this. His service record could have been accessed by the spy in whatever fashion. How exactly, McCrary didn't know, but it was possible. What confused him more was how did Ghost gain access to information this specific, and how could he predict it would be McCrary he would be working with?

"Reacquaint yourself with that old friend," Ghost had said. He turned away to prep other things in the moment, leaving McCrary to his own amazement.

The detective looked to his right from where he sat in the van, seeing the larger case that contained the sniper rifle. He reached out and patted it, like a trusty old friend he knew he could count on. His hand rested on the case for the duration of the ride, eyes closed, rehearsing the details of the strategy in his mind. When the van stopped McCrary came to life and shuffled to his knees. He took the Barrett's case in one hand and a case holding an M4 in the other, waiting patiently for the rear door of the van to swing open. That was when the night's mission would really sink in for McCrary, mimicking the days of his former deployment. He analyzed every aspect he could before it was time to go into action from the infiltration, stalking, setting up, the firing of the weapon, down to the extraction. It was his ritual, and tonight was no different. The goal was to live, and retrieve Stone as safely as possible. Anything else was inconsequential to him personally.

****

Ghost killed the engine of the van as soon as he stopped, and the headlights with it. The door creaked loudly as he exited the vehicle and his sheer size rocked it back and forth with his departure. He quick stepped to the back of the van and swung open the double doors. As he did so, McCrary sprang from the interior with surprising agility and wearing a stoic expression he didn't seem to possess an hour ago. He held two gun cases as he exited the van. No words were exchanged. Professionalism ruled the moment, and besides, Ghost had nothing else to say. McCrary didn't either.

Footsteps echoed from the woods off to Ghost's left. Branches cracked and snapped, resoundingly more thunderous in the quiet of the night. The vigilante gathered his rifle and a few other items secured in other cases. He paid no attention to where McCrary went as he'd given him specific instructions, and he knew the man had returned to his past as the night required. His footsteps slowly dissipated, one by one making less noise the farther he travelled. Not because he'd gone too far to hear, but because his sureness of foot and surroundings were restored from the depths of his muscle memory. As a Marine Scout Sniper, McCrary would have been able to move in silence for unprecedented distances over long periods of times undetected by the enemy. Ghost was well trained in the same manner, and he'd known other well-trained men in the same discipline, retired and active duty. One thing they shared in common, among many things the elite soldiers were trained in, was that the practice of their methods never left them. It stayed with them, even if it was shelved in the deepest darkest recesses of their being collecting dust. It would always be second nature to them. Like any skill it would deteriorate over time, however, its recovery came back quickly. And when it was a skill your life depended upon, it never truly rusted to the point where it couldn't be useful.

Ghost remained focused as he smiled in his mind's eye. He no longer heard anything beyond the callings of the night. It was unfortunate how McCrary fell into his plans. Ghost never intended for anyone so innocent to be dragged into the violent grandeur of his vengeance, let alone a public servant's wife. Of course, with the introduction of the Twins, everything had been given a bizarre shove into overdrive. Those two psychopaths were completely unpredictable, and when it came to human life, they would direct their course of fire in any and all directions. Given their involvement and what they had managed to take from the detective, Ghost expected McCrary to suspect something more sinister in play after Ghost provided the detective with a variation of the sniper rifle he once deployed with. To him it was a natural thought. He couldn't fault McCrary for having any suspicions. Even with being a master tactician, Ghost couldn't have predicted what the Twins would do, and he certainly wouldn't have fed into a narrative where McCrary's wife was taken from him. However, Ghost was simply happy the man was still incredibly capable. This was especially true in terms of him moving in silence because tonight Ghost was going to make more noise than he ever had.

Chapter 43
Ready or Not

Ghost passed McCrary bounding through the moderately wooded area with the agility of a panther. He whisked by the detective like a gust of wind and, surprisingly enough, barely made a sound. Branches and leaves of the underbrush clipped him as he passed, but they did so in a way that couldn't be mistaken for anything more than or breeze, or small woodland animal passing through the twilight of the moon's beaming illumination. McCrary didn't give the man's abilities much attention, although he was impressed. How the hell could someone so big be so stealthy in the woods? He was making a conscious effort with every step, letting the moonlight guide him. His pace wasn't nearly as exceptional as Ghost's, and it wasn't meant to be. Experience slowly churned beneath the surface for the former Marine, involuntarily taking control of his motor skills, guiding him with an excited return.

In the days of his service, McCrary would feel that sour stomach sensation resonate within him at first, letting the nerves run their course. The first handful of missions he was assigned came with a vomiting precursor. It typically garnered harassment from other team members, but the laughs were short lived when similar responses overtook them as well. The nervousness had an expiration date, but not the adrenaline. That was permanent. The trick was controlling it to keep a steady hand when the right moment came, if it came at all. More often than not he and his spotter would conduct missions of surveillance, gathering intelligence without engaging the enemy. Even under such orders they remained danger close, meaning they were within close proximity of their targets, and they would be tonight. Sometimes this was the case when they scouted ahead to mark a target for artillery fire. It applied mostly to McCrary and his spotter, who he rotated with at times depending on the mission when they were behind enemy lines. Over time they became numb to the deployment. Their nerves became reserved, and all that remained was collective calm and the mission at hand. Nothing else mattered. He was thankful that his biological functions remained in tune with this emotional detachment after so many years. By no means was he excited about the situation or his involvement, however, there was comfort in the resurrection of his training. McCrary hated to admit it, especially to himself, but tonight he was ready to kill.

His mission parameters were to set up around 400 yards out from Kurikova's estate from an elevated position off the hill behind the mobster's home. At the moment he was in the position of what was referred to as an unknown distance. By pure line of sight, McCrary estimated he was near his mark. It was crucial to be in the needed position. He took a knee as he looked out through a clearing of brush. Ghost had provided a pair of Bushnell Fusion Arc Laser Rangefinder binoculars, which McCrary removed from a large pouch attached to his vest via the interwoven MOLLE bands. Due to the bulky size of the binoculars the pouch was located on his back, left of center, in a position he could access single handedly.

The battery powered device was good up to 1760 yards, over a mile, which was far more than McCrary needed. It was also another testament to Ghost's resources. He prepped the device for the binoculars to locate his range at the moment, selecting the appropriate settings to zero in on the target area by utilizing the device's ARC technology. This gave him his true distance and horizontal distance for the heavy angle of his impending shots. The tech of the binoculars was incredibly helpful and time saving. When the setup was complete McCrary raised the optics to eye level. The readout told him he was within twenty-five yards of his targeted position. Mentally he patted himself on the back for coming so close to where he needed to be. He secured the binoculars in their pouch, picked up the two gun cases, and measured out the yardage with his steps. Within ninety seconds he was where he needed to be.

The illumination of the moon provided enough light for him to find a good placement for his concealment. He doubted very much that the security force patrolling Kurikova's estate was watching the surrounding hillsides with night vision goggles, but he pretended they were, making sure when he maneuvered that he remained out of any direct sight, hunching over to the level of the bushes and slipping seamlessly through the trees. Once he found a clear enough position, he sat on the ground laying the case out for the Light Fifty before him. He hefted the big rifle out of the case, setting it on his crossed legs to expand the bipod at the forward position of the lower receiver. McCrary then located one of the box magazines and slammed it home into the rifle.

Positioning was paramount. McCrary needed to have a full-scale view of the estate, but not protrude from his cover to give away his position. Once he started firing, if he needed to, the party would be officially underway. Ghost didn't have to tell the detective that firing wasn't necessary, except if he were somehow pinned down, or surrounded. The anti-material weapon would decimate anyone in its path, likely dusting them into a series of body parts of biological mist. McCrary had seen it before, even done it himself. He would fire if he needed to for the sake of their success in rescuing Stone. Ghost was a big part of that success, so McCrary couldn't let the man fail. The only difference for McCrary was that once he had Stone, he was getting the hell out of here. There was no waiting for the vigilante taking on the elite trained operatives and seeking his own form of justice.

McCrary adjusted to the position he selected, laying prone, legs extended behind him with his feet turned out so the inner placement of his boots rested on the ground in a half-Y position. His placement gave him an unobstructed view of the estate both vertically and horizontally. Next, he adjusted the scope to his range, utilizing the engrained skills of a Marine Scout Sniper to select the proper settings and adjust for a mild breeze. He adjusted the bipod's height as well so the rifle sat as level as possible, and then he fixed the butt-pad off the rear of the stock so it fit into his shoulder area just right. Lastly, he pulled back the bolt and loaded a round into the receiver.

There was a particular form of elation that overcame McCrary, elevating his heartrate as the adrenaline was re-introduced to his system. He took a series of deep breaths to steady himself against the force of his adrenaline, closing his eyes while each breath slowly entered and exhaled until the thumping in his chest became more restful. When he was ready McCrary opened his eyes and adjusted his right hand on the pistol grip of the Barrett rifle. With his free hand he reached up to the collar of his vest to activate the Motorola communications unit Ghost provided. He didn't need to worry about the volume of his words with his distance, but kept his tone just above a whisper anyway. The throat mic attachment and ear- piece were top notch accessories, enabling clear transmission and reception.

"Eagle-One in position," McCrary said. He rested his cheek along the stock as he looked through the scope, scanning the grounds of the estate.

Security lights illuminated the home very well, leaving very few dark spaces along its exterior. He guessed this was where any one of the sentries would be, if they weren't located farther out in the brush bordering the vast lawn. McCrary remembered the heat signature satellite photos Ghost provided displayed nearly two dozen men across the grounds in various locations. Some were closer to the home, which a handful patrolled its interior, and others were located farther outside of the perimeter. It only made sense to the detective that these highly trained men would relocate themselves at intermittent time periods. After nearly two years of guerrilla-like assaults on his operations, McCrary couldn't see Kurikova hiring men who sat in one place waiting for termination. Ghost was clear that the Russian only hired the best of the best. An assault on his mansion was obviously not a surprise. It was inevitable, whether Stone had been taken or not, and Kurikova was a smart man. He wasn't the type to lie in wait without a plan of his own, and for someone who had a brutal reputation but had never been criminally charged with the crimes he was surely responsible for, he couldn't be taken lightly.

A gurgling sound emitted through McCrary's earpiece followed by a response to his readiness. "Copy that, Eagle-One."

McCrary hated the sound preceding Ghost's transmission. He'd heard it before, in close quarters, and by his own hand. There were many sounds a man could experience throughout his lifetime that would remain embedded in his psyche, and the result of a well sharpened blade severing the throat and carotid artery of another human being was one such sound. It sent a shiver down his spine. McCrary shook it off like an involuntary tremble. Another deep breath followed, allowing him to reset.

"We're in the shit now, Marine," he told himself, forgetting the mic was now open both ways.

"Getting cold feet?" Ghost asked. There was a sense of amusement in his tone.

McCrary picked up on it immediately, and something Ghost had said earlier finally registered with him. '*It boils down to who I am…*' Ghost had explained to him. The comment was out of context, but McCrary found it quite applicable now. The man was a killing machine, quite literally, or at least from his exploits of mass murder spanning a varied portion of the country. Ghost was enjoying himself.

"The only cold feet I have are the ones I walk around on in the winter," McCrary said. And he left it at that.

"Good thing it's springtime," Ghost replied. Patches of his breathing came over the mic. He was moving quickly. A grunt transmitted over the frequency was followed by a slight growl. "That's two down."

"I have no visual at this time."

More breathing cast over the radio as Ghost mic'd up. "I'm approaching the house from the south. Your lower left corner."

The specificity of Ghost's description baffled McCrary. Curiosity forced him to shift his view, and sure enough a hulking shadow moved from the outskirts of the borderline. An arm extended forward, jolting ever so slightly with the recoil of a silenced pistol. McCrary scanned upwards, barely an adjustment from this distance, and watched a man hidden amongst the darkness collapse to one side. He continued to scan the immediate area to make sure Ghost was covered as he crouched just below the crest of a slight rolling incline in the yard where there was no cover.

Movement east of Ghost caught McCrary's eye. He quickly called it out over the coms. As he did Ghost had already dealt with the threat.

And then another caught the marksman's eye.

"Nine o'clock," McCrary said evenly.

Two more suppressed rounds dropped a man encased in the shadows, but they did not stop him. He must have been wearing body armor, as predicted. Ghost was on the sentry in less than a second. A flurry of hands shot out with blinding speed. McCrary watched through the green hue of the scope's night vision as the two shadows engaged in mortal combat. Their movement seemed similar, and their garb was nearly identical. The fight happened so quickly McCrary almost lost sight of which man was Ghost. The man he engaged appeared to be the same size, or close enough to it. Suddenly one man was knocked back, quickly taken into the other's grip by an arm lock, and then somersaulted in a singular space with such force McCrary thought he could hear the man's neck snap as he crashed into the ground. The entire display was a clinic on lethal hand to hand combat. The winner yanked the loser off the ground with one hand, finishing the engagement with two bullets shot upwards through the skull of the defeated. The body was then tossed into a darker space. Ghost then reloaded his pistol with swift precision.

McCrary was impressed, yet remained on task as he continued his over watch. Again, he forgot about the two-way mic being live as he gave life to his bewilderment. "Just who the fuck are you?"

A moment passed before Ghost replied. "Identities have no place in war, Randal. Not until it's won." Another flutter in time passed as Ghost added, "History is written by the victors."

McCrary couldn't argue as the man quoted phrases commonly heard throughout the branches of military service. He watched as Ghost moved closer to the home, making his way to one of nearest entrances on the back patio area. A full size in-ground pool occupied the outdoor area. Numerous sets of poolside lounges, chairs, and tables were setup on the stamped concrete area, bordered only by the well-manicured lawn. Ghost posted up near the corner of the house before it ventured into the covered space leading to a set of French doors. Dim light emitted from the interior of the home. McCrary caught sight of a black clad man walking across the inner threshold. Behind the man was the island counter of what appeared to be a large kitchen area. Lining the exterior of the covered patio portion of the backyard were two security lights facing out towards the pool. There was no way Ghost could get passed this sentry without first being seen. McCrary zeroed in on the target.

"Target in the kitchen," the detective said. "In my sights."

"No go," Ghost said.

McCrary panned his scope to his left a quarter of an inch, placing Ghost in his sights now. He watched the man apply a set of goggles, press a button on one side, and then the exterior screens glowed green in the infrared lens of the scope. They were a new kind of night vision goggles, something McCrary had never seen. Typically, the optical apparatus protruded outward and severely limited the wearer's range of vision from side to side, making it incredibly important to constantly be looking in all directions. These would give Ghost nearly full range of vision, and a great advantage. He'd given McCrary a pair as well, but he hadn't appropriated himself to them. There was a tinge of excitement to try the new equipment now.

He then watched as Ghost removed an item out of a vest pouch and activated it. He presented the item, which gave off a slight blue hue, as if he knew he was being watched. "Short range EMP grenade."

McCrary just shook his head, keeping his thoughts to himself. It figured the man had something like an electromagnetic pulse explosive. The mechanism had the capability of disrupting, if not destroying, electronic devices in the immediate area. This would neutralize the security lights, as well as the interior lights. It would also kill their communications for a short duration.

"When the lights go out get down here," Ghost instructed. "The attention will be on me, but keep your eyes up. We'll be off air for at least five minutes."

"Copy that," McCrary replied, shaking his head. Of course, Ghost was prepared for that, too. McCrary should have known better. The man covered every detail. The detective continued scanning for the moment, seeing movement along the east end of the home. "Company en route, three o'clock. Double bogies."

Ghost looked in the appropriate direction, holstering his pistol in a tactical thigh holster. He reached back with his right arm and easily freed his M4 from a U-shaped tactical clip. The rifle was swung into a forward low-ready firing position. The incoming sentries would come right around the corner of the home directly in front of him. He tossed the EMP grenade into the covered patio area nearest to the kitchen. The disc shaped explosive skipped across the stamped flooring made to look like granite rock, sliding along its stone etchings until it bounced off of the wall. The blue light caught the interior sentry's attention. McCrary watched him come to life with a desperate reaction, completely caught off guard.

"Going dark," Ghost reported, and then the glow of his goggles and the airwaves went dead.

The sentry in the kitchen stepped back and brought his rifle to bear, ready for anything beyond the French doors separating him from an impending threat. McCrary took this as a cue to let a round fly. He automatically lined up his shot. His pulse quickened even as he slowed his breathing in anticipation of firing, pausing as he squeezed the trigger. Ghost remained in place as the milliseconds ticked by, unmoving before the EMP blast came, prepped to address the surrounding threats.

The grenade exploded, but its pulse was undetectable. There was no sound. There was no flash. EMP's emit the same invisible pulse as a nuclear weapon, yet they only effect electronic devices. The results spoke for themselves as the security lights positioned on the south side of the home flashed out, and the interior lights died with them.

Directly in sync with the EMP grenade came McCrary's fifty caliber subsonic round. The suppressor on the rifle contained the report of the shot to a mere crackle similar to a .22 long rifle, or the clapping of a man's hands. Yet the 690-grain bullet traveled at a velocity of more than 1,000 feet per second and hit with a thunderous force in a flash. The timing couldn't have been better.

The round McCrary sent out was adjusted on the fly, but the target was hit with deadly precision. First the glass of the French doors shattered, destroying the entire square frame and cracking the surrounding sections. The sentry had no time to contemplate what a dangerous position he was in as the bullet punched him in square in the chest, snapping him off of his feet and tossing him backwards like a rag doll. His upper torso was eviscerated by the anti-material projectile, exploding into a crimson mist of organs and bone. The final mark he left on the world came in the form of a grisly splatter painting the kitchen of a man he was paid to protect, even as his body collided with the island counter nearly five feet behind him. His corpse folded forward and fell to one side as though someone had released the strings of a marionette. What remained inside him soon seeped out of the gaping cavity that once made up his torso, draining out into a puddle that would encompass the remains of his former vessel.

McCrary did not celebrate the success of dispatching his target. He did not enjoy killing anyone. But it was necessary tonight, and he'd made peace with that. He followed Ghost's plan, and he packed up to get moving.

The detective popped open the case holding the M4A1 rifle. He loaded and made it ready as he wove himself into the single point sling. Additional magazines were placed into the forward pouches of his ballistic carrier vest, and then McCrary was on the move. He took a few steps before he paused for a second, looking back at the Barrett rifle. He couldn't just leave it here in some random spot to be found by God-knows-who. Realistically, if he even engaged anyone inside Kurikova's home, the big gun wouldn't be useful in such close quarters. Something ate at him, and he decided he couldn't leave the gun. McCrary swung the M4 under his right arm and secured it into a U-shaped clip located on the bottom of his vest. This held the rifle on the lower end of the rail nearest to the barrel, lining his back in a vertical position with the stock directed skyward. He reached down and lifted the Light Fifty by the carry handle, adjusting the weapon in his hands so he was ready to put it to use.

Once the Barrett was in McCrary's grip, he began his descent from the hill. There was no concern for the amount of noise he made. He was too far out to be noticed anyway. All the attention would be on Ghost, the main infiltrator, which gave McCrary a better chance to enter without being noticed. He moved as quickly as he could, modifying his steps to work through the terrain so he wouldn't stumble. McCrary was never one to use his age as an excuse, but the Barrett made him think twice about that at the moment. Here he was, charging into an overrun hostile mansion protected by elite trained killers, hefting a fifty-caliber sniper rifle. The 400-yard sprinting would damn near tire him out before he reached the home, let alone carrying this damn gun. Near the bottom of the hill McCrary questioned his motivation, but dismissed it as his morals superseded the gun's necessity.

"Light Fifty, my ass!" he told himself, launching into another dreaded sprint once he cleared the decline of the hill.

Chapter 44
Den of Wolves

When the lights went out, Ghost paused for a single breath before moving. McCrary had done his job by removing any potential threats, and dispatched a man waiting inside the kitchen just beyond the patio. To his left Ghost could hear the shuffling of movement and the faint jangling of equipment projecting the approach of further incoming threats. There was a difference in pacing between the sounds, which confirmed McCrary's last transmission warning of at least two men coming his way.

Ghost surged forward, bringing his rifle to bear. He moved with quick, light steps betraying the agility of such a large man. In the brief moment leading to the impending engagement, Ghost travelled to a square support pillar designed to be a stone mosaic. This section of the massive dwelling was constructed in a more modern style as the southeastern corner expanded out into a lengthy rounded segment. The curved shape made it easy to follow along. Ghost assumed the men would likely be coming fast, tactically stalking their way around the bend in a stacked formation, one right behind the other, but slightly offline. Ghost listened hard as he leaned out from his covered position, timing their approach. At the first sign of movement he advanced.

The vigilante moved forward and remained in line with the edge of the home while tilting himself to his right. Keeping the M4A1 rifle shouldered, he switched the firing selector to semi-automatic. His position didn't move him far, but it was more than enough. He peered through the red dot scope, even though it wasn't entirely necessary. His line of sight was flawless.

At the first sign of movement Ghost seized the opportunity to strike. He squeezed the trigger twice, knocking the first sentry back into the other. He quickly adjusted targets in mid-fire, and punched four holes into the second man; two to the chest, which was protected by armor, and two more to the head. The suppressed rounds burst the man's head open with ease, releasing a dark mist of brain matter and blood. The lead man was close to recovering his footing by the time Ghost put down his partner, and raised his rifle to return fire. Ghost stepped forward a few paces, zeroed in his sights on the remaining sentry, and shot him four more times in the head as well. The overall engagement took a little more than two seconds, and neither sentry got a shot off.

Ghost immediately circled back and entered through the kitchen. There was no doubt the entire security force Kurikova hired was on full alert, and he expected to be swarmed over if he didn't keep moving. He kept in mind that the EMP blast only had a short range, which simply disrupted electronic devices. By this time Ghost figured he only had a few more minutes to take advantage of the darkness.

As he entered Kurikova's mansion Ghost felt swallowed by the pretentiousness of the man's ego. The infrared glasses switched on with the touch of a button, and gave Ghost a clear vision of the interior. Although greenly hued, he could assess that the grandiose tastes of the mob boss touched everything he owned from top to bottom. Ghost didn't care about the details, whether it was the gold laced Italian marbled counter tops and floors or the dark Mahogany cabinets with platinum handles. By the end of the night it would all come crumbling down. He rushed forward to the sentry McCrary had nearly blown in half, stepping around the increasingly large pool of blood oozing from the man's torso and the hunks of exploded entrails. Ghost pulled the man's earpiece from his head and the connecting radio from his belt. The device went into a cargo pocket on his BDU's for later use.

The body count was up to six.

A squeaking noise, like the kind made by misplaced steps against smooth flooring, resonated behind Ghost and caused him to move. The M4 came up as a man entered into the far end of the vast kitchen. If it weren't for Kurikova's luxurious tastes, he'd swear he was in the kitchen of the man's restaurant. Every appliance was industrial and stainless steel, which would have shone right along with the high-end accents of the crystal lighting fixtures. That is, if the lights were on. The faint creak of another door on the opposite end of the kitchen spun Ghost's attention back around. He kept low behind the large island counter at the center of the room. Either man was set on a path to converge on his position and would have no problem seeing him with their night vision headsets. Ghost considered the time, thinking of the lights flickering on sooner than later, and used what time remained to his advantage.

A gloved finger touched the left end of his goggles and the lenses became slightly darker. Less than a second later he launched two cylindrical canisters over the top of the island counter. Both objects arced out at forty five degree angles, tumbling end over end in their aerial pathways before they collided with the floor and skipped in the desired directions at the feet of their intended targets.

The sentries who had entered the kitchen were both caught off guard and stepped backwards. The seconds ticked away all too quickly. Alarming Russian exclamations were exchanged in controlled whispers, followed by harsh warnings. But it was too late.

The flash bang grenades burned like a thousand suns within the Kurikova kitchen and simultaneously echoed with the roar of a devastating thunderclap. Ghost rose from his position behind the island counter, firing two rounds at the sentry to his left, hitting the man high in his chest and esophagus. Blood spurted from his throat as he cried out and gurgled, arms gripping at the mortal wound as he fell.

Ghost spun to face the remaining sentry, stepping to his left around the counter to engage the disoriented man. The fierce light produced from the grenade would have blinded the man temporarily, and Ghost caught him at a disadvantage as he struggled to tear the night vision headset off to clear his eyes. The strap was set too tight and, in his frantic state, he couldn't slide it off his big head. Without hesitation Ghost advanced with his M4, placing the red dot scope on the man's head, and fired twice. There was no need for him to worry about the lights anymore.

Eight down.

Ghost suspected there were nearly a dozen more sentries, give or take. This didn't include the remaining twin responsible for abducting Stone, who was a handful all on his own. The vigilante hoped McCrary would catch the bastard from afar and do the world a favor, but hope didn't do any good in combat. Two things needed to happen: Stone needed to be extracted as soon as possible and remain alive, and he needed to send Kurikova to hell. Ghost speculated the remaining details in between, but they were inconsequential at the moment. Those were the goals of the night. And, if worst came to worst, Kurikova needed to die no matter what.

Movement was life, and Ghost did just that: he kept moving. He maneuvered to the eastern ward past the second man he'd dusted in the kitchen. He walked in a crouched, tactical stance while remaining vigilant with the M4 up and ready. A series of doors lined the hallway on either side; all of them were closed. Typically he would search them as he passed, but there was no time for that. Standard operating procedures had no place here tonight. He moved past them cautiously as most of the doors were offset from each other, staggered from left to right as he proceeded.

Sound was an important precursor to any attack, especially in dealing with the high skill level of the men Kurikova hired. Ghost listened hard. He was thankful for the noise-cancelling amenity of the earpieces he had selected. The device protected him from the deafening high decibel levels of gunfire, and amplified any lower sounds so he could hear at a nearly advanced level.

Which is why he heard them coming.

A black clad man maneuvered into the hallway in front of Ghost, mistakenly raising his rifle as he moved rather than acquiring the appropriate firing position first. He was cocky. The only thought Ghost assumed after the fact was that this sentry thought he had the upper hand of surprise. He gambled and lost.

Ghost stepped inside the man's workspace, deflecting the barrel of his rifle outward towards the far wall. At the same time Ghost jammed the hot tip of the M4's suppressed barrel under the man's chin, burning him as it tilted his head backwards. He screamed out as his flesh was singed before Ghost freely painted the wall and ceiling behind him with what little intelligence he had.

The sentry's back up did not make the same mistake of introducing his gun into the fray too late and, with the forward aggressiveness and tactical maturity that he moved with, Ghost knew he had met the first of a handful of Kurikova's Spetznaz warriors.

The Spetznaz soldier was a larger man, and heavily armed. A black mask covered his face, as many of the world's elite forces commonly did. It was the only lack of uniformity in his apparel, and it offset the woodland camouflage that he wore. Heavy rounds emitted from his blacked out AKS-74U rifle as he swept the hallway with bullets while emerging from the same direction as the man before him. The rounds punched into the sentry Ghost had killed seconds ago. The dead were never useless, and he served an honorable service of protecting Ghost while he used the body like a shield.

Ghost pressed forward into the advancing masked killer. He lifted the dead man slightly to better shield himself, and attempted to fire his M4 around the body. The experienced Spetznaz fighter returned Ghost's tactics by closing the distance between them to divert the barrel's trajectory towards the outside wall. A hard shove from the masked man forced Ghost to drop the M4 to adapt to the fight. Using both hands, Ghost pressed the dead man forward until the masked man slammed into the far wall at the end of the hall. A big hand butted the lifeless head of the first sentry into the second numerous times. The nose behind the mask bled profusely, but the disorienting tactic seemed to only piss off the Russian.

The masked man made a forward surge of his own, gaining only a few steps of space, which was more than enough. He raised the short-barreled Kalashnikov rifle over the dead man's shoulder to fire over the top. Ghost caught the barrel's advancement and pulled the gun his way while stepping inside the firing radius. The masked man fired it on full auto, blasting the hallway floor and walls until the bolt locked back and the magazine was empty. Ghost used the dead man as a shield once more, ramming the masked man back into the wall. The force and weight of them concaved the drywall just off-center of the supporting stud. The masked man grabbed the dead sentry by the collar and tossed the body from where they had originally come, grunting and growling as he pulled himself out of the wall.

It was not often that Ghost stood toe to toe with a man on his level of size, and possibly skill. In another life, in another time, he would have cherished the opportunity of such a contest. Whether it came from his extensive training, or it was something inherently engrained in his DNA, Ghost enjoyed a good fight. However, the life and death circumstances, compounded by the fact he was outnumbered, were not the kind he had time to relish.

A flurry of punches came Ghost's way. Some were blocked or deflected, while some landed or grazed him. The masked man was good. But he was nothing special. The titans clashed in the hall, filling the space with aggression and violence.

Ghost returned fire, continually moving even in the close quarters of a hallway so confining to its broad combatants. He parried punches and stepped inside them, delivering crushing elbows both to the body and the head, staggering the Russian adversary. A cannon-like knee delivered to the masked man's midsection drove him into the wall where damaged sheetrock dust escaped from within the structure and salted the tenderized opponent. A cry of pain echoed into the hallway, but it told nothing of the man's toughness. He immediately fired back, rising with what would have been a devastating uppercut. He quickly transitioned into a combination of punches. In the midst of the returned onslaught, the masked man seamlessly interjected a large combat knife. He held it in an overhand fashion so that he could strike when he attacked, as well as when he retracted the blade.

Sounds are important, and Ghost heard the introduction of a blade released from the safety of its sheath. He put what distance he could between them, calculating the man's reach, and what space there was to maneuver. There wasn't much.

The masked man jabbed and slashed with the blade, pressuring Ghost into the corner of the hall while positioning himself on the opposite side to prevent an escape into the opening of the doorway where he originated. There was no way for Ghost to get past him without paying dearly. He taunted Ghost, cursing at him in Russian with a growling pronunciation garbled by the mask's barrier.

"YA sobirayus' rasrezat' tebya na kroshnechnyye kusochki."

Ghost understood the masked man's words and let the overconfidence of his threat roll off him. Numerous operations in Russia had forced him to hone his linguistic abilities in the harsh sounding language. '*I'm going to cut you into tiny pieces*.' Ghost simply shook his head dismissively.

The masked man lunged in, swiping the blade from left to right, missing, and then attacked again with the tip of the knife as he rescinded the assault. Ghost delivered a well-timed push kick when the knife missed him. It grazed the masked man's mid-section, giving them space as he turned and deflected it with his non-knife wielding hand, and then stepped in with a barrage of fists and kicks. The counterattack was impulsive and aggressive, just as Ghost expected. He used the space he gained to avoid the attacks until he could take advantage of the right one.

Tides change in any battle when least expected, and Ghost had made a career of doing just that. The art of ensnaring an enemy was what allowed him to take on overwhelming odds. It was in the calculation of the skills he had honed over the years, what his enemy offered him in return, and why he was damn good at what he did. When the counter-attack came Ghost used his superior abilities to change the course of what this fool had designed to be his victory. A side-kick shot towards him like a spear, but the masked man's positioning wasn't ideal. Ghost turned ever so slightly, evading the strike while he caught the leg with his left arm. This position left the masked man exposed with his backside towards Ghost, and forced him to balance on one leg. Ghost stepped away, stretching the masked man's stance to the point of collapsing. As Ghost did so, he unsheathed his own knife and lacerated the flesh and connective tissue behind the knee. The blade cut deeply and with ease, severing the critical construction supporting the limb. A torrent of blood gushed from the wound and drenched the marble floor. The remaining sinew, bone, and cartilage popped and snapped as the man fell to the floor. The impact caused the flimsy knee joint to turn sideways, twisting the leg to the side like a limp noodle.

The Spetznaz soldier roared in agony, foregoing any combative aspects of the moment. He sat forward and reached out aimlessly for the site of the torturous pain. His focus was on the mangled leg, never having a chance to cradle it and pretend to ease his suffering. He did not have to wait long for mercy.

Once the masked man hit the floor, he let loose a guttural scream that resonated from an abyss of human suffering that would have made most men shiver with fear. Ghost was not most men, and he had heard it before. Then, just as abruptly as the screaming began, it stopped.

The vigilante launched a heavy kick into the side of the sentry's head, embedding it into the wall, immediately shutting off his pathetic whine. Drywall dusted the man's head as it rested inside the broken space at an awkward angle with his mouth still gaping open, twitching. Ghost reached behind his back and retrieved his snub-nosed Colt Python .357 revolver. The stainless steel gleamed with each muzzle flash of the three shots Ghost unleashed into the wall. He holstered the revolver and walked away without a second thought.

Ghost retrieved his M4 rifle, dropped the mag, cleared the chamber, and loaded a fresh magazine. He continued deeper into the massive home while he chambered a new round. The flash bangs and the machine gun report were incredibly loud and sent an appropriate announcement of his arrival. The dying man's grating outcry could still be heard throughout the halls of Kurikova's mansion. It was like an omen foreshadowing what was to come.

Chapter 45
Tremble

A home was supposed to be a place of solace in a time of grief. It was supposed to be the epicenter of safety and security to its residents, where life could flow seamlessly without regard to the outside world; a place where memories were made, and a head could rest peacefully and dream. The structure itself was a protectorate built under the strong-willed efforts of its family's patriarch, and deemed a fortress against the evils that would stand against him.

Not in Yuri Kurikova's world. Not in his home. Not anymore.

The moment the power shut off, blanketing his home in the dark reality of his misdeeds accumulated for the past quarter century, the Wolf felt as though the end was quite possibly that much nearer. Realistically it was inevitable. All kingdom's fell at some point, which made tonight's siege a revelation coming to pass even if Kurikova had wanted to turn a blind eye to it. The sensation radiated through him with an electric palpability, pumping him full of adrenaline fueled by fear and dread. He expected the attack to come, yet there was something ominously refreshing knowing that someone had the audacity to assault his home directly. It was a mistake made by Armenians long ago, however, tonight would not be the same.

Through the many years of his chosen profession it could be said that Kurikova knew he'd take losses over time. This included personal losses, such as Vlademir's recent death. *Was it ill of him to consider such things as a father, expecting his son to be stolen away from him in a life he'd willingly provided*? It was inevitable those kinds of transgressions would occur out in the world where he could not control everything. In his home it should have been different. He should have been able to protect *everything*, yet the darkness reminded him of a little-known fact he always chose to ignore; in a world filled with monsters, there are always bigger and badder monsters.

And one finally came knocking.

As was the protocol per Viktor, his security team's leader, Kurikova was immediately moved to a safe room. He'd chosen, and ordered it so, to remain free until a threat was viable. As for the safe room, there was only one way in, which meant there was only one way out. There were no hidden passageways, windows, or underground tunnels. This dorm of his mansion was literally a sealed bunker. Once they entered, he was the only person who could get them out. There was no possible escape, making this room the final destination for one or all of those in his presence.

Of the four masked men escorting Kurikova to the room, Viktor was at the lead. He was the most dangerous man Kurikova had ever known, and he had used his expertise a number of times. The former Spetznaz operator was made of iron will and had laser focus; a characteristic that caused great discomfort as the man's emerald green eyes saw through everyone who crossed his path. Kurikova was extremely confident in his abilities, even with the exploits of the man bringing his empire to its knees. Viktor's large stature, from the reports Kurikova had received, seemed to match up well with the vigilante. The overall skillset had yet to be seen. Kurikova thought he should have sent Viktor on a hunt for the man long ago, but having him close was much more important to the syndicate leader. If it came down to the two of them, Kurikova thought that he and Viktor would be far too much for the vigilante to handle. After all, it was his home, his *den*, and he had every intention of fighting to the end.

Kurikova thought of his home as the site of a final showdown, giving the evening a cinematic sensibility to the outcome of events accrued over a time span of nearly three years. Kurikova smiled through the fear and could not have thought of a more fitting environment to end everything once and for all. Yes, for the first time in a very long time, if ever, the Wolf was afraid. Dying was not the problem. He would go out with the ferocity of a pack's alpha, as he should. People like him did not deserve to die peacefully in their sleep, and he accepted that paradigm. What frightened him was losing everything he'd built; whether it was through legal or immoral means, he didn't care. His mark on the world would be snuffed out far sooner than he intended *if* the vigilante was successful.

When they reached the safe room, Kurikova used the secondary option of entry. The security system was set up with a formal key in case the power was cut off, a failsafe Viktor had taken the care to initiate. Typically, such a room would run off of its own power source, but it had hardly ever been used, and Viktor's paranoia in security measures had paid off with the keyed entry while the room's power remained switched off.

Kurikova removed a large, heavy metal key from his pocket and inserted it into the appropriate slot below the retina scanner. When the steel bolts rotated and unlocked the heavy security door masked to be a standard wooden portal, it opened slightly. Viktor pulled the large door open, and Kurikova patted the team leader on the shoulder as he passed him into the safe room. Flashlights quickly burned in all directions through the inky blackness of this asylum, lighting it with thousands of blinding white suns. The brightness of the tactical lights carried by the guards was too much, forcing Kurikova to close his eyes for a moment to protect them from the coming change in illumination. He heard the light snap of a switch, and the metallic creak of a breaker panel being opened. Three loud cracks sounded from the same corner as the breakers were flipped to the 'ON' position. A light hum comfortingly buzzed through the massive room. Kurikova exhaled a breath of relief, and opened his eyes to the soft lighting the room provided.

"*Dva snaruzhi, dva vnutri*," Viktor ordered. He pointed to two of his men, and then gestured to the door. "Two outside, two inside."

The two men designated by Viktor stand guard in the hall were also former Spetznaz operators. They followed the order without hesitation, and closed the door behind them. With the room now operating off of its own power the door's sensors quickly engaged, bolting the door shut automatically. The thrust of the steel bolts engaging into a secured position within the re-enforced walls echoed sharply with a mechanical tone, signaling the guise of their safety.

Viktor signaled to the remaining guard to move to the opposite side of the room with a nod of his head. He himself then moved to a parallel position, and the two sentries focused their attention on the door with their rifles in a ready position.

Kurikova sat behind the mahogany desk arranged at the back of the room, offline of the door, and arranged to be the room's centerpiece. He hadn't visited this place in a long time, yet it remained in immaculate condition. More bookshelves lined the walls behind the desk and were filled with reading material and pictures of the Old Country. Nostalgia was always comforting in the face of danger. A sense of ease filtered over Kurikova, but it was not relaxation. The oxygen pump was now running at full capacity, giving the room a more comfortable and livable atmosphere. The tank was large enough to sustain air for a dozen individuals for nearly six hours, more than enough for the three men, and far longer than any of them would need. He took in a deep breath, filling his lungs, and enjoyed the capability to do so while the possibility remained.

It was difficult not to take on the melancholic inevitability death presented, and Kurikova was not one to let such a feeling overcome him without a good drink. Off to one side of the desk sat a prestigious bottle of vodka he'd taken as partial payment five years earlier from a Chinese oil mogul for an atrocious import request to Moscow. Of all the things Kurikova dealt in, the sex trade was his least favorite, but it was undoubtedly lucrative. The shipment of Cambodian boys had turned his stomach, but the oil man's interests were none of his business, if the money was right. On top of two million dollars of U.S. currency, Kurikova took the bottle of Russo-Baltique Vodka the mogul had offered.

What made the vodka so unique was the twenty-pound pure gold flask encasement, and the diamond-encrusted Russian Imperial double headed eagle perched atop its cap. The design of the flask mimicked that of the Russo-Baltique's classic automobile design. The company was one of the first Russian car manufacturers of the 1900s. The bottle was one of only ten made in 2011, costing upwards of $740,000 with the accompaniment of a Dartz Prombron Iron Diamond SUV. Kurikova nearly took the vehicle for payment as well, but he decided against it. The Chinese oil mogul's arrogance and immoral compass disgusted Kurikova, despite his own amoral shortcomings. He later paid Viktor the cost of the bottle to kill the man inside the very vehicle that came with it. Wealth in and of itself came with its own troubles, but in these dark circles the consequences were much heavier when lines were crossed.

The irony forced Kurikova to halt pouring the drink. He snickered at the memory and weighed it against the atrocities he was responsible for. His eyes wandered around the safe room inside his mansion constructed on acres and acres of manicured land outside the greater Boston area, surrounded by the surreal beauty of the open forest and countryside. A slight grin curled one side of his mouth, and Kurikova set his dark eyes on the crystal tumbler while he shook his head.

"*Trakhni tebya, karma,*" the Wolf toasted. He raised the glass to no one in particular. Or perhaps he meant it to the circle of life — its choices and consequences. "Fuck you, karma."

Viktor heard the declaration from the back of the room, and briefly looked over to Kurikova. He witnessed his employer shaking his head as he sat back in the large leather chair and raised a glass to his lips. The Wolf was grinning as he did so, although any good reason escaped the sentry's mind. In his line of work observations told more truths, and the details of what he saw narrowed the scope of possibilities. The Wolf seemed joyous, or was it nearly insane? Viktor knew all too well that Kurikova was afraid. He sipped his expensive vodka, and his fear finally showed through with the tremble of his hand.

Chapter 46
Return to the Fold

At the edge of the lawn where the boundary of the estate filtered into the surrounding forest, McCrary took a knee as he huffed and puffed from physical exertion. Traversing through the thickets and controlling his movement down the sometimes-steep decline of the hill put him through more of a strain than he had expected. The older man considered how quickly Ghost descended from their vantage point, and the man's physicality became more impressive. McCrary had no delusions of grandeur floating through his mind regarding the possibility of keeping up with the agile mountain-of-a-man. The thought did make McCrary wish he were twenty years younger. Then there was the 'Light Fifty' he straddled across his thigh. Deciding to pack it along added an extra twenty-five pounds to his lazily fit and lanky frame, which put him over the two hundred mark. He combined these factors with the difficulty of the landscape and decided he had every reason to be tired. As McCrary regained the stillness of calmer breathing, he tapped into the essence of the former Marine Scout Sniper he once was and it pushed him on.

McCrary forced his way back up to his feet, never letting go of the Barret, and made his way along the western edge of the property. Ghost's plan was for them to attack the home from either side once he'd made his entry. The vigilante had utilized a contact well versed in computers to access blueprints from the Archives and Records Management Department of the Massachusetts's state government. McCrary thought they were likely stolen in some way, although building plans *were* public record. However, the details in the plans made all the difference and were not something he thought were found on standard documents.

A small map of the area occupied one corner of the blueprint, and based on the circled location marking Kurikova's property, McCrary suspected it was actually located outside of Boston. The drive had taken forty-five minutes, give or take if you included the time it took to get into position on the hill. Given the time frame and the encircled area on the tiny map, all the evidence indicated to him they were near Sudbury. It was more of a hunch, but his gut said it was a good one.

McCrary moved along the forest line keeping as low as he possibly could to avoid detection. He rounded the home and noticed a third upper level to the Federal styled design, which wasn't a farfetched feature of New England homes. He couldn't remember seeing this spectrum of the blueprints Ghost had provided. McCrary had a difficult time dismissing what should have been an important detail, but he didn't have time to think about it. The detective continued at a hurried pace. He focused on his breathing and searched the night as he moved towards his designated entry point.

The property included a tennis and basketball court that served as a buffer between a smaller version of the main home. The barn sized guest house west of the main home was as dark and empty looking as its primary counterpart. This reminded the detective that the power surge had to be near its end. The EMP's blast was light enough to disrupt the power delivery of the area where it was deployed, yet Ghost hoped it would stretch far enough to drop the entire property into darkness. He'd lucked out.

Loud explosions erupted from within the residence, and the flash of light that followed cast a white-hot flare through the kitchen windows. The disturbance in the home halted McCrary in his tracks. He instinctively dropped to one knee and turned to face the house while he prepped to put the Barret to use once more. His attention peaked to a higher state of alertness, as if it was possible, and he found himself instantly reverting to his habitual breathing pattern, prepared to shoot. For a moment he felt like a five-year-old who was afraid of the dark, wide eyed in bed after hearing a bump in the night. The response was futile, really, except his inspired hyper-awareness, which was incredibly helpful given the circumstances. The delusion quickly transitioned to his time of deployment in Iraq during Operation Desert Storm, where his failure meant lives were on the line if he didn't do his job. There was no difference now. A prideful sensation overcame him, and re-enforced the Marine he always was. It was a feeling that helped him fight past the fear that naturally arose in dangerous situations.

McCrary maneuvered to an upright sitting position, and pressed the rifle's stock firmly against his inner shoulder. With his right leg extended out in front of him, McCrary bent his left leg inward, placing the bottom of his boot flat against the inner thigh of the right. His seated arrangement created a tripod form giving him an elevated firing position that took into consideration the gradual incline from where he sat. Laying out prone would have taken away any opportunity to shoot over the knoll leading up to the back of the home, and he wanted to scout the area from a safe position where he still blended in with the dark scenery.

Between the house and the ball courts lay an open patio and large pool area overseen by a second story balcony that seemed too large for its placement designed to present a clear position of power. Despite the lack of lighting, this area was easy to see in the twilight of the night, and even clearer through infrared setting on the scope. In the back of his mind he wondered when the power would return, but he remained focused on looking for movement from any of Kurikova's guards. The notion paid off.

Gun shots from inside the home echoed furiously in the still of the night moments after the flash bang grenades were employed. McCrary's attention snapped his neck to the right towards the kitchen area where Ghost had entered. *There goes the silent approach.*

Just then two men appeared from the far side of the property opposite from McCrary. They rose into his view with precise tactical movement; not too slow, but not too urgent. The gun fire alarmed them, and naturally beckoned their response. They scanned the area as they approached a lower entry point off of the patio. Each step was methodical, and the men moved in a unison form displaying their integral training.

McCrary slowly raised the Barrett, breathing in a rhythmic fashion in preparation to dispatch the sentries. Once the rifle was in a firing position, he leveled the sites of the scope on the men. The moments ticked away like a countdown to forever, yet it passed far too quickly in reality. He watched one of the sentries remain focused on the door ahead of them while the other covered their exposed areas.

McCrary moved his index finger down to the trigger.

When he was satisfied, the second man turned towards the door along with his partner. For an instance in time their positions aligned perfectly.

And that's when McCrary squeezed the trigger.

The light crack of the suppressed fifty's subsonic round came too fast and too hard at such a close range for the two men to hear the report of the gun shot. They certainly felt its power as it tore through the secondary guard's left side, blew out his right, and eviscerated his partner all the same. Both men whipped through the air in a singular direction as their torso's erupted and flailed together like grisly windsocks in a storm, piling nearly five feet away from where they originally stood in a tangled heap of blank stares and bleeding meat.

McCrary turned his attention away from the scope to scan his surroundings, listening just as hard as he looked. He liked to think he'd have some semblance of a stone-cold killer within him, but it just wasn't becoming to a former combat Marine and veteran detective. It was now if someone was going to use lethal force against an innocent person, he was dedicated to being their sword and shield, and he would do what needed to be done. McCrary knew he was a good man who worked hard and lived with good intentions. He wasn't Ghost, but if he justified his actions once again by telling himself that Stone needed his help, albeit in the most unconventional manner, he could provide it. He would provide it.

The area appeared to be clear as best as the detective could tell, and he wasted no time hefting the big rifle as he ducked low and ran to the rear of Kurikova's home. He sought cover behind a large square pillar made up of an assortment of different rocks similar to those running along the perimeter of the kitchen. This position helped McCrary to avoid coming into direct sight of the back entrance in case any other sentries were inside the large glass French doors. There was no border to the entrance, giving it the appearance of a cosmic portal into another world, completely translucent with a wave-like impression from top to bottom. It reminded McCrary of mirrors in a funhouse, except he could see the interior in a blurred countenance.

McCrary lowered the big rifle, pointing it to the ground, so he could get a better concept of what waited for him inside. Even with the night vision goggles to combat the darkness within the wavy glass wall, it was too difficult to clearly distinguish anything threatening beyond it. The general shapes of some things could be speculated, such as a large table at the center of the room, couches and chairs, and maybe a bar on the far wall. With being stuck at such a disadvantage McCrary knew he'd have to push forward and risk immediate resistance. Tactically, if anyone witnessed the expiration of the two men on the patio, they would have secured a covered position of advantage from within and waited patiently. At least that's what he would have done, and as he considered the kind of men he was up against, McCrary quickly thought of how he could steal the advantage from them if they existed.

There was no way around it; McCrary was going to have to make some serious noise and go full Devil Dog by hitting them with shock and awe. Why? Because it didn't really make a difference whether he was quiet now or not. Ghost had seen to that already, and it was clear their presence was known. Surely the mercenaries guarding the home were on full alert to being assaulted by a one-man army. This gave McCrary a slight advantage if no one was actually waiting for him directly inside. There was no time to overthink things. He had a set course of action in his mind of what he was going to do, and he felt it gave him the best chance of survival.

First McCrary quickly unloaded the Barrett's fat, brick-like magazine and tossed it out into the grass. He then slowly ejected the loaded round so he could dispose of it. Once it was in hand, he tossed it into the pool and followed that up with dropping the rifle to the ground. He had no idea how things would play out. For all he knew he would die very shortly. And if he did, McCrary didn't want the powerful rifle easily falling into enemy hands. He looked over to see the mound of flesh he'd compiled, lifeless and resting in a large pool of blood that flooded into the intricate texture and cracks of the patio. And he dreaded the thought of dying like those men. *Dying like Audrey had.*

McCrary laid his head back against the rock pillar while he took in a series of deep breaths and let his hands go to work. The breathing helped to fight back the intimate terror building within him, and to balance the rush of adrenaline suddenly coursing through him. An attempt to control the way it disseminated was crucial to keep his hands as steady as possible. What he did know was that fear was healthy and the adrenaline would give him some necessary energy.

Focus and clarity was what McCrary truly strived for. Fine motor skills would go out the window once the heavy storm of fight or flight took over. Once he was in the shit, there was not going back. Anything requiring finer attention would be difficult. Tunnel vision would naturally set in and overcompensate focus, which was also a dangerous aspect of consideration. Being able to remain vigilant enough to look around, assess and then reassess, became a much narrower path to follow. He'd felt it many times while deployed, and during police raids. Knowing that his plan was simple enough helped him gain better composure before he made a hard entry.

While the detective's mind went a million miles an hour, his hands were busy. In one hand he unsecured a frag grenade, and in the other he now held two flash bang grenades. Feeling the devices in his hands assisted in bringing him to a slightly calmer state of mind. They also made him question everything. Here he was, in his home state, preparing to deploy a handful of grenades into a residential home that had nothing to do with an official police raid. The actions he was assisting in were every bit of illegal, but the purpose was what remained important. Save Stone. That's the goal. That's the mission. And then get the fuck out.

Quit stalling.

Despite the extensive overthinking he didn't want to do, McCrary arrived at the do or die moment. He pulled the pin on the frag grenade, held it for approximately two seconds of the five it was designated for, and then rolled the explosive towards the glass wall.

The theoretical construct of time had a way of taking on its own application when it was of the utmost importance, conspicuously slowing in the presence of a heightened state. McCrary pulled the pins on the flash bang grenades in preparation for their use while holding a tight grip on the safety levers that armed them. Forever ticked away within the spread of three seconds. Perhaps it was the anticipation of the explosion and the attention given to the moment like some kind of psychological trick of the mind.

The world around McCrary rumbled and boomed as though an angry dragon had been woken from a deep slumber, breaking the still of the night with a feral roar. The detonation spewed a breath of fire and glass in every direction that shredded and embedded into any soft or organic object in its path. In its wake it left disorientation and destruction masked in a fog of smoke and dust.

The protection from the pillar and the noise cancelling ear buds Ghost provided allowed McCrary to spring into action quickly. Once the explosion finally occurred his reality kicked into overdrive. The flash bangs were probably overkill, but McCrary had every intention of living as long as possible. He swung out from behind the pillar and lobbed the flash bang grenades into the interior of the home, crossing their directions like a large X. There was no telling where they landed. His visibility was still drowned in obscurity having been on the outside.

McCrary dropped to a knee and looked away from the impending flash. He brought the M4A1 rifle around to a ready position, charging the bolt with a fresh round, and waited. It didn't take nearly as long now that infiltrating Kurikova's home took on a more dynamic resonance.

The grenades exploded, barking in succession like angry attack dogs and flashing with the blinding force of a lightning bolt. McCrary heard the drowning sound of men crying out following the detonations. The outcries expressed shock and pain, which signaled McCrary to move quickly.

Glass shards sprinkled across the patio. The thick window shards were like stepping on ice cubes rolling underfoot, so McCrary altered his movements to sliding his feet over the patio to avoid a crucial misstep. He passed through the former barrier scanning from left to right, searching meticulously for any threats. The room was a large rectangular shape, deep, and set up to be some sort of game room. The night vision goggles helped with seeing the larger objects, but the remaining smoke and dust from the structural damage of the doorway lingered, clouding his vision.

Movement to his left near an alcove made McCrary startle. He turned quickly, taking a firm stance while keeping his sights up and on target. The form of a man ducked back beyond the doorway. McCrary adjusted his aim from the opening of the alcove, to the wall, a mere six inches where he suspected the man to be. As he did so he fingered the firing selector to full auto. When he pulled the trigger the M4A1 spat out a steady stream of armor piercing rounds. McCrary shouldered the rifle sturdily and guided the barrel in an upwards motion. The bullets peppered the wall in a slightly zig-zagged line from bottom to top, flouring the area with drywall particles.

Beyond the wall blood splattered against its parallel counterpart, and an armed man clad in camouflage and a ski mask tumbled to the floor. McCrary quick stepped to his left to remain mobile. It was basic firearms combatives to shoot and move; this way he would move off line of the reference point he'd given as his firing position and be would be somewhere else if the man had been able to return fire. McCrary couldn't see the total damage inflicted, which he appreciated.

You heard two screams.

McCrary returned his attention to clearing the room. There was another shooter somewhere inside here, and he'd already informed him of his arrival. A number of leather sofas were strewn about the room with arcade style games lining the outer walls. Foosball tables were positioned beyond the large pool table McCrary stood by. And then there was the bar at the end of the room; a perfect place for cover and concealment.

From his position the room opened into a hallway, and what lay beyond was another room. It seemed to be another living or play area, but it was too difficult to distinguish. Whatever its purpose in the home didn't matter. It was another space where the remaining shooter could be waiting to ambush McCrary. His eyes scanned frantically from left to right, from bar to tables to sofas.

Why are you standing still?

Movement was life. Staying in one place for too long gave the enemy better opportunity to zero in on your location and disseminate your absolution.

McCrary backed up, aware that there was nothing to obstruct his movement. He never took his eyes off of the arena before him. He side-stepped near the end of a long sofa set, not too close to give away his position, yet close enough to give him the advantage of surprise. His finger slipped down to the trigger, ready for action, and then he quickly breached the corner of the seating arrangement. The long space beyond was void of any presence, and McCrary quickly returned to an upright ready position.

Sweat began to form on his forehead. He could feel it dripping down to the goggles, and then rolling around the boundary set by their shape.

The power could come on at any minute.

McCrary stepped behind the couches positioned nearly two feet away from the wall. He didn't bother to speculate why, other than to give some form of walking path across the room without obstructing the obnoxiously large flat screen on the opposite wall. He used it to his benefit, continuing to scan the room as he walked in a tactically crouched posture. It would lead him to the end of the bar almost directly, save for a ten foot gap of open flooring.

As he neared the end of the oversized sofa configuration, McCrary paused. A metallic sound pierced the pounding rush of blood constantly surging through his head. It came from behind the bar, confirming his suspicions. McCrary dropped to a knee behind the sofa so that he was not deathly exposed. His mind raced. The other man was certainly there, and he had better coverage. The possibilities of attack and defense surged through McCrary's mind. Terror grasped hold of him, but not in a paralyzing manner. It could go either way if they both attacked simultaneously. Something told McCrary he was operating on more luck than skill at the moment. The hired gun behind the bar lived to kill. That was what he was hired to do. Period.

And your job is to stop people like him.

McCrary again wished he had the stone cold capabilities to confront violence with ice in his veins. It just wasn't there. Perhaps it was a testament to his humanity. But, then again, so was the fact that he'd dedicated his life to being a protector of others.

With his mind showing no signs of slowing down, McCrary worked to calm himself with a few deep breaths. He didn't have much time. At some point one of them were going to make a move, and that would be the end for one or both of them. Hitting first was to McCrary's advantage.

An epiphany hit him like a shot in the chest, and the detective rested on what was the best tactic at hand. It was so simple he felt foolish it hadn't occurred to him automatically. He chalked it up to being out of the fold of consistent combat for so long, and the mental toll taken by its chaos. But he knew what to do based on his knowledge under the circumstances.

McCrary knew the man's location, and he had the tools to make his idea a reality.

Once he made the decision, McCrary wasted no time implementing his strategy. Its usage arose from an age old principle deriving from the United States Navy, although it was allocated throughout the other military branches. The acronym was K.I.S.S., *keep it simple, stupid.* So, McCrary kept it simple.

After the hyper-sensitive seconds of overthinking were stripped away, the detective removed the last frag grenade from his vest. He armed it by pulling the safety pin and caught the safety level to avoid creating any noise. McCrary counted to two once again, allowing the fuse to *cook,* as they referred to it in the service, taking away any chance the man could return the explosive party favor before it detonated. He tossed it over the top of the bar in an overhand motion. The cylindrical mechanism ricocheted off of the back countertop before it dropped into the void separating the bar.

McCrary dropped to a prone position, burying his face into the intersection where the sofa met the hardwood floor, and covered his head.

The grenade had a blast radius of five meters, otherwise referred to as a kill radius. In this case, McCrary knew it would completely decimate everything in and around the bar. The explosion was preceded by a long, untamed scream loaded with desperation. The sentry had tried to get rid of the grenade; tried to get away, but in doing so only got closer to it. McCrary's tactic worked as he'd planned.

In detonation the grenade's concussion delivered a slew of shrapnel that minced through the guard instantly, wetting the room with what gore was left of him. There wasn't much. A portion of the bar blew outward, polluting the room with wood splinters combined with the already lethal chunks of metal shards penetrating the walls and couches and other furniture. The glass and mirrors decorating the bar shattered along with everything else affected by the discharge. Structurally the bar was left burned and blasted beyond repair.

McCrary took up his rifle and carefully moved from behind the couch. There was no way the man had survived, but it was tactically sound to make sure he was dead. The detective slowly crept over to the bar, turning with the rifle as he angled his view behind it. Body parts and building material were all that remained.

He ducked down behind the end of the counter, staying away from the biological mess greasing the floor, and checked the blueprint map located on his left forearm. It was a handy reference piece to have, and similar to one he'd used in the military. He folded up the cloth lining secured with Velcro to expose the map beneath a plastic safety barrier. With the night vision goggles McCrary could see it clearly several inches away from his face. Ghost insisted McCrary take it to remember where he needed to go. The detective insisted he wouldn't need it, but was glad he'd conceded. Being in unfamiliar territory was disorienting, and given the level of shock he'd endured already made it difficult to remember the layout he was intended to follow with certainty.

Prior planning had told him he wouldn't need to go far. Only the specific direction escaped him. Ghost's thorough reconnaissance suggested Stone would be taken somewhere out of sight, which made sense to the vigilante because of his extensive experience in taking hostages as a spy. At least, that's how McCrary justified it to himself. Kurikova had an elaborate wine cellar, and that was McCrary's intended target. He located the bar area on the map strapped to his forearm and followed the marker leading to a stairwell. He looked up and across the room to the alcove. *Shit.*

McCrary closed the map cover and double-timed it across the room. He paid no attention to the man he'd killed earlier, although it was difficult not to glimpse the gaping hole in the side of the man's face leaving his jaw unhinged. Beyond the body was a short, wide hallway that came to a boxed landing with an unluxuriously plain wooden door. McCrary slowly turned the handle and threw it open. He waited around the corner before turning to clear the space beyond.

When he did advance, he encountered a deeper form of darkness, inky black and thick. Closer inspection showed it was the stairwell leading down to the wine cellar. McCrary slowly and cautiously descended the carpeted steps. At the bottom he entered another long hallway. He disliked the exposure presented by the landing, but it was unavoidable. He crouched low to see as far as he could, his rifle shouldered and ready to fire if needed. So far, so good.

Once McCrary reached the bottom, he remembered something

crucial he needed to handle; a mistake often made in combat situations that got men killed. He ejected the magazine of the M4A1 and lightly inserted a new, fully loaded magazine. He'd probably only expended ten rounds beforehand in the alcove, but it was a rule of thumb to move on fully loaded.

In a crouched posture McCrary walked down the hall, feeling the pressure of the underground space close in on him. He paused, listened hard, and smelled something out of place. A hum radiated around him. The lights flickered on and off. He stripped away the goggles in preparation for the power to return, glimpsing the doorway to the cellar at the end of the hall in between the flashes of illumination. *Was that the smell of a cigarette, too*?

When the power returned, the door at the end of the hall could be seen. It was opened and just beyond its border was the burning tip of a cigarette hanging from the lips of a man who looked a lot like the one who'd killed his wife.

Chapter 47
Lights On

The reverberations of McCrary's thunderous assault on the mansion made Ghost grin. Multiple explosions had rattled the home on the west end. Ghost figured Kurikova was taking them seriously now. A man never expected his home to turn into a war zone, but the Russian mobster had chosen this life and he'd finally made the wrong kind of enemy. Beyond that, the need to be gentle and silent had passed once Ghost entered the home, and he hadn't expected the detective to follow suit.

Ghost violently wrenched the neck of a masked man to his right, nearly twisting the Spetznaz sentry's head all the way around. The echo of the cartilage and bones being forced beyond their design made Ghost sneer with disgust. He'd broken the bones of targets God only knows how many times and, although he'd done it, it was one thing that made him cringe every time. The sound of it stayed with him, replaying at times in his mind. Ghost did what was necessary, though not out of enjoyment.

The body went limp in his arms and he callously shoved the man down the winding staircase. He watched the lifeless shell tumble end over end, roll sideways, and twist into a mangled heap at the bottom as though a puppet had been cut free of its strings.

Bullet holes riddled the wall of the rounded wall. Family pictures had been knocked to the floor during the fight. Ghost had taken a few rounds across his torso, ripping holes in the armored vest, but he'd doubled up on his protection as usual. It was times like these he was grateful for his size and strength. Many operators didn't bother even wearing armor, instead opting to be lighter and quicker. He valued the benefit of the armor, padded with soft and hard plates alike. The weight didn't seem like much at first, until things became incredibly physical, then the armor took its toll. Ghost worked around the issue by training hard throughout his life and career, using the gifts he had to his advantage, and then advancing them by training with the added weight. The armor rarely came off on a mission, and accounted for extending his life far too many times to count.

Ghost now stood at the top of the second floor landing. The house was so large he could have fit at least two of his own homes, or what used to be his, inside of it. He checked his M4A1 rifle, recharging a new magazine. While he was at it Ghost removed the sling, detaching the quick release snap to carry the rifle freely. A knife slash had nearly destroyed the paracord material leaving it hanging by a few threads. He was lucky the blade had only done superficial damage near his upper right shoulder. The cut was bleeding, but it was of no concern.

Velcro crackled as Ghost pulled open his tactical armband to view the blueprint of Kurikova's home. He recalled McCrary stating he didn't need to carry one after being assigned to only go so far within the mansion. Ghost had insisted, knowing better, and the former Marine should have known better, too. Ghost had an additional flap on his arm band with the layout of the second floor. Remembering the floorplan wasn't difficult. However, Ghost preferred certainties over speculation, and when your life was on the line there was no time for guessing. He found his location quickly, looking up intermittently to scan his surroundings, remaining aware at all times.

The path he needed to follow was slightly off course. He'd only ascended to the second floor because of the threat he first encountered at the bottom, needing the space to take cover until the fight filtered into the stairwell and beyond. At the moment he was in a good enough position to fight or evade, depending on which direction presented the next threat. At the moment he was near where he suspected Kurikova to be locked down.

Building layouts are typically filed in accordance with the records office before construction providing complete specs of the home's square footage. Amendments to the blueprints are also filed in the same manner with any changes made, or at least they were supposed to be. What Ghost discovered was that the floorplan for Kurikova's home had an amended area, yet it wasn't labeled. On the blueprint it appeared as a simple dark blue area roughly the size of a large family living space. The walls had been drawn nearly twice as thick without any specific measurements.

Most people would probably overlook the extra room in the design, assuming it was an unfinished piece, except Ghost found a correlation that looked similar to the wine cellar. On the map the hallway was present, appearing to be accounted for, but the actual room was left blank. It was most likely considered unfinished, or scrapped from the plans altogether. Maybe the architect was lazy in removing it from the plans, or it wasn't necessary if it wasn't built. Or, in the case of a power hungry mob boss with a world full of enemies, the room was finished and ultimately left off of the books in the end.

Ghost surmised that a security company would have had to customize armored walls for a room of this size. In the midst of tearing Kurikova's life apart, Ghost found that Kurikova was a silent owner in a Russian owned security company called *Red Wolf Security* that specialized in corporate security and home engineering. That's all it took for him to confirm Kurikova's personalized safe room occupied this 'blank space' on the map. If Kurikova was there, Ghost came prepared to enter at all costs. Or bring everything down on top of the Wolf. Either way was fine. Although, Ghost preferred to look into the man's eyes when he snuffed Yuri from this world.

The lights flickered. Once. Twice. Ghost stripped the night vision goggles from his head and watched the power return. His vision adjusted well, but now the playing field had been leveled. Kurikova's mercenaries could see him just as easily as he could see them, and they were likely more familiar with the terrain. He imagined that the refreshed illumination would either embolden them to fan out to find him, or see them hole up and attempt an ambush leading to Kurikova.

Ghost took up the rifle and cleared the hall extending both directions of the home, east and west. In the western direction a marbled railing lined the walkway and overlooked the openness of what appeared to be the front entrance of the mansion. Either end of the railing acted as landings to the wide staircase that wound its way down. East was the direction Ghost needed to go, and the lack of illumination in the hallway worked to his advantage as the open loft became his proverbial light at the end of a tunnel.

The route to Ghost's destination from the second floor led to the north-eastern corner of the house where another stairway wound down to the first floor into a guest suite and secondary kitchen. Ghost passed other rooms that appeared to be empty as he quickly scanned them with the light mounted on the lower rail of his rifle. The firing selector was set on fully automatic, best for clearing rooms in close quarters combat, and for laying down cover fire if met with a threat.

He followed this path with pure destruction in mind, bursting through each door, scanning the immediate areas, then turning out into the hallway ready to fire. Logic told him the closer he got to Kurikova the more resistance he would face. In terms of numbers, depending on what kind of work McCrary was getting done, there were only a handful of killers left to disperse of, but they wouldn't necessarily die easily. Ghost never underestimated his enemy; he simply came more prepared. Preparation was everything, beyond training and developing the necessary skills, which were worthless if not put to proper use.

Movement up ahead caused him to move his index finger from lining the receiver to the trigger. The shuffling of feet made more noise than was necessary even for a hardwood floor. Was it a distraction? Ghost slowed his pace and stepped to the opposite side of the hall as softly as possible. He wasn't sure if he was seen, and being highly trained men, they wouldn't run and gun their way down the hallway in hopes of getting in a good shot on him. If his former position was their point of reference, he would now have a slight advantage.

Ghost stopped near an open door close to the end of the hall where it led into a vaulted loft. He twisted tightly inside the room, engaging the tactical light on the lower rail with a two second flash to clear the room, and then shut it down. Turning back towards the open door, Ghost took a fixed stance about two feet inside the room from the muzzle of his rifle to the wall. He stood ready to ambush anyone who stepped into the doorframe, which he designated as his immediate kill zone.

The loft was dimly lit, unlike the hallway, which created a problem for whoever took it up as a defensive position: light casts shadows. Turning off the light would also draw immediate attention to whoever waited for Ghost. At the moment, whoever waited on the other side of the wall was under the impression they had the element of surprise. They'd soon find out how wrong they were.

A masked guard moved first, having no other option but to clear the hall following his impatience, revealing his position with an unavoidable shadow. He moved methodically, cutting the corner with expertise — perfectly by the book. His barrel didn't protrude too far ahead of him, and he didn't lead with an over extended limb to give him away. If it weren't for the fact that Ghost knew someone was there and that damn shadow hadn't screamed out his position, the guy might have had a chance.

Might have.

Ghost dropped to a knee, and then whipped the sentry backwards with a vertical stream of automatic fire. The armor piercing rounds came with a metallic spit out of the M4A1's suppressor and punched holes in the guy from his pelvis to his jugular. The support hand under his own rifle jerked out to the side like a wet noodle after taking a round before punching into his chest, and the whole mess from his nuts to his neck sprayed blood against the wall behind him. The sentry never got off a shot before he met his end, but to Ghost he was still useful.

The man's body bounced off the adjacent wall, dropping his AK rifle. He remained standing with a mild amount of rigidness, fighting against the lethal symptoms of acute lead poisoning, but the combination of blood loss and compromised vital organs would ultimately kill him.

Ghost surged forward and pulled the man towards him with ease, using his own mass to support the limp body as he slid an arm inside the sentry's tactical vest the same way a Spartan took up his shield for battle. Inside the vest Ghost took hold of a handful of cloth to hold the body close while he tucked his rifle under the right armpit to be able to move forward and fire at the same time.

The maneuver was unconventional, and that's exactly why it generally worked. Using a human body as a shield atypically forced a man to hesitate shooting his own brother in arms, giving Ghost the upper hand. On top of the psychological advantage, the body protected him and allowed him to act defensively. He had a strength advantage in being able to hold the dead weight of the man. To most men it would be a difficult task, but he assessed the man's medium size the moment he saw him and put him at no more than 185 pounds in full kit.

As Ghost pushed forward into the loft area, he could see two couches were positioned parallel to one another. They were larger than most would have owned, but that was what the luxury of riches afforded the wealthy. Between them was a modern glass table void of any objects, framed in gleaming steel of an intricately round design. The end tables were smaller and identical.

Behind the farthest sofa a man fired and took cover as Ghost entered the room. The rounds went wide and punched holes in the wall over his head. Ghost returned fire immediately, shooting freely through the lower half of the sofa, and then adjusting his shots to blast the stuffing out the back. Blood lightly sprayed beyond the end of the obliterated furniture telling Ghost he'd hit his mark.

A third and more patient man concealed himself directly around the corner in Ghost's blind spot. He brought the fight to Ghost after having seen his comrades die so quickly. There was no doubt a surge of adrenaline and fury mixed with his years of elite training made his fight for survival more formidable than anyone before him.

The sentry opened fire, riddling the body Ghost used as a shield, forcing the vigilante's movement backwards. He pressed forward, turning out and away from his position while continuing to fire. Heavy AK 74 rounds *thwapped* into the lifeless body like rapid strikes of a whip, tearing into the armored vest and flesh in a melee of violence. The delivery was frantic and angry, and lacked any professional regard. The sentry didn't want to die tonight, and he was going to unleash everything he had to stay alive.

Ghost countered with his own gunfire, but the pressure of the bullets littering the body shield and its weight now put him at a disadvantage. His shots went wide and high, missing the intended target while blasting the far wall of the home and decimating random art and décor. Turning the body kept him alive long enough to coerce the sentry in closer, at which point he switched back to working offensively.

The body soared forwards in a cascading arc, rising high and curving through the air in a hail of flailing limbs and gaping, bloody wounds. As a projectile, the body forced the sentry to alter his direction of aggression. The flesh puppet traveled with such power he barely had time to maneuver out of its way.

A good distraction couldn't be lost, and Ghost took every benefit it afforded him. When the sentry sidestepped, he moved in close, and the real combative skills came to life.

He disarmed the sentry, tossing the AK to the side, and the sentry countered with a number of punches and a technique that stripped Ghost of his own weapon. Their mutual onslaught came with fast, heavy strikes, and intricate defensive techniques most men wouldn't be able to perform in a high stress situation. They utilized their fine motor skills over their large gross motor movements, defying the general logic of human capabilities in survival mode.

Their skillsets shone quickly, tossing each other from one direction to the other, delivering sneaky elbow and knee strikes. Neither man gave in. In the chaos of the confrontation they seemed to be equally matched, but it was in the finer details the eye missed with two fighters moving at such a high rate. The sentry was slowing down, fatigued by the adrenaline dump. Trying to keep up with the constant pressure his enemy provided was far too taxing.

Ghost, on the other hand, was impressed with the challenge, but he had no desire to let it drag out. Had he let his ego take control he'd entertain sustaining the inevitable. It wasn't a point for him to pat himself on the back, having absorbed a number of the sentry's blows periodically with the fast pace he kept, but the man was no match. Ghost knew the man's pattern and learned it quickly seconds after they engaged. The physical "tells" the sentry gave away sealed his fate, despite being a good combatant.

When the sentry whipped out a double-edged serrated knife, slashing and slicing at multiple angles, Ghost took a couple of them across his vest, the blade nicking a few of his rifle magazines with each swipe. Another barely missed one of his arms. He retaliated by stepping off the center line directly in front of the sentry so he was positioned on the outside of his knife hand. He drew the Colt Python from behind his back and shot from the hip as he stepped backwards, squeezing the trigger in succession as rapidly as he could. The .357 rounds hit the sentry's center mass, square in his sternum and stomach within a five inch grouping. It ultimately folded him over like a mule had kicked him in his guts, and dropped him to his knees.

The revolver went dry, clicking as Ghost continued to pull the trigger. He stopped when he saw the blood spewing out of the sentry's gaping mouth and pooling on the hardwood floor at his knees from the holes in his lower, unprotected torso.

For a moment Ghost paused to watch the man tremble as the realization that his life was over set in. Sadly for him, it hadn't happened in some hellish territory he had no business in under orders he didn't truly want to follow because his honor and pride for his homeland wouldn't let him do anything else. No, his death instead came in the home of the highest bidder; of a man he had no personal ties to, fighting for a cause that wasn't worth defending. Ghost looked at him with his head cocked to one side and pondered the irony of it. The man would still die in a hellish territory in a hellish way. Maybe it wasn't so different after all.

Ghost let the man die on his own, in his own blood, all alone. He could have ended things quickly for the sentry, but he felt there was a penance to be paid. There was no doubt the man had done horrible things in combat. Most soldiers had. Killing wasn't an easy task no matter how accustomed one became to it. There was a smaller percentage of men who enjoyed death as a thrill, like the Twins, who had killing deeply engrained into their psychotic DNA, or those who had been so desensitized to killing their humanity was lost altogether. Ghost knew he was not among these types of men. He placed the value of decency above their miserable existence. It's what allowed him to do the things he did.

A gurgling sound emanated behind Ghost. He paused as he recognized the wet bubbling of the sentry taking his last breaths while he not only bled out, but drowned in his own blood. Hiccups sounded like soaked cloth being slapped against concrete. Ghost half heard the sounds, and half remembered them from past executions by his hand. His memories amplified the things he remembered, and triggered images when he encountered similar situations.

The massive man turned to the dying sentry, who'd risen up to sit on the heels of his boots. He slouched pathetically, yet it was admirable he continued to fight on and die defiantly. Through the black ski mask holes his eyes cast out the weary curtain call death sometimes used to close the show. He scowled and grimaced, involuntarily incapable of keeping up the inherent toughness within him as he succumbed to dying.

Ghost watched as the man's spirit faded, slumping forward slowly until gravity dropped him into a contorted mess. The body faintly rose and fell with its last breaths. A sneer curled Ghost's lips, and a hard glare shot towards the dead man. It was then he was reminded why this was so easy for him, seeing an image that justified everything he had done, and would continue to do. As the sentry died it was not the man Ghost saw, but an image of his daughter, Chloe, frantically reaching for him, her little arms clawing and scratching for survival against an enemy she couldn't fight, crying, afraid and screaming for the one man who should have been there to save her. Her rosy-pink lips mocked the word he loved to hear her call out, the only name she knew him by; except terror fueled its projection instead of the love and joy he cherished hearing so much. All she could deliver was distorted into a morbid calling wrapped in silence. Tears bled down her flushed cheeks in a never-ending flood from her beautiful hazel eyes that highlighted the mask of her inextinguishable fear until it stretched out into unrecognizable nothingness.

The image died with the sentry, and Ghost moved on, satisfied, and coldly motivated.

Chapter 48
You're Not That Important

Predictability was in and of itself disappointing. Simon had hoped he was wrong about his strategy, but without having Richter around now forced him to exhibit the characteristics and focus he should have always had. He liked that change, being in control of himself a little more, or at least enough to display what he was truly capable of while still slightly unhinged. Everything occurred so quickly that it was difficult for him to completely process this new state of mind. Richter had always told him, '*If it feels right and it works, then go with it.*' And Simon was doing just that. Once he finished here at Kurikova's he could grieve and think things through more completely. In the moment, however, the detective had shown up as Simon thought he would, and by the sounds of things he and the vigilante were working as a team, yet separately.

God, I am good…

Richter would have been proud. In fact, Richter would have been the one to make the strategy, or at least he would have predicted McCrary's involvement. However, if his elder brother had survived there wouldn't have been anything else to finish. They would have killed the target and the detective and been on a plane to somewhere tropical and morally ambiguous before the end of the evening.

That was not the case, and as such, Simon's disappointment came with the predictability that McCrary would assist the vigilante, albeit voluntarily or not. This was the basis of the plan he'd laid out with the Wolf. While his target rampaged through the mercenary cannon fodder Kurikova supplied, he would entrap the detective with the FBI agent. Kurikova wanted to kill this Stone character with his own hands, but what difference did it really make? Simon looked forward to killing him for the Wolf, along with the detective, and then ambushing the vigilante afterwards before he could kill Kurikova.

"If he's still alive," Yuri offered.

They had in fact discussed the matter after Simon rudely interrupted Kurikova's initial beating of the FBI agent, at which point the deranged assassin had taken a seat on the agent's lap. After considering Kurikova's words Simon had to concede to the possibility, however unlikely he thought it was. And, unconvinced, he said, "But, of course."

The Russian went on expecting to die tonight. He was not unrealistic about the possible outcome after suffering from this mystery man's wrath for so long, yet he remained mildly optimistic. The Wolf said, "If he dies tonight instead it must be at my hand, even if you take him down."

Simon had a problem with that. The man killed his brother, the only person who ever loved him and looked out for him. Then again, Kurikova's entire organization had suffered from the damage the target had done, and the Wolf's son had been slaughtered, too. When Simon thought about it the vigilante was quite impressive. But he had to die. There was no question about that.

"Fine," Simon had agreed. It was a fair trade if he killed Stone, after all. "But only if it suits the moment. This man is a predator, and you don't waste time putting them down."

"We'll implement your plan with Viktor's," Yuri agreed. He had raised his glass of vodka to salute the arrangement. Simon lifted the limp arm of the unconscious Agent Stone and gave him a high five.

Hours later, with an assured rising body count throughout the mansion, Simon found himself face to face with McCrary. Their standoff began in the hallway leading to the wine cellar where Stone was being chilled in the climate controlled cellar storing Kurikova's massive and expensive collection. Simon maintained his composure, finishing a cigarette at the cellar's entrance. When their eyes met, Simon saw the shock of the moment overwhelm McCrary, who had him dead to rights with a rifle within twenty yards. It was fascinating for him being in the right place at the right time, the power enlightening them both to the other's presence the exact moment the lights came on, heightening the tension. The assassin would never forget such a priceless moment knowing that his presence brought on such a stunning and horrific response.

Simon simply turned away, grinning with the cigarette dangling from his lips, and disappeared into the dim atmosphere of the wine cellar. He partially expected some gun shots as a late response on behalf of McCrary. Nothing happened. Outside of the predictability of McCrary's presence, his lack of action was also disappointing to Simon. He expected the detective to want revenge for his wife even if the killing had been done by his brother. There wasn't a separation in that involvement as far as Simon was concerned. Then again, that was what separated ruthless people like him and Kurikova from the law abiding citizens of the world. They would have buried a town to avenge a loved one while the cop would likely seek the typical standard of justice. If McCrary only knew that his hesitation was going to get him killed, perhaps he would have acted when he should have.

****

When he drank in the details of the smoking man ahead of him, McCrary recognized the face and its features. Those would be burned into his memory forever. It was the eyes, however, that froze him. Those were the deadest eyes he'd ever seen, yet here they were again and somehow contradicted with a spark of insanity.

Who is he?

He wasn't the guy who killed Audrey. Of that he was certain. Ghost had killed him, and McCrary remembered it as Ghost had recalled it to him. But even with that, Ghost had gone on about McCrary getting revenge for his wife. Wasn't that already done? He'd never thought it out fully; resisting it every time it was mentioned as a ploy to further engage him on a personal level. A part of him wanted it, deeply, seeing the abomination before him smirking and alive. *Eye for an eye. That was justice, too, wasn't it*?

McCrary shook off the idea. It wasn't that he was thinking too much that led to him missing an opportunity to stop this guy. He was likely wildly dangerous, and in the circles the detective was running in at the moment, everyone seemed to be more dangerous than he was.

The bearded assassin had rolled to his right and stepped out of sight, fading into the bleakness of the wine cellar beyond. McCrary thought to charge after him, but that would be stupid. Someone like him wasn't the kind of person you rushed after. You had to be cautious, and McCrary was much safer keeping the guy at a distance and at the end of a gun.

He moved forward methodically, carefully approaching the cellar doorway. The flashlight on the lower rail cleared the space nicely with a quick blink on and off. McCrary moved through the door, checking the corner behind him for clearance, and then stepping behind the concealment of a row of wine. He couldn't believe the size of the cellar. It was a small underground warehouse with a twelve foot ceiling and had to be nearly the size of half a football field. There were countless bottles all encased in custom made refrigerated drawers. The humming from each industrial sized unit filled the room with a singular, low grade white noise. It wasn't overly loud, but it was distracting and enough to cover the sound of any movement.

The lighting made the cellar appear more like a dungeon than McCrary expected, but wine was something he knew little about. There were light strips lining the bottom of each row. They were iridescent, meant to simply guide one along their way. Other similar lighting was located at intersecting points between rows. McCrary looked up and saw dark bulbs above the row he occupied noting each section must have an individual switch. He shook his head in disbelief that something so elaborate had been constructed to house a fermented drink.

A piercing whistle reverberated through the cellar. It immediately caught McCrary's attention, and it wasn't far from him. Or so it seemed. He moved forward, deeper into the massive room, crossing an intersecting path to another row. He quick stepped to the end there and turned the corner to use the width of the wine encasement as cover.

"You're going to make me yell, aren't you?" the man called out.

McCrary didn't respond. He tried to use the man's voice to approximate its origin, but the humming of the wine encasements covered it too well.

"I hate yelling, detective," he stated. "It irritates me."

McCrary said nothing. He moved down the open aisle, rifle up and ready, quickly glancing down each row before he passed. The size of the wine encasements baffled him, and he couldn't even fathom how much money it had taken to build such a storage space.

"Detective," the man called, sounding more inviting than

threatening. "This doesn't have to end badly. We can make an arrangement. I'm flexible. You're here for the FBI agent, right?"

McCrary paused, partly enticed to respond, but more so to not give away his position.

"This is very aggravating, detective. I'm not interested in killing either of you," said the assassin. McCrary was buying it. The assassin continued, "We just need to come to an understanding is all."

McCrary moved towards the middle of the room, continuing to intermittently check his path as he crossed the rows of wine. He moved faster now, glimpsing in the direction the assassin likely occupied, looking for any silhouette of a figure instead of a solid position. Too much time would be wasted stopping and checking every row before moving on. Stone had to be somewhere, and his gut told him that he wasn't going to be hidden. The agent was likely the cheese in the trap; easy to see, but dangerous to get.

"Please, come to your senses, detective," the man called out. "We're waiting for you."

McCrary froze. Not only was the voice closer and much clearer now, his words stopped him in his tracks. *We're waiting for you*. He was with Stone. *Shit*!

"Please hurry," the man called out. "I have a more pressing matter to attend to."

It was then that the encompassing hum of the room slowly switched off, and the heavy weight of silence filled the room. McCrary heard the traction of his boots squeak against the concrete floor as he turned down an aisle three rows from the opening of the room's center. Being at the end of the row placed him at a better vantage point where he could see the shape of someone strapped to a chair and another walking around freely. Perhaps it was time to introduce himself.

McCrary moved out into the aisle cautiously, and moved towards the center slowly with the M4A1 in a low-ready position. It would take only a split second to have it up to fire if he needed to, and as far as he could tell this strange doppelganger of his wife's killer was walking around carelessly. He took a second to rethink his tactics, stopped at the corner of the last encasement, and dropped to a knee before steadying his aim on the man. The man appeared to be oblivious of McCrary's arrival, but he quickly proved to be fully aware.

"Glad you could make it, detective," the man said. He stood directly behind a slouched over Stone and held a pistol to the back of the agent's head. With his free hand he gestured to an open chair across from Stone. The area appeared to have a few long rectangular tables at the center once organized as a workspace. They were now disheveled and displaced to make room for Stone's apparent torture. "I'm Simon. Please, join us."

****

McCrary shook his head. "You've gotta' be outta' ye'r mind, pal."

Simon chuckled. *How observant.*

"Well, detective, you're not too far off," Simon said.

The low hanging light fixture cast off a yellow illumination that bathed the left side of Stone in its path, and cast over the right side of Simon. McCrary could make out that Simon wore some kind of suit, no jacket, a dark shade of blue for a shirt with the sleeves rolled up, and black slacks. He'd paid no attention to the details when he saw Simon in the hallway, but he excused that with the astonishment that overtook him at the time. Tight leather gloves encased Simon's hands, but McCrary focused on the one holding the gun to Stone's head.

"Let him go," McCrary said. "Back away and put the gun down."

Simon shook his head. "Really? You're really going to try your cop shit here."

"No one else has to die, asshole."

A confused look overcame Simon's. "No, everyone has to die, detective. That's what I do. It's what I'm going to do here to you and him…"

McCrary's finger moved to the trigger. He wanted to pull it; had every reason to do it. *Why can't I just fucking shoot him*?

"And that's what my brother did to your wife."

There was the insult again. The reminder of losing everything that mattered being tossed about like a meaningless pebble across a lake. And then Simon smiled.

McCrary pulled the trigger without any more hesitation, or any thought to it. All he felt was anger. All he wanted was revenge. Audrey wouldn't have approved, would she? Did it matter? No, not now. Now it was about life and death, and not just McCrary's life. Stone's was also hanging in the balance. Did he fire out of malice? Or was it because he had every reason in the moment to use lethal force?

None of the rationalizing mattered.

The shot hit Simon in the connecting tissue between his shoulder and neck, blowing out a chunk of the upper trapezius muscle. It sent the assassin reeling into a spin, and McCrary stepped to the side and fired again. His shot missed as Simon also continued to move, getting off a shot that went wide and hit the space McCrary once occupied. The bullet blew out the glass of a wine compartment and lodged deep inside the refrigeration encasement.

McCrary continued to move, as did Simon. The assassin rolled and fired. Two of his shots hit McCrary in the vest, barely stunting his motion, but he felt them.

The detective thanked Ghost for his over-preparedness, and continued to get a bead on Simon. He was wiry and fast, but he closed the distance easily. His next shot spun the assassin around as he tried to get away, winging him in his right shoulder. Simon barked in pain as the bullet ripped across the side of his limb leaving a bloody void where his flesh once occupied.

In the same instance Simon had also fired in rapid succession. Again, he hit McCrary in the heavily armored vest, but the last of the rounds nailed the upper receiver of the rifle, rendering it useless.

When the M4 ceased firing, McCrary quickly transitioned to his pistol, snapping the sling free from his body, tossing the rifle aside, and dropping his right hand down to the holster on his thigh. As he brought the gun up Simon crashed into him, knocking him backwards, and gripping his arm with two hands. McCrary slammed backwards into a wine encasement causing him to flail momentarily with the force of the impact. The lull in his control made him vulnerable.

McCrary was quickly redirected as Simon expertly trapped one of his arms, and then stepped inward to throw McCrary over his shoulder. He landed at Simon's feet, crashing hard against the concrete like a sack of potatoes. Simon maintained control of the gun hand, moving to disarm the detective. He underestimated McCrary's resolve as his big, heavy boot came up from the floor. The luck of the draw was a benefit for Simon as he blocked the kick with a forearm, simultaneously turning the barrel of the pistol offline from his head before McCrary pulled the trigger two times. The shells ejected in his face, but they were the least of Simon's concern. Another kick came up, knocking him backwards, and giving the detective the opportunity, he needed.

McCrary pulled his arm free from Simon, and rolled over to his stomach to push himself up. Simon countered quickly with kicks of his own, sending McCrary into a defensive position blocking his head from the onslaught. The assassin then stepped to the outside and kicked the pistol free from McCrary's hand, sending it across the room where it slid to a halt beneath the rectangular tables. Pain radiated through McCrary's arm, numbing his hand and wrist briefly, and forcing him to involuntarily retract it. Another kick struck him in the chest, knocking him to his back leaving him staring up into the maniacal eyes of the crazed killer.

"Well, done, detective," Simon hissed, seething with excitement. "That was a helluva try there."

McCrary kicked towards Simon's legs in an attempt to distract the assassin so he could stand, but he missed. "Fuck you, asshole!"

Simon shook his head. "You're not very original, detective."

McCrary flipped him the bird, defiant until the end.

Simon stutter stepped from one side to the other, faking the direction of his attack. McCrary fell for it in part because Simon was much quicker, and the detective couldn't recover the space he left undefended. Simon swooped in and dropped a heavy knee into McCrary's sternum, driving it in deep and hard. An attempt to push him away was made, but Simon easily navigated the defense, and began pummeling the detective. He struck him with stiff palm strikes to avoid hurting his hands, which proved to be more than effective as the force behind the attack bounced the detective's head off the concrete floor. One, two, three flush connections were all it took to daze the veteran officer.

While being at a distinct disadvantage, McCrary continued to mount some kind of offense, even though he looked more as though his arms were flailing in a never-ending fall into oblivion. Despair gripped him with each impact delivered upon him, and there was nothing he could do. Consciousness slipped away as Simon continued to strike him and the concrete compounded the assassin's efforts. Still, McCrary fought as much as he could, trying to get out from under the killer, and trying to deflect his powerful strikes. There was nothing he could do to change the outcome. He wasn't strong enough, or skilled enough, to stop Simon from killing him with his bare hands. Death seemed certain and, although he refused to give up, he was satisfied with knowing Audrey waited on the other side for him.

The beating stopped, and McCrary lay still for a moment. Confusion drowned him in a blurry mess. He was scrambled, but he was alive. His vision took a second to become clear, and then his hearing began to track what was happening.

Simon was no longer on top of him. McCrary looked to his right while he tried to sit up, still feeling the knee speared into his chest as his head spun out of control, even though the weight of Simon no longer pressed into him.

Beyond his splayed out feet McCrary saw two men fighting, realizing it was Stone and Simon. Stone roared with anger as he struck the down assassin. Then Simon countered, throwing the agent off of him, rising up and delivering a crushing stomp to Stone's chest.

"You two are full of a lot more life than I gave you credit for," Simon said standing over Stone and McCrary. He let out a celebratory scream in a tone laced with insanity before laughing wildly.

Simon turned his attention to the detective, looking down at the man with curiosity. "You, old man. You're a real pain in my ass. And I'm not having fun anymore."

McCrary blinked, seeing only one Simon before him. "Not the first time I've heard that, asshole."

Simon conceded with a bob of his head, weighing the possibility. "It's probably gonna' be the last."

McCrary pulled his legs underneath him, warily moving to a kneeling position. He hunched over breathing heavily, fighting the pain radiating through his head and body. Gasping, he watched Simon close the distance between them, snarling and glaring down on him with every step he took. This would have to be the end. There was no way he could continue fighting this animal with any hope to win, or even survive, for his or Stone's sake. Someone was going to have to die.

****

As Simon closed in, he reached out and took hold of McCrary's vest to pull him up and deliver a jarring knee strike to the man's head. An attempt to block it with an arm softened the blow, but there was no doubt it still rattled the detective. Simon delivered another and another. McCrary fell to one side, but Simon pulled him back up. Again, the knees were blocked, even partially, but the defensive attempt only made Simon throw them harder. And in that moment, he realized his mistake — his overconfidence. Richter had always told him it would be his downfall; that if he didn't focus and remain focused, he would slip up one day when he never should have. *But I'm in control. How could this happen*?

His jaw dropped in awe, and his eyes glazed over with bewilderment. He coughed, feeling the dryness caught in his throat before the warmth of his blood rose to change that sensation. His hands reached out for support, finding it with an unsteadiness that did not keep him from stumbling. Solid ground balanced him. Simon felt numbness and warmth and a chill all in succession radiating from his core. Again he hacked up more blood, bucking his body like a shot to his torso from a boxer, lifting him up on to his toes for a moment, and as he came back down there was no strength left in his legs to stand. He tumbled down to his knees, releasing the support he'd found before. Again, he wondered, *how could this happen*?

McCrary stumbled backwards away from the assassin, looking down on him through a mask of rage and pain. His body heaved with every breath he took, but the grimace on his face did not clear. He watched the stunned killer lost in translation on the losing end of a fight he should have never lost. Blood spilled out over the ledge of Simon's gaping mouth, wetting his teeth, and pooled at his knees. McCrary did not feel sorry for what he had to do. He was left with no other option. There was a sense of satisfaction in the outcome that it was not for revenge, but it was a subsidiary reason. He'd done what he needed to do out of the necessity to save his life and Stone's. Justice for Audrey was secondary, although in his heart she had always come first.

The midsection of the assassin was cut from his belt line to his sternum, and he shockingly attempted to hold in the crimson wave that leaked from the wound. Simon continued to cough, padding at his belly and negating that there was a knife embedded inside him. Blood soaked him and continued on to the floor, pooling outward around the space he knelt. He looked up to McCrary, shocked, angry, and relieved. It wasn't anything he could admit, but Simon had no issues with accepting his demise. He wasn't scared of dying. Richter had told him to never fear the end because it came for them all. *Embrace it.*

And that is what Simon did, taking what time he could to compose himself as the detective watched him bleed to death. He straightened his face, losing control of the tears that ran down his handsome features, and he smiled. At first it was thin and weak, and even then, Simon knew it wouldn't do. More effort was needed. He coughed up more blood, jerking his body with a violent hiccup, but he remained strong. *For Richter. For himself.* Simon regained his grin and let it spread farther and wider until the bloody chicklets of his teeth were exposed. His last breath arrived simultaneously, paralyzing him in the moment with his eyes glassed over devoid of life. Simon collapsed to one side and never moved again.

McCrary felt a lot of things in the moment, but he maintained what composure was necessary. He shook his head in disbelief, unable to compute what he'd just survived. He shook his head looking down on Simon. "Fuckin' psycho."

Chapter 49
Who's Afraid of the Big Bad Wolf?

"He's coming," Viktor said. When he spoke the words, it was like rolling thunder, full of strength and authority, demanding attention instantaneously.

The words broke the silence in the room, tearing away at the weight of the atmosphere. Viktor nodded to his comrade across the room obediently standing guard, statuesque without a single sway, who returned the gesture. A response also returned from the sentries outside of the safe room door echoed over the radio headset Viktor wore. He didn't necessarily need to tell them. His men were seasoned operators, and they knew that failure to report meant more men were down, which translated to this; the dangerous man was making his way to their location.

Viktor felt he was in the dark about the man pursuing Kurikova. Information was not only power, it was also survival, and not having every necessary detail put them all at a disadvantage. In no way did Viktor doubt his capabilities. He was prepared in every way possible. His skillset alone in hand to hand combat had garnered multiple combat Sambo championships in earlier years, as well as a confirmed kill rate in military combat upwards of 150. It wasn't an uncommon number as a member of an appointed kill squad to have such a success rate. Unofficially, Viktor could not keep count of the people he'd indiscriminately dispatched during his time of service. The numbers didn't matter to him anyway. He was great at what he did.

Black, hardened eyes stole a look at his distracted employer. Yuri 'the Wolf' Kurikova sat behind his oversized desk drinking himself into a calm state, or so it seemed. Viktor had witnessed the man's wrath many times and couldn't figure out why he was so shaken. Nearly twelve years ago an Armenian group had entered the Boston area and threatened

Kurikova's rule, going so far as to attack the syndicate leader at his prior home. There was no hiding then, and Kurikova knew those men were coming, too. The attack is what created the so called need for this safe room after relocating, but the Wolf had bloodied his teeth against the Armenian brutes, and he'd done so savagely. Kurikova had gone so far as to behead the group's leader in front of his wife and children. In succession, he did the same to the man's brothers to send a message that would never be forgotten. The Wolf's reign had not been challenged so decisively since.

Now they were under siege by one man, maybe two with the addition of the detective, if he were even involved. It disappointed Viktor to watch a man he'd known and protected for nearly fifteen years run and hide knowing Kurikova was no coward. With these thoughts the former Spetznaz soldier couldn't help but seek out the answers to the questions rattling around in his head. After all, the worst case scenario of the evening was that they were all going to die anyway, although he'd do everything in his power to thwart it.

"Why are we here?" Viktor demanded. His thick accent broke up his English pronunciations, but he was clear. There was no acknowledgement of his words, compelling him to bark at his master. "Yuri!"

Kurikova stopped drumming his fingers on the ledge of the glass set upon the vast landscape of the desk. His dead eyes rose from a place of concentration, staring into the clear alcohol and beyond, and settled on his most trusted bodyguard. He said nothing.

Frustrated, Viktor stepped towards the desk and repeated himself more emphatically. "*Why* are we here?"

Kurikova shook his head slowly as he sucked in a deep breath while pursing his lips. He didn't have an immediate answer even though he had already come to terms with the reality of the situation. His head bobbed from side to side while he wrestled with his thoughts. He wasn't certain of what to tell Viktor.

"Yuri," Viktor pleaded, his tone growing more aggressive.

"We're making a stand Viktor," Kurikova answered. "That was the plan. *Your* plan."

Viktor dismissed the accusation. "You wanted to be here, Yuri. I made that happen. But this is one man, supposedly. Why do we hide? *We* do not hide."

Kurikova felt the weight of his role crushing him, and he refused to fold beneath it. "We will live or die here based on our successes, Viktor. There is nowhere to run from here, and nowhere to hide. It will be him, or us. Simple."

Viktor shook off the absurdness. "We are sitting ducks here. I should have objected before."

Kurikova's eyes darkened as a menacing storm brewed within his irises. A primal demeanor encapsulated Viktor's leader as his facial features quickly became the snarling image of the pack's alpha. His heavy brow furled into an angry glare, and the slight reveal of his teeth. "That would have been a bad idea, Viktor."

A grin reshaped the hard line that made up Viktor's stoic mask. He nodded in agreement, saying, "*Da, ya vizhu eto seychas*." Viktor feared the man he'd followed for so long was lost. But it appeared he stirred beneath the surface of what he allowed them to see. "Yes, I can see that now."

Kurikova waved his hand, dismissing Viktor, and he said nothing more. Being questioned boiled his blood to some degree, but it was short lived. For his men, a certain appearance was needed. He could not show them he was afraid, although he acknowledged he let that slip for a moment. Being in this safe room presented a number of challenges in terms of his protection, and in terms of making it out alive. There was nowhere to go and Kurikova wanted it that way. It would be a fight to the death regardless of location, and he realized there was a chance they were simply prey awaiting the slaughter. He didn't care. In the end, he would be the last man standing, or the last of them to die. Even Viktor knew this.

The last of them to die…

The thought was both depressing and exhilarating, and it also instilled a fear that made him uncomfortable. Why now did he fear the end? And how could he also be excited by it? The answer was within him; at the heart of who he was. The Wolf was the answer, but it did not explain his fear. He slid the glass of vodka away from him, hearing it clash with the golden bottle of overpriced alcohol. Perhaps the potency of the drink was now messing with his mind. Over the course of the last few days Kurikova had consumed more than he typically would have, but business had been far from usual, and the circumstances were drastically different from the standard day to day operations.

Beyond all speculation of the safe room being the right place to make their final stand, Kurikova found it interesting no one questioned how its whereabouts could be known. It was installed secretly to some degree. Plans had been filed for a second underground room being built during the construction, but those were discarded officially with a convincing suitcase full of American currency. In his own mind, the Wolf never questioned whether the man would learn of the safe room's existence after having displayed intense attention to detail. With that vantage point Kurikova could better control the situation as long as things worked out in his favor. Otherwise he would die on his own terms, and there was nothing more satisfying to a man who craved the kind of power he had attained.

Kurikova envisioned the end being quick when it came for him or this vigilante. There was no way to get around that fact. Prolonging either man's death would only open up further opportunity to strike back and turn the tide. The crazy twin had mentioned that to him, altering his perspective. Hopefully that clown was able to follow through on his end by returning to finish his job. Kurikova didn't have much trust in the assassin, even though Simon was adamant about killing his target. He was no fool, and was well aware that for Simon it wasn't about finishing the job so much as it was about avenging his brother's death. If all worked out in their favor, Kurikova figured they could kill him together if nothing else. Vlademir needed redemption as well.

Dull gun shots made Kurikova turn his head to the main door. Through the vault they thumped liked drums in the distance, barely audible, yet distinguishable. The rapid fire of returned gun shots signaled a fire fight was underway beyond the safety of the room. Kurikova reached over to the glass of vodka and slammed back what remained. One way or another, the end was near.

****

Ghost descended from the loft with caution. He suspected all that remained of Kurikova's guards were those making up his personal guard, but there was no way to be sure until their paths crossed. Step by step the stairs wound down, and to see the real estate below he had to kneel to see beyond the threshold of the ceiling. The higher ground was universally considered a vantage point. However, in this dynamic, it also placed Ghost in a potentially harmful position. Clearing a lower area could have been costly if there were any hostiles downstairs. Stepping down exposed him first and therefore put him at a disadvantage. He knelt down and grabbed the railing with his left hand to hold himself in place, and then leaned over to his right with the rifle leading the way. The room below appeared to be empty, and was made up of a living suite that seamlessly transitioned into a small kitchen. He paused for a moment in anticipation of any movement beyond the large sofas or the island counter in the center of the kitchen.

The rifle scanned from left to right, and back again. Everything was still.

Once he felt comfortable with moving Ghost did so with rapid movement, springing down the stairs with the M4A1 trained on the open space of the room. A wall was directly behind him, so that removed any need to clear the space behind him. At the bottom of the stairs he sidestepped around the banister to keep the wall at his back, cross stepping to his left, knees bent and fluidly mobile. He paused a few feet from the end of the wall where an alcove led to a doorway that opened into a short hall. Another door led to the stairs where he'd find Kurikova's bunker.

The path to the end was simple enough, but more dangerous than ever. A feeling of excitement shot Ghost in the chest out of nowhere, anxiety and heartbreak and adrenaline all fusing together as one. At its core, Ghost's immediate quest for vengeance would be complete. Redemption, if it could be called that, would be fulfilled. He inhaled a deep breath to center himself. Now was not the time to let his thoughts wander; to think of his wife and daughter being thrown into a life of despair and horror. Another breath was taken in and exhaled. Ghost concentrated on the anger and the pain, molding them into a barrier around his heart and mind to create the protection he needed. He used what was left over as fuel to finish what he started. Within seconds he was seething once again with well targeted malice.

One more deep breath reclaimed a storm of fury and calm that, when appropriately directed, left nothing behind but casualties and destruction. Ghost was ready to continue.

Watching the living room and kitchen space for a moment longer, Ghost wanted to be certain there would be no followers before he exposed himself to clear the alcove. The seconds ticked away in long drawn out succession. When he found some semblance of satisfaction Ghost stepped away from the wall, giving himself space to clear the corner without needlessly overexposing himself. He tucked his right elbow tight to his body, shouldering the rifle snuggly, and then slowly leaned out. As soon as the space presented itself to be empty, Ghost stormed forward to the end and swung around to cover where he had come from.

Still no movement.

The remainder of Kurikova's guards must have been taken out by McCrary. Ghost wondered how the detective was fairing; whether he was still alive, and if he'd gotten to Stone yet. The older man was more resilient than he gave himself credit for. Ghost had faith in his ability to rescue Stone, but he was also prepared for him to fail. If nothing else, McCrary provided a necessary distraction so Ghost could do the heavy lifting. He maintained a position to be withdrawn from the detective's loss, if need be, although he found it terrible to have him wrapped up in this mess. Frankly, the situation was out of his league. McCrary knew it, too, which was why he was reluctant to agree to help. Ghost made it about seeking revenge for his wife. Manipulating his moral compass was done all too easily, even though deep down the former Marine wanted to fuck shit up tonight. Continually weighing the scales of justice is what guided McCrary. And then there was the tragedy he'd been exposed to. Sure, the detective agreed to help to get Stone back, not to murder the men responsible for his wife's death. When Ghost confronted the detective and agent in the cellar of the pawnshop, he could tell they'd bonded already. Good men don't leave other good men behind, and they didn't let the bad ones get away, either.

Ghost turned to address the door to his left. Beyond it would be the landing to the stairs where he'd make his final approach. Throughout the course of his career as a splinter cell operative, Ghost had developed enough sense to never barge through just any door. On many occasions there was no threat waiting directly on the other side, regardless of the situation, and it was safe to assume there wasn't any here. Assuming, like hesitation, could get you killed. Knowing that the more elite sentries Kurikova employed were former Spetznaz inherently directed Ghost to be more cautious. He'd come too far to let a careless mistake keep him from his goal, which forced him to anticipate this door to be the perfect point for a trap. Was it paranoia? Maybe. Better to err on the side of caution, though.

To check the door Ghost removed a device from a lower pocket on the outside of his vest. At first glance it resembled a small radio car controller. There were two fold up toggles for controls and a small screen at the center. Directly below the screen was a red power switch he slid to the right and the device blinked to life. From one end he pulled out a cord similar to that of a coaxial cable, but smaller in diameter. Attached to the end was a fixed HD camera capable of full color detail and infrared. He knelt down and slowly snaked the cord beneath the door.

Located in between the toggles and just below the power switch were two buttons, which Ghost used to feed the wire out further, and then to retract it. A silent motor inside the controller moved the cable in and out. Ghost could feel the small device vibrate from the mechanical action. He watched the screen as the high definition resolution picture beyond the door showed him everything he needed to see in full color. The camera was at floor level barely peeking out past the door. A quick toggle left and right showed him there was nothing immediately on the other side of the door.

Ghost worked the controls to feed the cable out further, and then he angled the camera up towards the door handle. The camera cord was capable of flexing upwards, but it couldn't be controlled to climb the door. A turn of the left toggle allowed the camera to zoom in, and it showed Ghost what he suspected was a magnetic strip charge just below the door handle. Sometimes he hated being right.

The charge itself was made up of two pieces; one attached to the doorframe and the other on the door. A magnetic strip linked them as a seal, and when the door opened, separating the connection, the charge would detonate. Ghost had used them before, and typically they were only powerful enough to immediately damage the initial person going through the door. He wasn't concerned with the explosive itself. What was bothersome was that it would alert the sentries surely waiting for him at the end of the hall. That couldn't happen.

"Motherfuckers'..." Ghost cursed to himself.

The wheels of his mind began to spin, racing through any and every option he could think of to find a quick solution. Very little came to mind that could practically be applied without making a disturbing amount of noise. Frustration attempted to set in, but Ghost refused to let it interfere. He came up with one option, slightly noisy, but it would get the job done. And the faster he acted the better.

Ghost stepped away from the door until his back pressed against the wall. He shouldered the rifle and looked down the sights six inches to the right of the door handle. His thumb switched the firing selector to semi-automatic. With all things considered Ghost figured the sound of the bullets punching through the door and into the parallel wall beyond was the best he could do in a pinch. If it alerted the sentries it was possible that he'd hear their boots on the hard wood flooring, at which point he'd use the charge to his advantage. Or, if he moved fast enough, the impromptu plan he devised would work in his favor, and he'd still use the charge to his advantage. Either way, with an initial plan and a backup, he needed to get moving.

In a succession of four expertly placed shots, each one above the last, a line streaked upwards and through the door. Each bullet spat from the suppressor of the rifle and punched the door with a dull thud. They surely embedded in the wall beyond, but Ghost paid no attention to them. He quickly squeezed out four more directly next to them going down creating a large enough notch to fit his fingers through. Ghost surged forward, inserted his fingers deeply through the door, and then tore a section of it free. He tossed the chunk of door far away, hearing it tumble off in the distance, and quickly ripped away a bigger chunk. The portal was made of solid wood, but it was thin and designed to appear fancier than it looked. Once a large enough space was created Ghost kicked through it, followed by his shoulder and the rifle. He paused standing halfway through the doorway with the M4A1 aimed at the bottom of the stairs where a ninety degree turn led down the hall.

Ghost kept the rifle trained forward as he finished passing through the door. There was no sign of disturbance from his position. He continued to pause, listening hard for any movement. Nothing gave him any cause for alert. He reached over to the magnetic charge and depressed a black switch located beneath a blinking red light. The arming indicator died, identifying the device as safe. Ghost squeezed the two pieces together and peeled them away from the door, holding onto them as he moved down the stairs.

At the bottom landing area Ghost alternated the rifle and the magnetic charge to the opposite hands. He raised the rifle in the grip of his left hand, securing the stock into his shoulder as he placed his back against the wall adjacent to the opening of the hallway. Ghost inched his way to his left, pausing to return the firing selector to automatic before he leaned out. The expectation was that there were at least two sentries posted outside of Kurikova's safe room, but until he saw them for himself, Ghost couldn't be sure. It was a common security standard. Any more than two men would congest the immediate area, especially in the case of a firefight, and that would impede on the line of fire between the would-be men out in front, and those behind.

All he had to do was to lean out and find out for himself.

Ghost bent slightly at the waist, breaking the cover provided by the wall across from him, and fired at the first sight of anyone. Two men were posted outside of the safe room, and his initial rounds knocked one of them backwards. The stream of bullets hit the sentry in the chest, but was stopped by his armored vest. The sentry quickly bounced back to return fire with the man to his right.

And with that Ghost's final confrontation was underway.

Chapter 50
Emergence

Before checking on Stone, McCrary crossed the open space of the wine cellar to retrieve his pistol from underneath one of the tables. He did so as quickly as he could, hobbling more than walking, aching from head to toe and squinting to see while his right eye threatened to finally swell shut. A thousand questions raced through his mind along with nearly as many emotions. It was all too much to process so, for the moment, all McCrary could do was concentrate on fighting through the pain. An old saying registered in his consciousness, and he couldn't help but grin. It was something his drill sergeant had said, which had likely been repeated across every entity of service and then some in one fashion or another:

Pain lets you know you're still alive. And if you're alive, you're still fighting!

McCrary hurt so badly that he wished he were dead. He checked the gun for any issues, ejected the magazine, cleared the barrel, and then reinserted the magazine. The final action was placing a fresh round into the chamber, and as he did so McCrary was forced to pause. Only a few feet away through blurry vision and one good eye, he saw the chair Stone had been attached to. Now it was toppled over and broken. At the foot of it were two large zip ties. The arms of it had been pulled away or splintered. It was undeniably a testament to Stone's own strength, but it wasn't the broken chair that stunned him. Yes, managing to somehow escape when it mattered most was impressive; it was a pure display of the will to live. What caught McCrary off guard was the amount of blood that stained the chair and the floor around it. Some, if not most of the sanguine fluid, was still wet.

The detective shook his head, astonished that the G-man had found some ungodly ability to rise from the brink of death. McCrary closed his eyes and breathed in deeply. Memories of men he'd served with, bonding in times of crisis and combat, losing good ones to a careless war waged on someone else's behalf, flooded his thoughts. Those moments were what seated the bond of brotherhood; men willing to live and die for one another regardless of the outcome. McCrary fondly added Stone to the ranks of the fighting men that occupied his mind. This was not something he would ever forget.

A hard look cast across the floor showed McCrary where Stone lay. Still, the agent was fighting, trying to pick himself up off of the ground even when he stumbled and couldn't find the strength. McCrary gritted his teeth and rose to his feet. *I'm coming, brother.*

His footsteps were heavy, but that was only because he had to be careful not to stumble and fall. McCrary attempted to preserve what tenacity and toughness he could, knowing that getting Stone out of here was going to be more difficult than he ever could have imagined. He could barely move on his own, let alone support someone else, too.

"Hey, you, sonofabitch," McCrary growled kneeling over the bloodied G-man.

Stone managed to lift his head and turn his face towards the familiar voice of the surly detective.

McCrary bit his lip and looked away for a few seconds, horrified to look at a man he would now call his friend until the day he died. Stone's once handsome face would have been a blanketed hematoma if it wasn't also cut and bleeding. He tried to talk. The sound was unrecognizable even for a mumble, and faded off into a high pitched grunt. Bloody spittle dripped from his swollen and split lips. Stone tried to talk again, but his mouth barely moved from the contusions. His head trembled as he tried to remain looking up, slowly fading back down to an outstretched arm beneath him where he used it as a pillow.

The sight overwhelmed McCrary. He couldn't imagine the pain Stone felt, or how he managed to endure so much and keep on kicking. But the agent had miraculously done so. Seeing Stone broken down, beyond fractured, told him his pain wasn't so bad. McCrary used it to muster up his own strength from a reserve a man never knew he had until it was needed.

McCrary turned back and knelt down to help Stone crawl onto all fours. The affair was painful to watch. McCrary didn't feel as though he was much help, fighting through the burning pain in his core and the imbalance in his head. He definitely had a broken rib or two, and a concussion. It was nothing in comparison to Stone. A heavy growl passed through clenched teeth as McCrary pulled Stone's right arm up high enough so he could get a shoulder underneath the agent. Howling pain squawked from Stone, but it had to be done. They couldn't stay here. McCrary and Stone rested in the first step of what seemed far too many just to stand. He thought of the help they needed, wondering if he could get it here on time. After everything leading up to this, after everything they'd survived so far, McCrary simply couldn't lose someone else now.

McCrary's big hand reached around Stone's back, and his long fingers gripped the belt line of the man's slacks, curling them into the ball of a fist. He straightened up as best he could, and Stone made more involuntary and terrible noises as the detective did so.

"I know, pal," McCrary sympathized. He took a series of deep breaths, heaving his big chest as much as he could, ignoring the burning around his ribs, to pump himself up for what he hoped to be the final step of rising to their feet. Collectively both men looked to one another, and McCrary narrated the obvious. "Sorry, but this is gonna' fuckin' hurt."

All of the detective's strength went into standing, applying the force to the one foot he had posted on the floor. He then got underneath Stone to stabilize the simultaneous lifting of his nearly dead weight. They both roared in unequal agony, kicking and clawing within their souls to rise up. Success seemed to be theirs, even if it were short lived.

Their momentum forced them to falter, and McCrary stumbled to his right dragging Stone with him. He called out against the fall, fearing the unsurmountable wave of pain that hitting the floor would cause. It didn't come. Instead, as McCrary reached out in the instinctive manner to soften the impact, his hand posted up against one of the wine refrigeration units, and they stopped. McCrary used the immovable object to steady himself and Stone — to re-grip his hold on the man and better support the agent with his broad shoulders.

Stone's feet shuffled beneath him to help sustain his position and carry what weight of his own that he could. A congratulatory pat on McCrary's stomach signaled he was as ready as he'd ever be to get moving. That same arm fell limply to his side

McCrary adjusted himself, getting his balance on both feet with Stone hanging off of his left side. A few more breaths were necessary to pump himself up for their hard earned exodus, stinging and painful, but nothing like what Stone was enduring.

"Alright, pal," McCrary grunted, bracing to shove off of the wine refrigeration unit. "Let's get tha' fuck outta' here."

****

There were many stops along the way. In the back of his mind McCrary knew there would be. There had to be. They weren't superhuman. And with every step he took, Stone's efforts to assist only drained the agent more. Soon Stone's weight leaned on McCrary more, and his footing became more uncertain. Stone's breaths became shallower as he exerted more energy. To be so battered and fractured and still have the will to go on was inspiring to McCrary. It kept the fire in him burning, and forced him to fight on, too. It hadn't occurred to him throughout this entire ordeal, but Stone had lost plenty along his way and it hurt him a little more.

The mansion was eerily still as McCrary half carried, half dragged Stone into the game room where he'd entered. Nothing had changed, and they hadn't encountered any threats. He suspected Ghost must have finished everyone off like the one man army he was touted to be. Or, better yet as far as McCrary was concerned, maybe Ghost and Kurikova had fucking killed each other. That was the happy ending McCrary envisioned to this nightmare. It gave him a sense of joy through all of the pain.

McCrary navigated their way through Kurikova's home blindly, opting to move towards the front entrance in hopes of finding a vehicle he could set Stone in without trying to lower him to the ground. They exited a hall and crossed an open marble floored foyer where a set of staircases wound down to the ground level on either side. McCrary had to stop for a moment to catch his breath, holding a strong stance to support Stone as best he could. He couldn't rest for too long because he didn't know if he could hold the agent up for a prolonged period of time. Or whether there were still any threats to be dealt with. Just a few breaths, that's all he needed.

The large front door to the home swung open easily. McCrary thought it would be heavier based on its size. Things were looking up. He and Stone stumbled out the door, scuffing their feet across the brick laid entry. Their energy was just about depleted, holding up long enough for them to collapse against an Escalade. The detective kept Stone pressed up against the vehicle and flung the passenger door wide open, desperately pulling Stone over to the seat. If it weren't for the agent's groans McCrary would have thought he'd passed out.

"We made it, pal," McCrary reassured. The words were more for himself than Stone. "I'm gonna' call fa' help. Hold on."

McCrary laid Stone back into the seat. He turned out to his right and collapsed against the SUV, exhausted. The weight of his eyelids was unbearable, forcing him to close them tightly. He fought to catch his breath while blindly searching the pouches on his vest for the burner phone Ghost had provided. At the same time, he also fought off the overwhelming feeling to give in to his scattered emotions. His hands fumbled with the phone, impatiently waiting for it to power on. Once the screen displayed a number of bars for reception McCrary stabbed at the phone icon and quickly dialed 9-1-1.

A number of satisfying sighs escaped from the detective. Finally, he was experiencing some semblance of civility, organization, and social stability. The voice that opened the line was rough with a smoker's rasp, and she answered with the standard dispatcher's spiel. To McCrary she sounded like an angel, and hearing the voice on the other end brought him into a brief calm.

"Yes, this is Lieutenant Randal McCrary with the Boston police department out of district C-11," the words came out with ease, almost practiced, although he'd never made an actual emergency call. All the years on the radio had prepped him, and his experience took over. "I need immediate assistance at my location. I have no address. Can you run a GPS locate on my phone?"

The dispatcher responded quickly. "I'm running you now, LT."

"I need back up units and a couple of ambis, ASAP. I have an FBI agent critical, an' I'm busted up pretty good, too. Possible multiple active shooters on scene including the Boston vigilante."

The events over the past few days encompassing her shifts had placed the dispatcher in an even more heightened state of mind, and increased her stress exponentially given the need for a rapid response. Most importantly, she recognized the LT's name from a previous B.O.L.O., or 'be on the lookout' bulletin that had been issued earlier in the evening for Detective Randal McCrary following a massive police response to his home address. She shook off the thought of what happened and said, "I have you just outside the Sudbury area, LT. Back up and paramedics are on the way."

McCrary nodded to himself, closing his eyes and sliding the palm of his free hand down his face to immediately wipe away the tears he suddenly produced. He turned and arched in a concerned attempt to check on Stone. The energy to stand and watch over the agent wasn't there. "How long?"

A tinge of frustration caused the dispatcher's voice to crack. She struggled for an answer as she worked to field radio responses. "Because of the location, LT, probably almost fifteen minutes."

McCrary could hear the disappointment in her voice, but she was only relaying what information she could. "It's okay, it's okay." He nodded his head as a subconscious bid to convince himself that the estimated time was adequate. Nothing could be done about it though. What mattered was that help was on the way.

"Is there anything else I can help you with, LT?" the dispatcher asked. There was no immediate reply, which she read as a cause for concern. "LT? Is there anything else I can help with?"

For a moment McCrary lowered the phone away from his ear, shaking his head. The action signified a non-verbal response, except it had nothing to do with the dispatcher. A flood of devastation washed over McCrary, breaking the levy that he'd built to maintain his composure. Everything he'd held in from the time Audrey was murdered rocketed to the surface out of control. McCrary released a powerful sob and held nothing back, continuing to wipe the tears away, and pinching his fingers deep into the bridge of his nose as if it would stop the pain. He fell apart with grief, sailing into uncharted waters he never thought he could possibly endure. The essence of a hardened man shattered, and Randal McCrary was overtaken with the loss of his wife.

The dispatcher grew more concerned without a response considering the circumstances. She yelled into the mic of her headset desperate for an answer. "LT? Answer me!"

All she could think was that something had happened to him. It did no good to speculate what exactly, but she couldn't help it. He had been there a few seconds ago, voice even toned and in control, and now he was just gone. She couldn't make sense of it. And then she heard the pain stricken cry reply.

"They killed my wife!" McCrary wailed. He tried to speak again, stuttering inadvertently until he could force the words out of his mouth. "They… Killed… My… Wife…"

McCrary wanted to say more, struggling to diversify his message, but the only words he could bring forth was what hurt him the most. He repeated them over and over again, his speech broken between words that stretched out longer with every painful pronunciation.

The dispatcher found herself covering her mouth in disbelief, choking back her own tears as she listened to a man crumble into pieces over the line. She looked around as if to suggest she needed help, but that wasn't the case at all. There was nothing anyone could do for Randal McCrary at this point; nothing at all.

She cleared her throat and listened to McCrary cry. There was something she could do, and she made sure he knew. "Don't worry, LT. Help is on the way. I'm not going anywhere."

Chapter 51
An Unstoppable Force

The return gunfire from the sentries at the end of the hall came in a fully automatic wave. One man shot while the other reloaded, and then they alternated, covering each other. The heavy rounds from their AK-74s ripped into the wall, obliterating the interior structure, and filling the hallway with the explosive clacking of their guns and a haze of drywall dust.

Ghost stepped back towards the stairs a few feet before bullets shredded through the corner where he sought cover. Wood splinters and white dust fogged the area. Despite the exhaustive gunfire rattling through the confined space, he could tell the sentries were getting closer, maneuvering down the hall in his direction, leap frogging from one position to the other. It wasn't a bad tactic, but it also wasn't ideal, either. Upon moving away from his corner spot where he initially opened fire, Ghost waited for the men to deploy some type of explosive or flash bang grenade to disorient him as he used so frequently. The obnoxious amount of forward moving rapid fire and the thick cloud of construction debris were effective, but it had no debilitating quality. He had a way to change things very quickly.

The device he'd removed from the stairway door operated by way of a magnetic detonator that connected the two pieces signaled through a low wave radio frequency. Once the connection between the magnetic strips separated a small, yet potentially lethal charge would explode. It was simple enough and mere child's play to operate. With the charge disarmed, Ghost pulled the pieces apart. The explosive was designed into the piece opposite of the power switch essentially creating a grenade for him to use at his leisure. A small amount of amusement made him shake his head. These guys made this too easy.

Ghost tossed the explosive end of the device into the cloud of dust encompassing the elbow of the hallway. He positioned himself on the far side of the wall to quickly move into the foggy atmosphere following the detonation. The sentries were getting closer. He could hear them communicate in Russian during the brief separation of gunfire. Ghost was uncertain of what they said due to the noise they made. Their gunfire suddenly hit a lull and the talking stopped. They were close.

When the power switch was activated the connection took a moment to recognize that the magnetic connection did not exist. A couple of seconds passed before the radio pulse transmitted, working in Ghost's favor. The curtain of dust shrouding the hallway in mystery was dissipating, and he could see movement through the damage inflicted on the infrastructure.

Ka-boom!

The explosive was more powerful than Ghost expected, and the sentries should have been standing directly over it. More damage bombarded the hallway as drywall dust plumed outward in every direction. Ghost pulled the collar of his undershirt up high to cover his mouth and nose while dropping the remainder of the explosive device as he charged forward into the chalky white mist.

The drywall provided great coverage in Ghost's favor, but it was just as much of a hindrance by doing the same for the sentries. At best he expected the two men to be badly wounded but not completely incapacitated. This way he wouldn't underestimate the kind of force he could possibly encounter. He moved with the M4A1 shouldered and ready with his left hand extended forward using it the way a blind man would a walking stick.

At the first sense of contact Ghost found one sentry staggering to his feet cussing in his native language. It wasn't difficult to tell the man was disoriented, and appropriately so. Ghost's left hand found the sentry, and by natural instinct and familiarity of human anatomy, he determined it was the left shoulder. This meant the wounded man who could barely stand had his back to Ghost. With a powerful force Ghost drove the shoulder forward, turning the sentry's face into the wall, and then pressed the barrel of the suppressed rifle to the back of his head. Two crisp mechanical whispers later and the sentry collapsed to the floor.

Beyond the haze of plaster material, the other sentry dragged himself down the hallway towards the door to Kurikova's safe room. He appeared to have taken the brunt of the explosive, possibly having been kneeling in the area of the detonation. Both of his legs were bloodied and useless, and his feet dangled from the wounded area by the threads of what remained of his black BDU's. The fractured bone and meat of his lower legs were now exposed. He didn't make a sound as he crawled away, or attempt to find another weapon to fight on with. The sentry simply moved away from the blast zone clinging to what little time he had left in this world as he maintained a glare of honor and determination he knew deep down was futile.

Ghost emerged from the wreckage, massive and menacing, squinting his eyes to protect against the debris. His determined pace quickly caught up with the impaired hostile, lowering the rifle to his side as he passed. Two more suppressed shots were delivered in passing as the barrel briefly hovered over the man's cranium. He immediately stopped moving.

****

Silence can be terrifying. It carried with it a limited array of meaning depending on the context. In combat it quite often signaled the end, or someone's end. Or, as cliché as it sounded, as the thought filled Kurikova's mind, it was the calm before the storm.

Viktor called out on his radio, barking orders in Russian to respond. There was no one left to hear him other than the men locked inside the safe room with him. A look of fury and concern melded together as he turned to his employer. "*Otvet' mne, chert voz'mi*!"

Kurikova shook his head, translating the meaning while he looked away. "Answer me, god damn it!"

"*Kakiye*?" Viktor sounded confused at first. Anger quickly replaced any concern.

Kurikova's head snapped back to his head of security. He saw the raw, seething rage boiling from within the large man, so powerful it curled one corner of his mouth and made him tremble.

"What is it?" he asked, standing from his chair behind the desk.

Viktor plainly looked to his boss. The answer was in his eyes, and

Kurikova knew. "It's him."

****

Ghost activated the earpiece he'd taken earlier from the sentry in the kitchen upon approaching the safe room door. In his left hand he held the radio Kurikova's men used and clipped it to his vest. He examined the door while he waited for the channel to connect, determining that he'd brought the right means to breach the door.

Out of a medium sized pouch Ghost removed two plastic lined rolls of putty material. What he held in his hands was a thermoplastic incendiary strip, which, in short, mimicked the effects of a plasma cutting tool used to slice through steel. When activated, using an electronic detonator similar to what he would also use for the breaching explosives he'd packed, the incendiary cord would ignite and burn through the door jamb of the safe room entrance. He began rolling out the strip, measuring it against the doorframe. Once the lengths were ready, he removed the plastic lining along the adhesive side to apply each strip.

As he prepped the door for a forced entry the radio channel came alive. A frantic and angry voice called out for responses, likely from the two men Ghost had just killed.

"*Oni mertvy,*" Ghost stated in perfectly pronounced Russian. His words were flat and cold, much like the open steppe of the Motherland. "*Ikh legch ubit', chem ya ohzidal. Day mne Yuri.*"

The channel went silent, and all that remained was the light static floating over the frequency. His words carried the desired effect being both chilling and stunning. "They're dead. They were easier to kill than I anticipated. Give me Yuri," he'd said.

It would have been easy to expect an explosive outburst in response, but Ghost held a trump card in his deck that he expected to compound the effect of his message once he made contact. He was familiar with his opposition, recognizing Viktor's voice, as well as knowing the former Spetznaz operator had been employed by Kurikova. They had history prior to Viktor's tenure within the Russian crime syndicate. The silence was not a surprise, but it did make Ghost smile. Despite the circumstances, it was important to enjoy the little things.

****

Viktor's silence was unsettling to Kurikova. Such a hardened man, a survivor of brutal atrocities in his youth and later in life a harbinger of such cruelties, he should not have frozen this way. The sullen look that overtook Viktor enraged Kurikova deep inside, not because he was angry with his head of security, but because he knew they both shared the same fear.

The former Spetznaz soldier walked to the far corner of Kurikova's desk. He paused, looking to Kurikova with questions that could not be answered. There was only one answer, and he knew it to be inevitable now. Viktor removed his earpiece and radio, folding them into one of his big hands, displaying his frustration with the shake of his fist. His eyes fell to the communication unit, and then slowly rose to meet Kurikova's.

"You have doomed us all," Viktor stated, dropping the radio onto the desk. He walked away to the other guard, keeping his back to his employer, as if his words explained the situation. Glaring eyes from the second sentry shot towards Kurikova.

The Wolf stared at the radio and its winding cord connecting to the earpiece. The gesture meant he was to pick it up. He didn't want to. It was obvious the man waited for him with a message conjured up to instill a deeper sense of his impending menace. Whatever he'd said to Viktor had a miraculous effect. How Viktor could be affected in such a manner was beyond Kurikova. The mystery in the thought forced him to shake his head. He couldn't imagine an answer that made sense to him, and he felt certain he wasn't going to ever do so.

A quick extension of the hand snatched the radio and earpiece off of the desk similar to the way a child would run from the door to their bed to avoid the monster beneath it. The difference here was that Kurikova brought the monster to him. He reconsidered administering contact as he held the radio, imagining that throwing it across the room would change everything and the killer at his door would simply go away. That, of course, was not the case. The Wolf needed to act like one. He was the leader, the alpha, and if death was coming, he would welcome it violently.

The earpiece slid into Kurikova's ear canal with ease, the soft silicone texture firmly squeezing into place. A deep breath preceded any words, and Kurikova immersed himself in the ruthless persona that had kept him at the head of the table for so long. His eyes went dark, and his brow furled into a furious grimace as his lips tightened.

"*Da*?" Kurikova spoke coldly; irritated. The greeting was nearly unintelligible, emanating from his mouth as more of a growl than a pronunciation. "Yes?"

"Knock, knock," came the equally cold response.

As soon as he heard the reply, Kurikova's attention snapped to the safe room entrance. The inner framing of the door came alive on either side, sizzling and sparking, emitting an inflammatory and metallic smoke beginning at the bottom of the jamb. A glowing orange hue followed the boundary line of the vault door like a countdown to the end of the world. Kurikova shot a fearsome look to his guards. Steely eyes returned his glare. Viktor separated himself from the other soldier, barking orders at the man simultaneously while he approached Kurikova.

"We're going to die," the head of security said. "But we will fight first."

****

The incendiary cord was a slow burn. Cutting through six inches of steel wasn't supposed to be easy. Ghost wasn't sure if the door would be entirely cut through, expecting some pieces to linger and remain attached similar to the way a can opener sometimes missed a notch or two. He had a remedy for that on standby that would ultimately lead to his entry.

Smoke from the effects of the incendiary cord began to fill the hallway. Again, Ghost was prepared. He unfolded a respirator mask and goggles from a cargo pocket located on his left thigh. From a short distance he watched the orange glow around the shape of the door, giving it an ethereal feel as though it would open a portal to another world. The cold reality was that in a way it would do just that. But instead of a new world, however, it would become a tomb.

The sizzling and popping of sparks stopped at the top of the door. Heat from the cord's destructive use glowed in between the gap it created. Ghost removed a small canister from another pouch on his vest, safely tucked towards the back of one side. His gloves fit tightly, and he would need them for protection. The canister contained an aerosol vapocoolant used for industrial work to quickly cool hot surfaces. It was necessary to cool the small gap left behind by the incendiary cord to apply the liquid foam explosive that would fully breach the door. The contents of the canister made a little bit go a long way, which gave Ghost plenty to use liberally.

In a less than thirty seconds the vapocoolant had crystalized around the edges of the door and cast off a light mist. Ghost quickly reframed the door with the liquid foam, using two cans simultaneously to line the door and connect them at the top. A benefit of the foam was that it would fill into the gap, and upon detonation it would compound the force of the explosion and fully remove the heavy door from the frame. With material to spare Ghost crossed the door diagonally from either upper corner to the lower end creating an X. Unconventionally, he created a four-by-four square on the ceiling about five feet away. He didn't want to have to wear the respirator the entire time he fought the elite men inside, only to then have to deal with Kurikova. The square would blow a hole overhead, directly leading outside to ventilate the area.

Next Ghost placed a detonator stick in each corner and at the center of the X, and two into the foam on the ceiling. A short twist of each cap signaled a blinking red light displayed activation where they were equipped with low frequency radio receivers.

Ghost moved to the end of the hallway and around the corner just beyond the space where the previous sentries had turned the drywall into Swiss cheese. He took a knee, turning his back to the direction of the blast, and found the detonation device for the explosive. A metallic toggle switch powered it on, and a short rubber coated antenna delivered the signal. Ghost tucked his head down into his chest as deeply as he could, and then depressed the red button on the device with his thumb.

****

The smoke that filled the safe room was toxic, and it burned lungs when inhaled. Every man had difficulty adjusting to it, and there was nothing that could be done. The air filtration system pumping in oxygen did not work quickly enough to suck out the harmful fumes polluting the air. They would have to live with it for at least a few more minutes. Viktor had not calculated what could essentially be considered a chemical attack. It was mildly debilitating, but effective, nonetheless. It was also inevitable that the door was going to be removed one way or another, allowing the smoke to spread outward. Once that happened, however, it wouldn't be long before the fumes were the least of their concerns.

Viktor took up position behind Kurikova's large desk while his only remaining comrade crouched near the far wall parallel to him. These positions kept them out of direct line with the door, which Viktor assumed would be blown inward by a powerful breaching explosive. The ensuing damage and blast would be further disorienting. He would have done the same thing if he were on the other side. The other advantage of their placement kept them out of each other's line of fire. There was only one way in, and they would both concentrate their fire on the single entrance. It would make an entry next to impossible. Knowing who he was dealing with now told Viktor that the prospective plan was not infallible.

Ghost, as the vigilante was known in secretive circles, was an unstoppable force. Viktor had witnessed this firsthand. The man laid waste to an entire Taliban village in the *Safed Koh* mountain range of Afghanistan near the Pakistani border after a joint mission dutifully went wrong.

Officially Viktor's squad, consisting of eight combat hardened men, was never there. Unofficially they worked in conjunction with an unknown American group, otherwise referred to as an O.G.A (other government agency), to hunt and capture a high ranking Taliban leader. The snatch and grab had gone as well as could have been expected. Viktor's Spetznaz kill squad led the operation and the American's provided back up consisting of one brutally skilled man, Ghost.

Once the Taliban leader was in custody Viktor had other orders outside of burning the village to the ground and sending a message. He was to extract the man known as Abu Zamal Muhammad without the American in tow, essentially double crossing the agreement made with the O.G.A. Both countries' interest in the man was similar and expansive, but Russia came first. The operative known as Ghost, however, had caught on to the betrayal in the middle of exterminating the village occupants made up of Taliban warriors, and a firefight ensued between him and everyone else.

Viktor had never seen such fury of violence and efficiency in killing. He was incredibly confident in his own abilities, later wondering if he could have mimicked the actions taken by the American. At the time it was all he could think of in recovery after being the only survivor. The Taliban leader had been executed mercilessly; coldly disposed of without a second's hesitation. Viktor had abandoned him to fight more effectively, which he did not do. The only thing that had saved him was when half a roof of a home he'd entered collapsed and pinned him into a corner, nearly crushing his left leg. Once he was out of sight there was nothing to worry about. The sounds of war echoed around him as he laid quietly in the confines of the dark. Time passed without him somehow being discovered. When silence overtook the area, signaling that the fighting had ceased, Viktor assumed everyone was dead. Still, he was strong and determined to live, and dug his way out through one of the fractured walls risking the remainder of the structure falling on top of him. He would never forget the man called Ghost, and never wanted to cross his path again.

Apparently, karma had other plans.

There was a lull in the breaching of the door. Silence lasted only seconds as an aerosol spray was applied. *He's cooling the door. Next will be the explosive breach.*

Within less than a minute the safe room filled with a godly clap of thunder, deafening, and powerful enough to shake the room. The steel vault door blasted out of the frame. The top end tipped downward as if it were going to roll end over end. Instead, the heavy portal moved with the force of a rocket in the one direction as if it couldn't be stopped. An upper corner raked through the wooden floor, yet it never slowed, splintering the floorboards with ease until it crashed into the steel reinforced wall of the safe room opposite from where it once hung. Sheetrock dust mixed into the air with the metallic fumes enveloping the room in a foggy haze.

Things happened so quickly Viktor almost forgot to react, having not completely returned from the memory he held of Ghost. Reality snapped him back into the here and now, losing the precious seconds it took for him to orientate himself into the moment, and he rose up over the desk with his rifle ready. Across from him the other guard was shaking his head as a way to loosen the cobwebs caused by the disorienting concussion of the explosion. Quickly he raised his rifle as well, focusing on the entryway.

It was difficult to see through the haze. Viktor knew the man would be coming though. He had to be. There was nowhere else to enter the safe room. *What a stupid name, safe room. More like death trap.*

The head of security looked behind him for a brief moment. He found Kurikova crouched on one knee wearing a mask of rage and disgust, coughing slightly from the corrupt air. He was gripping a fully loaded semi-automatic pistol. Viktor nodded and returned his focus to the door. He was happy to see the return of his employer. Not Yuri Kurikova, but the *Wolf*. It was in his eyes, the same wild glare he'd presented when he fought off the Armenians years ago. Still, Viktor figured if there was no chance of survival, at least they would die fighting to the end.

****

The pungent air made Kurikova want to throw up. Between the metallic fumes and the sheetrock dust it was difficult to take in a full breath. He waved a hand to keep the particles from settling in front of him, but it did no good. The entire room was contaminated now. Overall, it was the least of their worries. Any second now they would come face to face with their fate, whether it was destined to be the end, or not.

Gunshots roared to life, further assaulting Kurikova's senses. His ears rang already, and they naturally fought against the sharp increase brought on by fully automatic gun shots. Viktor yelled for him to stay down, standing, and then moving away from the cover of the desk. Kurikova had no intention of going anywhere. He was not equipped to join a gun fight with only eight rounds in his pistol while automatic rifles screamed and clacked and emitted more bullets per second than he carried on him. The pistol was for when the man got close to him, if he took that liberty, and if Kurikova could successfully put it to use.

He watched Viktor move out of his line of sight. The gun fire seemed to stagger now. Only one of them would shoot, and when that stopped the other would continue. Kurikova knew it to be a military technique to preserve their rounds, and to be strategically more effective. The man was crafty and well prepared. He'd shown the Kurikova syndicate his patience and dedication for nearly three years, and it appeared he wasn't going to rush things now.

Viktor yelled something unintelligible while firing his rifle and the other guard replied. Kurikova couldn't make out the words. Another explosion concussed the room and cast a blinding light throughout. Kurikova fell to one side, caught off guard by the force of the blast. He squinted as his vision fought to clear from the brilliant illumination, and then he returned to his crouched position behind the desk. He could see Viktor about ten feet away in the openness of the room dazed and on all fours.

A ghastly scream startled Kurikova, and he shrank down farther onto the floor. Viktor turned and rose onto one knee, screaming in return, "*NET*!"

Viktor spun to his feet, surging into the fight completely enveloped in rage. Kurikova listened to the Spetznaz warrior roar and growl, putting everything he had into what might be his final battle. The noises radiated throughout the room. Kurikova wasn't entirely sure what he heard, but the sounds were furious and brutal and they didn't last long.

A series of cracks echoed like broken branches in an empty forest. Each came one right after the other in succession, and occurred quick enough that the man receiving the pain couldn't react to the symphony of violence his body played to the room.

Again, an eerie stillness overcame Kurikova. His fear wrestled with his anger, nearly dispersing of the courage he had to manufacture. The pistol shook in his hand, and he wasn't sure which influenced him more. *You are the Wolf. You are the predator here. If it is your time, make him bleed to take it from you.*

Kurikova steeled his conviction and steadied his hand. The pistol stopped trembling in his grip. He could not cower here forever, and he refused to. Death would shake his hand tonight, and he would smile back at it.

As the mob boss slowly stood, he did so with the pistol in front of him, carefully aiming out into the center of the room with his finger ready to squeeze the trigger. Wild eyes looked beyond the gun sites, and took in the grisly scene before him.

Viktor's remaining guard sat slumped in the background against the far wall, catching Kurikova's attention with the vast amount of blood that surrounded his corpse. He had been shot from his torso to his toes. A compound fracture of his left leg twisted inward where bone protruded from the knee that was caved in sideways. The sight made the Wolf grimace with disgust, but that was not the worst of it. The guard's throat had been cut so viciously that the trachea dangled out of the damaged tissue, splattering blood across the wall, and leaving a meaty crater behind the torn flesh.

Kurikova fought the involuntary urge to tremble again. He continued to fight back his fear as he turned his focus on the star attraction.

At the center of the room Viktor stood with his back to Kurikova. Or, more likely, he was being held on his feet. Viktor was every inch as tall as the man, almost mirroring him. Yet there was obviously a world of differences between them. He could see the vigilante on the other side of Viktor, shadowing the former Spetznaz soldier. His head was lowered enough to remain protected by Viktor's body, but also so he could look beyond him.

Kurikova met the vigilante's gaze, trying to match the cold focus the man cast upon him. It wasn't possible. Looking into his eyes was like being engulfed in darkness. Kurikova had never seen anything like it before. He expected fire and fury — rage and ferocity. It wasn't there, or at least it wasn't being put on display in the moment. That feeling chilled the Wolf, bringing on an involuntary twitch that cast down his spine, making him shiver. And then the man spoke only two words, greeting Kurikova with a raw menace that did not disappoint: "Hello, Yuri."

Chapter 52
The Ghost and the Wolf

Fear, in its many forms, is widely considered to be a choice. Those with a stronger mental fortitude lean towards this belief, and in many situations, they're correct. Ghost was one such person. He also believed that there was a kind of fear you couldn't control. It was sudden and unmistakably devastating. There was no way to work around it, control any part of it, or stop it. That's the way Kurikova looked at Ghost, and a part of him reveled in it. The Wolf seemed to struggle with hiding it, putting up the effort to display what had made him a hardened *pakhan*, but Ghost saw through it.

Within the recesses of his mind Ghost imagined how his daughter had no choice in the fear she'd felt, far too young to be strong enough to fight back in anyway as she screamed and cried for her father.

I'm going to tear you apart.

Ghost exploded forward, lifting Viktor's body as he moved, and using the man as a shield.

Kurikova didn't hesitate to pull the trigger. He controlled his reaction despite his underlying panic, shooting three times and conserving the limited rounds he had. It became obvious he wasn't skillful enough to shoot around Viktor's body to hit the vigilante. As the man surged towards him, Kurikova did the only thing he could think of for his survival, and that was move. It was a futile tactic.

The distance between Ghost and Kurikova was a matter of fifteen feet, and it was covered in three long steps. Kurikova attempted to move out and away from the desk. His efforts were halted by the 250 pound body of a dead Russian soldier slamming into him. The impact knocked him off balance and backwards against the wall, stunning him momentarily. It was the only setback needed for Kurikova to be overtaken.

Ghost hurdled over the large desk effortlessly, landing on one foot while his momentum carried a heavy knee strike deep into Kurikova's torso, and folding him grievously. Ribs fractured instantly, and the Wolf vomited forcefully to the side as he went down. Ghost quickly transitioned to control Kurikova's pistol hand, turning the barrel offline from his body to avoid being shot, and then stripped it from the Russian's grip. He then struck Kurikova in the face with the weapon, first crushing his nose with the butt of the gun, and then striking him again. The force of the strikes nearly knocked him out, but Ghost was far from done.

Powerful hands took hold of the unstable Kurikova and lifted him off of the floor with ease, and then slammed him down on top of his pretentious desk. The sound of his body crashing into the fixed position of the unmoving object radiated pain with the undulating blitz of more bones popping and cracking. Kurikova gasped and groaned, but he never cried out.

Ghost held the *pakhan* in place with one hand and continued to beat him with the pistol. The unforgiving steel slide of the pistol lacerated Kurikova's face instantly, digging into his flesh, and bloodying him within seconds. The injuries accrued quickly, swelling on top of bleeding cuts, turning the Wolf's face into something resembling hammered meat on a butcher's board.

Kurikova's arms flailed wildly, displaying a haggard effort at fighting back. Ghost deflected the attempts with mere slaps, examining the pummeled man before him. One eye had turned red and glared up at him with a primal fixation while the other was already swelled shut. The heavy flesh above the ocular cavity inflated like a plum, and the cheekbone beneath it rose to meet it, sealing off any chance of being separated. His lips were torn apart, and the bridge of his sinuses resembled an S curve in a highway. Kurikova's gaping mouth presented Ghost with a view of a bleeding tongue and missing lower teeth.

A fluid laced rasp escaped Kurikova's savaged lips, growling and gurgling in its defiant pronunciation. "Fuck you!"

Ghost leaned backwards to keep from getting any of the bloody spittle in his face. He admired Kurikova's will to fight back. But it was useless. He was going to destroy the mob boss within the coming minutes. A strong grip forced Kurikova's limp right arm to the edge of the desk, and then he nonchalantly hyperextended it beyond its natural design, breaking it. Despite his venomous dislike for the Russian, Ghost couldn't help but respect his toughness. Kurikova simply groaned and grimaced.

Looking down on Kurikova, into his glaring eye, Ghost witnessed the alpha wolf's steely mask of calm. Ghost shook his head slowly and said, "It's not going to be quick."

Kurikova was taken up by his shirt and pulled off of the desk, flopping down to the floor. Ghost then sat along the edge of the desk and watched the mob boss struggle to his knees, grunting and growling in pain. Labored breathing wheezed from Kurikova's bloody mouth, periodically gurgling from the dark sanguine fluid building up in his lungs. He coughed horrifically, reminding Ghost of something out of a zombie film.

"The last time we talked you told me how my daughter cried," Ghost said. "You told me how she wet herself calling for her daddy."

The bewildered Kurikova turned his quivering attention to his would-be assassin. Pain blanketed him from head to toe, yet he felt numb and, somehow, angry. He said nothing in reply.

"I was supposed to be traded for your father back then," Ghost continued to summarize. "Captured and betrayed by my own government, supposedly, and traded for a gangster's piece of shit father."

A bloody grin curled one side of Kurikova's mouth.

"It was botched, and your father was killed." Ghost watched Kurikova's grin disappear. "And then *you* took *my* family."

Kurikova stared blankly at Ghost, confused. He shook his head and somehow managed to say, "When my father was killed in the assault there were two survivors." He bobbed his head to one side saying, "Agent Stone," and then he bobbed his head in the opposite direction, "and another agent. My business partner took care of the retaliation, killing both of their families. Not me."

Ghost considered the mob boss's admittance of involvement. It wasn't the same narrative that he'd known this entire time. Every bit of information he had firmly pointed back to Kurikova and his syndicate. There were a number of questions this new information raised, yet the details still kept Yuri 'the Wolf' Kurikova directly connected to the taking of Ghost's family. Still, throughout his extensive investigation, what Ghost learned now was that there was another influential figure involved. Whoever Yuri's 'business partner' was, it meant that there was someone else also responsible for forcing Veronica and Chloe into human trafficking.

"Who is it?" Ghost asked, blankly staring through the dying man.

Kurikova shook his head, denying Ghost an answer. The vigilante swiftly kicked Kurikova in the chest, knocking him backwards a few feet where he helplessly slouched into the corner of the floor and the wall. A violent coughing fit followed, and Kurikova used the involuntary momentum to sit up to vomit a dark excretion of blood. The frenzy was short lived and left him gasping and wheezing.

"You are going to kill me," Kurikova managed to say with blood cascading over his lower lip. His chin and chest were saturated and nearly black now. "Why should I say anything?"

Ghost said nothing.

Kurikova gestured with his one good eye, raising his eyebrow transiently to suggest that his logic was solid. "Why would I make your vengeance easier?" He raised his head up in a challenging and defiant manner to further beckon for a reply.

Ghost considered the question. The logic was solid, and he couldn't argue it. There was nothing for him to play in his favor to convince Kurikova to willingly give up his partner. It was inevitable that he was going to kill the mob boss, and they both knew it.

"I'm going to find him, Yuri," Ghost stated flatly. "And I'm going to make him pay for killing my family. I'm going to kill every one of them."

The Russian shook his head again. "We both know it doesn't matter anymore. Kill me." He looked away dismissively. "You bore me."

There were no longer any signs of fear in Kurikova. He'd truly accepted the outcome, and once the decision was made there was no turning back. Kurikova was simply waiting to die.

There was nothing left to discuss, and Ghost had no time or reason to press for more information. The wheels of his mind were already turning on how to find who he needed to search for next, automatically eliminating possibilities and keeping others in mind to research further. However, it was important not to get too far ahead of the task at hand,

and Ghost delayed his investigative thoughts to finish what he'd come here to do.

"You've lucked out, Yuri," Ghost said, crouching down to peer directly at Kurikova. "It's going to be quick after all."

Kurikova's body appeared to rock and tremble as if he were going into a seizure, but he was laughing at death as he'd intended to do. "How is that lucky?"

Ghost pondered his words carefully, considering at the same time if anything Kurikova had said about his daughter held any truth, and whether his admittance of a partner's involvement was an honest statement. The thoughts only raised more questions. He dismissed them as being momentarily inconsequential. After tonight, it appeared he had another target to seek out, and something about that challenge was oddly satisfying.

"That's lucky," Ghost said, standing to his full height and forcing the Wolf to look up at him from his knees, "because I took my time killing your son."

Chapter 53
Last Men Standing

"What do you want me to say?" McCrary asked. The embittered scowl he wore scanned the panel of four sitting across the table from him. Each Internal Affairs officer looked to poke and prod into the vigilante case, but he had no answers for them. Their professional duty was obviously more important than his need to grieve and heal physically, mentally, and emotionally. "Huh? What the fuck do you want me to tell you?"

Captain James O'Donnell led the investigation with the purpose of understanding Detective Lieutenant Randal McCrary's role in the vigilante investigation. The FBI had prohibited any questioning of Special Agent Connor Stone, so there was no way to learn his side of the story. This was followed by the service of a national security letter, which was an administrative subpoena restricting the Boston Police Department from releasing any detailed information on the case. Essentially, the gag order only prohibited the information being released to the public, but McCrary was using it as a crutch for his defense.

O'Donnell shook his head, frustrated. "Lieutenant, your language is not appreciated during this fact finding investigation." His tone hinted at a serious warning in almost a fatherly manner despite him being nearly ten years McCrary's junior.

McCrary dismissed Captain O'Donnell's admonishment with a spiteful shrug. It had been a week since the raid on Yuri 'the Wolf' Kurikova's estate and he'd kept his mouth shut the entire time. Considering his position in the matter he thought it best to discuss things with his union representative, as well as a lawyer. At first, he thought he would be received with open arms as a veteran cop who'd lost his wife in a string of killings connected to the vigilante responsible for the Boston Massacre event. He was wrong. The union refused to back him, and he couldn't afford a lawyer capable of representing him. When the gag order was issued to the department and every individual employee who arrived on scene at the estate that night, McCrary felt fairly confident he would be fine professionally.

The first two days following the incident found him resting to physically get around. Excessive amounts of bourbon had assisted with that process, and then he had to arrange Audrey's funeral and call family. After managing to get the ball rolling on the ceremony his sister flew in from Florida to take over. He was only one day removed from watching the love of his life being lowered into the ground before he was summoned to the I.A. investigation. At the heart of the matter, McCrary knew he was being ostracized for his past transgression with the department, as they hoped to learn the details of what the federal government had ordered to be restricted information. His stance came from the lack of trust in his administration, and he could take a fucking from them if he had to. It was the Feds' radar he wanted to stay off of.

"Cap'n'," McCrary began, pronouncing the title with as little respect as he could express, "you can ask your questions all day long. I ain't answering shit." O'Donnell barked again about his language, but McCrary ignored him. He removed his copy of the national security letter hand delivered to him by a team of FBI agents. "This here tells me to keep my mouth shut, especially with the level of my involvement. If I trusted you fuckin' turncoats with what I knew I have no doubt that information would be leaked to the public. The Feds are already gonna crawl up everybody's asses for their own investigation, and I prefer to only get ram-rodded once, thank you very much."

O'Donnell's irritation shone through with his flush red face. He was trying to refrain from exploding, dropping threats of insubordination and professional crucifixion, but he refused to smear himself in the process. McCrary didn't give him a chance to say anything, though.

"At least the government has some respect for my loss," McCrary finished. His anger rose to a level he could barely contain, trembling through him in ways he wasn't accustomed to experiencing. Or was it the pain from Audrey being gone? Anymore they were one and the same. "My wife was murdered in *my home*, Cap'n'. So, please excuse me, if I don't give a fuck about your investigation into my presence at that piece of shit mobsta's home."

O'Donnell overlooked the derogatory language in an attempt to capitalize on the opening McCrary presented. "So, you admit being on location and present during the assault on the Kurikova estate?"

The callousness of Captain O'Donnell overlooking the murder of McCrary's wife somehow calmed the detective. His lower lip no longer quivered, and his hands rested easy on the rectangular table where he sat. McCrary reminded himself these people weren't worth his frustration. A simple nod to no one in particular marked the end of his involvement in the investigation proceedings. McCrary then tucked the national security letter inside his jacket pocket as he stood.

"You're not dismissed, Lieutenant," O'Donnell informed. His tone attempted to intimidate the lieutenant. "Sit down."

McCrary sneered at the order and dismissed it with the shake of his head. "Nah. I'm done. Fuck off."

He turned and walked out of the conference room without slamming the door. His determined pace walked him towards his work desk, but he didn't stop for any of his possessions. The fallout of his actions would certainly result in his termination, and it was of no consequence to him. McCrary dropped his badge in the trash receptacle next to his desk when he passed by, saying nothing to the surrounding coworkers occupying the department. He ignored the stunned looks following in his wake, and he continued moving without speaking a single word to anyone as he exited the precinct for the last time. It was all a part of the plan.

****

Forty minutes later McCrary was on a private plane to an undisclosed location. He was joined by a small troop of FBI agents whose names he didn't bother to remember. They were more like human resource clerks as they adjusted his police pension to a federal retirement program, and uploaded his deputized special agent credentials into their system.

He watched the pretty young blond agent sitting next to him enter his information on the screen of her laptop, correcting her in the spelling of his name at least twice. She claimed her typing skills couldn't keep up with the speed of her thoughts. McCrary didn't care. He just wanted to make sure they got the name right on his new badge and increased check.

She smiled when he'd mentioned it, clearly catching onto the pride he took in his name. The smile faded almost as quickly as it had appeared.

"I'm sorry to tell you, sir," the agent said casually, losing the twinkle in her bright blue eyes, "but that's not going to matter anymore."

Before McCrary could object, he watched her press the enter button on the keyboard and all of his information was blacked out on the screen. Her smile returned having experienced this exact moment more times than McCrary could imagine.

"You don't exist anymore." Her words were matter-of-fact, and she meant them.

He turned his attention forward, and shrugged off the thought. He'd lost what meant the most to him when Audrey died, so what difference did not existing make?

****

Stone was a living, breathing bruise and human was the last thing he resembled as he slept in the slightly raised hospital bed. McCrary entered his hospital room coolly, nodding to the dark skinned man who'd been sitting at his side for the better half of the last week. The man nodded in return, expecting to see the detective again, and tossed his copy of *Guns and Ammo* onto the counter to his right.

"How'd it go?" Mason Jones asked. He was genuinely concerned with McCrary's situation after hearing from Stone what the former detective had been through, and who he'd lost.

McCrary hesitated to answer, grimly bobbing his head from side to side while he considered his answer. "As good as can be expected, I suppose."

Jones nodded. There wasn't much to say about a manufactured resignation. "What do you think about all of this?" He gestured with his head to their surroundings.

McCrary knew the former U.S. Marshal didn't mean the hospital room. It was a pretty standard room; bland and functional. What he meant was their location, and their new circumstances.

"It's a lot to take in so quickly," McCrary replied, shrugging. "But if this is the only way, then so be it."

Jones grinned and sat back in his chair. "You're taking this pretty good, man. Can't be easy."

There was suspicion in the air that told McCrary his emotional circumstances were about to be brought into question. The hunch made him uneasy, causing him to hesitate to answer and fidget with his right ear lobe. Audrey had caught on to all of his tells, and when he hesitated like this she would always say, "Grow up and say something." She hated a man who couldn't find his words, and he never disappointed her when he'd reply.

"Don't get me wrong," Jones interjected into the silence. "The government has a way of throwing in all this secret squirrel type shit that I always suspected to exist. It's like getting hit in the face with a fast ball."

Jones shot McCrary a look that told him the Marshal wouldn't pry. McCrary answered with a silent return of the gesture signaling his understanding.

"Yeah, but I always knew there was something out of place surrounding the boy scout here," Jones chuckled lightly.

McCrary looked at Stone, changing the subject and still in disbelief how badly the agent had been beaten. Empathy filled his tone as he finished saying, "Tough sonofabitch, though. No question."

Jones looked over to Stone with a compassion McCrary recognized as brotherly recognition.

"That he is," Jones agreed. "He always has been."

McCrary moved to a nearby wall to support his weariness, opting to remain standing so his exhaustion wouldn't overtake him. "What do you make of all of this? His plan?"

Jones wasn't sure what to say. He knew very little about the situation, still waiting on a briefing from their new supervisor. A recollection of his conversation with Stone before he left for Boston came to mind.

"All I know is that before he went to Boston, he told me he needed backup and that he wanted me to get qualified so I could transfer to the FBI. That damn sure didn't happen in this short amount of time. And, he said this case went *deep*." Jones opened his muscular arms, gesturing to the situation again. "Nuff said."

McCrary recalled what he'd learned in the cellar of the pawn shop. He tried to forget the disparaged women and children caged into slavery, but they came with the territory. After seeing such depravity, a part of him understood how driven Ghost could be in what he did, but McCrary couldn't agree with the man's methods. The horror they discovered in the cellar was what connected Ghost and Stone, but it was the depths of that connection on a familial level that was more disturbing. Once Stone was strong enough McCrary intended to confront him on that matter moving forward.

"I've worked a lot of strange cases," McCrary said, "and I'm sure you have as well. But I've never encountered anything like this. This has clusterfuck written all over it, and now…" He trailed off for a moment as he took in the room and considered the circumstances. "Now, this is a whole other level of strange I'm not sure I'm equipped to handle."

"I heard that," Jones agreed. "We're all former Marines, so at least the three of us will be in good company. Nothing brings us closer than a good ol' fashioned man-hunt." The idea put a smile on Jones' face, giving him an opportunity to display his bright teeth.

McCrary was amused by the declaration, and agreed with a Marine's battle cry. "Oorah!"

"Oorah, brotha'. Oorah." Jones nodded his head, pleased with the brotherhood that surrounded him.

The former marshal looked to Stone, who slept nearly endlessly it seemed. His rest was necessary. It pained Jones to see his friend in such bad shape, and stirred an anger within him he wasn't sure he'd felt before. He was stunned to have heard from Stone so soon, and discover the extent of the damaged state he was in. Albeit, he could barely understand Stone at the time, yet Jones was more than happy to take his friend's call and accept his invitation. The scope of what he was getting into was still beyond Jones, but if he knew the government well enough, which was a fluid concept at best, he likely would never truly know everything. He wasn't going to concern himself with the details right now. What mattered was that his friend needed him, and he answered the call. That's what real brothers did for one another.

****

Executing Yuri 'the Wolf' Kurikova came with a special feeling of pleasure. At first, Ghost thought he'd let his vengeance go too far by beheading the mob boss with a bowie knife, and leaving his head on display atop his desk. Then, after looking beyond the rage he felt, Ghost remembered the tragedies Kurikova's syndicate had inflicted across the world, and he wanted to desecrate the man's body more. Time, however, did not allow him to fully express the deepest and darkest thoughts he carried inside himself.

The arrival of the police interrupted Ghost's final actions, but they couldn't have arrived at a better moment. He had just barely made it out of the mansion and returned to the van before the State Police could set up a perimeter, or locate the vehicle McCrary had likely advised them of. The return to Boston gave him time to reflect on how far he could go, and also examine what he needed to restrain. He wasn't a barbarian from the dark ages, and he couldn't allow himself to fall deeper into the abyss he swam in on a daily basis. It was his personal hell; a hell he controlled as much as he possibly could, regulated by the pain he felt.

At times he wondered what Veronica and Chloe might think of the punishment he doled out in their names. The answer was overwhelmingly negative, naturally. Ghost couldn't imagine they would be able to understand the way he justified his actions. Hell, even in the domestic life he led with them they were never made privy to the details of his profession. Veronica knew most of it in a roundabout way, which she was comfortable with. And Chloe had been far too young to have any inkling of his violent profession. They knew what mattered most to him, and that was how he loved them more than he deserved to love anyone.

Was that a good enough reason to murder men who made their living in an industry dedicated to ripping other lives apart for blood money? Ghost thought so, and that ended the debate he held in his mind about his actions.

In the days following Kurikova's death, Ghost noticed there was a limited amount of information reported by the media. A made up story revolving around an implosion of the Kurikova syndicate was the widespread cause of the mob boss' death from an assault on the house with no survivors. It was an open and shut case, which law enforcement compared to a similar assault by an Armenian hit squad approximately twelve years prior. Ghost immediately recognized it as a cover-up, so farfetched that it was completely believable. He'd been responsible for implementing similar tactics in other countries for American allies throughout his former career. On top of that, assassinations he was responsible for weren't always carried out in a straightforward manner. They had to be handled delicately depending on the purpose.

As for his personal vendetta, Ghost had every intention of continuing with the least amount of delicacy of action.

He kept himself busy with deeper research into Kurikova's businesses. It was one of his strongest traits, and something he enjoyed. In the world of espionage Ghost had learned early and quickly that the phrase 'knowledge is power' applied to every facet of the game. The gathering of information heightened his anticipation with a rare intensity. On his professional operations it had mostly been done for him, while at other times he did his own reconnaissance in the field, depending on the matter he was addressing. His personal agenda made hunting down his target, then systematically dispatching them along with everyone involved, far more satisfying.

This time around, however, Ghost would not work through an organization so methodically before going for the head of the snake. Would he tear it apart as he went? Yes. Would he go straight through everyone and everything directly to end the life of whoever was responsible for taking his family from him? Yes. However, he wouldn't follow the same blueprint he'd laid out for Kurikova, exposing the human trafficking trade piece-by-piece and peppering the Russian's name along the way.

Stone was likely not going to be of any use any time soon, which was really of no consequence. Ghost had used him to subjugate the local law enforcement, mostly, so they didn't get in his way, and he would be all too easy to find when the time came.

The discoveries Ghost made originated with Kurikova's records. He'd taken the liberty of excavating a number of ledgers from the desk in the safe room, and they provided some good leads. The Russian's money also paid for good information acquired by skilled *grey hats* that loyal contacts had connected Ghost with. These computer security experts operated without any malicious intent, unlike *black hat* hackers, yet they were still outliers from the professional spectrum leaving no connection to their daily lives. Like black hat hackers, grey hats were typically difficult to reach, and essentially worked as computer mercenaries. Ghost simply wanted to extract information from higher government access points he did not have the skillset to acquire. His technological abilities were fairly vast, but he was not on the level of these experts. His cause proved to be noble enough, and the cold hard cash wasn't bad either.

The days had turned to weeks, and the weeks to months, but it was time well spent. Kurikova was involved with a network that was far more advanced than Ghost had realized, and tracking anyone down who worked with him from the shadows was no simple task. He'd added in multiple factors of whose pockets needed to be padded, and dug into the familiar criminal underworld where he was used to playing in order to narrow the search. The payoff came down to an enigmatic figure within the international crime world, famously known for his exploits in all activities that benefitted him. This man went by an equally cryptic moniker, Mr. X.

****

There wasn't a time of the year in the countryside outside of Madrid that the man secretively known as Mr. X didn't enjoy. The nights in Central Spain could be cold, and the days humid and hot, but the overall expanse of the weather and lush surroundings of the *meseta*, or plateau, was something he found to be magnificent. He loved the scenery and found it quite calming. The undulating hills of the property he'd acquired long ago was littered with Pyrenean oak along the outskirts of the property's boundary otherwise bordered by long stretches of white three railed horse fencing. His collection of pure bred Andalusians had nearly sixty acres of controlled space to roam to their hearts content, if they weren't being schooled or trained in the arena.

He overlooked the opened space in the midst of a mild seventy-five degree day. A light breeze kept the restrictions of the humidity at bay with strong, periodic intervals allowing him to survey the playful work being done from the shade of a second floor balcony located at the back of his substantial hacienda. Ever a businessman at heart, courting relationships of all kinds on a global scale, Mr. X remained impeccably dressed. Today he'd donned a dark blue Armani suit, custom fitted of course, in an Italian cut with a burgundy tie, belt, and Oxfords offsetting the color scheme with an Autumnal tone. He preferred the blue colored arrangements to the typical black or greys as these shades somehow enhanced his mood.

Due to the tepid heat, Mr. X was *sans* the jacket, yet remained in the slightly glossier vest. And because he was not working at the moment, he ventured into the casual by rolling up the sleeves of the white cotton dress shirt high into his forearms. White scars littered the flesh between his elbows and wrists as reminders of more dangerous days; days when he'd taken more physical risks than he did anymore. Occasionally he still engaged in the physicality the life of crime provided to reignite that old flame of days long past.

It was mid-afternoon, which gave him the allowance to enjoy a vodka tonic. He enjoyed a generous amount of lime in the drink, opting for two wedges rather than the typical one. He raised the icy tumbler to his lips while he watched the work in the arena. Behind him the light humming of a motorized wheelchair announced the presence of the patriarch figure of his home. Without turning Mr. X said, "Hello, father."

A well-dressed man drove the wheelchair onto the balcony and stopped beside Mr. X. His suit was equally impeccable, and despite the warmth, he wore the entire three piece suit. They shared an elongated appearance in the framing of their faces, and a tight square jaw. Being twenty years to Mr. X's senior, his father appeared to be a fit man, long and lean just like his son. He also had an olive hue to his barely wrinkled skin from lengthy amounts of time in the sun. Their Sicilian heritage passed this on, although there was also a slight Scandinavian connection in the white-blond hair that they shared in their more youthful years. The father's hair was now simply white. Beyond appearing to be physically fit, the elderly man in the wheelchair was forever bound to its dependency. The family trade saw to that with a bullet in his spine many years ago.

"Good afternoon," the father replied. His naturally grim expression set him apart from the charismatic joy his son employed. He had never been certain if his son was inherently happy, or if it was a character trait to the near psychopathy he had been tethered to throughout his lifetime. Either way, his son had always used it to his advantage. "Anything new today?"

Mr. X turned to his father with a joyous grin. "It's another beautiful day, father; business as usual. Although, I am taking some time to relax."

A judgmental grunt was the only reply.

"You don't approve of the down time?" Mr. X inquired in mid-sip.

"After the events in Boston, do you think it's wise?" the old man's surly tone came with the impact of being more orderly than suggestive.

Mr. X continued to grin, watching the prized Andalusian stud, Khan, gallop around the arena under the watchful eye of Julio, the residential *entrenador de caballos*, or horse trainer. "I think it's necessary to stop and enjoy the life we've built, especially during climates such as this." He took a heavier sip of the vodka tonic, not so much out of thirst, but to assist with his patience.

"This has gotten out of hand," the father stated. He wanted to say more, but knew better. His position at the table had been far removed, and he was allowed access for consulting purposes only.

Mr. X looked down to his father, his grin never fading, exuding a charisma many never quite understood. In tighter circles it had been attributed to some form of lunacy, but he'd always held to the belief of attracting more with honey than shit. "It will be handled appropriately, father. Don't worry."

The innocence of childish laughter floated in the breeze from the horse arena, catching Mr. X's ear and beckoning him forward to the garish stone railing. He leaned forward on its wide top, enthralled with the sight before him while filled with a depth of pride and love. It was rare to feel this way, or at least it had been before he was surrounded with the newer joys of his life. Having them in this home had made his professional efforts more fruitful, which in turn translated to life moving beyond the organizations he oversaw. It was a pipe dream really. But Mr. X relished the thought of a rainy day when he wouldn't have to make shady deals between killers and spies, or regulate them to keep worldly peace in the shadows. The fantasy was given hope with having family near.

Mr. X waved gleefully towards the arena. "You're doing fantastic, my dear!" he encouraged, laughing with prideful amusement.

His father shook his head. He truly thought his son had lost his mind. However, it was also that sensibility that made his son so proficient, and that gave the patriarch little to truly be concerned with on most occasions. The newest threat to them, however, was not one to be taken lightly. He wheeled himself forward, turning the chair so he could look beyond the stone railing down to the horse arena. A submissive sigh escaped his thin lips, frustrated.

"Be wary of the hearts you trifle with. Some of the gentlest hearts belong to the most beastly of men," the father advised. Satisfied with his viewing, he pulled away from the railing and retreated into the depths of the massive home.

Mr. X continued to smile and wave, giving no attention to his father's dismissal. He shook his head with reverence, overwhelmed with excitement for the youth and her mother waving back to him. Their raven black locks blew in a breeze as it filtered through the arena, swept to one side giving full exposure to smiles so bright they rivaled the sun. As he gazed outward, the words of Mr. X's father did not go unheard. In fact, they couldn't have been truer, nor could there have been a weightier warning laced into them. Mr. X continued to smile and wave regardless, not that he ignored the disclaimer, but he was well beyond it. It was too late to be warned, and his father knew that already. Perhaps it was simply meant to be a reminder.

"Grandpa, come ride with me!" called the little girl. She rode atop Khan with supreme confidence for an eight year old, tutored only by the best, and under the deepest of care from Julio.

Mr. X stood, somehow feeling his smile growing brighter. "I'll be right down, sweetheart."

A moment passed as Mr. X continued to observe the heartwarming scene; lost in wonderment of how blessed he was by the child and her beautiful mother being a part of his life for the better half of the last three years. The contradiction of waging war in the darkest of trenches of his mind gnawed at him momentarily. *Some of the gentlest of hearts belong to the most beastly of men*. The words lingered in his consciousness, and his head bounced with a subtle agreeance to himself. He set down the alcoholic beverage on a nearby table and retreated from the balcony en route to the arena. While he had the time, he needed to enjoy as much as he could. The girl's father was coming for her, and he wanted to make as many joyous memories as he could before he needed to make horrifying decisions to ensure his survival.

In the time it took Mr. X to navigate the hacienda's elaborate floor plan from the second story to the ground level, his phone rang on three separate occasions. He ignored it every time as he bypassed the wonderful aroma of lunch seducing his senses from the kitchen made by Julio's angelic wife, Valencia, who he simply could not resist stopping and hugging, either for the ampleness of her bosom or the fact that she always lovingly pecked him on the cheek with her equally voluptuous lips. After this delightful detour, he then had to maneuver around the pool and patio furniture to exit the steel gate to get to the arena across the wide driveway. His direct focus at the moment was to create some memories with his granddaughter to stow away for safe keeping. The idea kept a smile plastered onto his face throughout the entire journey.

Mr. X crossed the pea gravel drive, maintaining a watchful eye on the young rider atop the nearly mystical appearing Khan. She was meant to ride, fearlessly taking to the equestrian fortitude with a strong interest, and demonstrating skillful potential at such a young age. Her radiant innocence was practically unmatched, but to him, the ebony shade of Khan's opulent coat came close.

Julio was the man to attribute for her early abilities. He was masterful in his guidance, and Mr. X had never known anyone to be more caring or close to these beautiful beasts. He swore Julio could speak to them, or *whisper* as he'd heard it called, because the man could do magical things with the steeds.

The phone alerted him of another call with its incessant buzzing, which turned out to be the same number he'd recently dismissed three times prior. *Someone's persistent.* The crunching of the gravel beneath his feet ceased as he stopped to consider taking the call. His number was known by a select few, and those people only made contact in case of necessity, or an emergency. The number heading the top of the screen was one he didn't recognize and it raised a number of red flags. *What the hell…*

"I'm an admirer of persistence, which you seem to have in droves on this fine day," Mr. X greeted, still smiling and watching the arena ahead of him. "I hope this call is important. If you're not sure who you're talking to it could have consequences you're not prepared to deal with."

A tinge of static crackled in a moment of respite. Mr. X considered hanging up. He didn't have the patience for such trivialities. However, when the call showed signs of life, he was glad he stayed on the line.

"This is the most important call you'll ever take, *Mr. X*," the growly voice stated. It was laced with malice, especially in the pronunciation of the moniker, giving its listener a reason to pause.

"Hmm, that is dreadfully interesting. Perhaps you really don't know who I am." Mr. X maintained a jovial tone, purposely adding a laugh at the end. He hated overstating his position with entitled phrases, but he was becoming annoyed beneath the cover of his openly good mood. "And, please, before you move into the cliché threats I'm certain are coming my way, know that if you were going to kill me, you should just do it instead of forewarning me. I'd respect you more that way."

Another pause in the call followed.

"I'm going to assume you've realized that you've dialed the wrong number and reached out to the wrong person," Mr. X stated. "In that case, I'm going to forgive this transgression assaulting my precious time. I bid you good day."

Mr. X removed the phone from his ear to visibly press the red 'end call' button upon the touch screen. Before he could end anything, a terrifying scream radiated from the speaker so horrific, it startled him. The buzzing and grinding of machinery echoed and rumbled over the line, drawing out an even deeper and more horrifying sound. He would have mistaken it to be animalistic if it weren't for the faint utterance of garbled words mixed into the agonized shrieking. Much of it was unintelligible, yet there was a certain aspect he understood clearly; a point likely meant for him to hear specifically. It was his name.

Concerned, Mr. X turned away from the arena and returned the phone to his ear, unable to hide the drastic change in his expression. His mind raced thinking of everyone who could be on the other end experiencing such savagery. Only those who *truly knew him* knew his name, and not the *nom de plume* that had granted him the anonymity outside of his business dealings.

"Do I have the wrong number now?" the mystery caller asked. There was a sense of satisfaction in his voice that was unsettling.

Mr. X gathered himself to a more neutral state of mind. It was the only way to deal with violent people, and he didn't want to let the caller know how bothered he actually was. Displays of such frustration and emotion did no good in discussions, especially when he needed to find out who was on the other end. Whether it was for himself, or the suspected lunacy he was rumored to be ill with, Mr. X didn't know, but he smiled once again. "You have my attention."

"Is that all?"

He considered what other options there were, and had no offering. "What else could you want?"

Another pause.

"My family," the caller stated. The anger returned in his words, and it was quite obvious he spoke in a restrained manner somehow suspecting those two words would tell an entire story all by themselves.

And they did.

The answer was all too relevant to Mr. X, and he became irrationally ecstatic. "My god, what a piece of work you are. I didn't think we'd correspond so soon, my boy!" He turned back towards the arena, laughing, forgetting about the hair-raising scream previously broadcasted. "Goodness, this is a treat, I'll tell you what! Mmm, I have an idea! Hold on one second, won't you?"

Mr. X continued on towards the arena, moving faster, each step crunching across the gravel beneath his rapid pace. He was more excited than he had been in a long time. His heart pounded so ferociously it would have been hard to determine if it were literally going to explode. A hand waved to Julio gesturing for him to escort Kahn to meet him at the fencing, and the horse trainer followed the non-verbal cue.

Before he reached the arena border, Mr. X extended the cell phone into the air ahead of him and said, "Say hello!"

The pleasant invitation garnered the dual voices of the granddaughter and her mother, who were within a reasonable enough distance to be heard clearly over the phone. Mr. X smiled grandly, stopping in his tracks while he dramatized his laughter with an over exaggerated arch backwards. He used the ostentatious maneuver to act as though he had to turn away to catch his balance, mocking the clowning around he did for his granddaughter's amusement so often.

Instead, what Mr. X had done was steal himself the opportunity to drop the happy act for the briefest of moments, and icily end the call by saying, "Come and get them."

WE'RE NOT DONE YET!

Thank you for reading *A Dangerous Man!*

I hope you enjoyed it, and that I have you hooked for the sequel, *A Violent Man.*

While I have your attention, I'd like to get real for a moment…

I am naturally and incredibly protective of the ones I love, and that aspect of me grew exponentially when I became a father. It was in this time that I became aware of many new horrors of the world, or perhaps I just opened my eyes to them and saw them as tangible threats. Regardless, among these murky fears I found myself disgusted at the reality of human trafficking, and the lack of justice for its victims. In this fire is where *A Dangerous Man* was forged. My research taught me about a subject I never really understood, and one that cannot be overlooked.

While I've written this story in the hopes of creating a compelling and thrilling ride to escape the world around you one page at a time, there is a reality-based facet that swirls within it. The subject of human trafficking is all too real, and all too horrific. Modern day slavery is at an all-time high, and is a heinous disease plaguing the moral ambivalence of mankind that proves these wicked people truly do exist. The monsters who are responsible for this, both men and women, have built a multi-billion dollar industry off of the pain and suffering of men, women, and children; one where victims are torn from their everyday lives through force, fraud, and coercion only to disappear into obscurity. In many cases, there's no telling where they'll go, or what they'll be subjected to.

There are many organizations across the globe battling on the front lines of this war to save humanity, and they could use our help. Please consider seeking out an organization and supporting them however you can, whether it be with donations or volunteerism.

I hope you've enjoyed my novel, and I truly hope there's a part of you that wants to join the fight against human trafficking. Together we can fight alongside Ghost and make a tangible impact on the lives of those who cannot help themselves.

Sincerely,

J. L. Engel

P.S.

In the time it has taken you to read this letter, another individual will have been enslaved, and of this 40 million, 2 million are children who are being sexually exploited, and every 10 minutes an adolescent girl dies from violence related to human trafficking.

Made in the USA
Middletown, DE
23 January 2022